Pass...
Succ...
These h...
a lo...

Enjoy!

Mediterranean Men:

Gorgeous Greeks

*Two fabulous, sun-drenched novels come from
international bestselling authors*
Helen Bianchin and Julia James

'Helen Bianchin brings readers a dynamite
story in *The Greek Bridegroom* that will
pin you in your seat.'
—*Romantic Times*

'This entertaining book boasts powerful chemistry,
a great plot and high-energy characters.'
—*Romantic Times* on *The Greek Tycoon's Mistress*
by Julia James

Mediterranean Men:

Gorgeous
Greeks

featuring

THE GREEK BRIDEGROOM
by
Helen Bianchin

&

THE GREEK TYCOON'S
MISTRESS
by
Julia James

M&B™ and M&B™ with the Rose Device
are trademarks of the publisher.
Harlequin Mills & Boon Limited, Eton House,
18-24 Paradise Road, Richmond, Surrey TW9 1SR

MEDITERRANEAN MEN: GORGEOUS GREEKS
© by Harlequin Books SA 2007

The Greek Bridegroom and *The Greek Tycoon's Mistress* were first published in Great Britain in separate, single volumes.

The Greek Bridegroom © Helen Bianchin 2002
The Greek Tycoon's Mistress © Julia James 2003

ISBN: 978 0 263 85842 6

009-0807

Printed and bound in Spain
by Litografia Rosés S.A., Barcelona

The Greek Bridegroom

by
Helen Bianchin

Helen Bianchin was born in New Zealand and travelled to Australia before marrying her Italian-born husband. After three years they moved, returned to New Zealand with their daughter, had two sons, then resettled in Australia. Encouraged by friends to recount anecdotes of her years as a tobacco sharefarmer's wife living in an Italian community, Helen began setting words on paper and her first novel was published in 1975. An animal lover, she says her terrier and Persian cat regard her study as as much theirs as hers.

Don't miss Helen Bianchin's new novel,
The Greek Tycoon's Virgin Wife,
out in October 2007
from Mills & Boon® Modern™!

For Helga,
friend, and talented florist

CHAPTER ONE

THERE were some days when it just didn't pay to get out of bed, Rebekah groaned as she lifted her head from the pillow and caught sight of the digital clock.

It was blinking, indicating a power failure through the night had disrupted the alarm mechanism.

She fumbled for her watch, checked the time and uttered a muffled oath as she slid from the bed, then cursed out loud as she stubbed her toe on her way to the *en suite*.

The icy blast of water ensured the quickest shower on record, and, dressed, she raced into the kitchen, dished out fresh food for the cat, snatched a container of orange juice from the refrigerator, gulped a mouthful, then she collected her bag and took the lift down to the underground car park.

Seconds later she slid in behind the wheel of the Blooms and Bouquets van, inserted the key into the ignition…and nothing.

Don't do this to me, she begged as the engine refused to kick over. *Please* don't do this to me! During the ensuing minutes she coaxed, cajoled, promised, and still it remained as dead as a doornail.

She restrained the urge to scream in frustration. Talk about having Friday the thirteenth on a Tuesday!

Raising her head heavenward and praying to the deity didn't work either.

What else could go wrong?

It was better she didn't ask, for it might tempt fate to fling another disaster in her path.

There was nothing else to do but get behind the wheel of her MG and send the sleek red sports car purring through Sydney's suburban streets.

Not exactly a suitable vehicle in which to transport flowers to the Double Bay florist shop she co-owned with her sister, Ana.

In the early pre-dawn hours there wasn't much traffic, and already the city was stirring to life. Pie-carts were closing up after the long night, the council street-sweeping trucks whined along, clearing debris from the gutters, and fruit and vegetable vendors transported their supplies from the city markets. Taxis carrying businessmen to catch the early flights interstate, petrol tankers beginning deliveries.

It was a time of day Rebekah enjoyed, and she activated a popular radio station on the console and felt her spirits lift with the upbeat music.

Soon the sun would lift above the horizon, and the grey shadows would disperse, bestowing everything with light and colour.

A sweeping glance was all it took at the markets to determine the best of the blooms were gone, and she figured her order, placed it, then turned the car towards Double Bay.

The shop was situated in a trendy élite area, and

thanks to a bequest from her late mother the business was free from any loan encumbrances.

It was six-thirty when she unlocked the outer door and she tripped the lights, filled the coffee percolator, then set to work.

While the percolator took its time, she booted up the computer and downloaded email orders, then she checked the fax machine.

They were in for a busy day, and there was a need to adjust her order. She crossed to the phone, made the call, then she rang a mechanic to go check the van.

Hot, sweet black coffee boosted her energy levels, and she was on her third and last cup for the day when Ana arrived.

Looking at her sister was akin to seeing a mirror image of herself...almost. They shared the same petite height, fine-boned features, slender curves and naturally blonde hair. Two years separated them in age, with Ana the eldest and twenty-seven. Their natural personalities were similar, although Rebekah felt she held an edge when it came to determined resolve.

The necessity for self-survival in an abusive relationship had provided a strength of will she hadn't been aware she possessed. It had also implanted an ingrained distrust of men.

A year's engagement to Brad Somerville, a beautiful wedding, embarking on a dream honeymoon...nothing prepared her for the sudden change in the man she'd vowed to love and honour less than ten hours before.

At first she'd thought it was something she'd done or said. Verbal abuse was bad enough; physical abuse was something else. Jealous, possessive to the point of obsessiveness, he soon killed any feelings she had for him, and after three months of living in a hellish marriage she'd simply packed a bag and walked out of his life.

Following the divorce she'd legally reverted to her maiden name, bought an apartment, adopted a beautiful Burmilla kitten whom she'd named Millie, and lived to work.

'Hi.' Rebekah summoned a sympathetic smile as she glimpsed the slight air of fatigue evident in Ana's expression. 'Late night? Morning sickness?'

'That bad, huh?' her sister queried as she crossed to the computer and began cross-checking the day's orders.

'Maybe you should listen to Luc and cut down your hours.'

Ana shot her a telling glance. 'You're supposed to be on my side.'

Rebekah wrinkled her nose in humour. 'I am, believe me.'

'What would I do in that great house all day? Petros is the ultimate manservant.'

The phone rang, and Ana picked up, listened, then handed over the cordless receiver. 'For you.'

It was the mechanic with word all the van needed was a new battery, which he'd install, and mail her the account.

'Problems?'

'The van wouldn't start.' She relayed the repercussions, then took the next phone call.

It didn't get better as the morning wore on. A difficult customer took most of her patience, and another complained bitterly about the cost of florists' delivery charges.

Food, she needed food. It was almost midday, and the energy boost from juice, coffee and a cereal bar had clearly dissipated.

'I'll go pick up a salad sandwich. Then you can take a lunch break.'

Ana glanced up from the computer. 'I can eat lunch on the run just as well as you.'

'But you won't,' Rebekah said firmly. 'You'll buy a magazine, seat yourself at any one of the nearby café's, and take your time over a latte and something sensible to eat.'

Ana rolled her eyes. 'Tea,' she amended with a grimace. 'And if you begin treating me like a precious pregnant princess, I'll hit you!'

She laughed, a low, throaty chuckle, and her eyes held a mischievous gleam. 'Petros?' she hazarded. The middle-aged manservant had been part of Luc's household for years, well before she'd first met Ana's inimitable husband. 'Does he still refer to you as Ms Dimitriades?'

Ana's laughter was infectious. 'He considers anything less would be regarded as undignified.'

She adored her sister, and they'd been the best of friends since she could remember, sharing, caring, *close.* Ana's marriage to Luc Dimitriades a year ago had been one of the happiest moments of her life.

'Luc has made a booking for dinner this evening.'

Ana named the restaurant, and Rebekah's eyebrows rose a fraction. It numbered as one of the ritziest places in town. 'We'd like you to join us. Please,' she added. '*Two* Dimitriades men are too much for one woman to handle.'

Rebekah felt an icy shiver slither the length of her spine, and the nerves in her stomach tightened into a painful ball. Please let her voice give no hint to her inner turmoil. 'One of Luc's cousins is in town?' Amazing she could sound so calm, when her defence mechanism had already moved to *alert*, and her mind issued the silent scream *Please don't let it be Jace.*

'Yes. Jace arrived yesterday from the States.'

No. The silent scream rose and died in her throat as Jace Dimitriades' image rose to the fore to taunt her.

Tall, broad shoulders, chiselled features, piercing dark grey eyes, and a mouth to die for.

She had reason to know how it felt to have that mouth possess her own. Even now, a year later, she still retained a vivid memory of Luc and Ana's wedding, partnered as her sister's maid of honour with Jace as Luc's best man. How for several hours she'd been aware of Jace's close proximity, the touch of his hand at her waist, the brush of his body against her own as they assembled for bridal group photos.

Dancing with him had been a nightmare. Sensual

heat spiked her blood and sent it racing through her veins. Sexual chemistry at its most base level.

Hadn't that been the real reason for her momentary escape onto the terrace within minutes of Luc and Ana taking their leave?

Yet Jace was there, standing close, almost caging her against the terrace railing as she turned to move away.

That had been her mistake, for it brought her much too close to him. The next instant his lips brushed her cheek, then slid to savour her mouth, and in a moment of sheer madness she angled her mouth to his own.

His instant response was devastating.

Shocked didn't cover it. No one had kissed her quite like that. As if somehow he'd reached down into the depths of her soul, tasted, savoured, with intent to conquer. It left her feeling as if she'd leapt off a high cliff and was in dangerous free fall. Exhilarated by the instinctive knowledge he would catch her...before she hit the ground.

Who was the first to break contact? To this day she couldn't be sure. All she remembered was something inexplicable in those dark grey eyes, a stillness that held a waiting, *watching* quality as she went from shock to dismay in a few seconds flat.

Anger kicked in, and she slapped him...hard. Then she walked away, aware that he made no effort to stop her. She rejoined the wedding guests, and smiled until her facial muscles ached.

Afterwards had come the rage...with herself for initiating something so foolish, and with him for indulging it.

Now Jace Dimitriades was back in town, and Ana and Luc expected her to make up a foursome for dinner?

'No,' she reiterated aloud.

'No...you don't want to.' Ana's gaze narrowed as she attempted to analyse her sister's expression. 'Or no, you can't?'

'Choose whichever one you like.'

Ana appeared to take a deep breath. 'OK. Are you going to tell me about it, or do I have to drag it out of you?'

'Neither. Simply accept I decline your invitation.'

'That won't wash, and you know it. You haven't seen Jace since the wedding.' Her sister's eyes assumed a speculative gleam. 'What did he do? Kiss you?'

Oh, my. 'On what do you base that assumption?' she managed calmly, and saw Ana's gaze narrow.

There was a telling silence. 'It's not like you to wimp out,' her sister said at last.

Wimp? 'Forgive me, but I'm not in the mood to embark on a verbal fencing match with a man who'd enjoy every thrust and parry!'

'Think of the fun you'll have in besting him,' Ana offered persuasively.

Rebekah glimpsed the mischievous challenge in those guileless blue eyes, and her lips curved into a slow smile. 'You're wicked.'

Ana grinned. 'The black Versace halter-neck will be fine.'

A backless creation which didn't allow for wearing a bra? 'I haven't said *yes*.'

'We'll come by and collect you. And drop you home again.'

She could imagine how easily, *smoothly* Jace could intercede and insist he escort her home in a taxi.

'*If* I agree,' she qualified, shooting Ana a warning glance. 'I'll drive my own car.'

'*Brava.*' Ana's eyes gleamed with humour, and Rebekah shook her head in mock-despair as her sister executed the *victory* sign.

It was almost seven when Rebekah slid from behind the wheel of her MG and allowed the uniformed attendant tend to valet parking.

For the umpteenth time she silently questioned her sanity. Except *retreat* at this late stage wasn't part of her agenda.

How had the past year affected Jace Dimitriades?

Did he have a lover? Was he between relationships?

Fool, she mentally derided as she entered the restaurant foyer. Men of Jace Dimitriades' calibre were never without a woman for long. She recollected Ana relaying Jace regularly commuted between London, Paris and Athens. He probably had a mistress in each major city.

The *maître d'* greeted her with polite regard, elicited her name, the booking, and directed her to the lounge bar, where patrons lingered over drinks.

The ambience spelt *money*...serious money. The floral displays were real, not silk imitation. The carpet thick-piled and luxurious, the furniture expensive.

A pianist was seated at a baby grand, effortlessly providing muted background music, and the drinks stewards were groomed to the nth degree.

Refined class, Rebekah conceded as a steward enquired if he could assist locating her friends.

He succeeded with smooth efficiency, and she followed in his wake.

'Mr Dimitriades.' His acknowledgement held deferential respect, and she had a ready smile in place, polite words of gratitude on her lips as she tilted her head.

Only to have the smile freeze as she saw it was Jace, not Luc, who had moved forward to greet her.

'Rebekah.'

In one fluid movement he came close, lowered his head and brushed his lips to her cheek. The contact was stunningly brief, but it robbed the breath from her throat for all of five seconds before anger hit.

'How dare you?' The words escaped as little more than a vehement whisper.

One dark eyebrow slanted, although his eyes held a watchful expression. 'You expected formality?'

She didn't trust herself to respond. Her attention was held, *trapped,* by the man standing within touching distance.

Tall, so tall her eyes were on a level with the loop of his impeccably knotted silk tie, and his breadth of shoulder was impressive sheathed in exclusive tailoring.

In his mid-thirties, his broad, chiselled facial bone structure gave hint to his Grecian ancestry, and there was an inherent quality in those dark grey, almost black eyes that took hold of her equilibrium and tore it to shreds.

No one man deserved to exude quite this degree of power...nor possess such riveting physical magnetism.

Sexual alchemy at its zenith, she acknowledged shakily as she attempted to gain a measure of control over her rioting emotions.

One look at him was all it took for her to remember how it felt to have that mouth close over her own with diabolical finesse. Exploring, coaxing...and staking a claim.

She was suddenly aware of every breath she took, every heightened pulse-beat, and the way her heart seemed to thud against her ribcage.

It was crazy, *insane* to feel like this. In the name of heaven, *get a grip*. To allow him to see just how deeply he affected her was impossible.

Why, suddenly, did she feel as if she'd walked into a danger zone? And that it was *he*, and not she, in command of the situation?

Dammit, she'd accepted Ana's invitation, and she owed it to her sister and Luc to be a pleasant guest. Hadn't she dressed accordingly, and given a promise to sparkle?

CHAPTER TWO

PROJECTING *joie de vivre* required effort, and there was a very real danger she'd verge towards overkill.

A glass of wine would help dull the edges, but she'd had nothing to eat since lunch. Consequently iced water seemed a wise choice, especially as she'd need all her wits to parry words with Luc's inimitable cousin.

The restaurant's chef was reputed to be one of the city's best, and numbered among the country's finest. Hence, the selection offered was meant to tempt a gourmand's palate.

Rebekah ordered soup as a starter, requested an entrée-size meal as a main, and deferred a decision on dessert.

She settled back in her chair and glanced towards Jace. 'You're in Sydney on business, I believe?'

There was nothing like taking control and initiating conversation.

'Yes.' He met her level gaze, held it, and wondered if she had any idea how well he could read her. 'Also Melbourne, Cairns, Brisbane and the Gold Coast.'

'Interesting. Presumably matters which require your personal attention?'

How would she react if he revealed *she* was one

16

of them? He inclined his head. 'I'm unable to delegate in this instance.'

Property he wanted to sight? Yet in a high-tech age, it was possible to scan digital images at the speed of light, and as he shared some investment interests with Luc, why couldn't Luc act on his cousin's behalf?

The waiter delivered their starters, and Rebekah toyed with the soup, spooning the contents automatically without affording it the appreciation it truly deserved.

'Tell me something about floristry.' Jace's voice was pure New York, and she waited a beat before countering,

'An idle query, or genuine interest?'

His eyes held a humorous gleam. 'The latter.'

'The art, or a day in the life of...?'

'Both.'

'Floral artistry comprises a good eye for colour and design, shapes appealing to the customer's wants and needs, the specific occasion.' If he wanted facts, she'd supply them. 'Which blooms suit, room temperature, the effect the customer wants to achieve.'

She lifted her shoulders and effected a light shrug. 'Knowledge where exotic out-of-season stock can be bought and how long it takes to air-freight it in. And the expense involved. Unfortunately there are always those who want the best at minimum cost.'

'I'm sure you manage to apprise them that quality comes with a price?'

'Don't be fooled by Ana and Rebekah's petite stature,' Luc drawled. His mouth curved into a warm smile. 'I can assure both sisters pack a powerful verbal punch.' He turned towards Ana and brushed light fingers down her cheek. 'My wife, especially.'

'It's a defence mechanism,' Ana responded sweetly. The waiter removed their plates, and Rebekah's gaze shifted to Jace in a deliberate attempt at dispassionate appraisal.

Superb tailoring emphasised an impressive breadth of shoulder, and the deep blue shirt with its impeccably knotted silk tie accented his olive textured skin.

All she had to do was look at him, and warmth flared to uncomfortable heat as her mind spun into overdrive, remembering how it felt to have his mouth on hers. From there it was just a step away for her mind to spiral out of control, imagining what lay beneath the trappings of his conventional attire.

Don't go there. Dear heaven, what was *wrong* with her? No one, not even her ex-husband in the heightened throes of pre-marital passion, had been able to arouse such an intense reaction.

She was conscious of every breath she took, and co-ordinating cutlery with morsels of food and the actual eating process was fraught with nervous tension.

Was Jace aware of her inner turmoil? Dear God, she hoped not.

Oh, for heaven's sake, she mentally chastised. You're only sharing dinner with him, and acute vulnerability could be conquered...couldn't it? Or at least successfully masked. Besides, Jace Dimitriades was only a man like any other man, and hadn't Brad been charm personified in the beginning? Only to turn into a wolf in sheep's clothing.

Except instinct warned comparing her ex-husband to Jace Dimitriades was akin to associating an ill-bred canine with a powerful panther.

There was a part of her that wanted to replace her cutlery, stand to her feet, and leave. Retreat to the safety of her car, return to her apartment with her sanity intact.

Except such an action was a cop-out, and besides, what excuse could she present? *Act,* she commanded silently. You deal with people every day in the shop and utilise psychological skill to handle difficult customers. How difficult could it be to deal with Jace Dimitriades for a few hours? There was the added advantage of Ana and Luc's presence to provide a buffer. It should be a breeze.

Fat chance! She felt about as relaxed as a cat on hot bricks!

Why hadn't she listened to her initial instinct and remained adamant at not doing this? Because she cared for her sister. At least, that was the simple answer. The more complex one didn't bear contemplating.

Maybe some wine would loosen her nerves a little, and she indicated the wine steward could fill her glass. Seconds later she took an appreciative sip, and felt the grape's delicate bouquet slip into her bloodstream.

It was a relief when the waiter presented the next course. Her appetite was non-existent, and although her meal was a decorative vision in cuisine artistry, her tastebuds appeared to be on strike.

Travelled south for the duration, she accorded with silent wry humour, aware to an alarming degree just where they'd chosen to settle.

Eat, she commanded silently. Focus on the food. The evening would eventually come to a close, and she'd never have to place herself in this position again.

She may as well have told herself to go jump over the moon for all the good it did, for she was supremely conscious of every movement he made. The economical use of his hands as he apportioned each morsel of food. The way the muscles at the edge of his jaw bunched as he ate. His hands were broad, tanned with a sprinkling of hair, the fingers tapered with neatly shaped nails.

How would those hands caress a woman's skin? Lightly skim the silken surface, discover each pleasure pulse and linger there?

Her mind came to a screeching halt. What was the matter with her? She couldn't blame the wine, for she'd only consumed a few sips, and alternated it with chilled water.

'You have an early start in the morning?' Luc queried solicitously.

Could she conceivably use that as an excuse to slip away soon? 'I have to be at the flower market around four-thirty.'

Jace's gaze narrowed. 'Every day?'

'Six out of seven.' It didn't bother her. Never had,

for she was a morning person. However, after a fourteen-hour day on her feet anything less than six hours' sleep and she was wrecked.

'I'll order coffee.' Luc signalled the waiter, and she joined Ana in choosing tea, all too aware coffee would keep her awake. How long had they been here? Two hours? Three?

They were almost done, and within half an hour she'd be free to slip behind the wheel of her car and drive home.

Wonderful, she determined as Luc fixed the bill, and she stood to her feet, collected her evening purse, and followed Ana to the foyer.

Her skin prickled in awareness of Jace's close proximity, and it took considerable effort to move at a leisurely pace. She could almost feel the warmth of his body, and her own stiffened at the light touch of his hand at the back of her waist as they gained the pavement.

'I'll see you to your car.'

'I had a valet attendant park it for me.'

Ana tilted her face as Jace leant down to brush his lips to her cheek. 'Luc and I can give you a lift back to the hotel.'

'I'm sure Rebekah won't mind.' Jace straightened and shot his cousin a measured look. 'I'll be in touch tomorrow.'

Rebekah uttered a silent prayer that Luc would intercede, only the deity wasn't listening. Ana leant forward and brushed her lips to her sister's cheek, accepted Jace's affectionate 'Goodnight', then she moved with Luc towards their car.

It was so smoothly effected, she could hardly believe she'd been cleverly manipulated. His hotel *was en route* to her apartment. Given she had to pass right by the main entrance, it would be churlish to refuse.

However, her mind screamed in silent denial as she waited for the attendant to fetch her car. She didn't want to be alone with him, ever, and especially not in the close confines of her MG sports car.

What had prompted him to suggest it when she'd been so painstakingly polite all evening? She hadn't flirted, or given him any reason to think she coveted his attention.

Dammit, just get in the car, drop him off at the hotel, then that'll be the end of it. Ten, fifteen minutes was all it would take.

There wasn't a lot of leg-room, and it gave her a degree of satisfaction as he folded his lengthy frame into the front passenger seat.

Rebekah didn't waste a second, and she gained the street, then headed towards Double Bay. Idle conversation, simply for the sake of it, wasn't on her agenda, and she didn't offer a word as she took liberties with the speed limit.

Ten minutes and counting.

It was a beautiful late-spring evening, the dark sky a clear indigo sprinkled with stars. Cool, sharp temperatures promised another fine day, and she directed her mind to the shop's orders and the stock she'd need to purchase from the markets.

It didn't work, for she was supremely conscious of the man seated beside her. In the close confines of the car she was aware of the subtle tones of his cologne, the clean smell of his clothes...and the faint male muskiness that was his alone.

Rebekah felt the tell-tale prickle of her skin as her body began an unbidden response. There was warmth, and heat pooled deep inside, intensifying with damning speed as her pulse accelerated to a crazy beat.

His hand rested on one knee, which was close, much too close to the gear-shift, making it impossible not to touch him whenever she changed gears. Avoiding contact without appearing to do so required care, and she wondered if he sensed her disquiet.

What if he did, and he was silently amused? Oh, dammit, just *drive*. In another five minutes she'd be free of his disturbing presence.

One more set of traffic lights and she'd enter the outer fringes of suburban Double Bay. A sense of intense relief began to descend as she turned into the street housing the main entrance to his hotel, and she drew to a halt in the impressive forecourt.

A uniformed bellboy moved towards the car, and Rebekah turned towards Jace. 'Goodnight.'

In one fluid movement he captured her face with his hands, then lowered his mouth to hers in an evocative kiss that invaded and seduced. All too brief, it held the promise of *more*.

Shocked surprise encompassed her features as he lifted his head, and her mouth parted, only to close again as he offered a huskily voiced *au revoir* before sliding out from the low-slung seat.

She caught the faint gleam in those dark eyes before he turned and walked towards the main entrance.

Damn him. What did he think he was playing at?

She moved the gear-stick with unnecessary force, then sent the car into the street. Her apartment was situated two blocks distant, and she reached it in record time, easing the MG down into the underground car park.

In the lift she castigated herself for not predicting Jace's move. He'd bargained on the element of surprise, and had won.

So what did it matter? She was unlikely to see him again. But it irked unbearably he'd caught her unawares, and provided a not so subtle reminder that he was aware of her vulnerability, and, even more galling, susceptible to him.

She should have slapped his face. Would have, if his action hadn't rendered her momentarily speechless.

Ten o'clock wasn't *late*, and with only six hours' sleep ahead of her she should go straight to bed. Instead, she slid off her stilettos and roamed the apartment, too emotionally wound up to settle to an easy sleep.

Nothing on television held her interest for long, and after utilising the remote to flick through every channel she simply switched off the set, collected a magazine and flipped through the pages with equal uninterest before discarding it in disgust.

A derisive sound emerged from her throat as she doused the lights and made for her bedroom.

She could still *feel* Jace Dimitriades' touch when she began removing her clothes. As she cleansed her face of make-up she was positive she could still *taste* him, and she took up her toothbrush and cleaned her teeth, twice.

So vivid was his powerful image, she was prepared to swear he was there with her as she lay in bed staring into the room's darkness.

Over and over the evening replayed itself, and the memory of his kiss taunted her, awakening her imagination to such a level it became impossible to sleep.

Jace Dimitriades drained the last of his coffee, reached for his suit jacket and shrugged it on, collected his wallet and cellphone, then he exited his hotel suite, took the lift down to ground level and walked out into the sunshine.

He had an hour before he was due to join Luc at a business meeting in the city. Time enough to achieve his objective, he determined as he crossed the street and walked the block and a half to his intended destination.

Blooms and Bouquets was ideally sited, the window display colourful with expertly arranged blooms in numerous vases on stands of varying heights. A background wall held a similar display, and the overall look from outside was a mass of floor-to-ceiling flowers.

The result was visually stunning, and a testament to the two sisters who owned the boutique.

He pushed open the door, registered the electronic buzzer, and offered a greeting to Ana, swivelled his head to include Rebekah, who was deftly assembling a bouquet of orchids at the work table.

'Jace, how wonderful to see you.' Ana slid off her chair behind the computer and joined him. 'Is this a social call?'

He leant down and brushed his lips to her temple. 'How are you?' His smile held affectionate warmth. 'In answer to your question...social and business.'

'Then let's get business out of the way first.'

The phone rang, providing a convenient interruption. Not that he really needed one, but it helped. 'Answer that. Rebekah can organise the order.'

Could she, indeed? From the moment he stepped into the boutique all her senses had snapped into full alert. It was crazy the way her body reacted to the sight of him. Amend that to just *thinking* about him, she admitted wryly. Hadn't that very thing kept her awake last night?

Any hope of having Ana deal with him was shot, leaving her with little option but to place the bouquet taking shape onto the work table and move forward to assist him.

He looked...incredible, the dark grey business suit fashioned by a master tailor, fine cotton shirt, impeccably knotted silk tie. But it was the man himself who took hold of her composure and tore it to shreds.

She didn't like the feeling at all. It had taken two

years to repair the damage Brad had wrought and restore a measure of confidence. To have it undermined in any way was something she'd defend to the death.

Rebekah slipped into the polite, professional role with practised ease. 'Do you have anything particular in mind?'

Good, his presence rattled her. He'd caught the faint tremble in those capable hands, sighted a glimpse of her inner struggle as she geared herself to deal with him. Signs she wasn't anywhere near as calm as she'd have him believe.

'A journey is but a series of many steps.' The quote teased his brain, although he couldn't be sure of its accuracy or its origin, only that the words were pertinent.

Rebekah Stanford intrigued him. He admired the look of her, the strength of character apparent. The exigent sexual chemistry. But it was more than mere physical attraction. There was mystery surrounding her, something he couldn't quite pin down.

During the past year he hadn't been able to dismiss her from his mind. Her features teased his subconscious, the scent and feel of her. The way she'd responded to his touch haunted him...and destroyed anything he thought he could feel for another woman. Plural, he amended ruefully, aware of the few women he'd sought to fill a void.

Now he was back, intent on combining business with pleasure...or was it the other way round? Intent on determining if memory of an emotion still existed, and if it did, just what he intended to do about it.

'Roses.' Their velvety texture, exotic perfume, the exquisite petals so tightly budded just waiting to unfold.

'What colour do you have in mind?'

Rebekah moved towards the temperature-controlled cabinet and indicated several vases holding a variety of colours.

There was the perfection of white, glorious pinks and corals in their various shadings, and deep, dark red.

He didn't hesitate. 'The red.'

She opened the glass door, removed the vase and carried it to the work table. 'How many would you like? The cost—'

'Is immaterial,' Jace concluded. 'Three dozen.'

'Would you like them delivered? An extra charge applies.'

'I'll handle delivery.'

A woman undoubtedly. Hostess, friend, or lover?

If it was a lover, he must possess all the right moves. He'd only been in the country two days.

Rebekah gestured towards a stand containing cards for every occasion. 'Perhaps you'd like to choose a card and write on it while I fix these.' She was already reaching for Cellophane, and mentally selecting ribbon.

Within minutes the bouquet was ready, and she attached the card, accepted payment, then handed him the roses.

Jace took time to admire their assembled artistry, then he presented her with them. 'For you.' He observed a gamut of emotions chase across her expressive features, and saw her struggle with each and every one of them.

'Excuse me?'

'The roses are for you. I suggest you read the card.'

Rebekah read the words with a sense of mounting disbelief. *'Dinner tonight. Seven.'*

'I'll collect you.'

'You don't know where I live.' *What was she saying?* She had no intention of sharing dinner with him.

'Ana will give me the address.'

'No.'

One eyebrow slanted in mocking humour. 'No, Ana won't give me the address?'

'No, I won't accept your invitation.' The thought of spending time with him wasn't a good idea.

'I promise not to bite.'

'Thanks, but no, thanks.' She held out the magnificent sheaf of roses. 'Please take these. I can't accept them.'

'Can't, or won't?' His New York-accented drawl held humour, and something else she couldn't define.

Ana? Where was her sister when she needed her?

It took only a glance to determine Ana was still on the phone. 'I don't date.'

The stark admission appeared to have no effect at all. 'Seven, Rebekah.' He turned and walked from the shop, and her reiterated *no* fell on deaf ears.

She swore, and followed it with a husky litany that damned the male species in general and one of them in particular.

'Oh, my,' Ana declared as she replaced the receiver. 'What did he do? Issue an indecent proposal?'

'He asked me out.' Rebekah's voice came out as an impassioned hiss.

'And that's the extent of his crime?'

Rebekah tossed the bouquet of roses onto the work table. 'I'm not going.'

'Of course not.'

'How dare he come in here and order roses…?' She could hardly contain her anger. '*Three dozen* of them.' Her eyes flashed blue fire. 'Then give them to *me*?'

Ana clicked her tongue and shook her head. 'Very bad taste.'

Rebekah's mouth tightened. 'I'm not accepting them.' She pushed the bouquet into her sister's hands. 'You take them home.'

'Why not you?' Ana queried reasonably.

'I'll return them to stock.' She spared them a glance, and her artist's eye admired the blooms' beauty. Just for a moment she felt a twinge of remorse.

No man had gifted her anything in a while. And never flowers.

'Who does Jace Dimitriades think he is?' It was a question that required no answer, and she banked down a further tirade as a customer entered the boutique.

Rebekah was glad of the interruption, although she seethed in silence for the rest of the day. A number of scenarios as to how she'd deal with him crossed her mind. Some of which, should she put them into effect, would be sure to get her arrested for causing grievous bodily harm.

'Do you have a number where I can contact him?'

It was late afternoon, and Ana was about to leave.

'Jace?'

'Of course, *Jace.*'

Ana's features assumed a thoughtful expression.

'It's been two years since your divorce. Don't you think it's time you emerged into the real world again?'

'You're advocating I have an affair?'

'Who are you afraid of?' Ana queried gently. 'Jace or yourself?' She walked to the door, paused and turned to give her sister a warm smile. 'Think about it.'

Rebekah opened her mouth, then closed it again.

As an exit line, it was without equal.

CHAPTER THREE

IT WAS after six when Rebekah eased the MG into the underground car park and rode the lift to the seventh floor.

Indecisiveness was not one of her traits, yet for the past hour she'd changed her mind at least a dozen times.

On entering her apartment she crossed to the phone, looked up the number for Jace's hotel, punched in the digits, only to replace the receiver minutes later. Jace Dimitriades didn't appear to be in his room, and a request for his cellphone number was politely declined.

Damn. Failure to contact him meant she had little option but to shower and dress in record time. Or stand him up.

Oh, for heaven's sake, she chided silently. A few hours, good food, pleasant conversation... What did she have to lose?

Her sanity, she conceded half an hour later as she replaced the in-house phone, gathered up her evening purse, car keys, then rode the lift down to the lobby.

He stood tall, the image of masculine strength, emanating a sense of power only those totally at ease with themselves were able to exude.

Rebekah met his probing gaze, caught his warm smile, and felt her stomach execute a slow somersault.

Any mental assurance she could survive the evening began to dissipate. Was it too late to change her mind? *Way too late,* an inner voice mocked with derision.

Jace watched the fleeting emotions evident, defined each and every one of them, and felt a sense of male satisfaction in knowing he affected her.

'Rebekah.' He moved forward, appreciating the cut and style of her clothes. The slim black skirt and matching jacket highlighted the creamy texture of her skin, and her make-up was minimal. A touch of gold at her ears and her throat added a pleasing addition. Her hair was drawn into a smooth twist, and his fingers itched to remove the pins and let it fall free.

What would she do if he drew her into his arms and covered that pretty mouth with his own? Undoubtedly she'd react like a frightened gazelle, he decided grimly.

What damage had her ex-husband done to kill her natural spontaneity? Something hardened inside him at the array of possibilities, resulting in a surge of anger against a man he'd never met.

'We'll take my car.'

'I've hired a vehicle for the duration of my stay,' Jace said smoothly, and glimpsed her faint disconcerted glance before it was quickly masked.

She wanted to retain control. It made her feel secure, and she suppressed the momentary uneasiness at Jace's increasing ability to undermine her confidence.

Together they walked through the entrance doors, and Jace led her towards a gleaming Jaguar, unlocked the passenger door and saw her seated, then he crossed in front of the car and slid in behind the wheel.

Rebekah's awareness of him became more pronounced within the close confines of the car, and she banked down the onset of nervous tension. Difficult, when her pulse had already increased its beat and she could feel the thud of her heart.

This was madness. She should have said an emphatic *no*, and, failing that, not left it until the last minute to rescind his invitation.

Except on reflection, his inaccessibility hadn't really given her much choice.

In the restaurant, Jace deferred to her preference in wine, ordered, then requested the menu.

Rebekah wasn't sure she could eat a thing, for her digestive system seemed to be in a mildly chaotic state. And it wasn't just her digestive system!

Oh, *move along,* an inner voice prompted. You're here with him. At least try to enjoy the evening. *Pretend.* Surely it can't be too difficult. You managed OK last night.

Yes, but then Luc and Ana had been present. Now she was on her own, and she'd been out of the social scene for too long. It was two years since she'd exercised her social skills to any great degree. One date soon after her divorce had proven to be disastrous, and at the time she'd vowed not to repeat it.

'Tell me what made you choose to be a florist.'

She took a sip of superb chardonnay, and replaced the goblet onto the table. Blooms and Bouquets...she could do shop-talk. 'The perfection of professionally grown blooms, their textures, colours and scents. The skill in assembling them together so the image conveys something special to the person to whom they're gifted.'

Jace watched her features become animated, her blue eyes deepen and gleam like blue topaz as she elaborated on her craft. Did she know how attractive she was? Or how deeply she appealed to him?

On every level, not just the physical.

'The pleasure, comfort and solace they provide for every occasion,' she continued, smiling in reflection of the many memories she'd shared where warmth and the sheer joy of making someone's day a little brighter became paramount.

'One imagines there's a downside?' he probed, and watched as she wrinkled her nose.

'Early starts, long days on your feet, dish-pan hands from having them constantly in and out of water.' She offered him a wry smile. 'Difficult customers who are impossible to please. The rush to get orders out on time. Incorrect addresses, mistakes made with deliveries by the courier.' She effected a negligible shrug. 'Like any business, there are the accompanying problems.'

The waiter delivered their starters, and they each

began eating. The prawn cocktail was succulent with a delicate sauce on a bed of shredded lettuce, and Jace forked his with evident enjoyment.

Did he enjoy women as much as he enjoyed food? She almost choked at the thought. *Where had that come from?*

She lifted her goblet and took a sip of wine. 'Your turn, I think.'

He set his empty dish aside and regarded her with a thoughtful gaze. 'New York-born to Greek immigrant parents. Graduated from university with a degree in business management.'

Rebekah held his gaze and attempted to define what lay beneath his composed exterior. 'The condensed version,' she acknowledged. '*Business management* covers a broad spectrum.'

'I specialise in takeovers and buy-outs.'

'Large companies with their backs against the wall?'

'Something like that.'

'It fits,' she said simply.

'On what do you base that assumption?'

'You have a ruthless streak,' she inclined with thoughtful contemplation, aware it was more than that. Leashed strength meshed with an animalistic sense of power, a combination which boded ill for any adversary.

'I imagine you wheel and deal with cut-throat determination.' She paused a beat. 'Mostly you win.' She doubted he ever lost...unless it was a deliberate tactical manoeuvre.

'An interesting character analysis,' Jace accorded with musing cynicism.

The waiter removed dishes, and the wine steward refilled their goblets.

Soft piano music provided a pleasant background for the muted buzz of conversation.

'You have family in New York?'

'Parents, one brother, two sisters, and several nieces and nephews.'

Was he removed from them, too caught up being a high-flying entrepreneur and too involved in his own life?

'My mother insists we all get together once a fortnight for a family dinner,' Jace drawled. 'Madness and mayhem would be an accurate description.'

'But fun?' She had a mental image of adults laughing, chiding children, noisy chatter and a table groaning with food and wine.

'Very much so.'

Did he take his women...it had to be plural, although presumably he was discriminative...to visit?

'Not often, no.'

Rebekah endeavoured to still her surprise, and failed. 'You read minds?'

'It's an acquired skill.'

'One in which you excel.'

Jace inclined his head, but there was no arrogance apparent, just the assurance of a man well-versed in the vagaries of human nature and possessed of the ability to deal with them.

It was during dessert that Rebekah happened to

glance towards the restaurant entrance. Afterwards she couldn't say what drew her attention there. Instinct, perhaps? Some deep, inner, protective element alerting her to danger?

For a few heart-stopping seconds she prayed she was mistaken, but she'd have known that profile anywhere, the angle of his head...

'What is it?'

She registered Jace's voice, and tried to tamp down the sick feeling that filled her stomach.

'Rebekah?'

Oh, God. *Think,* she bade silently. There's a good chance he won't see you, and if he does, what can he do?

Plenty.

Jace witnessed her pale features as the colour leeched from her cheeks, and her eyes had dulled an instant before she veiled them with her lashes. What, more relevantly *who* was responsible for rendering her as still as stone?

'Do you want to leave?' His voice was quiet, but serious in its intent.

She wanted to say *yes.* Now, quickly, quietly.

Except that was a coward's way out, and she'd vowed the day she legally severed all ties with him she'd never allow Brad Somerville to intimidate her again. Ever.

'My ex-husband has just walked in the door.'

Was she aware that with so few words she'd conveyed so much? Somehow he doubted it.

'Is it a problem?'

If she stuck with the truth, how would Jace Dimitriades deal with it? A hollow laugh rose and died in her throat. Why in hell would he *want* to?

'No,' she denied, and knew she lied.

Jace's eyes narrowed as he observed her monitor her ex-husband's progress towards a reserved table, and witnessed her fleeting expression the moment the man recognised her presence. It was neither embarrassment nor awkwardness...but fear.

'Well, *hello*.'

Rebekah kept her head erect, her eyes wide and steady. The action was a well-practised one, for she could never be sure what Brad's next move might be.

'Brad.' The acknowledgement was stilted, remote.

'Introduce me to your...companion.'

'Jace Dimitriades.' Jace's voice held a faintly inflected drawl and was dangerously quiet, almost lethal. He made no effort to rise to his feet or take Brad's extended hand.

Rebekah saw something move in Brad's gleaming gaze, recognised the early-warning sign of his temper, and felt her apprehension accelerate.

Brad focused his attention on Rebekah. 'Keeping it all in the family, darling?'

'The *maître d'* is waiting to show you to your table,' Jace intimated with deceptive mildness. Although anyone with any nous would see it as a dismissal. Those who knew him would have quailed at the leashed savagery lurking just beneath the surface.

Brad inclined his head. 'Of course.' His voice softened with silky threat. 'Take care, Rebekah.'

She hadn't realised she'd been holding her breath until she released it, and she forced herself to pick up her spoon and scoop a small serving of fruit, then eat it.

Calm? She felt the antithesis of *calm*. Yet she'd learned her lessons well, and it was far better to attempt normality. In the beginning, after the shock of discovering Brad's dual personality, she'd gone through an entire gamut of emotions...from heartbreaking tears, to anger, remorse, dislike, only to discover it made things worse.

'We can go somewhere else for coffee.'

Rebekah picked up her water glass with a steady hand. 'It's OK.'

Not, Jace determined as he surveyed her features. She was far too pale, and her actions were too rigidly controlled for his liking.

Almost as if she guessed his intention to summon the waiter and request the bill, she voiced quietly, 'Please, don't.'

'His presence here is making you feel uncomfortable.'

Now, that had to be the understatement of the year.

'You don't understand.'

His eyes narrowed, and she sensed a watchful quality evident. 'You think if we leave, he'll have won?'

He was too astute for her peace of mind. 'Yes.'

'Meanwhile you eat food you no longer taste, sip water or wine while we wait for coffee,' he pursued in a silky voice. 'And tie your stomach in knots during the process.'

She knew Brad's *modus operandi* only too well. Interpretation of her ex-husband's wild mood swings, anticipating his reactions had become an integral part of her survival.

'It's better this way,' she said coolly.

'Not for you,' Jace declared with certainty, and saw the slight lift of her chin as she met his gaze.

His own didn't waver from hers as he ordered coffee from a hovering waiter, and he settled the bill, waited patiently for her to finish, then he led her from the restaurant.

'I'll take a taxi,' Rebekah said stiffly, and incurred his swift dark glance.

'The hell you will.'

She didn't say a word, couldn't, for her throat was tight with nerves, and she walked at his side in silence, then slid into the passenger seat the instant he unlocked the car.

It didn't take long to reach her apartment building, and during the short drive she stared sightlessly out the window, unaware of the familiar scenery, the traffic.

Her mind was filled with the scene in the restaurant, Brad, and the electric presence of the man seated within touching distance.

'Thanks for dinner.' Politeness had been ingrained from a young age. She reached for the door-clasp, and froze as his hand captured her wrist.

'Is your ex-husband likely to confront you?'

She paused a few seconds too long. 'Why would he do that? He has no control over my life.'

Jace had questions he wanted to ask, but now was not the right time to get answers...even if she'd be willing to give them to him. 'I'll be in Melbourne for a few days with Luc. I'll ring you.'

'There's no need.'

He leaned closer and slid a hand to capture her nape, tilting her head so she had to look at him. 'Yes,' he said quietly. 'There is.'

For a heart-stopping second she thought he was going to kiss her, and she unconsciously held her breath, aware that a part of her craved the feel of his mouth on her own.

There was a hunger she couldn't quite control, and she trembled with it, wanting in that moment to be absorbed by this man. To have him take her to a place where she could temporarily forget the vindictiveness that lived inside Brad Somerville, and begin to repair the damage caused to her emotional heart.

She heard a faint sound emerge from his throat, and she swallowed painfully as he brushed his thumb over the curve of her lower lip, tracing its fullness.

His eyes were dark, too dark to determine his intent, and she felt the tension in him, the restraint, and knew instinctively the next move was hers.

All she had to do was use the edge of her teeth, the tip of her tongue on the tip of this finger to offer an unspoken invitation.

Dear God, she wanted to, she wanted *him*. Except she hesitated too long, and she thought she glimpsed the gleam of a faint smile, sensed the slight edge of his regret as she pulled back.

Then he did smile, and the hand holding her nape gentled and soothed the tension there for a few seconds, then he released her and eased back in his seat.

She felt as if her limbs were fused together, restricting mobility, and she was intensely aware of the sensual electricity apparent. Explosive and primitive, it shimmered as an elusive force, poised to shatter the shell she'd painstakingly erected around her fragile heart.

'Goodnight.' The word emerged as little more than a strangled sound, and she fumbled for the door-clasp, almost breathless in the need to escape.

Except the constraint of the seat belt stopped her, and she uttered a silent cry as his fingers sought the safety clip and unfastened it.

Within seconds she slid from the car and she almost ran the few steps to the haven offered by the entrance to her apartment building. The keys were plucked free from her purse and she selected the appropriate one as she punched the security code freeing the external door into the lobby.

From there it took only a moment to use her key to gain the area leading to the triple bank of lifts.

She was trembling by the time she reached her apartment, and inside she made for the kitchen, extracted bottled water from the refrigerator and gulped several mouthfuls before seeking a chair.

The evening was over. Although instinct warned whatever she shared with Jace was far from done.

It was as if something deep and primal was being resurrected from her soul, *his*. The sane, sensible part of her brain questioned any metaphysical connection, but the illogical part queried if they hadn't been joined together in a previous life, and their souls were forcing recognition.

Then there was Brad. She tamped down the memories and the pain. A few years was but a small window in the picture of her life. Hadn't that been the professional advice given at the time?

The sudden peal of the phone startled her, and she stood to her feet to take the call, except she was unable to reach the handset and pick up before the answering machine cut in.

Her automated greeting was brief, and she hesitated, wary as to who would be calling at this time of night.

'Having fun with your new man, sweetheart?'

It was followed by a click as the caller replaced the receiver.

Rebekah felt the blood drain from her face.

Brad. There was no mistaking his voice.

Shock jolted her senses and was quickly replaced by a sickening fear.

Her telephone number was unlisted. What ruse had he used to gain it? Had he also gained access to her cell-net number?

She crossed her arms and hugged them together across her midriff as her mind whirled with facts and possibilities.

The restraining order she'd had to take out against

him was still in place. If he chose to violate it he'd face the legal consequences.

Her body began to rock a little until she stilled the movements and crossed to sink down into a chair.

Please, *please,* she begged silently. Don't let the nuisance calls begin again.

Once, only *once* following her divorce had she dated another man. Immediately afterwards Brad had begun a series of phone calls. It had taken complaints to the police, written reports, warnings, and finally the filing of a restraining order to get him to stop.

Now, tonight, a chance meeting had started it all over again.

Thank God she was safe in her apartment. She'd chosen it deliberately for its high-tech security measures, and had installed double locks on her door as well as a safety chain.

She wrapped her arms around her knees and hugged hard. It was *coincidence*...wasn't it? Brad couldn't be having her followed? Even more frightening, monitoring her every move away from Blooms and Bouquets?

CHAPTER FOUR

THE day began much as any other, with the usual pre-dawn visit to the flower market, followed by setting all the blooms into troughs of water at the boutique.

Rebekah booted up the computer, downloaded orders, printed out hard copies, then checked whether she needed to order more stock.

Ana arrived around nine, and together they dealt with orders, customers, and the many phone calls that made up a typical day.

'Are you going to tell me how dinner with Jace went last night, or must I prise it out of you?' Ana queried during a momentary lull.

Rebekah added another spray of baby's breath to the bouquet she was assembling, made a deft adjustment, then gathered in the sheet of Cellophane. 'It was OK.'

'Just...*OK*?' her sister teased.

'If you're asking whether it became deep and meaningful... No.'

Jace was far too astute to move too fast too soon, Ana approved, silently applauding his style as Rebekah anticipated the next query.

'He said he'll phone. Am I seeing him again? I don't think so.'

'Why not?'

Because it'll cause problems for which there's no solution. The very reason she'd scaled her life down to a simplistic level. 'Why?' she countered. 'He's only here for a brief stay, then he'll return to New York. What's the point of starting something that has nowhere to go?'

She desperately wanted to confide about Brad's appearance in the restaurant, his phone call, and the disturbing fact he'd somehow gained access to her private line.

Except something held her back. There was concern for Ana's pregnancy, and besides it was too soon to determine whether Brad was bent on a single nuisance call or if he intended to resort to a repeat of his former behaviour.

She could only pray it wasn't the latter.

At that moment a customer entered the shop, and within minutes everything went to hell in a handbasket.

Luc's former mistress, the glamorous, unpredictable Celine, confronted Ana verbally, then launched into a physical attack that happened so quickly Rebekah wasn't swift enough to prevent it.

It was akin to a horror scene in a movie as Celine swept a glass vase to the floor, where it shattered, and a hard shove sent Ana down among scattered countless shards.

Rebekah gave an involuntary cry and flew to her sister's side, at the same time castigating Celine with pithy, unladylike language. 'You *bitch*,' just didn't begin to cut it.

Everything after that became a blur as Rebekah phoned Petros, Luc's manservant, contacted Luc on his cellphone, then she closed the shop and drove to the hospital, where she paced the visiting-room floor with all the pent-up anger of the demented as she waited for a medical professional to appear and provide a lucid report on Ana's condition.

'Your sister is fine. The ultrasound shows no sign of foetal distress. She's being transferred to a room, and one of the nursing staff will take you to see her soon.'

Rebekah's relief was a palpable thing, and she uttered a silent prayer in thanks.

It took only seconds to punch in Luc's number, relay the update and learn he was about to board a flight back to Sydney.

There was time to call the owner of the boutique adjacent Blooms and Bouquets, explain and request she tape a notice detailing a family emergency to the door.

With that taken care of, she began to relax, and she crossed to the coffee machine, inserted coins and sugared the black brew.

Hot and sweet was the best compliment she could offer, but it served to soothe in the aftermath of the past traumatic hour.

With smooth efficiency she made a series of calls, arranged replacement staff during Ana's enforced absence and notified a few regular customers their orders would be delayed.

Tears filled her eyes the instant she saw her sister

sitting upright in bed with bandages covering her hand and forearm.

'Don't you *dare* cry,' Ana warned, tempering the threat with a warm smile. 'I'm OK.'

'You might very well not have been.' The hug was a very careful one, then she stood back and brought the shaky feeling under control. Just thinking about Celine's crazy attack made her impossibly angry.

'The shop—'

'Is shut, and Jana has taped an explanation to the door.' She met Ana's clear gaze. 'Don't even think of suggesting I go back and leave you here on your own.' A determined smile lightened her features. 'I'm here until they throw me out.' Or at least until Luc arrives, she added silently.

'Promise me you won't work late tonight.'

Rebekah crossed fingers behind her back. 'You've got it.' Did it matter her interpretation of *late* wouldn't match that of her sister? A small transgression from the truth shouldn't count.

She deliberately made no mention of Celine. If Ana wanted to talk about it, so be it. Otherwise the subject was best left alone...for now. Luc, no doubt, would take appropriate action.

Various members of the nursing staff moved in and out of the suite as they conducted routine checks, and a proffered tray of tea and biscuits proved welcome.

Not long afterwards Ana drifted into a light doze, and Rebekah slipped into the corridor to use her cellphone.

A tall, dark-suited figure strode towards her, and

for a split-second her heart stopped. The two Dimitriades men were alike in height and breadth of shoulder, with similar features. Except this was Ana's husband, not Jace.

'Rebekah.' Luc clasped a hand over her shoulder. 'How is she?'

The words were almost cursory in his urgency to see his wife, and she offered him an understanding smile. 'OK,' she assured, and her eyes hardened. 'You're going to deal with Celine?'

His expression became harsh, almost lethal. 'It's done.'

She didn't want to contemplate what action he'd taken, and didn't ask. Whatever it was, she could only be glad she wasn't the one on the receiving end of Luc's wrath. He had the look of a predator who'd staked the kill, and by the time he finished with his quarry all that would remain would be skeletal bones.

'Ana is asleep.' She touched a light hand to his. 'I'll check in later.'

'Thanks.' Momentary warmth lightened his eyes, then he turned and entered the suite.

Rebekah drove to Blooms and Bouquets, popped in quickly to thank Jana for her help, then she unlocked the shop and set to work. A few regular customers were understanding of the circumstances and took up her offer for free delivery. The rest would have to wait until morning.

She took time to ring the hospital, spoke to Ana, then Luc, and learnt her sister would be discharged the next morning.

It must have been after seven when she realised she'd hardly eaten all day, and she rummaged in the small refrigerator beneath the counter, discovered a pot of yoghurt and an apple, demolished both, then continued working.

At nine she locked up the shop and began deliveries. Fortunately they were contained within a fifteen-kilometre radius. Consequently it was almost ten-thirty when she entered her apartment, and she fed Millie before heading for the *en suite*, where she shed her clothes, then she took a leisurely shower and let the heated spray of water ease the kinks from a long, hard day.

Afterwards she donned a silk robe, then padded out to the kitchen. It was way too late to eat a meal, but something light with a cup of tea would take the edge off her hunger.

The message light on her answering machine was blinking, and she filled the electric kettle, popped bread into the toaster, then depressed the message-button in order for it to rewind.

Five, she determined as the first began to play.

A friend, suggesting they go to a foreign art film on Sunday; her doctor's receptionist with a reminder to make an appointment for her annual check-up; Luc, with an update and quietly chiding her for working late.

The fourth message sent her heart slamming against her ribs. 'Two nights in a row, darling? Unusual for you, isn't it?' A click as the message concluded. Then the fifth call ran... 'Taken him to bed yet?'

Brad.

She clenched her hands until the knuckles showed white.

Just then the phone rang, and she stood locked into immobility for a few seconds, then, mindful it could be Luc, she snatched up the receiver, muttered a strangled greeting, then sank down onto the floor as Brad's voice filtered through the receiver.

'Nice of you to pick up, darling.'

Rebekah replaced the receiver, disconnected the handset, then retrieved her cellphone and rang the telephone company's twenty-four-hour number, reported the nuisance calls, cited the restraining order, waited while her details underwent a computer check, and carefully wrote down the digits of her newly assigned private number.

Then she made a cup of tea, carried it into the lounge and switched on the television set in the hope of finding something light and humorous to view.

At midnight she crawled into bed and slept until the alarm woke her four hours later.

Habit was responsible for her mechanical movements as she dressed, drank strong, sweet coffee, dished fresh food for Millie, then she rode the lift down to the car park.

Dark streets with minimal traffic ensured a smooth drive to the flower markets, and with the day's stock stored in the van she did the return journey to Double Bay.

Rebekah worked with efficient speed, paused at seven-thirty to call Luc and give him her newly assigned number.

'Brad?' Luc queried sharply, and she cut in before he could continue.

'I've taken care of it. Don't tell Ana, OK?'

'Want me to intervene on your behalf?'

He was a force to be reckoned with, but she doubted even he could achieve any more than she already had.

'Thanks, but it's done. Give Ana my love. I'll call in to see her after I close the shop.'

'I'm taking her straight from the hospital to the beach house for a few days.'

'Good idea. Tell her I'll phone later this morning.'

'Rebekah.' His voice became clipped, serious. 'Don't be a hero. Brad calls you again, I want to know.'

'You've got it.' She replaced the receiver, dialled the hospital and was put through to her sister, whose reassurance was cheering.

'I'll be back at the shop on Monday.'

'We'll see.'

'Oh, lord, don't you start,' Ana groaned in response. 'If Luc had his way, he'd wrap me in cotton wool and confine me to the house.'

She managed a chuckle. 'That's not such a bad idea.'

'Got to go. The medics have arrived to prod, intrude and note down personal questions.'

Rebekah laughed out loud. 'Sounds like fun.'

'Oh, yeah? Wait until it's your turn, sister, dear.'

For a moment she caught a glimpse of the future, a family gathering on the lawn at Luc and Ana's home, two small children scampering in the sunshine; herself holding a baby...her own, and beside her a man whose face was obscured as he looked down at her.

The image faded, then disappeared, and she shivered.

As if! It was fanciful thinking, stimulated by Ana's pregnancy. And a desire for a child of her own? a tiny voice taunted.

Fool, she chastised as she turned back to the work table and ran a check of the day's orders.

Ana's replacement arrived at eight, a slim, dark-haired girl in her twenties named Suzie, and Rebekah breathed a sigh of relief as the girl proved to be quick and competent.

Together they coped with customers, readied orders for delivery, and Rebekah manned the phone.

When it rang for the umpteenth time she picked up and intoned her customary greeting.

'Rebekah?'

The New York accent gave him away, and the timbre of his voice sent her pulse racing to a faster beat as she managed a cool acknowledgement. 'Jace.'

'I'll be back in Sydney by late afternoon. Share dinner and a movie with me tonight.'

She tightened her grip on the receiver. 'I don't think that's a good idea.'

'Dinner, or the movie?'

'Both. Neither.' Oh, lord, she was losing it! 'No.'

She closed her eyes, then opened them again. 'I have to go,' she said with a hint of desperation, and hung up.

Ana rang mid-afternoon, her voice light, warm, *alive*. It was wonderful to hear her sound so happy, and Rebekah said as much.

'I am,' her sister assured. 'How are things at the shop? No problems? Is the temporary girl panning out OK?'

'So many questions,' Rebekah teased. 'Fine, no, very well. Does that cover it?'

'And you? Are *you* OK?'

Sisterly intuition? 'Of course.'

'Uh-huh.'

'I can take care of myself.'

'I know. With one hand tied behind your back.'

Rebekah choked back a laugh. 'Go give your husband the attention he deserves.'

'I intend to. I'll call you Sunday.'

The afternoon deliveries went out, they tidied up the shop, and Suzie left at five-thirty with a cheery wave and a promise to report early next morning.

Rebekah began moving in some of the outdoor displays, varied coloured cyclamen in decorative pots, Australian natives, ferns, and placed them inside, watered and tended to them.

It was almost time to lock up and go home, and she admitted to a feeling of relief the day was almost over.

The peal of the phone sounded above the muted

background music emitting from the CD player, and she crossed to the counter to pick up.

'I suppose you think you're smart, changing your number,' Brad intoned without preamble.

A sickened feeling invaded her stomach, and she drew a calming breath. Logic, not anger, she'd been advised. State facts clearly, then hang up.

'What you're doing is harassment, and there are legal measures in place to prevent you from bothering me. Why buck the law and invite trouble for yourself?'

She returned the receiver to its cradle, then moved towards the door, only to pause as the phone rang again.

At that moment the door swung inwards and she glanced up to see Jace framed in the aperture for an instant before he entered the shop.

No, Rebekah groaned silently, wishing him anywhere else but here, *now*.

'Aren't you going to answer that?'

The sound of his voice raised all her fine body hairs, and she suppressed the shiver of nerves threatening to visibly shake her slim frame.

Brad *and* Jace? It was too much. Without a word she retraced her steps and snatched up the phone.

'You sound agitated, darling. Am I finally getting to you?'

'You're wasting your time, and mine,' Rebekah added, and cut the connection.

'Problems?'

He couldn't begin to understand the hornets' nest

he'd disturbed, and she took a second to square her shoulders before turning slowly to face him.

Jace didn't like the tension creasing her forehead, the darkness in her eyes, or the edge of pain evident.

'What are you doing here?'

'No *hello*?' he drawled, staying exactly where he was. Crowding her right now would be the height of foolishness.

'I'm about to shut up shop and go home.'

He took a moment to scan the interior before bringing his attention back to her.

'Is there anything I can do to help?'

'Go away and leave me alone?' Rebekah posed, and saw his faint smile.

'I don't consider that as an option.'

The phone rang again, and she chose to ignore it.

'Want me to take it?' Jace queried smoothly, and saw her face pale. 'Brad?' He didn't need her confirmation, the shadows dulling her eyes were sufficient.

'It'll only make things worse if he hears your voice.'

His gaze hardened and his features assumed a grim implacability. 'How bad is it likely to get?'

You can't begin to know. Except the words never left her lips.

'Go collect your purse and we'll get out of here,' Jace commanded quietly.

'You should leave.' Please, she added silently. Can't you see I can't deal with you right now?

'I will, when you do.'

The insistent ring of the telephone proved the deciding factor, and she retrieved her purse, removed the afternoon's takings from the cash register, picked up her keys, then followed him out the door.

Locking up took a few seconds, and she turned towards him. 'Goodnight.' She stepped around him and began walking to her car, only to have him fall into step beside her.

'I thought we'd pick up a pizza somewhere.'

'You do that…solo. I've had a long day.' She unconsciously flexed her shoulders. 'Yesterday was even longer.' And tomorrow she had two weddings scheduled.

'You need to eat.'

'I plan to.' She reached her car, slid in the key and unlocked it. 'Alone.'

'In that case, perhaps you wouldn't mind dropping me off at the hotel on your way home. I caught a cab here.'

She retrieved her cellphone and punched in a series of digits, miscalculated one of them, and reached a wrong number.

Jace watched her expressive features, caught the fleeting emotions, and reached forward to open the car door.

'Who are you afraid of, Rebekah? I can promise not to harm a hair on your head.'

Why did she suddenly feel as if she couldn't breathe? 'Maybe it's not my head I'm worried about.'

A husky chuckle sounded low in his throat, and he spread his hands in silent surrender. 'Pizza, Rebekah. That's all. We both need to eat. Why not together?'

She looked at him. 'That's it? Pizza?'

'Pizza,' he drawled in acquiescence.

She made a split-second decision she had a feeling she might later regret. 'I know a place. Get in.'

King's Cross wasn't too far distant, and at this early hour it would be incredibly ordinary. It wasn't until post-midnight the Cross began to show its true colours, with the pimps, prostitutes, touts displaying their talents. In the back streets lay the dives and dens where the less salubrious deals were made. A place where a wrong move could mean a knife in the ribs, or worse.

Already the surroundings were beginning to change.

Graceful old residences were left behind, with small brick cottages appearing, terrace houses, and the element of care began to diminish.

'I get the feeling you're intent on showing me another side of this beautiful city,' Jace drawled as they neared the Cross.

'A landmark,' Rebekah corrected. 'Ana and I ate pizza here a few nights ago.'

'With Luc's knowledge?'

She began searching for a vacant space to park the car. 'I imagine she told him.'

Jace checked the flashing neon, the floodlit doorways. 'Afterwards, rather than before.'

'You're a snob.'

'No.' New York contained areas where you put your life on the line in daylight. After dark merely trebled the danger. 'I wouldn't want any woman of mine wandering around here after dark.'

'As long as you're moving,' Rebekah assured with a wicked grin. 'Standing still for more than a few minutes isn't recommended, unless you want someone to approach and ask your going rate for sex.'

She spotted an empty space and swung into it, then cut the engine.

'Pizza, you said?'

She led the way to a small shop on the opposite side of the street where the owner's oven-fired pizzas rated as the best she'd ever sampled anywhere. Bright red-and-white-checked tablecloths covered small square tables, empty Chianti bottles held lit candles in various stages of meltdown.

However, the aromas were redolent with spices and garlic, the service warm and friendly, and if you were fortunate enough to gain a window-seat it was a great vantage point to watch the people walk by.

'Rebekah! *Comè sta?*'

A tall Italian Adonis moved from behind the counter and enveloped her in an affectionate hug. '*Bella,* twice in one week?' the man teased. 'If I didn't know you visit only for the pizza, I might begin to think you fancy me.'

She laughed, a glorious, husky, free sound that caught Jace unawares. The frown that had been evident from the moment he walked into Blooms and Bouquets disappeared, and gone was the tension from her eyes.

'Angelo.' The mild admonishment held affection, and he shook his head with mock-regret.

'But I see this is not so,' he said as he moved her to arm's length. 'For you have brought someone with you.' There was a pause as he examined Jace, and something silent passed between them, then it was gone as he returned his attention to her. 'If you seek my approval, you have it.'

Jace saw the soft pink that coloured her cheeks as she smiled and shook her head in silent remonstrance.

'Jace Dimitriades, Angelo Benedetti.'

Angelo extended his hand and Jace shook it. 'Rebekah and I are friends from way back. *Friends,*' he emphasised quietly. 'The window table is yours.' His smile broadened as he held Rebekah's gaze. 'Go take a seat. I have pizza to make.' He moved ahead of them to the table, removed the *reserved* sign, pulled out a chair for Rebekah, indicated the one opposite to Jace, then he crossed behind the counter.

'I gather acquiring the window table is something of an honour?' Jace inclined.

'No one sits here without Angelo's personal invitation to do so.'

He picked up the menu and scanned the varieties listed. 'What do you recommend?'

'The works,' she said without hesitation. 'It's something else.'

It was, and when Angelo personally presented the aromatic masterpiece she watched as Jace savoured it with delighted satisfaction.

He fitted right into the atmosphere, spurning cutlery as he demolished the initial piece. 'Sheer ambrosia.'

'*La dolce vita,*' Rebekah accorded, and went on to reveal, 'Angelo refuses to get into the pizza-delivery game. If you want to sample his pizza, you have to come here to eat it. You get to drink Chianti or coffee, and watch the world go by.' She offered a warm smile. 'The total experience.'

Jace picked up another slice and bit into it. 'Worth it.'

The smile became a husky chuckle. 'I'm glad you think so.'

He stilled, and his gaze was dark, serious. 'Are you?'

The query was quietly voiced, but there was something in his underlying tone that brought all her defences to the fore.

He saw the shutters come down on her expression, and the smile faded from her lips. Such a soft mouth, so many fragile emotions. There was a brief moment when he wanted to smash a fist into her ex-husband's face for the damage he'd done. The little information he'd managed to prise from Luc had made him incredibly angry.

The silence stretched between them, and he ate steadily, aware that she pushed her plate to one side.

He could almost see the conscious effort she summoned to move the conversation on to a safe plane.

'Your trip to Melbourne proved successful?'

'Yes. I have meetings here early next week, then

it's Brisbane, Cairns, Port Douglas, Brisbane and the Gold Coast.'

Idle conversation. The need for it beat silence and eased the tension steadily building inside her.

'Whereupon you return to New York.'

'Yes.'

Nothing explained the sudden pain that pierced her heart, or the sensation of impending loss. What was the matter with her? Jace Dimitriades had no place in her life, any more than she had a place in his. They resided continents apart. Besides, sexual awareness was no basis on which to build...*what*? A relationship?

Dear heaven. Even the thought of sharing sensual intimacy with such a man fired the blood in her veins and sent her nervous system into cataclysmic overload.

Imagining that strong, muscled body naked, his arousal large, hard and pulsing with need. The touch of his mouth on hers, his hands shaping her breasts...

Would he hurt her as Brad had? Take his own satisfaction without any thought for hers? Cruelly taunt her to compensate for his inadequacies?

Somehow she doubted Jace was anything but an experienced and skilled lover. He exuded the confident sensual intensity of a man at ease with himself, and possessed of an intuitive awareness of what it took to please a woman.

How could she explain the yearning deep inside to discover if it was true? To give herself unconditionally to his seduction, exult in the pleasure of it as they soared towards the heights of passion together, shared a mutual shattering climax, followed by the infinitely languorous warmth of drifting fingers, the gentle touch of lips to skin...the exquisite liquid feeling that accompanied lovemaking. Very good lovemaking.

'The pizza is good?'

The sound of Angelo's voice was a stark intrusion and brought her tumbling back to reality. It took a second to marshal her thoughts together and summon a smile.

'Superb, as always,' she reassured, not quite meeting his steady gaze. She needed several more seconds before she could look at Jace.

'Can I bring you coffee? Tea?'

'Tea,' Rebekah ordered. She needed to sleep tonight.

'Make it two,' Jace added, reaching for his wallet.

'Mine,' she insisted, and extracted a note from her purse to cover the bill. 'Don't take his money,' she insisted to Angelo, who laughed with delight and pushed the note towards her.

'What if I refuse altogether?' He inclined his head towards Rebekah. 'Tonight is on the house, my friend. For old times' sake.' He turned to Jace and offered a hard glance. 'Take care of her.'

'Count on it.' Jace's voice was a silky drawl laced with intent, and drew Angelo's silent approval.

The tea arrived, a fine Ceylon blend Angelo kept

for special customers, and she savoured it with genuine enjoyment.

'Do you come here often?'

'Occasionally.'

She liked his hands, the shape and texture of them, their strength. A shiver feathered its way over her skin as she remembered how they felt threading through her hair, capturing her nape the instant before his mouth lowered to hers. Magic. He had the touch, the degree of *tendresse* to melt a woman's heart.

But not hers, she determined with quiet resolve.

'I'll drop you back to your hotel,' Rebekah offered as they farewelled Angelo before emerging outdoors onto the street pavement.

It was still light, but the sky had acquired the dull patina of approaching dusk. Soon the streetlights would spring on, and the regular patrons of the Cross would begin to appear.

Together they crossed the street to her van, and she ignited the engine then eased into the steady flow of traffic.

'How will you manage at the shop until Ana returns?' Jace queried, watching her competent handling of the vehicle, the traffic.

'I was able to get another florist to fill in today, and she's agreeable to work tomorrow.' She drew to a halt at a set of lights. 'I'm seriously considering asking if she'll work part-time. I'll need to discuss it with Ana.'

'And Brad?' He slipped that in, because he felt the need to know.

'I can handle it,' Rebekah assured tightly.

'And if you can't?' Jace pursued.

She spared him a hard glance as the lights changed up ahead. 'The legal authorities will do it for me.'

It didn't make him breathe any easier. There was something primitively evil beneath the layers of Brad Somerville's projected sophistication. Obviously well-hidden to have fooled the woman seated beside him.

The cars up front began to move, and she shifted gears, then followed the main arterial road leading to Double Bay.

It was with a sense of relief she pulled into the entrance immediately out front of the Ritz-Carlton, and she looked in silent askance as Jace removed his wallet, extracted a business card, and penned a series of digits before handing it to her.

'My cellphone number. It'll reach me any time, anywhere.' He cast her a look that was serious in the extreme. 'Call if you need me.'

He reached for the door-clasp, then turned back and fastened his mouth on hers, conducting a slow sweep of the sweet inner moistness with his tongue before deepening the kiss into something frankly sensual.

How long did it last? Scant minutes, but it left him wanting more, much more than the taste of her mouth.

He stifled a sound deep in his throat that was pure regret as he gentled her lips with his own, then he broke the contact and stepped out from the van to stand watching as she sent the vehicle moving out onto the street.

Then he turned and entered the hotel lobby, acknowledged the concierge with a curt nod, and took the lift up to his suite.

CHAPTER FIVE

REBEKAH locked her apartment door and re-set the security alarm before crossing to the kitchen to feed the cat.

A sense of trepidation tied her stomach in knots as she forced herself to check the answering machine, and she expelled some pent-up breath at the sight of its unblinking message light.

Thank God. She closed her eyes, then opened them again in a gesture of innate relief.

Although how long would it take Brad to bypass the telephone company's security and determine her new unlisted number? Technically, it wasn't supposed to happen...which didn't necessarily mean that it couldn't be done.

She lifted her arms high and stretched her body in an effort to dispel kinks from sore muscles, then she moved through to the *en suite* adjoining her bedroom and began filling the spa-bath. Half an hour relaxing there with a glossy magazine and a cup of tea was just what she needed to help her unwind from the day.

It worked just fine, and she crawled into bed, snapped off the bedside light...and lay staring into the darkness as Jace's image filled her mind.

She fell asleep with the vivid memory of how it felt to have his mouth invade hers, and sheer exhaustion was responsible for uninterrupted somnolence until the alarm rang early next morning.

Saturday numbered one of the busiest days of the week, and today didn't prove any different. Suzie was a jewel, and they worked together getting the orders organised, completed, and boxed the two wedding orders ready for the courier, dealt with customers who came in off the street, and even managed to snatch something to eat at reasonable intervals.

There was no lull, little time to think, just the need for smooth efficiency.

Ana checked in around midday, and Rebekah was delighted to hear the happiness emanate from her voice.

There was the opportunity to mention Suzie's suitability to assist part-time, and Ana's *'hire her'* clinched the decision.

'Mornings and all day Fridays and Saturdays,' Rebekah offered, named the rate of pay, and gave a relieved sigh at Suzie's enthusiastic acceptance.

There was a sense of satisfaction and achievement in that Ana was fine with her life back on track; Blooms and Bouquets would continue to operate efficiently.

Two down and two to go, Rebekah rationalised, hoping, praying that her ex-husband's nuisance calls would cease and he'd fade back into the woodwork.

That left Jace Dimitriades, and she had no idea how she was going to deal with *Jace*. If she had any sense and an iota of self-preservation she'd refuse to see him and put him out of her mind.

Fat chance. He was already there, firmly embedded in the recesses of her brain. He made her want something she couldn't have. His image teased her with endless possibilities of what it would be like to *be* with him.

Take that step, and she'd be irretrievably lost. Caught up in a sensual madness that could very well lead to her destruction.

But what a way to go.

'See you Monday.'

Rebekah glanced up from the computer and smiled as Suzie caught up her bag. 'Goodnight. Enjoy the rest of the weekend.'

'Shall do. You, too.'

The glass door swung shut, and Rebekah returned her attention to the computer. She'd save the data onto disk and take it home, where she'd load it into the laptop tomorrow and key in the appropriate accounting entries.

Three customers entered the shop to secure last-minute purchases, and she tended to the last one, then just as she was about to secure the lock Jace appeared at the door.

Just the sight of him sent her pulse racing, and set the butterflies fluttering madly in her stomach. Heat suffused her body, and she deliberately regulated her breathing in a bid to control her wayward emotions. 'I'm just about to close,' she managed evenly. 'Is there something you want?'

His answering smile did strange things to her equilibrium. 'You, to join me for dinner tonight.'

Forget control. His *you* sent her imagination into a tailspin, and she banked down riotous images of tangled sheets, naked bodies…his, *hers,* coupled together in the throes of passion.

What was *wrong* with her? The silent castigation was heartfelt. Had she been locked too long in denial? Was that it? And if so, why *this* man?

Don't answer that.

Her only weapon was humour. She lifted a hand to her chin and tilted her head.

'Ah, you're all alone in the city with no one to call, and I'll do?' What was she doing, for heaven's sake? One didn't tease men of Jace Dimitriades' calibre. 'What if I've made other plans?'

'Have you?'

Honesty came to the fore. 'No.'

'Good.'

'Don't count your chickens too soon,' she warned. 'I haven't said *yes.*'

He lifted a hand and pushed a stray tendril of hair back behind her ear. 'But you will.'

What did she have to lose? Stupid question. Maybe Ana was right, and it was time to loosen a few strings.

'Can we negotiate on a movie?'

'Done.'

'OK.'

Jace gave a deep, husky chuckle. 'You want to be chauffeur, or shall I?'

She pretended to consider both options. 'Oh, let's go for role reversal. Besides, I have a better knowledge of the city than you do.' She checked her watch. 'Pick you up at seven?'

'I'll be waiting.' He glanced around the shop's interior. 'Now, let's get you out of here.'

'I've done it a thousand times on my own.' More, if anyone was counting.

'Then indulge me and let's do it together.'

Five minutes later Rebekah walked to her van as Jace slid behind the wheel of his car.

Neither of them noticed the man seated in a vehicle thirty metres distant. If they had, it would have taken more than a casual glance to determine his identity. A cap worn backwards and wrap-around sunglasses provided a very good disguise.

There were no messages recorded on the answering machine, and Rebekah hit the shower, stepped into clean underwear, tended to her make-up, swept her hair into a smooth knot, then dressed in black evening trousers, a red camisole and matching evening jacket. She added stiletto heels, caught up an evening purse and her keys, then she took the lift down to the underground car park.

The MG was parked in its customary space, and she fired the engine and sent the sleek little sports car onto street level, then drove the few blocks to Jace's hotel.

He emerged from the lobby as soon as she drew into the entrance bay, and within minutes she rejoined the traffic.

'Where to?'

'Darling Harbour.'

'Yessir.'

Jace wondered if she had any idea how her features

lightened? Or how the darkness that was a lurking constant in her eyes disappeared when she smiled?

'Don't be sassy.'

She shot him a grin. 'Just acting out the *chauffeur* part.'

It was a beautiful evening, cool, but not uncomfortably so, and they ate seafood at an elegant restaurant overlooking the inner harbour, drank a little chilled white wine, then took in a top-rated movie guaranteed to earn the lead actors, the producer and director major award honours.

'That was great,' Rebekah accorded as they emerged from the cinema complex and began walking to where she'd parked the MG.

Fine food, beautiful ambience, fantastic movie... great date, *great man,* she reflected, aware this was her first date in a long while. Too long.

She'd played her private life so carefully since her divorce. Brad's erratic behaviour had diminished her self-image, damaged her trust in men, and left her with a heightened sense of the need for self-preservation.

Rebekah reached the MG, unlocked both doors, and slid in behind the wheel as Jace folded his lengthy frame into the passenger seat.

It wasn't a car for a tall, well-built male frame, and it brought him far too close for comfort. She was supremely conscious of his thigh close to the gear-shift, making it difficult for the edges of her fingers not to brush against him each time she changed gears.

There was an acute awareness of his clean male scent combined with the hint of his exclusive brand of cologne. Above all was the intense sensual chemistry apparent…a latent entity that threatened her libido, not to mention her peace of mind.

'Shall we stop off somewhere for coffee?'

Rebekah brought her jangling thoughts together and focused on his words, faltered for a few telling seconds, and offered hesitantly, 'It's late. I—'

'Just…coffee,' Jace reiterated quietly, aware of her escalating nervous tension. 'There are a number of cafés close to the Ritz-Carlton. We'll choose one, and when we're done I'll walk back to the hotel.'

It sounded reasonable, no strings, just the sharing of coffee as a pleasant conclusion to a very enjoyable evening.

Double Bay was known for its trendy cafés, where the day-time clientele lunched and the social élite met and lingered over coffee during the evening. Whatever the time, it was an opportunity to be *seen*.

Finding a parking space took a while, and they strolled along the street-front, chose a café and selected a table.

Coffee at its finest, Rebekah acknowledged silently as she savoured the sweet, aromatic brew. Discussing the merits of the film they'd just seen seemed a safe topic of conversation, and they engaged in an interesting exchange of views.

'You have tomorrow off?'

She stilled, and for a second her eyes assumed a wary expression. 'Yes.'

'I've booked a harbour cruise. It takes approximately six hours and leaves at ten.'

Such cruises were very popular among the tourists, and crew served lunch on board as well as morning and afternoon tea. 'You'll enjoy it.' It was a great way to see the many coves and bays around the inner harbour, view prime real estate, and relax in pleasant surroundings.

Jace held her gaze. 'Join me.'

She was willing to swear her heart stopped for a few seconds before racing into a thudding beat. 'There'll be a running commentary informing passengers of various vantage points throughout the day. You won't need me along.'

His smile held warmth and something she was reluctant to define. 'I want you along.'

'Jace…' She paused, then stumbled over the words, 'I can't keep seeing you.'

'Can't, or won't?'

Oh, lord, this was getting out of hand. *'Why?'*

There was despair in the query, and it angered him to think her ex-husband had done such a number on her.

'The truth?' His gaze speared hers. 'I want to spend time with you.'

To what end? The obvious one wasn't an option. 'I won't have sex with you.' Stark words that matched his in honesty.

'If I just wanted sex, there are several numbers I could call.'

So he could. Numbers listed in the trade papers, the telephone yellow pages...and failing that, all he had to do was ask a discreet question of the hotel staff to have the relevant information supplied.

'So,' he drawled silkily. 'Shall we start over?'

She took a deep breath and slowly released it. 'I usually do domestic chores on a Sunday.' Go to the gym, meet a friend for coffee, take in a foreign film, read, relax. It was a token excuse, and they both knew it.

Oh, *dammit*. She spread her hands in a gesture of surrender. 'All right, OK.' She was angry, with herself, *him,* for being manoeuvred into a position where it would seem churlish to refuse. 'I'll go.'

Rebekah glimpsed the gleam of humour in that dark gaze, and she could have sworn the edge of his mouth twitched. 'Such a gracious acceptance.'

She drained the last of her coffee. 'I think it's time I went home.' She stood to her feet. 'Thanks for an enjoyable evening.'

He duplicated her movements, extracted a note and anchored it on the table. 'I'll walk you to your car.'

'I'll be fine,' she stated firmly. 'Goodnight.' She turned away from him and quickened her steps, aware that he fell in beside her.

'Has anyone told you you're impossible?' she flung tersely, and missed the fleeting amusement apparent.

'Rarely to my face.'

'Obviously it's high time someone did.'

There were people seated outdoors beneath large shaded umbrellas, and she was conscious of background chatter, music emitting from speakers, and cars cruising the street searching for a parking space.

Within minutes they reached the MG, and she unlocked the door, then slid in behind the wheel, slipping the key into the ignition without pause.

Jace leaned down towards her. 'Join me for breakfast at the hotel. Eight. Then we'll head for the pier.'

Rebekah looked at him steadily. 'I'll eat at home, and meet you in the hotel lobby after nine.'

She fired the engine as he stood upright and closed the door. With consummate skill she eased the car out from its parking space and resisted the temptation to check the rear-vision mirror as she entered the flow of traffic.

Rebekah slept well and woke feeling refreshed and ready to meet the day. Choosing to wear dress-jeans and a T-shirt, she tied a sweater over her shoulders, applied sun-screen beneath her minimum make-up, and swept her hair into a careless knot atop her head.

Shortly after nine she slid her feet into joggers, caught up her shoulder bag, her keys, then took the lift down to the underground car park.

Jace had also chosen casual attire, and her heart jolted at the sight of him in jeans and a polo shirt. He held a jacket hooked over one shoulder, and he was something else.

He walked towards her, and she admired the way the jeans moulded his thighs, hugged his hips, while the polo shirt clung to his hard-muscled torso, emphasising an enviable breadth of shoulder.

'Hi.' As a greeting, it fell short by a mile, but it was the best she could do with her breath caught in her throat as he slid into the passenger seat.

'Morning.' His appraisal was swift, encompassing. 'You slept well?'

Oh, my, how did she answer that? Admit his image had filled her imagination and her last waking thought had been of him?

'Yes, thank you.' Why was she sounding so excruciatingly polite? 'And you?'

'Fine.'

His smile broadened, and her stomach curled as the grooves slashing each cheek became more defined, and tiny lines fanned out from the corners of his eyes.

Rebekah moved the gear-shift and sent the MG out onto the street, driving with practised ease as she headed towards the city pier.

He exuded latent strength…not only of the body, but of the mind. A man who went after what he wanted with steel-willed resolve, she perceived, and wondered at his strategy with regard to *her*.

A convenient but brief affair while he tended to business? Why go for emotional entanglement when he could pay for sex, then walk away?

It didn't make sense. None of his actions made sense.

Unless… No, she dismissed instantly. He wasn't attracted to her. *Intrigued,* possibly. Was he aware of the sexual chemistry that shimmered between them? Or was it one-sided and all *hers*?

Oh, for heaven's sake, get a grip, she mentally chastised. He's Luc's cousin, he's in Sydney on business, you're the sister of his cousin's wife. He's simply being kind.

So why didn't it feel like *kind* when he touched her? *Kissed* her?

So how *did* it feel? a tiny imp taunted.

Like she'd caught a glimpse of heaven on earth. Something she dared not hope for, in a place she was afraid to occupy.

Fear of rejection? Afraid it wouldn't, *couldn't* last?

She'd experienced one particular taste of hell. She wasn't keen to sample another.

But what if you're wrong? What if you're choosing to deny something incredibly wonderful simply because one man fooled you with a Jekyll-and-Hyde personality?

Just enjoy the day, why don't you? she admonished silently as they walked out onto the pier and boarded the large cruise boat equipped to carry up to fifty passengers and crew.

The sun shone brightly with the warmth of an early summer, and the sky was a clear azure. A breeze became evident as the boat moved out into the harbour, and Rebekah pointed out prime real estate built on the rocky cliff-face that bordered the many coves and inlets.

There were numerous craft moored, some small, others large and luxurious, and she indicated various landmarks, homes of the rich and famous as the boat cruised the inner harbour.

For a while they moved out on deck, and she was conscious of Jace's presence, the light touch of his hand on her arm, the way her body reacted to his as he leaned in close to follow her line of vision as she indicated certain focal points of interest.

Way out in the distance a huge tanker was slowly making its way in, and as they returned city-side there were two tugboats steaming out to meet a luxury liner, a solid, oft-used ferry boat chugging towards the North Shore, and a sleek hydrofoil bringing passengers in from Manly.

Where better to view the wide, distinctive arch of the Harbour Bridge, the graceful architectural curves of the Opera House?

Sydney was a beautiful city with one of the finest harbours in the world. Today, looking at it from a visitor's viewpoint, there was a sense of pride in the familiar, an innate feeling of patriotism.

The sun had moved overhead and was now shifting towards the west, washing the buildings, some old, some new in towers of concrete, steel and glass.

Glorious by day, stunning at night when electric light shaped the many buildings against an indigo sky, and multicoloured flashing neon added colour and interest to an intriguing night-scape.

'Beautiful.' Jace's voice was quiet, almost husky, and Rebekah turned towards him, words of agreement escaping her lips.

Except he wasn't admiring the view, he was looking at her.

For one brief minute it seemed as if the world shifted slightly, and she barely refrained from reaching out a hand to steady herself.

Crazy. Perhaps she imagined it, and it was the boat?

But no, it was moving steadily, there was no backwash, and the harbour waters were as smooth as glass.

This was bad. Really bad.

She leaned forward against the railing and concentrated on a small liner as it lay moored, then she shifted her attention to the row of city buildings.

Most all of the passengers had emerged onto the deck, and she gave a surprised start as Jace moved to position himself behind her.

It was, she realised, a polite gesture to allow others room to share the view, and his arms caged her body as he fastened his hands on the railing.

His body wasn't touching hers, but she was supremely aware just how easy it would be to lean back against him. Have him link his arms at her waist, and rest his chin against her head.

For a moment she felt as if she couldn't breathe, and panic that he might sense her discomfort forced her to regulate every breath in an effort to slow her rapidly beating pulse.

The cruise boat docked at four, and the passengers lined up ready to disembark. Jace stood behind her, and he put a hand to her waist to steady her as they stepped down the gangplank.

She felt the heat of his touch, and her stomach executed a backward flip.

Nerves, she decided, were hell and damnation. Her body seemed to be in a permanent state of flux whenever Jace Dimitriades was within touching distance.

'We're not far from the aquarium,' Jace declared. 'I checked out its location this morning. We've time for a quick tour before it closes.'

'*We?*' She shot him a startled glance. 'I don't think—'

'You have an aversion to sea creatures?'

'No.'

'You visited last week, and can't bear to do it again so soon?'

Dammit, he was teasing her. Well, two could play at that game. 'Fish?' she queried sweetly. 'You want to go see *fish*?'

His warm smile tore the breath from her throat. 'With my favourite tour guide for company.'

Rebekah gave a small mock-bow. 'Australian residents have a duty to please their overseas visitors.' She indicated a flight of steps. 'Shall we proceed?'

The staff member manning the aquarium ticket box shook her head doubtfully and reminded there was less than an hour before closing time.

'We'll walk very quickly,' Rebekah assured as Jace picked up the tickets.

Some exhibits were exotic specimens, others fearsome, especially in the large aquarium housing various predators. The enclosed areas held a damp salty smell, and Rebekah breathed in fresh air as they emerged out into the sunshine and began walking to where she'd parked the car.

'How dedicated are you to playing tour guide?' Jace queried as he slid into the passenger seat.

She turned towards him. 'You don't want to go back to the hotel?'

'I'd like to explore the Rocks,' Jace declared, and saw her eyes widen.

The area was in an old part of the city bordering on the harbour and held a variety of shops, stalls and numerous cafés and restaurants.

'You're kidding me, right?'

'We could grab something to eat there.'

This was going a bit too far. 'We've spent all day together,' she managed evenly.

'So, what's a few more hours?'

Common sense urged her to refuse. 'I have things to do at home.' It was a token protest.

'Want for me to help out?'

There was a part of her that was tempted to call his bluff just to see him undertake domestic chores.

'Somehow I can't summon an image of you handling a vacuum cleaner or wielding an iron.'

'I managed both during my years at university.'

Caution rose to the fore at the thought of him visiting at her apartment. Mutual ground, *public* ground was infinitely safer.

Rebekah ignited the engine. 'OK, the Rocks it is.' Two hours, she qualified.

They stayed twice as long, wandering at ease, pausing here and there, then Jace chose a restaurant where the food was superb, and they lingered over coffee, enjoying the ambience, the background music.

A sense of latent intimacy seemed to manifest itself, something she put down to the glass of wine she consumed during the course of the meal. She was acutely conscious of the man seated opposite, aware to a finite degree of the inherent vitality beneath his sophisticated façade. Primitive sexuality meshed with elemental sensuality...a dangerous combination, and more than most women could handle.

Yet it awakened something deep within her, an entity she was almost afraid to explore for fear of being burnt.

Safe meant not seeing him again. And, dear heaven, she had every reason to covet safety.

'Shall we leave?'

Jace's voice intruded, and she pushed her empty cup to one side. 'Yes. I have an early start tomorrow.'

He took care of the bill, and they exited the restaurant, choosing to walk the esplanade path to where she'd parked the MG.

Rebekah felt the touch of his hand at her waist, and she experienced a feeling of surprise, almost shock when it slid to capture her own.

For a moment she froze, her first instinct being to pull free, except she hesitated too long and his fingers shifted to thread themselves through hers in a loose linking that was warm, intimate.

It made her want to shift closer, feel the strength, the heat, of his body. More than anything, she longed for his arms close around her, to sink in against him, have his mouth capture her own and wreak sensual devastation.

Yet she hesitated, aware any move on her part would invite more than she was prepared to give.

At that moment his thumb slid against the sensitive veins at her wrist, then began an evocative caress as her pulse jumped and skidded to a heavy beat.

Could he tell? How could he not? she groaned inaudibly. She couldn't disguise the response of her body, and almost as if he knew he lifted her hand to his lips, lightly brushed them to her fingers, then let their joined hands fall.

Oh, my. She felt as if rockets were being launched inside her head, with the aftershocks reverberating through her entire body.

It was a fine kind of madness, fed by desire and fuelled by too vivid an imagination.

Rebekah was grateful when they reached the car, for it enabled her to break contact and slide in behind the wheel.

She wasn't capable of uttering so much as a word, and she didn't even try. Instead she focused on negotiating the traffic, and there was a sense of relief as she drew into the hotel entrance.

Short-lived, she discovered as Jace slid the gearshift into neutral, then he leaned towards her and captured her head, angling it as he fastened his mouth over hers in a kiss that tore her vulnerable emotions to shreds.

Seconds or minutes? She had no idea how long it

lasted, only that she felt cast adrift like a rudderless boat in the open sea.

Did she kiss him back? Perhaps she had. All she knew was that when he released her she felt totally lost.

She couldn't speak, and her eyes felt impossibly large as she simply looked at him, and she gave a start of surprise as he touched a finger to her lips.

His smile held incredible warmth, and she felt herself begin to melt...which was crazy.

'I'll phone you tomorrow.' He reached for the door-clasp and slid out from the car.

For a heart-stopping second she couldn't move, then she became conscious of the concierge standing at the entrance, valet parking staff, and she shifted gears then put the MG in motion.

Rebekah entered her apartment a short while later and crossed to the kitchen for a cool drink. It was then she saw the message light blinking on her answering machine.

Ana? Unlikely, given her sister preferred direct contact to her cellphone.

She crossed to the machine and depressed the 'replay' button, waiting as the tape automatically rewound.

'How was your day with lover-boy?' Brad's voice was low and ugly. 'Don't bother changing your silent number again.' There was a click as he ended the call.

Rebekah stood still for what seemed an age, then she located the number she'd been advised to call, day or night, and filed a report.

It did little to ease her mind. Nothing to stem the sense of frustrated anger that rose to the fore as she re-set the answering machine.

She took a shower, then slid into bed to lie staring at the darkened ceiling for what seemed *hours* before she succumbed to sleep, where nightmarish dreams invaded her subconscious, and when she woke to the sound of the alarm it was as if she hadn't slept at all.

CHAPTER SIX

'BITCH. You'll pay for this.'

Rebekah clutched the receiver as the male voice vented in a sibilant tone that held more threat than if Brad had screamed the words in her ear.

The shop held two customers, Suzie was dealing with one, and the other was examining a glorious stand of gladioli.

Rationalising with him was a waste of time, but she tried. 'You're in violation—' a click indicated he'd ended the call '—of the restraining order,' she finished to an empty line.

The electronic door buzzer sounded, and she replaced the receiver, summoned a smile and turned to see Jace standing inside the door.

Her senses stirred at the sight of him. The dark three-piece suit, deep blue shirt and silk tie indicated he'd come straight from a business meeting, and he removed the lightly tinted sunglasses, silently indicated she serve the waiting customer, then browsed the various bouquets on display.

It took a while for the customer to make a choice, and Rebekah completed the purchase, then crossed to Jace's side.

She looked pale, and her eyes bore the lacklustre appearance of someone battling tiredness and, unless he was mistaken, a headache. He doubted she'd slept any better than he had.

He lifted a hand and tucked back a stray lock of hair that had escaped the knot atop her head. And watched her eyes dilate at his touch.

'Feel up to sharing one of Angelo's pizzas?'

All she wanted to do was go home, soak in a hot tub, then grab a salad, veg out in front of the television for an hour, and make up on lost sleep.

'I'd planned on an early night.'

'You've got it. I've at least an hour's work on the laptop, and I'm due to take the early-morning flight to Cairns.' He didn't add that he'd originally intended flying out tonight, but had shifted the booking to tomorrow. 'I'll be here when you close.'

His smile made her toes curl. She should refuse, but she didn't. 'OK.'

'Wow,' Suzie said with genuine awe when Jace had left the shop. 'Who *is* that man?'

Rebekah explained the connection, and Suzie rolled her eyes.

'Is your sister's husband equally attractive?'

'Equally,' she assured solemnly.

'I don't suppose there are any more male cousins here or abroad?'

'A few.'

Suzie gave an impish grin. 'I *know* I'm going to enjoy working here.'

Jace reappeared just as Rebekah was about to lock up, and gone was the formal business suit. In its place were jeans and a casual chambray shirt left unbut-

toned at the neck. He'd rolled the cuffs back and discarded shoes for joggers.

'All done?'

Luck saw them park close to Angelo's pizzeria, and
they ordered, choosing take-out rather than electing
to eat in, and strolled along the main street while they
waited on the pizza.

'Tough day?'

Jace caught hold of her hand, and she didn't object.
'Not really. Ana insisted on putting in a few hours,
against Luc's and my wishes. Fortunately Suzie is
good at taking up the slack.' She spared him a direct
glance. 'Yours?'

'Bearable.' He didn't add he'd spent most of it
wanting the day done so he could spend time with
her.

A tout called out to them from an open doorway,
only to halt his outrageous spiel as Jace directed him
a chilling look.

Angelo had the pizza boxed and ready to go when
they returned to the shop.

'Where do you suggest we eat this?' Rebekah
asked as she eased the van into the flow of traffic.

'Your apartment?'

It was her own private domain, and only family
visited her there. When it came to joining friends, she
chose a restaurant, café, cinema or shopping complex
as a meeting place.

'I don't think that's a good idea.'

'My hotel?'

A park bench? Drive out to one of the beaches? By then the pizza would be cold.

'We'll go to my place.' She shot him a direct look. 'Just be warned I intend chucking you out at nine.'

'So noted.' His drawl held an element of husky humour.

Minutes later she used her key to unlock the sliding steel grille guarding entrance to the underground car park, eased in beside the MG, then they rode the lift to the seventh floor.

As soon as she opened the apartment door Millie was there, rubbing her head against Rebekah's leg, only to back up and regard Jace with feline curiosity.

'The kitchen's through the lounge to the right.' She led the way. 'I'll show you where the plates are kept, and you can apportion the pizza while I feed Millie.'

The message light on the answering machine was blinking, and her stomach tightened.

'You want to get that?' Jace asked, indicating the machine, and she shook her head.

'It won't be anything that can't wait.' If it was Brad, she'd prefer to run it when she was alone.

They ate pizza seated at the dining-room table, and she unearthed a bottle of red Lambrusco, extracted two wine glasses, filled both, and handed him one.

There was an easy familiarity in the gesture, although nothing discounted the electric tension fizzing along her nerve threads.

'How long will you be away?' It was the only thing she could think to offer, and he finished the mouthful he was eating before responding,

'Four days. I fly direct to Cairns tomorrow, visit Port Douglas Tuesday morning, take the late-afternoon flight Wednesday to Brisbane, visit the Gold Coast Friday morning, and return to Sydney late afternoon.'

'Real estate?'

'Shopping complexes, warehouses,' Jace added as he reached for another slice of pizza.

'You assess, buy at a low price, move in a team to upgrade, promote, then sell when they're showing a handsome profit.' It was just a guess, but she imagined it to be a fairly accurate one.

Rebekah demolished two slices, then slowly sipped her wine.

'Something like that,' he declared indolently. He didn't add that he headed a family consortium with global business interests, and he kept a personal check on all of them. The Sydney arm had initiated some major staff changes at its top level, and he'd chosen to cast a personal eye over the new MD's purchase proposals. And check out if his attraction for Ana's sister was as tantalising now as it had been a year ago.

The answer was easy. The solution, however, was anything but.

The women in his life had been eager, willing, and practised in the art of seduction. Relationships clear-cut, boundaries established and recognised, and while affection formed a base, *love,* the everlasting kind, had never rated a mention.

Until the event of Luc and Ana's marriage he'd

been content with the status quo. There were any number of women he'd be satisfied to have as his wife. But none he'd covet as the mother of his children. Which had to tell him something.

For the past year he'd immersed himself in work, dated few women more than a token once or twice, indulged in selective sex, and become very aware that while it might satisfy his libido, any emotional pleasure was sadly lacking.

'Would you like some coffee?'

'Thanks. Black, one sugar.'

Rebekah stood to her feet, gathered up the plates and cutlery and carried them through to the kitchen.

The headache she'd fought against most of the afternoon intensified, and she opened a cupboard, retrieved painkillers, popped two from the pack and swallowed them down with water.

'Headache?'

She hadn't heard him leave the dining room, and her hand shook a little. 'It's nothing a good night's sleep won't fix.'

His mouth curved into a faint smile. 'Is that a hint I've outstayed my welcome?'

'No,' she managed quietly. 'No, of course not.'

The smile reached his eyes. 'Good.' He moved round the servery, took the glass from her hand and put it down, then he captured her face in his hands and began gently massaging her temples.

She opened her mouth to protest, only to have him press his thumb against her lips.

'Shh. Just relax.'

It felt like heaven as his fingers moved to massage her scalp, and she instinctively lowered her lashes so her gaze fastened on the hollow at the base of his throat where a pulse beat so strongly there.

His touch held a mesmeric quality, almost as if a part of him was invading her senses, and she swayed slightly, caught in the sensual magic he was able to evoke.

A slight sound brought her lashes sweeping wide, and she almost died at the magnetising warmth evident in his slumberous gaze.

Her lips parted involuntarily, and she glimpsed the warmth turn to heat, then his mouth slanted over hers, gently at first as his tongue took an exploratory sweep before tangling with her own in an evocative dance that demanded more, much more.

One hand fisted her hair while the other slid down past her waist to hold her fast against him, and she lifted her arms and linked her hands together at his nape as she leaned into him, exulting in the feel, the taste, the sensual heat of him.

It was like nothing else she'd experienced before as he wrapped her close, so close, his hands shaping her waist, her hips, buttocks.

His mouth left hers and nuzzled the sensitive curve at the edge of her neck, then trailed a path to nibble her earlobe before seeking her mouth as he took her deep in a sensual imitation of the sex act itself.

Almost as if he sensed he was going too far too fast he eased up a little, locking her hips close to his own so she couldn't help but be aware of his arousal.

Its potent force took her breath away, and she wondered what it would feel like to have him inside her, moving in an ever-increasing rhythm until he reached his peak.

There was a part of her that wanted to be swept away by the tide of passion. To have no thought, no scruples, no reservations. Just follow wherever he chose to lead.

Would the reality exceed the limits of her experience, and prove to be as mesmeric as she imagined it could be?

Somehow the answer had to be *yes*. This man possessed the touch, the sexual expertise to indulge a woman in a feast of the senses. From acutely sensitive to the raw and primitive.

A shiver feathered its way over the surface of her skin, raising all her fine body hairs in anticipation as treacherous desire pulsed from deep within.

She wanted the tactile touch of skin on skin, and the need for it drove her to seek the opening of his shirt. There was a primal urge to fist the material and tug it free from his jeans then drag it off so she could rain his torso with the heated pressure of her mouth. To gently nip the hard muscle tissue close to a male nipple, then caress each one with her tongue, teasing mercilessly until he groaned at her touch.

More than anything, she wanted him to bestow her the same favour, to drive her sensually wild until there could be only one end.

Her audio-visual senses were so caught up in the mindless fantasy she was only dimly aware of a ring-

ing in her ears, and she gave a despairing groan as
Jace gently broke contact.

'Should you get that?'

The phone. Dear heaven, it was the *phone*.

The answering machine picked up, and she froze.
Please, *please* don't let it be Brad.

Jace held her loosely, his gaze intent as he witnessed her disquiet.

'Inviting him into your apartment isn't a good
move, darling.' Brad's voice was unmistakable. 'Has
he discovered you're a frigid little bitch?' There was
a click as he cut the connection, the faint whirr of the
answering machine as it rewound the tape.

Rebekah wanted to curl up and die. She closed her
eyes in an involuntary gesture of self-defence, then
opened them again to focus on the third button of
Jace's shirt.

A hand cupped her chin, tilting it so she had to
look at him, and she fought to hold back the moisture
shimmering in her eyes.

'Don't.' Jace framed her face between his hands,
and smoothed a thumb over lips made slightly swollen from his kiss.

She wasn't capable of uttering a word, and her eyes
ached with unshed tears.

He saw her lashes lower to form a protective veil,
and pain stabbed his gut as a single tear escaped and
rolled slowly down one cheek.

'Please,' she said huskily. 'Just go.'

She felt his thumb erase the trail of moisture, and

his hands were incredibly gentle as he cradled her face.

'No.'

'Please,' she reiterated as he tilted her face.

'Look at me.'

The command was softly voiced, and she felt his fingers trail the slope of her neck, linger at its edge, then return.

The peal of the phone was an intrusive, strident sound in the stillness of the room, and he felt the tremor that ran through her body.

With one economical movement Jace reached forward, lifted the receiver, listened, then ventured in a deadly soft voice, 'Don't ring again if you value your skin.' He cut the connection and didn't return the receiver to the handset.

'I suggest you change your number.'

'I've already done that twice in the past two days.' He may as well hear the rest of it. 'The police have been notified, and my lawyer.'

He understood too clearly. 'Who each advise keeping your answering machine on to record each of his calls.'

'Yes.'

'Which have only accelerated since he saw us together at the restaurant last week.'

Rebekah didn't concur, she had no need to. Brad's reaction was self-explanatory.

'Is there a possibility he might attempt to physically hurt you?'

She paused a second too long. 'I don't think so.'

'He doesn't have a key to your apartment?'

She shook her head. 'I bought it following the divorce.' And lived with Ana between leaving Brad and obtaining her legal freedom. It had been a fraught time, laced with various incidents involving her ex-husband's harassment. She'd neither sighted nor heard from him in ages. Until Wednesday of last week. Now the torment seemed set to begin all over again.

'Would you like me to stay over tonight?'

Shocked surprise widened her eyes. 'No, of course not.'

A gleam of humour lit his gaze. 'I imagine you have a spare bedroom.'

She did, but she didn't intend for him to occupy it tonight or any other night. 'I'll be fine.'

Would she? Somehow he doubted she'd sleep easily.

'Only a fool blames another for his own inadequacies.' The words slipped quietly from his lips, and when she didn't answer, he smoothed his palm along the edge of her cheek. 'And it would take an incompetent fool to allude to a woman's frigidity.' He waited a beat. 'Especially when the woman is *you*.'

He wanted to show her how it could be between a man and a woman, watch as she came alive beneath his touch. To kiss and caress every inch of her, awaken each nerve-end, and be aware only of him. Malleable, mindless, *his*.

Except he wanted her *with* him, mind, body and

soul. Not on edge with nervous tension, or emotionally shaken.

'I think you should leave.' She just wanted to be alone, secure within these four walls, where she could sink into the hot tub, then pull on a robe, view television for an hour before slipping into bed.

'Not yet,' Jace said quietly. Not until she'd regained some colour and her eyes didn't resemble huge pools mirroring a mixture of hurt and shame.

'We were going to have coffee.' A return to the prosaic was the wisest course, and he moved round her, collected the carafe from the coffee-maker and filled it with water.

Rebekah collected her shattered thoughts together and crossed to extract coffee mugs from a cupboard, coffee beans, a fresh filter, and set it all in place.

The automatic movements helped, and within minutes they faced each other across the table as they sipped aromatic coffee.

'Tell me what it was like for you as a child.'

She recognised his diversionary tactic, and cast him a level glance. 'The usual things that shape most children's lives. Love and laughter, a few tears, happy family, school. My mother died a few years ago. Dad has very recently taken a new job in New York.'

'You and Ana are very close.' It was a statement based on his own observation, and her gaze softened.

'We're best friends as well as business partners.'

It was difficult to look at him and not be startlingly aware of the way it had felt to be in his arms, his touch, the intensity of his kiss, and the way he'd been able to transport her to a place where sheer sensation ruled.

There was a part of her that wanted to be taken there again. By him, only him. Just thinking of Jace as a lover brought a flood of heat to her body, and yet instinct warned if she allowed him into her life she'd never be the same again.

Was it worth the risk? Not if she wanted to survive emotionally. This man would invade her senses, her heart, and forever leave his mark.

'You haven't mentioned your marriage.'

The sound of his accented drawl brought her back to the present with a sudden jolt, and she tightened her grip on the coffee mug.

'What do you want to hear? That I was courted by a man for several months, engaged to him for a year, and in all that time I had no inkling a few hours after the wedding he'd turn into an abusive monster?'

He was silent for several long seconds as he held her gaze. 'It must have been hell to deal with.'

And then some. 'And you, Jace? No skeletons in your cupboard?'

'A few regrets.' Everyone had some. 'None of any consequence.'

He wanted to ease the pain he glimpsed in her eyes, but knew she'd deny him if he did. Instead, he drained his coffee, then stood to his feet.

'Time for me to call it a night.' He took his mug into the kitchen and put it in the sink, then he pre-ceded her to the door.

Rebekah caught up her keys and followed him. 'I'll drive you back to the hotel.'

'I'll call a cab from the downstairs lobby.'

'Don't be ridiculous.'

He turned towards her and pressed a finger to her lips, then he lowered his head and brushed his mouth to her temple. 'I'll phone tomorrow.'

She opened her mouth to protest, but he was already walking towards the bank of lifts, and she waited there until the lift doors opened. Then she retreated into the apartment, locked up, set the alarm, and headed for the hot tub.

CHAPTER SEVEN

'HAS Brad been bothering you again?'

Rebekah caught the fierce sisterly concern in Ana's voice, and tried to diffuse a potentially sensitive subject. 'Why do you ask?'

'This is *me*, remember? And I don't fool easily. So spill it.'

Suzie was on a lunch break, and they were alone in the shop.

Rebekah refrained from prevaricating, but she kept it simple. 'You know the score. Every now and again Brad decides to ride the nuisance wagon. So I changed my silent number to minimise the hassle.'

'Uh-huh. This wouldn't have anything to do with the fact you've been seeing Jace?'

It was a rhetorical question, and they both knew it.

'I'm not *seeing* Jace,' she refuted, paying far more attention than necessary to the bouquet she was assembling.

'OK, we won't go there just now.' Ana's gaze held a degree of anxiety. 'Watch your back, Rebekah,' she warned gently. 'Brad is a loose cannon just waiting to explode.'

She controlled the shaky sensation that threatened to visibly exert itself, and met her sister's gaze.

'I'm doing everything I've been legally advised to

do,' she assured quietly. 'It's been two years since the divorce. I'm entitled to a life of my own.'

Ana's expression softened. '*Brava.* You, more than most.' There were assurances she wanted to reiterate, but she wisely held her counsel. 'Promise you'll phone me at the slightest hint of a problem. OK?'

Rebekah offered a wry smile. 'Want me to write it in blood?'

The phone rang, and Ana picked up, intoned the customary greeting, conversed for a few minutes, then held out the cordless receiver. 'For you. Jace.'

'Hi. How are you?'

'Do you really want to know?' His voice was low and husky, almost intimate, and she barely controlled the spiralling sensation deep within.

'How was the flight? Cairns?'

'Fine. Better if you were with me.'

The breath stopped in her throat. 'I have to go, we're really busy.'

She thought she heard his faint chuckle. 'Take care, Rebekah. I'll call you on your cellphone tonight.'

Rebekah handed the cordless receiver to Ana with a lift of her eyebrows. 'Nothing to say?'

'And risk having you jump down my throat?' There was humour in her voice, and her eyes danced with silent mischief. 'No way.'

The afternoon was busy, so much so it was almost seven when Rebekah locked up shop and slid into the van. She planned a shower, then she'd fix a steak salad and eat it with a fresh, crunchy bread roll she'd picked up from the bakery, maybe watch a video she'd rented out.

Summer was definitely on its way, for the days were becoming warmer, she perceived as she swung the van into the driveway leading down to the apartment underground car park.

It took only seconds to insert her key and have the security grille lift to allow her entry, and she eased into her allotted parking bay, cut the engine and gathered her shoulder bag, the leather briefcase with the day's computer print-outs, then she slid from the van and began walking towards the lift.

'Think you're pretty smart, dating another man, don't you?'

Rebekah froze, caught in the grip of fear as Brad stepped out from behind a concrete pillar. Calm, she had to remain calm. Try logic, a silent voice screamed.

'How did you get in here?'

'Use your imagination.'

He was taller, bigger than her, and she recognised the hard glitter in those pale grey eyes, the cruel tilt of his mouth.

Instinct had her gauging the distance to the lift well.

'Forget it,' Brad advised harshly. 'You'll never make it.'

The van...if only she could lock herself in there, she'd be safe. Except she'd locked the door, and by the time she reached it, inserted the key, he'd have caught her.

OK, if she couldn't escape, she had two options. Talk first; if that failed, *fight*.

'I can't think of anything we have to discuss.'

'Wrong, baby.'

She hated his smile, it hid pure venom. 'If I don't ring my sister within five minutes, she'll call the police.'

He recognised her bluff. 'So—call her.'

Rebekah slid open the zip fastening her bag, felt for and found the small canister, then she palmed it as she withdrew her hand, aimed and pressed the spray button.

The mace hit him in the face, and his howl of pain was animal-like in its rage.

Rebekah didn't hesitate, she ran to the lift, hit and held down the button…and prayed. If only she could get inside, she'd be safe.

Oh, come *on*, she begged, agonising if she'd have been wiser to have sought the van and locked herself in. At least she could have used her cellphone to call for help.

There was a faint electronic whine heralding the lift's descent, and she felt her heart thud in her chest as she counted off the seconds to its arrival.

She could hear Brad swearing, his voice rising to a raging crescendo, and then she didn't care any more as the lift doors swung open and she raced inside the cubicle, pushed the seventh-floor button, only to see Brad put his arm between the closing doors.

A scream left her throat, and she stabbed the *close doors* button. To little avail. His strength was accelerated by rage, and she batted his hands with the briefcase, drawing blood.

Fear drove her, and for a few seconds she thought she'd won. Except one herculean burst of strength on Brad's part pushed the doors open sufficiently for him to squeeze through.

She still had the can of mace in her hand, and she used it mercilessly before he had a chance to bring the lift to a stop mid-floor.

The cubicle wasn't large, and even blinded by the stinging mace Brad roared with rage as he lurched, arms spread wide, circling as she strove to evade him in the confined space.

Her only hope was to escape as soon as the lift stopped at the seventh floor, and she quickly identified her apartment key on its keyring, and held it poised in readiness.

There was nowhere to hide, and the timing proved lousy as Brad's hand groped her shoulder, then closed over it with steel-like strength.

A random punch slammed into her ribs, quickly followed by another to her upper arm.

At that moment the lift drew to a halt, and he dragged her out into the foyer.

'Where's your damned key?'

She'd die before she willingly gave it to him, and she wrestled with him, taking a cracking slap to the side of her face.

'Give it to me, bitch!'

Rebekah swung the briefcase at him and he

wrenched it from her grasp, then tackled and knocked her to the floor.

In one desperate move she tossed the keys as hard as she could, uncaring where they landed as long as he couldn't find them.

She heard them hit something with a resounding clunk, felt the bruising grip of Brad's fingers on her flesh, then a loud voice demanding,

'What the hell is going on here?' Followed by, '*Rebekah?* George, get out here!'

There was noise, voices, the sound of scuffling, then mercifully she was free, and hands were soothing her, Maisie, her neighbour, was issuing instructions like a nursing sister-in-charge, her chosen vocation. And her partner, George, an ex-wrestler with a body that was all muscle, held Brad in a bone-crunching grip.

Maisie called the police, helped Rebekah into her apartment, called a doctor, then she collected her camera and took photos for evidence.

Rebekah didn't argue, although she was sufficiently familiar with police procedure to know they'd do the same.

When they came, she gave a statement, which had to be typed up and signed at the police station within the next twenty-four hours. The doctor arrived and examined her, dressed a few abrasions, suggested ice-packs for the bruising, and gave her a sedative to take to help her sleep.

Maisie fussed over her, plying her with water and painkillers.

'Is there someone I should call? Your sister, brother-in-law?'

'I'll do it later.'

Maisie looked doubtful. 'You really should have someone stay with you tonight. Or you should go to your sister's place.'

'I'll be fine.'

'Sure you will. You're as pale as a ghost, and as cold as charity.' She gave a derisive snort. 'If I had anything to do with it, you'd be in hospital overnight.'

Rebekah tried for a smile and didn't quite make it. 'I promise I'll ring Ana the moment you leave.'

'Hmm. Why don't you go take a shower, and I'll rustle up something light for you to eat?' She held up her hand. 'I'll be offended if you refuse.'

It was easier to capitulate. 'Thanks.'

She stayed beneath the hot spray for a while, then, towelled dry, she donned jeans, added a cotton top, and emerged into the kitchen to discover her neighbour removing a plate of delicious-smelling goulash with rice.

'Your sister rang while you were in the shower.'

Rebekah knew the answer even before she posed the question. 'You told her?'

'She had to know. She's on her way over.' Maisie indicated the plate which she set down on the dining-room table. 'Sit and eat.'

'Yes, Mother.'

'I could be, if I'd been a child bride.' She tried to look fierce. 'You need someone to look after you.'

'I have you and George just across the hall.' She

took a mouthful of food and closed her eyes at the taste. 'I know why George married you.'

'Don't change the subject. You need a man in your life.'

'I had one, and look at the way that turned out.'

'A real man, one who'll take care of you.'

'Perhaps I'm content taking care of myself?'

Maisie gave another snort, and filled the kettle to make tea.

In no time at all the intercom buzzed, and Rebekah threw her neighbour a wry glance. 'The cavalry have arrived.'

Ana *and* Luc? There were hugs, expressions of concern, reassurances given, and decisions made.

'You're coming back with us,' Ana said firmly. 'And if you argue, I'll hit you.'

'I rather think she's had more than her fair share of that, *agape mou*,' Luc chided gently, and watched his wife's face crease with remorse.

'I didn't mean— Oh, God, Rebekah,' Ana groaned out loud.

'I know, you just love me to death, is all.'

Rebekah's cellphone pealed, and Luc moved to retrieve it from the coffee-table, where Maisie had placed everything that had spilled from her bag.

'I'll take it, shall I?' He picked up, and moved to one side of the room. His conversation was muted and spanned several minutes, then he retraced his steps and handed her the unit. 'Jace.'

She closed her eyes, then she opened them again and voiced a restrained greeting into the mouthpiece.

'Rebekah—'

Even from a distance she could sense the quiet anger beneath the surface of his control. 'I'm fine.'

'And daisies grow upside-down in the ground.' His voice held an edge she couldn't define. 'Give me your word you'll stay with Luc and Ana for a few days.'

She almost said she'd suffered worse than this. 'Tonight,' she conceded, and heard him mutter something unintelligible. Suddenly she'd had enough, and there wasn't another thing she wanted to hear...much less from a man who'd caused her more emotional highs and lows in one short week than anyone she'd ever known. 'Goodnight.'

Maisie took care of her plate, Ana fed Millie and put down fresh water, while Rebekah gathered up a change of clothes, a few essentials and pushed them into an overnight bag.

Luc crossed to her side as she re-entered the kitchen. 'Ready?'

She inclined her head, thanked Maisie, gave Millie a gentle pat, then she followed everyone out into the lobby while Luc locked up.

Ana sat in the back seat of the Mercedes and caught hold of Rebekah's hand as Luc drove to their palatial home in suburban Vaucluse.

'Do you want to talk about it?'

'Not particularly.' There was little point in rehashing it.

Ana's fingers tightened, and her voice held an uncustomary hardness. 'This isn't going to happen again.'

It was nice, Rebekah had to admit, to be taken care of. Luc and Ana's home was an architectural masterpiece set in beautiful grounds high on a hill with splendid views out over the harbour.

Petros, their politically correct manservant, fussed over her as if she were a precious piece of china. Within minutes of arrival he prepared tea and exquisite bite-size sandwiches.

Luc joined them for a while, then at a telling glance from his wife he excused himself on the pretext of dealing with business email. He brushed a light kiss to Ana's cheek, then crossed to gift Rebekah a similar salutation and departed the room.

Rebekah allowed Petros to refill her cup, and declined anything further to eat.

Ana waited only long enough for the manservant to wheel the tea-trolley from the room before leaning forward in her chair.

'Tell me exactly what happened,' she insisted sternly. 'And don't leave anything out.'

Reliving the episode was emotionally draining, although it helped her deal with it.

'The *bastard*,' Ana derided huskily when Rebekah finished. 'Luc and Jace will ensure he never comes near you again.'

Hang on a minute... '*Jace?* What does Jace have to do with it?' She drew in a deep breath in the hope of assembling a sense of calm. 'While I appreciate Luc's help, I'm quite able to take care of everything myself.'

'It's done,' Ana said simply. 'And you can stop with the fierce expression.'

'Ana—'

'It's time to bring out the big guns,' her sister remonstrated gently. 'Luc and Jace have them...in spades.'

This was getting out of hand. 'Look—'

'No,' Ana declared emphatically. '*You* look. I don't want to wake up one morning and hear Brad has somehow got to you and you're just another statistic in the assault and battery records.' She leaned forward and caught hold of Rebekah's hands. 'I was *there*, remember? When you walked out on him, and afterwards.' Tears filled her eyes. 'Jace is the first man you've dated in a long time. Only to have Brad emerge out of the woodwork and stalk you.' A tear escaped and rolled down her cheek. 'No one, *no one* is ever going to hurt you again. Ever.'

Rebekah felt her stomach curl into a tight ball at her sister's distress. 'Ana, don't. I'm OK. The police have arrested him.'

'Sure, you're OK. Bruised ribs, multiple contusions. Not to mention shock and trauma.' Her voice rose. 'I hate to think what would have happened if he'd dragged you inside the apartment. Or if Maisie and George hadn't been home.'

She caught the fierce determination apparent, and stayed any further protest...for now. *She* might be the victim, but Ana was hurting too. 'You haven't shown me the latest print-out of the babe's ultrasound. Or the radiographer's video clip.'

Ana offered a shaky smile. 'Changing the subject won't change my mind.' She stood to her feet and extended her hand. 'Come on. Let's go see pictures of your foetal niece or nephew.'

It helped to take both their minds off the earlier part of the evening, and it was there Luc found them rewinding the video tape for the third or fourth time.

'Time to call it a night for both of you, hmm?'

Rebekah caught the way his features softened as he took Ana's hands in his and gently pulled her to her feet. He would, she knew, ease his wife's apprehension and be there for her when she stirred through the night.

An ache began deep inside at the thought of being able to sink into the comfort of a man's arms, have his lips brush her forehead, trail over her cheek and settle on her mouth.

'You're to rest tomorrow,' Ana insisted as they ascended the stairs. 'Suzie is competent, and we'll manage. Coming into the shop is a no-no. OK?'

'I'll see how I feel in the morning.' It was a compromise at best, and Ana shot her a dark glance as if divining her thoughts.

'I mean it.'

Rebekah caught her sister's hand and gently squeezed it. 'I know you do.'

'Petros has made up the front guest suite for you, and you're to sleep in. Just come downstairs whenever you feel like breakfast.' Ana's features sharpened a little. 'Are you sure you're OK?'

'Yes,' she reassured. In truth every bone in her

body ached. 'I'm going to have that sedative, hop into bed, and sleep like a baby.'

She did take the sedative, and she did sleep for a few hours, only to wake in the early dawn hours feeling as if her body had been pummelled like a punching bag.

Which it pretty much had, she conceded as she slipped gingerly out of bed and made for the *en suite*.

She snapped on the light and examined her face in the mirror. A bit of concealer would cover the emerging bruise. As to the rest of her...she lifted the nightshirt and grimaced at the swelling on her ribs, the blueish-purplish colour, and knew she was fortunate none of the ribs was broken. Shallow breathing was the order of the day for a while.

There were scratches on her arm, a large, reddish welt on one forearm.

Not nice, not nice at all. But the swelling would subside, the bruises yellow and disappear. Give it a few weeks and all that would remain was the memory.

Rebekah checked her watch and saw it was much too early to dress and go downstairs. Returning to bed and trying to sleep wasn't an option, so she switched on the bedside lamp and leafed through a few glossy magazines Petros had thoughtfully provided.

Rebekah waited until Luc left the house at eight, saw Ana follow him minutes later, then she quickly gathered up her bag and moved quickly downstairs.

Petros was in the midst of clearing the dining-room table, and he turned as she entered the room.

'Good morning,' he greeted warmly. 'I trust you slept well? Ana insisted I shouldn't disturb you.' His gaze took in the bag. 'What can I get you for breakfast?'

It would be useless to say she wasn't hungry. 'Orange juice, toast and coffee will be great.'

One eyebrow arched. 'Might I suggest some fruit and cereal? Eggs with a little ham or bacon? A croissant, perhaps?'

'You're bent on spoiling me.' She took a seat and poured herself a glass of juice. There was fruit on the table, and she selected a banana, peeled and ate it.

'But toast and coffee is fine.'

There was a folded newspaper near by, and she flicked through the pages, read the headlines, her horoscope for the day, and scanned the comic strips. By which time she'd eaten two pieces of toast and had almost finished her second cup of coffee.

Rebekah retrieved her cellphone and punched in the relevant digits to summon a taxi, and she was relaying the address when Petros re-entered the room.

'You intend going somewhere this morning?' the manservant asked as he began clearing dishes.

'I need to go back to my apartment and feed my cat.'

'Luc would be most upset if I allowed you to take a taxi. I'll drive you, whenever you're ready to leave.'

'Nonsense.'

'Please, in this instance I must insist. If you'll tell me which company you called, I'll ring and cancel.'

It seemed easier to capitulate, and twenty minutes

later she slid out of the four-wheel-drive Petros used for transport.

'I'll wait until you're ready to return.'

He wasn't going to like the next part at all. 'I intend remaining at the apartment, Petros.'

His lips pursed in visible disapproval. 'Luc and Ana will be most displeased.'

'I promise I'll ring and explain.' Ana she could handle, and Ana would handle Luc. *Fait accompli.* Besides, in less than half an hour she'd be at the shop.

'Ms Rebekah, I don't think this is a good idea.'

She offered him a sweet smile. 'Thanks for the lift.' Then she turned and used her key to enter the main lobby.

Home, she breathed as she entered her apartment. There was no place quite like your own, and Millie bounded towards her, curling back and forth around her ankles, purring in delighted welcome.

The apartment looked achingly familiar, and she moved through it, straightening a vase on the chiffonier as she made her way to the kitchen.

Fifteen minutes later she'd fed Millie, changed into work clothes, and was on her way to the shop.

'You aren't supposed to be here,' Ana remonstrated the instant Rebekah walked through the door.

'I know everything you're going to say,' she responded firmly as she crossed to the work table and stowed her bag. 'But I'd rather be doing something constructive than swanning on the chaise lounge, idly flipping through the pages of a magazine.'

Take control. Hadn't that been the essence of any

professional advice she'd ever received? 'OK, where are we at?' she queried briskly.

'You've got the morning,' Ana conceded, trying for a fierce look that didn't quite come off. 'Then you're going home.'

'I've got the day,' Rebekah corrected gently. 'And I'll go home when I'm ready.'

'You're impossibly stubborn.'

'And I love you, too.'

Suzie looked from one to the other. 'Are you two going to fight, then make up? Or is this serious stuff and I should take five to let you sort it out alone?'

'Stay,' Rebekah and Ana ordered in unison.

'If you insist. Shall I mediate, or referee?'

'Neither.'

The phone rang, and Ana declared *sotto voce*, 'Saved by the bell.'

The morning was busier than usual with a number of customers coming in from the street. It was late morning when Rebekah took a quick check of their stock and reached for the phone to place an order, then arrange for the courier for delivery.

The electronic buzzer heralded the arrival of another customer, and she glanced towards the door, then stilled as Jace entered the shop.

Shock, surprise were just two of the emotions she experienced. Not the least was speculation as to why he was here when he was supposed to be in Cairns. Had his meetings concluded earlier than he'd anticipated? Yet if so, why wasn't he in Brisbane?

For a moment her gaze locked with his as he stood exuding a silent power that was vaguely frightening.

She watched as he moved towards Ana and offered an affectionate greeting, then he turned and moved towards the table where Rebekah was in the midst of gathering sprays of orchids into a large bouquet.

The nerves inside her stomach gave every impression of performing a series of complicated somersaults, and her fingers faltered as he paused within touching distance.

What could she say? Anything would be superfluous, so she didn't even try as she bore his raking appraisal.

A muscle bunched at the edge of his jaw, and she saw his eyes harden briefly, then he lifted a hand and trailed light fingers over her cheek.

'Get your bag,' he commanded gently. 'I'm taking you home.' He pressed his thumb over her lips as they parted to voice a refusal. 'No argument.' He increased the pressure slightly. 'I'll carry you out of here if I have to.'

Rebekah removed his hand, only, she suspected, because he let her. 'You don't have the right to give me orders.'

'It's a self-appointed role.' His voice was a silky drawl that feathered sensation down the length of her spine.

Everything faded from her peripheral vision. There were just the two of them, fused by an electric awareness that had everything to do with heightened sensuality. Right now she didn't need or want it.

'Go away.'

'Not a chance.'

'Jace—'

'Do you really want to do this the hard way?'

He was capable of implementing his threat despite any resistance on her part, and, given the choice, she'd opt for dignity over embarrassment.

'How did you—?'

'Find out where you were?' he completed. 'It was a process of elimination. First Luc, then Petros, and Ana.'

Rebekah moved slightly, shot her sister a dark glance and was met with a blithe smile. It was nothing less than a conspiracy, and one where the odds were stacked against her.

'There's a lot of work to get through.'

'Nothing Suzie and I can't handle,' Ana assured.

'There you go,' Jace drawled with hateful ease. 'Now collect your bag and we'll get on our way.'

'I have the van. And there is no *we*.'

'Arguing this back and forth isn't going to change a thing.'

'So concede defeat and follow you like a little lamb?' She refrained from adding *to the slaughter*... To no one, least of all this Greek-born American, would she admit she ached all over, her head thumped with pain, and she was fast approaching the need for serious time out.

'I have the car double-parked outside,' Jace informed as she reached for her bag.

'I hope the traffic officer has issued you with a

ticket.' She offered Suzie a wry smile, brushed her lips to Ana's cheek, then preceded Jace from the shop.

'None of this is *your* business,' Rebekah declared as he eased the car out from the busy thoroughfare. She was unsure whether to be relieved or disappointed there hadn't been a parking-violation ticket attached to his windscreen.

'Wrong. My involvement with you started all this.'

'What *involvement*?'

'Don't split hairs, *pedhaki mou*.'

The affectionate 'little one' got to her as she turned towards him. 'You mean you postponed business meetings and flew back to Sydney because you felt *responsible*? That's ridiculous.'

He met her gaze and held it for a few seemingly long seconds. 'Is it?' He returned his attention to negotiating traffic. 'I don't think so.'

'I fail to see the reasons for everyone's concern. I'm OK.' She was tempted to tell him there had been more damaging attacks in the past, only to refrain from the admission.

'Sure you are,' Jace discounted in a dry, mocking tone. 'You were barely standing up in there, pale as a ghost, your eyes dark with pain.' There was underlying anger apparent. 'What were you trying to prove?'

Should she tell him the truth? 'I didn't want to sit and brood.' And I didn't want to be alone, she added silently.

Jace swept the car into the entrance adjacent her apartment.

'Here's fine.' She already had her hand on the door-clasp.

'The hell it is.' He eased the car down the incline leading to the underground car park, and indicated the security lock. 'Give me your key.'

'There's no need for you to personally see me to my apartment door.'

She was a prickly young woman, and one he wanted to kiss senseless one minute and shake sense into the next. 'Just…do it, Rebekah.'

'I don't—'

'Your ex-husband has been released on bail.'

Rebekah stilled at his words, then drew in a slight breath…anything other than *slight* hurt like hell. 'Why am I not surprised?'

Brad's mother was a rich society matron who engaged high-ranking lawyers to protect her only son. On the past two occasions Wilma Somerville had rushed to his defence, blamed Rebekah for instigating the attacks, and threatened dire consequences if an official complaint was filed.

The next time Ana took matters into her own hands and persuaded Rebekah to press charges, only to have Wilma's lawyer release him hours later on bail and later persuade judge and jury Brad was a well-educated, caring man who simply needed a course in anger management. A hefty fine, and he was free.

'You're determined to personally check out my

apartment to see Brad hasn't slipped past security un-
detected and may be lurking in wait for me?'

'Something like that.'

Rebekah handed him her key in silence, then when
the security grille lifted he drove into the parking bay
alongside her MG.

'I very much doubt he'd be so foolish,' she offered
as they walked towards the lift.

Jace spared her a direct look. 'I'm not prepared to
let you take the risk,' he assured with chilling softness.

She'd decorated her apartment in soft green, cream
with a touch of apricot in muted tones. Complemented
by modern furniture and same-tone drapes. Her own
individual touch, rather than the ascetic perfection of an
interior decorator. The ambience was calming and
peaceful…her personal sanctuary.

Her small, pale grey-tipped cat sat up on the sofa,
surveying him with unblinking solemnity.

'Millie,' Rebekah indicated. 'She's very spoilt, and
not used to you yet.' Whereupon Millie proved her
mistress wrong by jumping down onto the carpet,
padding over to Jace and began winding herself
around his legs.

He bent down and fondled Millie's ears. An action
which sent the cat into feline ecstasy.

'Must be your natural masculine charm,' Rebekah
accorded with wry humour.

Jace straightened and one eyebrow slanted in mocking cynicism. 'Why don't you sit down and relax?'

Relax, with you here? she demanded silently. Fat chance. 'Thanks for bringing me home.'

'But please leave?'

'Yes.'

'Think again.'

Her eyes flew wide. 'Excuse me?'

'Independence is a fine thing,' he opined quietly. 'In this instance, there's no way you're staying anywhere alone.'

Anger flared, and it showed in her eyes, the tightening of her mouth. 'Now, look—'

'We've done that,' Jace said in a deceptively mild voice. 'We're not going to do it again.'

'Just who gave you permission to take charge of my life?'

'The decision is mine.'

'Well, you can absolve yourself from any misguided responsibility and go leave me alone.'

'No.'

She was angry before, now she was steaming. 'Brad is unlikely to do anything while he's out on bail. Even his mother's lawyer would have a hard job extricating him from jail if he did.'

His gaze focused on her features, noting the tilt of her chin and the proud determination in those deep sapphire-blue eyes. 'I'm not prepared to risk a repeat of last night.'

She wanted to lash out at him, *hurt* as she'd been hurt. Yet this was the wrong man, and her mind was spiralling in a way that made no sense at all. 'Next you'll tell me you intend staying here all day.'

He was silent for a few long seconds, then he ventured silkily, 'That's the plan.'

It was then she noticed the laptop in his hand. 'You've brought work with you?' Her voice seemed to have acquired a higher pitch, and she met his steady gaze with something akin to disbelief.

'I can work anywhere. Why not here?'

The anger bubbled over. 'You've appointed yourself *babysitter*? I don't believe this...any of it!'

His eyes hardened fractionally. 'Believe it's not open to negotiation.'

CHAPTER EIGHT

REBEKAH reacted without thought and the palm of her hand connected with his cheekbone in a stinging slap.

An entire gamut of emotions chased fleetingly across her expressive features, and Jace divined each and every one of them.

Dear lord in heaven, she'd actually *hit* him! In her eyes it made her no better than Brad. 'I'm sorry.'

The words were huskily voiced so as to be barely audible.

The air seemed filled with electric tension, and she was hardly conscious of breathing.

'Feel better?' he drawled with deceptive mildness.

Innate honesty came to the fore. 'No.'

She missed the faint gleam of humour lurking in the depths of his eyes.

'I picked up some filled bagels on my way to the shop. Why don't we have lunch?' he suggested quietly. 'Afterwards you can rest while I put in a few hours on the laptop.'

'I'm not an invalid,' she protested at once, wanting the afternoon done with so she could be alone. His presence in the apartment unsettled her. *He* unsettled her.

He shot her a level look, then he moved through

to the kitchen, set the bagels on plates and placed them on the dining-room table.

They ate in relative silence, and washed the food down with hot, sweet tea, then Rebekah curled up on the sofa with a magazine while Jace settled himself at the escritoire on the far side of the room.

She must have slipped into a fitful doze, for she woke feeling refreshed, albeit stiff and sore. A quick glance at her watch revealed it was almost five, and she experienced shock to think she'd slept for so long.

Jace glanced up from the computer screen at her first sign of movement, his appraisal swift and encompassing as she straightened and stood to her feet.

He caught the careful way she moved, and contained a renewed surge of anger against the man who'd caused her such pain.

'Feeling rested?'

She looked better, her pale features had acquired a healthy colour, although her eyes were still too dark.

'Yes.'

'Good.' He turned back to the screen and re-immersed himself in scrolling through data.

Rebekah felt the need to freshen up, and she took her time, declining the use of lipstick as she changed into jeans and a cotton-knit top.

As soon as Jace left she'd fill the hot tub, then after a long, leisurely soak she'd grab a bite to eat and crawl into bed with a book.

Millie followed her out into the lounge, then padded towards the kitchen and waited to be fed. Jace barely glanced up from the screen as she passed through.

A slight frown creased her brow as she crossed into the laundry and extracted clothes from the drier, folded and put them away.

'I've ordered in,' Jace informed minutes later. 'I hope you like Chinese.'

She turned towards him slowly. 'I thought you'd return to the hotel.'

'You thought wrong.'

A sudden suspicion occurred. 'I'm fine, if you'd prefer to leave.'

He made two more keystrokes, then closed down the program. 'No.'

'Excuse me?'

'I have no intention of leaving you here alone.'

She felt her stomach execute a few painful somersaults. 'We already had this argument.'

'Then we'll have it again.'

'I don't need to go out from the apartment before tomorrow.' She gestured in the direction of the apartment entrance. 'There's no way anyone can get in unless I open that door.'

'It doesn't change a thing.'

'You can't stay here!'

'Why not? You have a spare bedroom.'

And she could sleep easily in her bed knowing he occupied the room directly across the hall?

'Unless, of course, you invite me to share your bed?'

The element of mockery evident brought her to flashpoint. 'As if that's going to happen!'

The apartment intercom buzzer was an insistent, intrusive sound, and after a moment's hesitation she crossed to pick up the receiver, only to have Jace lift it from her hand.

Minutes later he collected their Chinese take-out, paid the delivery boy, then he unpacked the bag onto the table.

Not long after they'd eaten she gathered clean sheets from the linen cupboard and handed them to him.

'The spare room is down the hallway on the left. Feel free to watch television. I'm going to bed. Goodnight.'

She turned and walked towards her room, closed the door, then she took a shower, slid into bed and snapped off the light.

She was running, but she didn't seem to be gaining distance in her attempt to reach a safe place. And it was dark, very dark, with only brief prisms of light.

Where was she? Nothing was familiar. Only an awareness of being outdoors, damp grass, tall trees, then there was dense undergrowth that caught on her clothes, gnarled tree roots, and the dank smell associated with the cyclic rebirth, growth and decay of plant life.

Thunder rolled across the sky, followed by forked lightning, and behind her she could hear the echo of her own frantic passage towards safety.

Except it was foe, not friend, and a mental image of Brad in the role of her attacker flooded her brain.

She tripped over an exposed tree root, and she cried out as she went down. There was an imperviousness to pain as she scrambled to her feet and staggered into a running gait, fleeing as he gained on her.

Then, miraculously, the undergrowth cleared, the trees disappeared, and there was smooth lawn, a house with all its lights blazing. A beacon offering her sanctuary.

She picked up speed and ran towards it, but no matter how hard she tried she couldn't close the distance and the house remained out of her reach.

Just as she began to despair she drew close, and she was at the front door, her hand on the knob, praying it would open and not be locked.

Her relief was palpable as it swung open to her touch, and as she turned to close it Brad was there, wrenching the door from her grasp.

She screamed, pushing all her weight against it in an attempt to prevent his entry. Except it was hopeless, her strength no match for his as he forced it open.

Then she turned and ran, blindly seeking the stairs in the hope of reaching a bedroom where she could close and lock herself in.

Only to have him catch her just as she reached the landing, and she cried out as his hands closed over her arms. Screamed as they moved to her shoulders.

She heard him swear, then his voice calling her name…

The scene began to change and fade, and she was no longer on the floor, she was in her bed in the apartment, the voice repeating her name bore an American accent, and the man grasping her shoulders wasn't Brad.

This man's features portrayed concern, his facial muscles reassembling over broad-sculptured bone as concern was replaced with relief. Chillingly bleak eyes riveted hers, trapping her in his gaze for seemingly long seconds before the bleakness faded.

'Jace?' What was he doing here? It was late, she was in bed, the bedside lamp was switched on...and then she remembered.

He caught each fleeting emotion and gauged every one. 'You were having a nightmare.'

Rebekah shivered, still partly caught up in it. All she'd need to do was close her eyes and she'd become immersed in the darkness again.

'Would you like a drink?'

She became aware of the man sitting on the edge of her bed, his jeans, the unbuttoned shirt, the slightly tousled hair.

This close she was suddenly conscious of her own attire, the thin cotton nightshirt, the rumpled bedcovers.

There was a sense of intimacy apparent, something exigent beneath the surface that would ignite and flare at the slightest touch, the faintest move.

Rebekah unconsciously held her breath, unable to tear her eyes away from his. She swallowed the lump that had risen in her throat. 'Please.' Anything to have him shift away.

Yet when he did she felt a strange sense of loss, which was crazy. There was a compulsive need to straighten the bedcovers, and she finger-combed her hair, then winced as bruised muscles made themselves felt.

Jace returned with a glass part-filled with chilled water, and she took it from him, had several sips before placing the glass onto the bedside pedestal.

'Thanks.' *Please,* just go, she begged silently. She felt acutely vulnerable, and way too disturbed by his presence.

'Want to talk about it?' His dark eyes seared hers, lingered, then trailed to her mouth.

'Not particularly.'

He lifted a hand and brushed the tips of his fingers to a large bruise on her arm, and she quivered beneath his touch.

'How often did he do this to you?'

She wanted to protest it was none of his business, except the words never left her lips. An admission would raise the query as to why she'd stayed after the first attack. Brad's tears, his apparent horror and remorse at his actions, together with his fervent promise it would never happen again had influenced her to forgive him. Until the next time.

'Does it matter?'

'Yes.' There was steel beneath the silkiness, an expression she couldn't define in those dark eyes.

His hand moved to cup her jaw, and his thumb

caressed the tender flesh Brad had slapped with a hard palm, then he threaded his fingers through her hair.

Rebekah felt as if they were enmeshed in some elusive sensual spell. 'I think you'd better leave,' she voiced shakily.

Yet the words were at variance with her emotions.

There was a part of her that ached to invite this man's touch, to reach out and seek the comfort he could provide.

Oh, dear lord, just to be held close and feel the press of his lips against her temple, the beat of his heart against her own. To feel safe and protected.

Except it was more than that, much more.

She wanted, *needed* the touch of his hands, his lips on her body. She wanted *him*.

She didn't want to analyse the *why* of it. To agonise whether she should or shouldn't, or what might come after.

There was no room for wisdom, just innate need.

Her eyes ached with it, and tears rose to the surface to shimmer in the lamp-light.

He leant forward and brushed his lips to hers in a kiss that was gently evocative, and her mouth trembled slightly as she sought control over her wayward emotions.

Her lashes fluttered down in a desperate bid to close out the sight of him. It didn't work, nothing worked, for she still did battle with her sensory perception of him...his clean male scent, the warmth and the passion. Especially the passion, *there* but held in tight control.

She felt his mouth shift to the bruise on her shoulder, then slip to caress another, and something deep inside slowly unfurled and began to melt.

Were some of the carefully erected barriers coming down? Her skin was silk, and scented with a delicate perfume he failed to recognise. He wanted to obliterate the taint of Brad's touch, replace it with his own and show her how the loving could be. The intense pleasure, the acute ecstasy experienced by two people in complete accord.

The words could come later. For now there was only the tactile sensation of touch, the silent communication of want and need in the slight tremor of her body, the fast-beating pulse at the edge of her throat, and heat…hers, his, as he trailed his lips up to fasten on her own in a kiss that dispensed with any inhibitions and encouraged her response.

It was everything she craved for, evocative, erotic, with an edge of hunger that tugged at her soul. A sigh rose and died in her throat as she angled her mouth to his and deepened the kiss.

The only part of him touching her was his mouth, and he used it to devastating effect, sweeping her to a place where there was only the moment and the electrifying sensual chemistry they shared.

Rebekah cupped his face and kept his mouth on hers until he gently removed her hands as he trailed kisses down her throat and edged to the soft swell of her breast.

He eased the edges of her nightshirt aside and savoured the rounded contours before laving a tender peak.

Sensation arrowed through her body and she arched against him, only to groan out loud as he shamelessly suckled there.

With care he freed the remaining buttons on her nightshirt and the breath hissed between his teeth as he caught sight of the bruised swelling on her ribcage.

Rebekah closed her eyes against the dark anger evident, only to have them open in stunned surprise as he pressed his lips to each and every bruise in turn.

Jace trailed a hand to the curve of her waist, then rested over her hip before slipping low to tangle in the soft hair at the apex of her thighs.

It was almost too much as his lips traced a similar path, and she cried out loud as he bestowed the most intimate kiss of all.

He sensed her shocked disbelief, the sudden stillness, and felt something twist in his gut at the instinctive knowledge her ex-husband had never gifted her this form of oral pleasure. A man who was selfishly insensitive to consider his own satisfaction without thought for his partner?

Her climax when it came took her unawares, for she hadn't imagined there could be more, much more than she'd already experienced, and she gasped as he took her high again and again until she reached for him.

His skin was smooth as thick-textured satin, and she exulted in the feel of hard sinew and muscle as she freed him of his shirt.

Dear heaven, he was built with well-developed musculature, a taut waist, and washboard midriff.

It was easy to unsnap his jeans and slide the zip down, then pull them off with his help. His briefs followed, and she had a bad moment wondering if she could accommodate him.

There was an elemental quality apparent, a base, primitive need she was unable to ignore as she became caught up in the sexual thrall of him.

His hands skimmed the surface of her skin, shaping her body as he explored all the pleasure spots with the sureness of a man who knew where and how to touch to drive a woman wild.

He took her to the brink of sexual anticipation, and held her there until she begged for release, then he entered her with exquisite care, moving slowly as she stretched to fit him.

It was like nothing she'd experienced before as she absorbed his length, and she cried out as he began to withdraw, only to ease forward in a slow rhythm as old as time, lengthening each stroke and increasing its pace until she accepted and matched it.

Together they moved in unison towards a climactic explosion that shattered all of her preconceived beliefs.

Her whole body was like a finely tuned instrument beneath a master's touch, responding as it never had before. As she'd never imagined it could, she decided hazily as every nerve sang with elated pleasure.

This...*this* was how it was supposed to be. Two

people together, sharing a sensual feast that culminated in the ultimate pleasure.

Not the quick slaking of lust that Brad had subjected her to in the name of love before he rolled off her and fell asleep.

Jace was still joined with her, his lips intent on trailing a lingering path to her breasts, where they caressed and teased, then suckled there.

Tiny darts of sensation arrowed through her body, and she traced the length of his spine with her fingertips, exploring each indentation until she reached his buttocks.

She felt them clench beneath her touch, and her lips parted in a secret smile, only to gasp out loud as he began to move, slowly stroking deep within until she caught the rhythm and joined him in the ride.

Afterwards he kissed her, taking her mouth in a gentle imitation of the sexual act itself, then he gathered her in close against him and held her until she slipped into an exhausted sleep.

It was in the early dawn hours that she stirred, and, half-asleep, began to move a little, unconsciously changing position…hazily aware something was preventing her. *Someone,* she determined seconds later.

Instant recall followed, and with it came the inevitable *ohmygod* moment. *What had she done?*

Like a giant jigsaw puzzle the pieces fell into place. The nightmare, crying out, Jace, and sex. Hell, she had a vivid recollection of the sex!

'Don't,' a husky male voice adjured close to her ear.

Rebekah stilled at the sound of that deep, slightly accented drawl, and her breath seemed to lock in her throat as one hand slid to her hip while the other took possession of her breast.

'Please. Let me go.'

His lips brushed her temple and trailed to settle at the sensitive curve at her neck. 'Stay, *agape mou*.'

'My lover'. This was all wrong. It was he who should go, not her.

'Last night was—'

'A mistake?'

Oh, God. She closed her eyes, then opened them again. It had been the most beautiful experience of her life. And she could hardly blame him for the seduction. She'd wanted him as much as he appeared to want her.

'No.'

She felt his lips move to form a smile. 'Your honesty is charming.'

'It—can't happen again,' she managed, feeling wretched. She'd never been promiscuous in her life. Brad had been her first and only lover.

'Why not, *pedhaki mou*?'

He sounded vaguely amused, and she shifted, then froze as she became aware of his arousal. 'Because it can't.' It didn't help that his mouth was intent on completing a treacherous path along the slope of her shoulder.

'Uh-huh. *Because*, hmm?'

Warmth was stealing through her veins. 'Stop that.' It was a weak admonition, and they both knew it.

'You don't want me to do this?' He shifted, drawing her to lay on her back as he leaned over her and let his lips drift over her breast. 'Or this?' He caught one tender peak between his teeth and took her to the edge between pleasure and pain.

One hand splayed over her stomach, then moved low to tangle in the soft curls, and pleasure arrowed through her body as he effortlessly located the sensitive clitoris.

It took only seconds for her to scale the heights, and he held her there, enjoying her delectation, then he took possession of her mouth as she began to fall.

It wasn't enough, Rebekah decided hazily. It would never be enough. And she reached for him, welcoming the sure, hard length of him as he slid inside her.

Afterwards Rebekah lay entwined in post-coital languor, enjoying the gentle drift of fingers in a lazy, exploratory path over his warm skin.

It felt so *right*, being here like this.

They were both adults, they weren't in a relationship with someone else... At least, she wasn't. But what about Jace?

She wasn't prepared for the way apprehension feathered along the edge of her spine. What if he was just amusing himself—?

'No.' Jace slid a hand beneath her chin and tilted it so she had to look at him. 'No,' he reiterated quietly, and her eyes widened.

'No—what?'

'I number several women among my friends, but none to whom I owe my fidelity.'

'You read minds?'

'Yours isn't difficult to interpret.' With a slow smile Jace slid to his feet and strolled naked into the *en suite*.

Rebekah took pleasure in the look of him, the breadth of shoulder, the splendid musculature of his back, the tapered waist and lean, tight butt.

Just thinking about the intimacy they'd shared brought a renewed surge of heat, and a repeated longing to experience once again the incandescent sensation he was able to arouse.

Soon she'd go take a shower, dress, make breakfast, then head into the shop. And Jace? Would he take a flight back to Cairns or Brisbane and complete his reorganised business meetings?

Then what would happen? She'd return to her day-to-day life while he tied up his Australian connection, after which he'd return to New York.

Rebekah was unprepared for the devastation that hit at the thought of him leaving. Even more unconscionable was the possibility of not seeing him again.

Maybe she could have survived with her emotions intact if it hadn't been for last night. Now she didn't have a hope in hell.

Fool, she castigated in silence. She should never have allowed him to stay, and should have banished him from her bedroom the moment he entered it.

Except she hadn't. Now she had to live with it.

Jace re-entered the room and his gaze narrowed as he interpreted her expressive features. Doubts and re-

flective thought he could deal with. Regret was something else.

He watched her eyes widen as he closed the distance between them, and he resisted the temptation to
join her in bed. Instead he tugged the sheet free and
scooped her into his arms and returned to the *en suite*.

'What are you doing?'

Another woman would have offered a feline purr,
wound her arms round his neck and pressed her
mouth to his.

Rebekah sounded apprehensive, and totally devoid
of any musing coquetry.

A muscle clenched at the edge of his jaw in recognition of what she'd become beneath her ex-
husband's hand.

'Sharing the hot tub with you.' His drawl held an
element of humour, and he successfully prevented any
protest by the simple expediency of closing her mouth
with his own.

It was sheer magic. The pulsing water, the touch
of his hands as he gently massaged scented bath oil
into her skin. She wanted to close her eyes and have
him administer to her forever.

How long did she have? Three, four days…a week
at the most.

Rebekah knew she should stop it now. Climb out
of the hot tub, catch up a towel, advise him to do the
same, then say…*what? Thanks, that was great.
Maybe we can do it again some time?*

There could be no doubt this was just a brief interlude. To think it could be anything else was ridiculous.

Besides, her life was all mapped out. Blooms and Bouquets was her focal priority. She had a flourishing business, a nice apartment, a late-model car. What else could she want?

A man she could trust. Someone to be there for her, as she would be for him. To share the love and the laughter, the few tears and sorrow fate might provide in their lifetime. Children. The whole package.

Was it too much to hope for?

Not just any man. *This* man.

The revelation poleaxed her. For a shock-filled second she thought she might actually have blacked out.

'Rebekah?'

Oh, God. Get a grip on reality. 'It must be getting late. I need to get to the flower market, organise the day's orders.' She was babbling, her hands already reaching for the marbled surround as she rose to her feet.

A startled yelp emerged from her throat as Jace's hands closed over her waist, and she struggled as he pulled her down in front of him, then caged her within his arms.

'I have to go.'

'No,' he refuted. 'You don't.'

'Jace…' She broke off with a groan of despair as his mouth savoured the sensitive curve of her neck.

'An hour, hmm? Just an hour.'

It was closer to two before she slid behind the

wheel, fired the engine and sent the MG up onto street level.

Jace occupied the passenger seat, and minutes later she eased the car to a smooth halt outside his hotel entrance.

'Have a good day.' It was an automatic phrase, and when he leaned forward she offered her cheek, only to have him take her face in his hands and bestow an evocatively deep open-mouthed kiss.

When he released her there was delicate pink colouring her cheeks, a soft, tremulous smile parted her lips, and her eyes held slumberous warmth.

It was a look he'd deliberately sought, and one he could easily become accustomed to without any trouble at all.

CHAPTER NINE

THE rising sun coloured the landscape, promising warmth as the day progressed, and Rebekah covered the relatively short distance to the shop in record time.

The Blooms and Bouquets van was already parked out back, which meant Ana had completed an early run to the flower markets. Something she'd intended to take care of, except something...*someone*, she corrected, had caused a delay.

The scent of flowers filled her nostrils as soon as she opened the shop door, and she breathed it in, loving the delicate fragrances.

'You shouldn't be here,' Ana protested. 'At least not this early.' Her gaze sharpened, then narrowed fractionally. 'There's something different about you.'

Rebekah crossed to the work table and stowed her bag. 'I'm fine.'

'Very much *fine*. You're almost glowing.'

Her sister was a kindred soul and far too perceptive for Rebekah's peace of mind. 'A good night's sleep works wonders.'

'Or not much sleep and a long night's loving,' Ana teased. 'Ah, you're blushing.' Her smile held a witching mischievousness. 'It has to be Jace.' The man was incredibly resourceful if he'd managed to infiltrate the emotional barriers Rebekah had erected. If he toyed with her and broke her heart, she'd kill him.

'Are you going to tell me?'

Rebekah shot her sister a steady look. 'Yes, it's Jace. And no, I'm not going to tell you.'

'Spoilsport.' Her expression sobered. 'How are the bruises?'

'It'll take a few days.'

'More like a week or two,' Ana corrected. 'Luc has employed private security to keep a watchful eye on the premises.'

It was understandable Luc wouldn't risk anything happening to his wife or unborn child.

'Shall we get to work?' Rebekah suggested.

The day proved to be busier than usual, and the phone calls many. Mostly business-oriented, but Rebekah took a call from the police relating to a required clarification in her statement, and her lawyer.

Jace rang mid-morning, and again mid-afternoon.

Just the sound of his voice was enough to send her pulse racing to a faster beat.

All day she'd been caught up with the memory of what they'd shared through the night and early this morning. After almost three years of celibacy she was conscious of highly sensitised tissues and nerve-endings as a result of his possession. Each shattering climax had been more intense than the last, and even now just the thought brought heat pooling deep inside.

There was no contact from Brad, but then she hadn't expected there to be. His mother, his lawyer, the police...each would have warned him of the consequences involved if he dared risk another personal confrontation.

Looking back, she damned herself for not realising Brad had an obsessive-possessive personality. He'd been a consummate actor, fooling everyone. Except his mother and the medical and legal advisors hired to protect him.

Jace walked into the shop just as she was about to close up for the evening, and she felt the familiar jolt of her heart at his presence as he stood waiting while she shut down the computer, checked the locks, then set the alarm prior to vacating the premises.

He brushed his lips to her temple. 'Busy day?'

'Yes.' Her stomach turned a somersault or two, then settled down. 'We filled more than the usual orders.'

Jace pressed a finger to the generous curve of her mouth. 'How are you?'

So intensely aware of you, I feel as if every nerve-end is fizzing with active life. 'Fine.'

His slow smile held a degree of sensual warmth. 'Feel like driving to Watson's Bay and eating seafood while the sun goes down over the ocean?'

'You don't need to do this,' Rebekah said quietly as they walked to her car.

'Take you out to dinner?' he queried as he slid into the passenger seat beside her.

'Act the part of bodyguard,' she qualified, and sensed a sudden stillness apparent.

'You want to run that by me again?'

There was silk in that accented drawl, and it raised all her fine body hairs in self-protective defence.

'I don't want you to feel obligated in any way just because—'

'We had sex?'

It hadn't been just *sex*. She'd had sex with Brad for the few brief months she'd lived with him as his wife. Last night she'd been made love to for the first time in her life. There was, she had to admit, a world of difference between sex and lovemaking.

'Want to start over?' Jace offered with dangerous softness.

She waited a beat as she released her breath. 'I think so.'

Jace caught the slight quiver at the edge of her mouth, and wasn't sure at that precise moment whether he wanted to shake her or kiss her senseless.

'Good.' He indicated the key she held poised in her hand ready to insert into the ignition. 'Suppose you drive, and we'll discuss this further over dinner.'

The restaurant Jace suggested was a converted bath-house erected in the days long gone by to service the day trippers who visited the bay to swim and picnic.

Now it was a fashionably trendy place to eat, with an excellent menu and superb food.

It was a pretty beach, and the ocean waters were dappled with reflected sunlight. Soon the natural light would fade, and the moon would rise to provide a silver pathway from the horizon.

Jace managed to secure a table by the window, and

he ordered wine while Rebekah checked out the menu.

A prawn risotto and side salad appealed, and Jace selected something more substantial containing a variety of seafood.

'Let's dispense with the obligation issue,' he began as soon as the waiter retreated in the direction of the kitchen. He leaned back in his chair and subjected her to a thoughtful appraisal. 'My interest in you is entirely personal. Not a misguided sense of responsibility or duty due to an extended family loyalty. Or merely a means of protecting you from your ex-husband,' he revealed with dispassionate imperturbability, then added with deadly softness,

'What we shared last night. What was that? Just great sex, no emotional involvement?'

There was knowledge apparent in his dark gaze she couldn't deny. 'No.'

The waiter brought their starters and presented them with practised flair, while the drinks steward topped their glasses.

'I want to be with you. My hotel suite,' Jace elaborated. 'Your apartment. It hardly matters which, as long as we're together.'

She swallowed the lump that had suddenly risen in her throat. 'You're taking a lot for granted.'

His gaze seared hers. 'You think I'm playing a game? Using you for sex? *Amusing* myself with you?'

Oh, my, he didn't hesitate to spell it out. In a boardroom he'd be a ruthless aggressor, a feared adversary.

'Which one, Rebekah?' he pursued relentlessly. 'Or do you imagine it's all three?'

Dear heaven. 'I don't know.' She could be equally fearless. 'Only that whatever it is, it has a very limited time-span.'

'Does it?'

She was breaking up inside. 'Your life is in New York. Mine is here.'

His gaze narrowed, and when he spoke his voice was a silk drawl. 'With no possibility of a compromise?'

She met his gaze and held it. 'Your definition of *compromise* is what? You fly into Sydney when you can spare the time between cementing corporate deals? I take a week's break here and there throughout the year and visit New York?' She was on a roll, and couldn't stop. 'We meet halfway? Enjoy full-on sex for as long as it takes, then bid each other a fond farewell at the airport, smile and say *that was great, we'll consult our schedules and work out another date*, then take separate flights to different destinations on opposite sides of the world?'

He was silent for so long she became increasingly nervous. 'Are you done?' he queried with deceptive mildness.

'Yes.'

Rebekah picked up her cutlery and began eating, although her tastebuds appeared to have gone on strike, and she had to consciously control her hands to prevent them from shaking.

She had only to look at Jace to vividly recall his

kiss, the touch of his hands, his mouth on her body. It was almost indecent to feel the heat sing through her veins, tripping her pulse and causing her heart to thud in her chest.

The degree of intimacy they'd shared brought a tinge of soft pink to her cheeks.

After last night her life would never be the same. And that was an admission she had no intention of verbalising.

Rebekah finished her starter, picked at her main, declined dessert, and ordered coffee.

'I didn't thank you,' she ventured quietly as she spooned sugar into the dark brew.

'For what, specifically?'

Coming to my rescue? Dropping everything and flying to Sydney? Putting me first above important business meetings? 'Ensuring my safety.' It didn't seem adequate. 'It was kind of you.'

He considered the word, reflected on it a little. 'I think we've gone way past *kind*.'

'I hope it hasn't interrupted your business meetings.'

'So polite,' Jace gently mocked. 'I have an early-morning flight to Brisbane, followed by an afternoon meeting on the Gold Coast. I'll be back early evening.'

She needed to ask. 'When do you return to New York?'

'Sunday.'

That left only a few days. She felt as if her whole world had suddenly shifted on its axis. Soon he'd be gone, and the thought of him not being a constant in her life affected her more than she was prepared to admit.

How could she be so contrary? Fighting against allowing him into her life for days, and now she didn't want him to leave. It hardly made any sense.

A hollow feeling settled in her stomach, and she pushed her coffee to one side, unable to swallow another mouthful.

Jace watched the fleeting emotions chase each other across her expressive features. She was a piece of work, so incredibly beautiful with a sweetness that went right to the depths of her soul. Was she aware how easily he could read her? It was the one thing that had kept him sane during the past ten days.

'Finished?' He didn't wait for her answer as he signalled the *maître d'* for the bill, paid it on presentation, then he caught hold of her hand and led her out to the car.

'I'll drop you at the hotel,' Rebekah indicated as they entered the outskirts of Double Bay.

'A token resistance?'

Her stomach executed a backwards flip at his drawled query. 'I have to be at the flower markets before five in the morning, and I need some sleep.'

'So, we sleep,' Jace said imperturbably.

'I really think—'

'We've done this already.'

'*You* might have. The jury's still out with me.'

She was aware he shifted slightly in his seat. 'All

you have to say is you don't want to share the same bed with me.'

Rebekah opened her mouth to say the words, then bit them off before the first one could escape her lips. She couldn't do it, for to deny him was to deny herself.

Millie greeted them as soon as they entered the apartment, miaowing in protest because she hadn't been fed. Something Rebekah attended to at once, and was rewarded with a brief purr and a swishing tail as the cat tucked into her food.

The message-light on the answering machine was blinking, and showed three recorded messages. The first was her father in New York, then Ana with a reminder for the morning. Brad followed with sibilant invective damning Luc and Jace Dimitriades, and promising Rebekah would pay, big-time.

'Don't erase it,' Jace commanded quietly. 'Let it run in case he rings again.'

'He will.' She was certain of it.

'Each call will become another strike against him in court.'

Not too much of a strike, she accorded silently. His mother and her lawyers were a formidable team.

'I'm going to hit the shower.' Rebekah turned and moved down the hall to her bedroom.

Minutes later she stood beneath the warm spray of water, soap in hand as she lathered her skin. The subtle rose-scent misted with the steam, and she gave a startled yelp as the door slid open and Jace stepped behind her.

She didn't have a chance to say a word as he turned her round to face him, then his mouth captured hers in a gentle, evocative kiss that tugged at her heart-strings.

'You shouldn't be here,' Rebekah managed the instant he lifted his head a little, and she glimpsed his musing smile as he shaped her face with his hands.

'Uh-huh.'

He angled his mouth over hers, and this time he went deep, sweeping her emotions to unbelievable heights where there was no sense of time or place, just the heat of intense eroticism.

How long had they remained like this? she wondered with bemused bewilderment when he slowly broke the kiss. Long seconds, or several minutes?

He had the most beautiful face, she decided, taking her fill of him. Dark eyes merging from the deepest grey to black, a facial bone structure to die for, and a mouth that was heaven on earth.

She possessed the strongest inclination to lean in against him, press her head to the curve of his shoulder, and just rest there. To have him close his arms around her, and know nothing, no one, could touch her.

Jace put his hands on her shoulders and turned her away from him, then he began massaging her nape, the tense muscles at the edge of her neck, her shoulders.

There were kinks, and he eased them out, working at each one until she sighed in gratitude.

It felt so darned good, she simply closed her eyes

and went with it, exulting in his touch, the magic he seemed able to generate without any effort at all.

'Better?'

Rebekah lifted her head and breathed an almost inaudible, 'Yes,' as he gently turned her round to face him. 'Thanks.'

He caught up the soap and placed it in her hand.

'Return the favour, *pedhaki mou.*'

Her eyes widened as she registered a delightful mix of surprise and reservation.

'Too big an ask?'

To soap that masculine frame...all over? Maybe she could skip certain parts of his anatomy... Although it seemed ludicrous to feel reticent after last night.

She didn't trust herself to speak, and began lathering his chest, completing the upper part of his body, his arms, shoulders, then she stepped behind him and rubbed the soap over the muscular curve of his back, his buttocks, the backs of his thighs. Then she moved in front of him and handed him the soap.

'You can do the rest.'

His arousal was a potent force, and a soft pink coloured her cheeks.

'Too shy?'

The pink deepened, and she reached for the shower door, only to have him halt her escape.

'Stay, *agape mou.*' The husky plea undid her, and she looked at him blindly as he drew her round to face him. 'I want to pleasure you a little, then I'll take you to bed...to sleep, I promise.'

She stood mesmerised as his hands shaped her breasts, and brushed the tender peaks with the pad of his thumbs.

Liquid fire coursed through her veins, and a husky groan sighed from her throat as his lips sought the vulnerable hollow at the base of her neck, savoured there, then gently bit the soft flesh, soothed it, then trailed to the slope of her breast, where he suckled until she dragged his head away and pulled his mouth down to hers.

Her mouth was firm, her tongue an exploratory tease, and he let her run free with it, enjoying her touch as his hand trailed low over her hip, then slipped low to caress the sensitive moist folds, felt the clitoris swell and harden...and absorbed her cries as she went up and over. Again, and again.

She *ached* to feel him deep inside her, and in one fluid movement she linked her hands together at his nape, then lifted herself to straddle his hips, where she created a sensual friction that had him groaning out loud.

'Witch,' he accorded in a husky voice an instant before she sank down onto him, absorbing his length to the hilt in one slow slide. His hands cupped her buttocks as they began to rock, long, leisurely movements that increased in pace as they scaled the heights, poised at the brink, then tumbled together into a glorious free fall.

Afterwards they stepped from the shower stall, and Jace caught up a towel, fastened it at his hips, then he caught up another and dried the moisture from her body.

The bruises had become more colourful, and looked vivid against the paleness of her skin.

Jace swore low in his throat and would have said more in castigation, except Rebekah pressed a finger to his lips.

'Don't. It's done.'

He swept an arm beneath her knees and carried her into the bedroom, then he pulled back the covers, settled her down onto the mattress and slid in to curl her close in against him.

Exhaustion brought an easy sleep, and contentment kept her there until the alarm buzzed loud in the early pre-dawn hours.

'Stay there,' Rebekah bade as Jace slid from the bed and pulled on his trousers.

'I'll make coffee while you dress.' He snapped the waist fastening closed, and she gathered up fresh underwear and headed towards the *en suite*.

There was coffee perking in the coffee-maker when she entered the kitchen, and she tried not to be caught up by the look of him as she collected a cup and filled it with the aromatic brew.

Lean-hipped, bare-chested, olive-textured skin covering splendid musculature, his hair tousled, and a night's beard shadowing his features, he was something else.

'Problem?'

He was the problem. A very big problem. And it was getting worse with every day, and *night*, that passed.

Sunday. The word seemed to reverberate inside her head. On Sunday he leaves. Two nights he'd stayed over, and already she couldn't bear the thought of him not being here.

How could she become so attached to someone so soon? It didn't make sense. None of it made any sense.

Rebekah finished her coffee, then she crossed to the sink, rinsed the cup, then caught up her shoulder bag.

'I have to go.'

'You didn't answer the question.'

How could she say she'd miss him dreadfully? Or that her heart would break a little when he left?

His gaze was steady, his eyes dark with an expression she couldn't define as she stumbled to find the words.

'I appreciate you being here.' It was as close as she could get, and his mouth curved at the edges.

'I'll come down to see you safely into your car.'

He glimpsed her slight confusion. 'Have you got a spare key I can use to get back in here?'

She did, and she fetched it, gave it to him, then walked to the door.

The basement car park was well-lit, and as silent as a concrete tomb. This morning it seemed eerie, and she suppressed a faint shiver as she slid in behind the wheel.

Jace shut the door, and watched as she reversed out, then drove towards the ramp leading up to street level.

CHAPTER TEN

FRIDAY was always a busy day at the shop, with numerous orders to fill, deliveries to be ready on time for the courier, and they had two weddings booked for Saturday.

'We'd like to have you and Jace join us for dinner tonight,'

Ana issued soon after she arrived. 'Luc spoke to Jace before I left and he's deferred the decision to you.'

It sounded a lovely idea. 'Thanks, that'll be great. What time?'

'Seven?' Ana's eyes sparkled with humour. 'Petros said to tell you he'll make moussaka.'

'And dolmades?' Rebekah said hopefully.

'I'll ring and tell him.'

With Ana manning the telephone and the computer, Rebekah and Suzie worked with efficient speed, taking minimum breaks for lunch. By day's end everything was done, preparations were in place for Saturday, the market requirements tabled.

'All done,' Suzie said with satisfaction. 'Will you be OK if I leave now?'

'Sure. See you tomorrow.'

Jace was waiting as Rebekah locked up, and she

handed him the keys to the MG while she slid into the van.

Ten minutes later they rode the lift up to her apartment, and after a quick shower she selected a simple bias-cut dress in topaz-blue, added stiletto-heeled pumps, applied minimum make-up, then she caught up an evening purse and emerged into the lounge.

Jace was intent on televised news coverage, and he turned towards her as she entered the room. His smile was warm and her pulse tripped then raced to a faster beat.

'Ready?'

It was a few minutes before seven as Jace brought the MG to a smooth halt immediately adjacent the main entrance to Luc and Ana's home.

Petros opened the front door before they had a chance to ring the bell, then Ana was there with Luc to greet and usher them indoors.

'We'll have time for a drink before Petros serves dinner,' Ana informed as she moved into the lounge.

True to Ana's promise, Petros served dolmades as a starter, followed it with moussaka and delicate slices of lamb, and presented a magnificent fruit flan for dessert.

Rebekah chose to join her sister and accepted mineral water, leaving the men to drink superb red wine with their meal.

Petros was in the midst of clearing the table prior to serving coffee when the house cellphone rang, and he moved to one side, extracted the unit, spoke briefly, then handed it to Luc.

The conversation was brief, and Luc's tone sufficiently serious to warrant concern as he ended the call.

'That was the police reporting a break-in at Blooms and Bouquets. Someone was seen hurling a brick through the front window.' Luc spared Rebekah a level look. 'The culprit's been caught and identified.'

'Brad.' It was more of a statement than a question, and Luc inclined his head in acquiescence.

'We need to organise for someone to board up the window,' Ana said at once. 'Is there any other damage?'

'I'll go down with Rebekah,' Jace indicated as Luc put through a call to an emergency repair service.

Please God, don't let it be too bad, Rebekah pleaded silently as Jace drove down to the shop. It wasn't any great distance, and he pulled the car to a halt on the opposite side of the road.

A police car was parked adjacent the shop doorway, and Rebekah presented documentation as proof of ownership, then she unlocked the front door and entered the shop.

It was a mess. Vases were overturned, flowers strewn on the floor, and there was water pooling everywhere.

She felt sick, sickened at the degree of vengeance that had caused Brad to go to this extreme. The risk of being seen and caught was high, for the area bordered on the trendy café district, and was consequently well-lit and frequented by several passers-by.

Had he wanted to hurt her so much he was prepared

to go to jail? She doubted even his mother and her high-flying lawyer would be able to save Brad this time.

Maybe it would turn out to be a good thing, and he'd finally get the help he needed. But at what price?

Police procedure took a while, an emergency contractor arrived to board up the window, then Rebekah received clearance to clean up.

There was a sense of unreality, that the whole episode was merely a bad dream from which she'd awaken.

With methodical efficiency she began noting down ruined blooms, and made a list of what she'd need to re-order. Now it was a matter of physical work, clearing broken glass and floral debris.

'Where do you want me to start?' Jace asked as he discarded his jacket and began rolling up his shirt-sleeves.

She fetched a broom and handed it to him. 'You sweep, I'll dispose of the glass.'

They worked together, and it didn't take as long to clean up as she'd first thought. When it was done, she rang Ana and gave her sister a personal report, then she checked the locks and preceded Jace to the car.

'Thanks for your help,' she said quietly as she slid into the passenger seat.

'You imagine I'd have let you come down here and tackle this alone?'

His voice held a quality she didn't want to examine right now, and she retained silence for the short ride back to her apartment.

Inside, she moved straight through to the bedroom, stepped out of her stilettos, slipped off her clothes, and donned a silk robe.

Bed had never looked so good, and there was the temptation to slip between the sheets, snap off the light and drift into a dreamless sleep.

'I've made coffee.'

Rebekah turned at the sound of Jace's deep drawl, and tried for a faint smile, only to fail miserably.

He closed the distance between them and gathered her in against him. He'd expected reaction to set in, but hadn't bargained on it leaving her dark-eyed and white-faced.

'That bad, huh?' He felt a tremor rake her slim body and rested his cheek against the top of her head.

Just hold me, she begged silently. She needed to borrow some of his strength for a while. Even a few minutes would do while she replenished her own. Then she'd sip coffee, maybe put on a video in the hope of losing herself in a light, frivolous movie.

At that moment the phone rang, and she stiffened, wondering who could be calling at this hour. Then common sense prevailed as Jace released her.

'Want me to take that?' He didn't wait for her to answer as he crossed to pick up the bedroom extension.

His end of the conversation was incredibly brief, just a word here and there in confirmation, and she stood quietly as he replaced the handset.

There was a part of her that noticed the broad set of his shoulders, his stance, the way he exuded an animalistic sense of power. Inherent vitality meshed with blatant sensuality to compile a forceful image any sane person would prefer as friend rather than foe.

'Luc,' he revealed. 'Brad has been denied bail.'

The relief was palpable. This time he'd gone too far, and he hadn't been able to slip free of the legal net.

'It's over,' Jace assured quietly. 'Your statement and the evidence is sufficient to ensure he'll go to jail.'

'His mother—'

'Even her lawyer won't be able to swing anything. That's a given.'

'You can't be sure of that.'

'Yes,' he said with grim inflexibility. 'I can.' Brad Somerville would never have the chance to hurt her again. If he so much as tried, the law would come down on him so hard life as he knew it would never be the same again.

'Now,' Jace inclined as he pulled her close. 'Where were we?'

'I think we should go to bed.'

A husky chuckle sounded low in his throat. 'My thoughts, exactly.'

She shook her head. 'To sleep.'

'OK.' He swept an arm beneath her knees and carried her through to the bedroom, switching off lights as he went.

'I can walk,' Rebekah protested.

'Indulge me.'

Yet it was he who indulged her, and for a while she forgot the ugliness of the earlier hours, then he held her as she slept.

Saturday proved to be exceptionally hectic, and a few of the regular clientele called in to commiserate over the broken shop window, the break-in. Rebekah and Ana were circumspect in their explanation, even to Suzie, and it was business as usual as the orders were met, deliveries made.

It was late when Rebekah finished for the day, and she walked out of the shop into Jace's arms, laughing a little as he drew her close, bestowed a lingering kiss, then caught hold of her hand as he led her to the car.

Did he have something planned for his last night in Sydney?

She hoped so. She felt like dressing up, going somewhere special in order to hold the memory of the night forever in her mind.

He didn't disappoint. An hour later she sat sipping champagne in one of the finest restaurants the city had to offer.

The food was exceptional, the ambience fantastic, and the man seated opposite was the embodiment of everything she could ever hope for.

Yet there was a sad poignancy to the night. This was their last meal together, the last time they'd share the same bed.

Unless... No, she wouldn't even go there. Their lives, where they resided, they were too far apart for it to be possible to sustain a successful relationship.

Sure, they'd call each other. Email, fax, phone. For a while. Then the contact would dwindle down to practically nothing, and eventually cease.

But it had been great while it lasted. Better than great, she admitted. So much so, she wasn't sure she'd be able to exist without him.

They lingered, and returned late to her apartment.

The loving was the sweetest, the most sensual experience of her life. He made it so good, it was all she could do not to weep from the joy of it.

They slept for a while, then woke to pleasure each other again before hitting the shower.

'I'll make breakfast,' Rebekah declared, and he pressed a finger to her lips.

'We'll do it together.'

Bacon, eggs, hash browns, juice and strong black coffee. Except she could hardly eat a thing as she conducted a mental countdown to the time they'd need to leave for the airport.

They talked, although afterwards she couldn't recall a word she'd said, and she cleared the table, stacked the dishes, blindly forcing herself to focus on the mundane as he collected his wet-pack from the *en suite*.

She heard him re-enter the kitchen, followed by the soft sound of his overnight bag hitting the floor, then his hands curved over her shoulders as he turned her round to face him.

His hands slid up to cup her nape, then he covered her mouth with his own in a kiss that seared her soul.

When he lifted his head she could only look at him

in silence, too afraid to say the words bubbling up in her throat.

'Marry me.'

Rebekah's jaw dropped, and she struggled to find her voice. An impossibility with a host of random thoughts chasing each other inside her head.

'What did you say?' she managed at last.

'Marry me,' Jace reiterated quietly, and witnessed the gamut of her emotions. Shock, confusion, fear. He could accept the first two, but he wanted to wipe out the third.

'You can't be serious.'

'I am. Very serious.'

She was lost for words. There was one part of her that wanted to shout an unconditional 'yes'. Except sanity demanded a different answer.

He didn't give her the chance to utter it. 'You stole my heart when I partnered you at Luc and Ana's wedding. If I could have, I'd have swept you off to live with me in New York then. But it wasn't the right time...for you.'

'And you imagine it is now?' she queried sadly.

'I want to make it the right time. The question is...do you?'

'Jace—'

'I love you,' he vowed gently. 'The everlasting, "till death do us part" kind.' He made no attempt to touch her. He could, he knew, use unfair persuasion. But he wanted nothing she'd regret on reflection. 'I want to be in your life, and have you in mine.'

Was she brave enough to reach out with both hands

and accept what he offered? She wanted to, desperately.

The thought of never seeing him again was earth-shattering. Yet...*marriage*?

Rebekah met and held his gaze, aware of the strength, the perceptive quality apparent and the integrity. This man wasn't of Brad's ilk, and never would be.

Dared she take that step forward? She didn't think she could...at least, not right now. Maybe in a few months' time, when she'd become used to the idea.

'No conditions, Rebekah.'

He was adept at reading her mind, and to offer him anything less than total honesty wasn't an option.

'I can't do that.' She was breaking up inside. 'I love you.' She felt her mouth tremble, glimpsed sight of the sudden darkness in his eyes, and recognised the effort it cost him to retain control. 'The past week with you...' She faltered, unable to find the words. 'I couldn't bear to lose what we share.' She was dying, slowly, as surely as if the lifeblood was flowing from her body.

'But?'

Rebekah wasn't capable of saying a word.

A muscle tightened at the edge of his jaw. 'You must know I find "no" unacceptable.'

'Jace...' His name emerged from her lips as a husky entreaty.

He caught up his bag and slid the strap over one

shoulder. 'I have to collect my stuff from the hotel, check out, then get to the airport.'

'I'll take you.'

'No.' He leaned forward and kissed her, hard, briefly, then he straightened and walked to the door. He turned and cast her a long, steady look. 'If you want to make it ''yes''...call me.' He opened the door, and closed it quietly behind him without so much as a backward glance.

Rebekah stood there in stunned silence, battling with herself to go running after him. Except she hesitated too long.

It seemed an age before she gathered sufficient energy to re-enter the lounge, and she curled up in a chair, buried her head in her arms and cried...for everything she'd just lost.

At least half a dozen times during the next hour she picked up the phone to call him, only to cut the connection before she'd keyed in the requisite digits.

Then it was too late, he'd already have boarded, and his cellphone would be switched off.

Millie jumped up into her lap, padded until she found a comfortable position, then settled and began to purr.

Rebekah abstractedly fondled the cat's ears, and didn't even try to stem the silent tears.

She had little idea of the passage of time. Eventually she stirred and began taking care of household chores, then, not content, she embarked on a thorough spring-clean of the apartment.

Food was something she couldn't face, and at seven she curled up in a chair and switched television channels until she found something that held her interest.

She must have slept, for she woke to the distant sound of the alarm ringing in the bedroom and she scrambled to her feet to go switch it off.

CHAPTER ELEVEN

ANOTHER day. Her first without Jace. Where was he now? On a stop-over at Los Angeles?

Oh, dear God, *what had she done*?

It was a first to display uninterest at the flower markets; at the shop she assembled blooms and bouquets automatically, devoid of her usual enthusiasm. At night she ate little, showered, then climbed into bed in the spare room after lying awake in her own for hours agonising that Jace wasn't there to share it with her.

Two, three days, four. Each one becoming more unbearable. She couldn't sleep, she didn't eat.

On the fifth day Ana took her by the shoulders, shook her a little, then demanded,

'OK, what gives?' She took a deep breath. 'And don't feed me any garbage about missing Jace. It's more than that.'

Sisterhood was a wonderful thing. Rebekah didn't know whether to laugh or cry. She did neither, and went straight to the truth.

'Jace asked me to marry him, and I said *no*,' she said starkly.

'You *what*?' Ana demanded in disbelief.

'I said no,' Rebekah reiterated, adding, 'For now.'

'Jace asked you to marry him, and you *refused*? Are you mad?'

'Wary. Scared,' she qualified wretchedly.

'Of loving him, and being loved in return?'

'All of that.' And more. 'His base is New York. It's a long way from home.'

'If you love him,' Ana began, then clicked her tongue in silent remonstrance. 'You *do* love him?'

Did she breathe? 'Yes.'

'Then what in hell are you doing here? Book the next flight out and go tell him.'

In her mind she was already winging her way there. 'The shop—'

'Suzie and I can manage.'

'Luc—'

'Leave Luc to me. Maybe we need to consider our options,' Ana suggested. 'Whether we want to sell, or have someone manage the place on our behalf.'

'But Blooms and Bouquets is—'

'Ours? It can still be ours, if that's what we both want. Just not run exclusively by us.'

'We've put so much into this place.'

'Maybe it's time to move on. I have a husband and soon there'll be a child. Both of whom are my life.' Ana drew in a deep breath, keyed in a few strokes, and brought up an internet site.

'What are you doing?'

'Booking you on a flight to New York.'

'I can't—'

'Yes, you can.' Her fingers flew over the keyboard, poised, then she added keystrokes, muttered to herself, added a keystroke or two more, then waited for confirmation. 'Done,' she said with satisfaction a short while later. 'You fly out tomorrow morning.' She named the airline, the flight number and departure time. 'Your electronic ticket will be despatched by courier within the hour.'

It was all going too fast, and she opened her mouth to say so, except Ana got in first.

'Don't,' she cautioned. 'For once in your life take hold of the day and go with it. What do you have to lose?'

What, indeed? she queried as she checked her bag, showed her passport, and moved through Customs into the departure lounge early next morning.

Her initial protest that Jace might be in another city...hell, another country, were dispensed with at once by Ana, who'd assured she'd already checked such details with Luc.

'Surprise him,' Ana had insisted. 'You have his office address, and that of his apartment. If by chance he's not at either place, you have his cellphone number. You can call him.'

So here she was, in a state of high anxiety, about to board a flight to the other side of the world.

Was she doing the right thing? Worse, would he still want her? They were questions she'd asked herself constantly during the past fifteen hours. Twice, she'd almost cancelled out.

The agony and the ecstasy, she accorded wryly as the plane soared into the air. Knowing that it was mostly of her own making didn't help at all.

If she'd listened to her heart instead of her head, she'd have shouted a joyous *yes* when Jace asked her to be his wife. Instead, she'd applied numerous reasons why she shouldn't be with him, rather than all the reasons she should.

Dammit, she was a fool.

Words that sprang to mind repeatedly during the long flight, the disembarkation process, and the cab ride to her hotel.

If you want to make it 'yes', call me. Except she hadn't called, nor had he called her.

What if he'd decided she was too much work, and had taken up with another woman?

If he could do that in so short a time, he wasn't worth having, she decided as she slid from the cab and followed the concierge's direction to Reception.

Her suite was on a high floor overlooking Central Park, but she barely glanced at the view before she unpacked a few essentials, then took a shower.

Ring him, a silent voice urged when she emerged dressed and feeling marginally refreshed.

It was crazy to be so nervous, she decided as she checked his cellphone number, then keyed in the digits.

Her hand shook a little as she waited for him to pick up.

'Dimitriades.'

Hell, he sounded different. Hard, inflexible.

Rebekah swallowed, then found her voice. 'Jace?'

There was a second's silence. 'Where are you?'

Oh lord. 'In a hotel.'

'*Where,* Rebekah?'

For a moment she couldn't think. 'It's opposite Central Park.' Memory kicked in, and she named it, then added her room number.

'Don't move. I'm on my way.'

He ended the call, and she replaced the handset, aware she had no idea where his office was situated in relation to the hotel. Or even if he was in his office.

It could take him up to an hour or longer to get here.

Time she could use to call her father, and catch up. On the other hand she could leave it until tomorrow to ring him. A call to Ana held more importance, and she checked the time difference, calculated it was the middle of the night in Sydney, then opted to send a text message instead.

As the minutes ticked by she was conscious of the onset of nervous tension. Her stomach felt as if it was tying itself in knots, and she couldn't keep her hands still for longer than a few seconds.

Rebekah examined the contents of the bar-fridge, checked out the cupboards and drawers, leafed through the complimentary magazines, and scanned the hotel directory folder, the breakfast menu.

Perhaps if she made herself a cup of coffee—

The doorbell rang, and she almost dropped the cup.

Then she was at the door, unfastening the lock with fingers that shook a little.

Jace seemed to fill the doorway, and her gaze became trapped in his. Held there by some mesmeric force.

For a moment neither of them moved, and everything faded from her peripheral vision. There was only the man, nothing else.

'Are you going to ask me in?'

His slightly accented drawl broke the spell, and she stood aside.

'Of course.'

He closed the door carefully behind him, then turned to face her, seeing her uncertainty, the nervousness, knew he could dispense with it, and would any time soon.

'Would you like coffee?' Rebekah asked in a strained voice.

Whisky would be more appropriate. Had she any idea what he'd gone through in the past week? The hour it had taken for him to get here?

'Coffee isn't a priority right now.'

Oh, to hell with it. She hadn't come all this way to play verbal games. If he was waiting for her to make the first move then, dammit, she would!

Without thought she reached out a hand, fisted it in his shirt and pulled him close. Then she drew his head down and sought his mouth. Her heart and soul went into the kiss, slaking a need that had been denied too long.

It took only seconds for his hands to settle over her shoulders, then ease down her back to cup her buttocks as he held her against him, and it was he who took control in a devastating oral supplication that tore the breath from her body.

Her lips were soft and slightly swollen when he

lifted his head, and he traced the lower curve with a gentle finger.

'What took you so long?'

'Stupidity,' Rebekah said with innate honesty, and Jace smiled as he pressed a light kiss to the tip of her nose.

She locked her arms around his waist and pressed her hips in against his, felt the power of his arousal, and exulted in his need.

'Are you going to say the words,' he drawled gently, 'or do I have to drag them out of you?'

'Yes. The answer's *yes*.'

His mouth found hers, and this time there was such an element of *tendresse*, her heart softened and began to melt.

'Good.' His hands shaped her body, lingered, then moved up to capture her face. 'When?'

'When...*what*?' she queried, definitely distracted by the way his lips were caressing her closed eyelids, a temple, before trailing down to the edge of her mouth.

'Will you make an honest man of me?'

His fingers were toying with the buttons on her blouse in seemingly slow motion. There was all the time in the world, and he was in no hurry.

'Early next year?' she posed, not really focusing on planning a wedding date right now.

'Uh-huh.' He tugged the blouse free from the waistband of her skirt, then gently pulled it free.

'The end of the week.' He began working the zip on her skirt. 'A traditional ceremony in Sydney.' The skirt slid down to the carpet. 'I initiated the requisite paperwork while I was there.'

'You're crazy,' Rebekah said huskily as he undid her bra fastening.

His mouth closed over hers fleetingly. 'Crazy in love with you.'

She was willing to swear her heart stopped for a few seconds before kicking into a faster beat. 'Thank you.'

Jace lifted his head. 'For what?'

'For having enough faith in what we share to walk away and let me realise for myself that what I feel for you is *love*.'

He brushed his lips to her cheek. 'I don't think you have any conception just how hard it was for me to do that.'

She thought of the long, lonely nights when she woke and realised he wasn't there. How she jumped at every ring of the phone. The meals she wasn't able to eat because of an aching heart. And the knowledge that life without Jace in it would be no life at all.

'Yes, I do.' She eased his jacket off, then began unbuttoning his shirt. 'You're wearing too many clothes.'

'Want some help?' he asked quizzically, and she shook her head.

'Believe me, the pleasure is all mine.'

And it was. She took it slow, savouring the removal of each item until he stood naked before her. Then she pushed him down onto the bed and straddled him, watching in delight as his eyes dilated and became heavy with passion.

Instinct ruled as she tasted him, and she savoured each moment the breath hissed between his teeth, the faint groan, the slight tremor as she embarked on a sensual feast where boundaries and inhibitions didn't exist.

Then it was Jace's turn, and he showed no mercy in his pursuit of gifting her the ultimate in primitive pleasure. It was she who cried out, she who reached for him and begged his possession.

When they came together it was with raw, primeval desire. Brazen, tumultuous. *Magic*.

The long aftermath held a dreamy quality, a gentle, tactile exploration with drifting finger-pads, soft kisses, and such an acute sensitivity it made her want to cry.

'Hungry?' Jace murmured as he nuzzled the soft hollow at the edge of her neck.

'For you, or food?'

She felt his mouth curve against her throat.

'When did you last eat, *agape mou*?'

'On the plane.' How many hours ago? Eight, ten?

'I'll order Room Service.' He bestowed a brief hard kiss. 'Then we'll shower, and you get to grab some sleep.'

He chose a light meal, and he extracted a half-magnum of champagne from the bar-fridge, opened it and poured the contents into two flutes.

'To us.'

He touched the rim of his flute to hers, and her

bones melted at the wealth of passion evident in his dark gaze.

'I love you.' She wanted, needed to say the words, and Jace took hold of her hand and brought it to his lips.

'You're everything to me,' he vowed quietly. 'More than I ever dreamed it was possible to have.' He turned her hand over and buried his lips in her palm. 'My life.'

She wanted to cry, and the tears welled up and shimmered there, threatening to spill.

He lifted his head, saw them, and pressed his lips to each eyelid in turn. 'Don't.'

The long flight, the nervous excitement, the love-making had taken its toll, and she was helpless to stem the flow as they spilled over and trickled down each cheek in twin rivulets.

He smoothed them with his thumb, then fastened his mouth on hers in a gentle, evocative kiss.

Their meal was delivered a short while later, and they fed each other morsels of the light, fluffy mushroom omelette, the salad, and Rebekah alternated the champagne with bottled water.

She was almost asleep on the chair, and it was all she could do to remain awake as they showered together, then, dry, she let Jace carry her to bed, where she curled up against him and was asleep within seconds of her head touching the pillow.

It was a while before Jace gently freed himself from her embrace and slid from the bed. He extracted his cellphone and made a series of calls. Then he rejoined her in bed and gathered her close.

There was, Rebekah accepted, nothing quite like the power and prestige of serious money.

Jace used it mercilessly to ensure everything went according to plan, and she experienced a sense of stunned disbelief as he organised return flights to Sydney the next day for them both, accepted Luc and Ana's offer to have the wedding at their home, gave them carte blanche to have Petros arrange caterers and liaised with the guest list.

The phone calls were lengthy and many, with Ana relaying she'd seen a wedding gown to die for, and everything down to the finest detail would be successfully organised in time for *the* day.

The fact that it was seemed nothing short of a miracle.

Even the weather was perfect, with brilliant blue skies, sunshine, and the merest hint of a breeze to temper the day's warmth.

'Ready?'

The gown, as Ana had promised, was something else.

Ivory silk with an ivory lace overlay that had a scalloped hemline resting just below the knee. Elbow-length sleeves in ivory lace, and a high neckline. The headpiece was a pearl band with a short fingertip veil bunched at the back of her head, and she carried a single long-stemmed white rose. Her only jewellery was a diamond pendant and matching earrings.

'Yes.' Rebekah turned to her sister and gathered her close in an affectionate hug. 'Thanks for everything.'

'You're welcome,' Ana responded gently. 'OK, let's get this show on the road.'

Luc was waiting downstairs to lead her out into the grounds, where the guests were assembled on chairs either side of a red carpet facing a delicate wrought-iron gazebo.

'Beautiful,' Luc complimented quietly as he took her arm. His gaze slid to his wife, and the warmth of his smile brought a lump to Rebekah's throat.

Together they walked out onto the terrace, traversed the short flight of steps, and made their way towards the gazebo. The guests stood and those lining the red carpet threw rose petals in Rebekah's path.

She saw Jace standing at the assembled altar, and she caught his gaze and held it as she made her way towards him.

A light, husky laugh escaped her lips as he drew her close and kissed her, thoroughly.

The celebrant cleared his throat, and they broke apart.

It was a simple ceremony, the words deeply moving, and Rebekah fought back the faint shimmer of tears as Jace slid a wide diamond-encrusted ring onto her finger.

There was the flash of cameras, voiced congratulations, and a shower of rose petals as they trod the red carpet as man and wife.

Champagne and food were served in a marquee

erected close by, guests greeted and thanked, then all too soon it was time to change and leave for the airport.

Ana helped her remove the headpiece and veil, then assisted with the zip fastening of the gown.

Rebekah freshened up, then slipped into an elegant trouser suit, added comfortable heeled shoes, then turned towards her sister.

'I'm going to miss you dreadfully.'

'We'll email each other every day, and talk on the phone. Jace has promised me you'll both visit at least twice a year.'

Rebekah's expression sobered a little. 'A month ago—'

'Don't look back,' Ana cautioned gently. 'You have today, and all the tomorrows.' She brushed her lips to Rebekah's cheek. 'Embrace them and be happy.'

'How did you get to be so wise?' Rebekah asked shakily.

'If you cry, I'll hit you.'

'Sisterly love,' Luc drawled from the doorway, whilst Jace offered,

'Shall we divide and conquer?'

'I think so,' Luc said with musing indolence as he crossed to his wife's side and drew her close.

Jace extended his hand, and Rebekah's toes curled at the way he looked at her. 'Ready, *agape mou*?'

'Yes.' And she was. Ready to go anywhere he chose to lead.

Together they made their way downstairs, and as they reached the car Rebekah turned to her sister.

'OK, this is it. The last goodbye.' She gave Ana a quick hug. 'I'll ring you from Paris.' Then it was Luc's turn. 'Look after her,' she said fiercely.

'Every minute of every day,' he promised solemnly.

'Go,' Ana pleaded, on the verge of tears.

Two sisters, two destinies, Rebekah mused as Jace took the main road leading towards the airport.

'We'll visit soon. And you have my word we'll return for the birth of Ana's child.'

Rebekah felt something begin to soar deep within, and she turned to look at him. 'Have I told you how much I love you?'

She had, several times through the night. They were words he'd never tire of hearing. Words he'd say to her, over and again for the rest of his life.

'If you do, I'll pull the car to the side of the road and kiss you.'

Her eyes assumed a wicked sparkle. 'An act that would probably cause a public spectacle.'

'Count on it.'

'Then I guess we need to wait for a more appropriate moment?' She began counting off each finger. 'Let's see, there's the long flight, with a brief stopover in Los Angeles. Thirty-six hours in total before we reach Paris.'

'Forty-eight,' Jace corrected with a musing smile. 'We have a not-so-brief stop-over in Los Angeles.'

Rebekah gave a laugh that was part delight, all mischief. 'Can't keep your hands off me, huh?'

He shot her a gleaming glance. 'Want me to try?'

Her expression sobered. 'No,' she assured quietly. 'Not in this lifetime.'

He waited until he passed the hire car in at the airport before he gathered her close and kissed her, thoroughly. So thoroughly she temporarily lost any sense of time or place.

Then he unloaded their bags from the boot, hefted the strap of one bag over his shoulder and gathered up the other, and caught her hand in his.

Together, as they would always be, for the rest of their lives.

EPILOGUE

SYDNEY in the spring reminded Rebekah of new beginnings as seasonal plants came into bud with the promise of life and colour. The trees began to blossom as nature prepared for yet another rebirth.

The gardens in the grounds of Luc and Ana's beautiful home were carefully tended, the lawns fresh and green and clipped with manicured precision.

It was a glorious day, the sun shone and there was only the merest drift of cloud in a stunning blue sky.

A baby's wail pierced the air, loud and protesting, as the celebrant performed the naming ceremony of Luc and Ana's young son. Marcus Lucien Dimitriades possessed a strong pair of lungs, and at three months of age he was his parents' pride and joy.

'Beautiful,' Jace accorded softly as he curved an arm along the back of her waist, and she turned to him with a smile, about to concur, when she saw he was looking at her, not the babe Ana held in her arms.

It was almost a year since their marriage, and there were times when she felt the need to pinch herself to see if she was living in a dream or the real world.

'Definitely *real*,' Jace assured quietly as he brushed his lips to her temple, and she lifted her face to slant her mouth into his, briefly savoured their warmth and reluctantly broke the contact.

'I love you.'

She felt his arm muscles tighten at the back of her waist. 'You certainly pick your moments, *agape mou.*'

'Bothers you, huh?' she teased, and almost drowned in the passion evident in his dark gaze. 'You can exact your revenge later.'

'Count on it.'

Later that night she lay in his arms, replete in the aftermath of lovemaking.

'Have you told Ana our news?'

Rebekah pressed her lips to his shoulder, nibbled a little, then soothed the love-nip with a soft kiss.

'Today was special, and very much her day. I'll tell her over lunch tomorrow.'

Jace's hand shifted to her waist and settled there, and she covered it with her own.

A child, theirs. A unique gift they would nurture and watch grow. Share the joys, the fun, the laughter, and hopefully few tears. And love unconditionally for the rest of their lives.

'No regrets?'

'None,' she vowed gently. 'You're the love of my life. My present, my future. Everything.'

Brad, her brief marriage, and its repercussions no longer existed.

'As you are mine,' Jace reciprocated gently.

The Greek
Tycoon's Mistress

by
Julia James

Julia James lives in England with her family. Mills & Boon were the first 'grown up' books she read as a teenager, alongside Georgette Heyer and Daphne du Maurier, and she's been reading them ever since. Julia adores the English and Celtic countryside, in all its seasons, and is fascinated by all things historical, from castles to cottages. She also has a special love for the Mediterranean – 'The most perfect landscape after England!' – and she considers both ideal settings for romance stories. In between writing she enjoys walking, gardening, needlework, baking extremely gooey cakes and trying to stay fit!

**Don't miss Julia James's new novel,
Bedded or Wedded?, out in November 2007
from Mills & Boon® Modern™!**

For IHV

CHAPTER ONE

THEO ATRIDES narrowed his dark eyes. Fabulously wealthy, dangerous to cross, he was unfairly blessed with a sexual magnetism that had as much to do with the aura of raw power that surrounded him as the physical attributes with which he was so shamelessly endowed.

He paused at the head of the flight of wide-sweeping stairs, looking down into the hotel's crowded banqueting suite. It was a sea of men in black tie, women in rainbow evening dress. Chandeliers caught the glitter of jewels everywhere.

From his vantage point, like an eagle poised in its eyrie, Theo let his alert gaze systematically quarter the throng below, searching with steady purpose. Suddenly he stilled. Beneath the silk-smooth covering of his superbly tailored tuxedo, his tall, powerfully built frame tensed.

Yes, they were there! Both of them.

It was the woman he studied, and as he did so his jaw tightened.

She was dressed to kill. Of that there was no doubt. His expert eye looked her over. Medium height, with a figure both slender and generous—and very, very much on show. Blonde hair cascaded down her bare back in rippling waves. Her skin was pale, like an opalescent pearl against the thigh-length little black dress which dipped so low over the swelling orbs of her breasts that only their delicate tips were veiled by the clinging satin. Likewise, her pert little bottom was tightly, and barely, sheathed, while shimmering stockings covered her legs from exposed thigh to provocative black satin stiletto heels.

A perfect package. So skimpily wrapped. So tempting to unwrap.

5

She laughed, throwing her head back, letting that fabulous fall of hair ripple down that naked back, exposing the tender line of her throat, the dazzle of diamonds hanging from the succulent morsels of her earlobes.

Theo couldn't even see her face yet, and already he felt his loins tightening. Hardening.

The rush of sensual pleasure of his own ultra-masculine reaction warred with a hard, tight shaft, not of desire, but anger, mingling explosively. Women like that were trouble. Especially for the men they caught in their toils.

He should know…

Slowly, he began to walk down the wide sweep of stairs.

Leandra had never felt more naked in her life. With every breath she feared that her breasts would finally escape her low-cut bodice completely, and every movement of her legs would make the tight sheath of her skirt ride up over her bottom. Chris must have been mad to make her wear a dress like this!

But he had been adamant that she should look as brazenly sexy as she could, or there was no point in any of this charade at all.

Even so, she hated the way she looked in the tarty get-up!

She took a quick but deep, controlled breath—the same technique she used to subdue stage fright. For that was all this was, Leandra reminded herself—a stage performance. Certainly a glitzy charity gala at one of London's top hotels was not her customary stamping ground.

She was more used to pub theatres and grimy green rooms—the usual lot of a struggling actress. Now, thanks to Chris, she was standing beside a handsome young Greek millionaire—and almost sick with nerves.

Demos Atrides, who ran the UK subsidiary of the vast Atrides business empire, turned to her with a reassuring smile. She gave him a wide smile back, the way her role demanded.

She liked him a lot, and not just because of Chris. For all

his wealth Demos was very diffident—he needed Chris's buoyant confidence to keep his spirits up, Leandra knew. She wasn't the only one dreading the coming confrontation.

Would their charade be convincing? Leandra swallowed. She mustn't be the one to let them down—after all, she *was* the professional actress.

Demos's light touch on her arm made her start slightly.

'He's here,' he said in his soft, mellifluous voice, the Greek accent distinct. As was the tension in his face.

Leandra drew in her breath. 'Here goes,' she said, and wished herself luck.

As he approached them Theo Atrides felt his mood darken. He didn't want to be here, but his grandfather Milo had insisted. As patriarch of the Atrides clan he was used to getting his own way. That was why, Theo knew, Milo was taking it so hard that his younger grandson refused to come to heel.

Not that it was like Demos to cause trouble. He'd always done everything Theo had asked of him, running the London office diligently and competently. His affairs had always been conducted with discretion; even Theo knew nothing about them.

Why make such a fuss about this one?

Theo's mouth thinned. The reason was right in front of him. Blonde, lush and very, very sexy. No wonder his little cousin didn't want to come home and marry Sofia Allessandros, the bride Milo had chosen for him. What man would want to give up a mistress like this?

Demos Atrides felt the heavy hand on his shoulder, and for a moment it felt like the clap of doom. Then he recovered.

'Theo!' he exclaimed, with a forced expression of delight. 'It's good to see you. My PA told me you'd phoned from the jet to ask where I'd be tonight.' He glanced beyond his cousin. 'Where is Milo?'

'Resting,' returned his cousin tersely. 'The flight was a strain. You shouldn't have made it necessary, Demos.'

The words were a reproof, and Demos coloured slightly.

'There was no need for him to come,' he replied defensively.

'Wasn't there?'

Deliberately Theo shifted his focus to the woman hanging on to Demos's arm like a gilded limpet. As his eyes lit full on her face for the first time he felt, like an electric shock, a response that was like a kick in the gut.

For a moment his brain churned. She wasn't in the least what he'd been expecting from what he'd seen of her so far. He'd assumed that the brazenly sexy body would be accompanied by nothing more than a vacuous expression and an avaricious nature.

Instead, a pair of intelligent amber-coloured eyes flashed up at him, deep-set and lustrous, catching him with an unexpected beauty despite being caked in eyeshadow and their lashes clotted with too much mascara. Something showed in their depths, but before his scrambled brain could identify it it was gone. Theo dismissed it, and went on studying the rest of her face. It was layered in make-up, far too much of it, but the excess could not camouflage the height of her cheekbones and the fine, straight line of her nose. Nor could the sticky scarlet lipstick disguise the tender curve of her mouth.

Theo suddenly felt an odd desire to take a tissue and sweep away the acres of gunk smeared all over her extraordinary natural beauty...

For a moment, the merest instant, something stirred in him that had nothing to do with his immediate and all too easily identifiable reaction to the lush physical charms of the woman in front of him. Something that disturbed him—moved him...

He snapped his mind away. It didn't matter an iota what he thought of Demos's mistress. It only mattered that he got his cousin away from her and back to Athens and his engagement to Sofia Allessandros.

It was what everyone expected—especially Milo. He was

desperate to see the next Atrides generation secure. He had never, Theo knew, recovered from the tragedy that had almost overwhelmed the family eight years ago, when both his sons and their wives had been killed when the Atrides jet had crashed. Theo himself had hardly had time to grieve. At the age of twenty-four he had found himself single-handedly in charge of the entire Atrides business empire as Milo suffered a near-fatal stroke at the loss of his sons. Business rivals, seeing the Atrides clan so stricken, had swooped.

Theo had fought them off, swiftly becoming battle hardened, and now, at thirty-two, the Atrides empire was stronger and wealthier than ever. No one dared challenge its ruthless boss these days.

All it needed now was a new heir for the next generation— Milo was right.

But it would not be Theo who provided one.

Marriage was not for Theo. Never would be.

If anyone was going to give Milo the great-grandsons he craved, it would have to be Demos—and Sofia Allessandros. As for the foxy piece clinging to Demos's arm—well, she'd just have to look for another rich lover!

His eyes swept over her again. With looks like that it shouldn't take her long to find one…

Leandra stared at the man looking her over with those dark, heavy-lidded eyes. Just stared. Oh, good grief, but he was devastating! Absolutely devastating! She'd heard enough about Big Bad Cousin Theo from Demos, heaven knew. He wasn't just a tough, ruthless businessman.

Women flocked around Theo Atrides, and he helped himself to the ones he wanted, sampled them, then discarded them for fresh sweetmeats. Leandra could see why—and it was not, definitely not, just because he was stinking rich. Theo Atrides could have pulled women by the bucketload without a drachma to his name!

Leandra felt herself helpless under the impact of his sheer physical presence, from the commanding height of his six-foot-plus frame to the subtle but heady scent of his aftershave mingled with raw, potent maleness. The photos she'd seen of him—family shots in Demos's apartment, glossy spreads in celebrity magazines—whilst capturing his eye-catching good looks, had not prepared her for the real Theo Atrides. Let alone for his effect on her.

She'd blithely assumed, because she was totally unattracted by Demos's looks, that she'd be as immune to his cousin's.

Oh, boy, what a mistake! Theo Atrides's features were much stronger, his eyes keen and hooded, darker than his twenty-six-year-old cousin's and far, far more knowing. His nose was a strong slash, his cheekbones powerful and high, and his jaw might have been hewn with a chisel. His mouth had none of Demos's fullness, but was wide and mobile and, Leandra registered with a hollow feeling, a million times sexier...

In fact, in just about every atom of his being, Theo Atrides was a million times sexier than his cousin.

And a million times more dangerous. In an act of unconscious self-preservation Leandra veiled her assessing eyes, adopting instead the vacuous expression of a bimbo that fitted the charade she was acting out. Doing so had its compensations. It allowed her to look him over just the way she wanted to—needed to.

Not that he'd look twice at her. All his women, however briefly they lasted, were either celebrities in their own right— a couple of supermodels, an opera singer and an Oscar-winning movie star sprang effortlessly to mind—or else they were blue-blooded scions of Europe's cosmopolitan aristocracy and America's Wall Street plutocrats.

Except that he *was* looking at her. Theo Atrides was looking her over very, very thoroughly, with all the expertise of a practised connoisseur of the very best in female beauty.

It was a nerve-tingling experience.

As she felt, almost physically, those dark, knowing eyes wash over her, Leandra could feel her legs jellify. Her breath had frozen solid in her throat, making it impossible to breathe. Her heart, it seemed, slewed to a stop in her chest and her eyes were stretched so wide she must be goggling. Then, just as she started to go into complete meltdown under his blatantly sexual appraisal, she realised she could see contempt openly sitting in his eyes. It was obvious what he thought of a woman dressed as revealingly as she was.

Two impulses warred within her. One was to grab the nearest tablecloth and cover herself up. The other was to slap his face so hard it would spin the stars for him!

Of course she did neither—she could not afford to.

Instead, she behaved in the way that her role in this elaborate charade required her to behave. Badly.

'Demos,' she husked, pressing into his side more closely, unconsciously seeking his protection from such an arrant sexual predator, 'who is this gorgeous, gorgeous man?'

Leandra's voice was slightly breathy. It was not entirely put on. Her body was out of control, reacting to this man's presence in ways she had only ever read about, never experienced. It was a mix of terrifying and exhilarating.

Demos opened his mouth to answer, but was forestalled.

'Theo Atrides,' murmured his cousin. His voice had dropped a register and taken on a deep, dark husk of its own, heavy with his drawling Greek accent. The raw sexiness of it made Leandra's toes curl, accompanied as it was by a kilowatt's worth of sexual charge blazing through eyes which were suddenly, devastatingly, heavy-lidded and half closed.

He turned to Demos.

'And this is…?' He paused expectantly, the purring note still deep in his voice.

His appeal to his cousin sent a frisson of waspish anger through Leandra. Doesn't he think me capable of answering for myself? she thought indignantly.

'Leandra,' supplied Demos. He said her name reluctantly.

'Ross—' completed Leandra, with the very slightest bite to her voice.

'Leandra,' echoed Theo Atrides drawlingly, ignoring the

irrelevance of her surname. Women like her had no need of anything other than a first name—preferably something exotic.

'You are very lovely, Leandra.' He paused infinitesimally. 'Very lovely. All over.'

The heavy-lidded dark eyes washed over her. She felt they were stripping off every last vestige of clothing. Then he helped himself to her hand.

His touch was as electric as his look. To her shame, Leandra believed that she actually trembled as he made contact.

His hand was large and smooth. Warm and strong. And very powerful. Hers looked pale and fragile within its olive-tanned grasp.

Leisurely, Theo lifted her scarlet-tipped, freshly manicured fingers to his lips. But instead of grazing her knuckles in a courtly fashion, as Leandra was steeling herself to expect, he turned her hand over to expose her palm and bent his head.

As his lips touched her flesh she felt them part slightly. Then, in a caress that exploded every nerve-ending in her palm, they laved her skin softly and sensuously. She felt a prickle of arousal all over her body, delicious and enticing. Warm, liquid coils of heat pooled in her veins. Then suddenly, shockingly, she felt the tip of his tongue flicker exploringly at the junctions of her fingers.

Shock, outrage and a sizzle of raw sexual excitement electrified her, searing the breath in her fractured lungs. She couldn't move even as he released her from his shockingly intimate caress.

She grabbed her hand back into her own possession. It felt as if every nerve-ending in it had been set on fire, humming like flame racing along her veins. For one long, overwhelming moment she felt as if the world was whirling round her, and the only still point was the flare of sensation echoing in her hand.

Her lips parted and she stared, helplessly, at Theo Atrides.

He smiled down at her. A warm, intimate smile. A knowing, indulgent smile. A dangerous, sexy smile.

Almost, almost she felt herself moving blindly towards him, to press herself up against his lean, hard body and give herself to him absolutely. He was like a powerful magnet sucking her towards him.

But she had to resist. She must! She was here to play his cousin's mistress—nothing more. Forcibly she relaxed her muscles, and by sheer effort of will—still reeling from the sensual onslaught of Theo Atrides's terrifyingly skilful, insolent mouth on her exposed, defenceless skin—she managed to pull her body back from leaning into his.

Thee mou, thought Theo, as she drew back with obvious reluctance, the girl couldn't have come on stronger if she'd given him her telephone number! She'd all but gone up in flames for him! What the hell would she be like if he got her horizontal?

A sudden, overpowering image of her lying beneath him, naked and aching for him, yielding her body to him with soft moans, filled his mind with devastating, vivid clarity. He thrust it aside brutally. This was no time to get the hots for a woman who was threatening the stability of his family and its very future! All her sizzling reaction to his deliberate sexual provocation had proved was that, whatever she felt for Demos, it wasn't anything that stopped her lighting up for any other man. The faithful type she wasn't!

He turned back to his cousin.

As his attention snapped off Leandra wondered why she felt bereft, instead of relieved—as if a source of heat suddenly turned off had revealed how cold she had been feeling.

All her life.

In a daze she tried to make herself concentrate on what Theo was saying to his cousin. It was hard, because her brain felt like mush.

'So,' Theo said to Demos, his deep voice sounding amused, 'this is what is keeping you in London so long, I see! I can't say I'm surprised, now I've met this delicious morsel of female flesh—' His eyes worked over Leandra once more, so brazenly she felt her stomach drop even as anger leapt in her throat at such a description. 'But,' he went on, holding up a hand peremptorily and focusing back on his cousin, 'all good things come to an end, Demos. Sofia is waiting for you. It's time to come home.'

Leandra could feel Demos tense.

'I'm not ready,' he replied tersely. His usually mild voice sounded strained.

'Then *be* ready,' said Theo unforgivingly. He reached out and closed his hand around his cousin's shoulder, turning him slightly away from Leandra as if she were an intruder on the scene.

He switched to Greek, reinforcing her exclusion.

'Milo's on the way out, Demos. It's only a matter of time. His doctors know it and he knows it. He's old—he's had too much to bear in his life—don't do this to him. Come home and get engaged to Sofia. It's all he asks. He needs to know that the next generation is assured—you can't blame him for being anxious. He knows, *Christos,* he knows, just how uncertain life is! He needs to know that a great-grandson could be on the way soon—he needs an heir.'

He spoke rapidly, in a low voice.

Stiffly, Demos answered. 'Milo has two grandsons, Theo. Why don't you oblige?'

Theo's jaw tightened. 'I'm not the marrying kind, little cousin.'

For a second something showed in Demos's eyes.

'And suppose I'm not either?' he said.

There was something in Demos's voice that stayed his cousin. Theo looked at him narrowly.

'What's that supposed to mean?' he asked slowly.

For a long moment Demos just looked across at him, as if he was going to say something. Then, with a fling of his hand, he shook Theo off his shoulder.

'It means I'm having too much fun to want to settle down!

'm not ready to marry anyone, let alone Sofia Allessandros!' An urgent note entered his voice. 'Make Milo see that, Theo. Make him!'

Anger lashed through Theo. Anger at both of them—Milo for wanting to arrange other people's lives because he was taking leave of his own, and Demos for insisting on living his own life when he had responsibilities to meet!

And most of all anger, irrational but powerful, against the girl plastered against Demos—the cause of all this trouble.

He wanted out of this! He hadn't wanted to come here, and now he was here he wanted to wash his hands of the whole business. He wanted to get away—away from the endless demands of family, of business—go some place where all he had to do was gaze out over the blue Aegean, hear the cicadas calling, inhale the heady scent of the maquis, feel the zephyred wind from the south on his body.

With a soft, compliant woman in his arms...

Like the one at Demos's side...

He gave a rasp in his throat, banishing the dangerously enticing vision.

'Enough!' His hand slashed the air with a short, brusque slash. 'I'll expect you tomorrow, Demos. Milo wants to see you at nine. We're in the penthouse suite here. Be on time.' He eyed his cousin darkly, his harsh gaze sweeping out to Leandra. 'And get some sleep tonight!' he finished, reverting to English.

His eyes flickered briefly over her face. The expression in them made her want to hit him. His thoughts were naked. With a woman like her at his side what man would want to sleep?

He, for one, could think of a thousand better things to do with her—

He snapped his mind away again. The woman was an irrelevance.

Soon her brief intrusion into his family affairs would be over—permanently.

*   *   *

Demos Atrides opened the door to his apartment and ushered Leandra inside. Immediately she was tightly enveloped in a bear hug.

'Well,' demanded the extremely handsome blond embracing her with long familiarity. 'How did it go? Did he show?'

Leandra extricated herself, tossing her evening bag on the silk-covered sofa, and kicked off one of her high heels. Her feet were killing her. She said nothing. She didn't think she could for the moment.

'Oh, yes, he showed all right,' said Demos behind her. His voice was tight.

'And?' demanded the other young man. 'Did he fall for it?'

Demos gave a short laugh, displaying the tension he was still under.

'Hook, line and sinker—isn't that what you say?'

The blond laughed, showing an expanse of gleaming white teeth in a brilliant smile that lit his handsome face. Leandra laughed too, but hers was short, with an edge to it.

'With the emphasis on hook—as in hooker,' she said bitingly. 'God, Chris.' She kicked off her other shoe and flexed her aching ankles. 'Thanks to that dress you poured me into, Theo Atrides looked at me like I was some kind of tart!'

A shiver went through her at the memory of the way Demos's cousin had looked her over—and more than looked...

But Chris was not dismayed. 'That's brilliant, Lea—just what we wanted! He's got to think Demos is totally captivated by his sexy little mistress! Speaking of sexy—' he caught her shoulders '—you, darling, look absolutely edible! Yum, yum!'

Leandra was in no mood for his foolery. Reaction and revulsion were setting in with a vengeance.

'Leave off, Chris!' she said, pushing his hands off her shoulders and heading towards the bathroom. 'I need to get out of this ridiculous costume!'

*   *   *

The evening had been far more of an ordeal than she had thought it would be—thanks to that wretched dress and Theo Atrides! She stepped out of the shower and towelled herself vigorously. It had seemed so easy, as well as a good deed, to pretend to be Demos's mistress. All she'd had to do was move into the spare bedroom in Demos's luxury apartment and spend the last three weeks appearing to be living with him—until his family finally got the message that he wasn't coming home to marry Sofia Allessandros.

Leandra stared at her reflection as she combed out the knots in her wet hair, her face set. Had tonight's performance been sufficiently convincing? Would the Atrideses finally leave him in peace now?

She hoped so—with a shudder she knew she couldn't face another encounter with Theo Atrides. Her nerves couldn't stand it.

A sudden shaft of depression hit her. Theo Atrides was the most incredibly attractive male she'd ever laid eyes on, and he'd seen her as nothing more than a sexy, trashy tart.

But what if he hadn't?

Her comb paused and her imagination took flight. She saw herself, gowned in black still, but soft velvet, long, sweeping the ground, its modest *décolletage* set with a single white rose, her hair caught in a low, elegant chignon at the nape of her neck, her make-up subtle, her perfume elusive…

If Theo Atrides had seen her looking like that then perhaps those heavy-lidded eyes would have gazed at her quite differently, mused Leandra dreamily. Sensually, yes, but without that offensive glint of contempt he hadn't bothered to hide. His eyes would have shown nothing but the desire of man for woman. As old as time. An eternal hunger yearning to be sated.

She sighed, beguiled by her own impossible vision. Then, abruptly, she sobered. Struggling actresses, whatever they wore, were not his fare. And even if they were, she added crushingly, it wouldn't do you any good! Even filmstar Madeleine Fareham with her precious Oscar hadn't gone the

distance! The papers were full of her marrying her latest co-
star on the rebound from Theo Atrides!

Decisively, Leandra tugged the last of the knots from her
newly washed hair as if she were tugging something out of
her that had just taken root—a weed that looked like an or-
chid but was really nothing more than poison ivy.

Back in the lounge, Chris and Demos were drinking coffee.
Leandra, swathed in a towelling robe, poured herself a cup
and collapsed next to Chris. He put his arm around her shoulder.

'Better now?' he asked sympathetically.

She nodded. 'Yes. Sorry—but, honestly, the way you
dressed me up—I just felt so exposed! And Demos's cousin
looked at me like I was some kind of total floozie! It was
horrible! Still…' she took a deep breath '…it's all over now.
Thank goodness. Oh, Demos.' She leant forward and tossed
the diamond earrings in his lap. 'Here you go.'

He caught them and put them on the coffee table. Then he
met Leandra's eyes.

'Lea—thank you. Thank you a thousand times.' He
sounded embarrassed. 'And I am sorry that my cousin behaved towards you in such a disrespectful way.'

Leandra held up a hand. She didn't want Demos feeling
bad about it.

'It's OK,' she said lightly, playing it down. 'I'll survive.
And, hey, it's like Chris says—that was the whole plan—to
make me look like a rich man's sex toy. I should be glad he
believed it!'

She looked down into her coffee cup. Oh, Theo Atrides
had believed she was a sex toy all right! Memory leapt at
her, searing her belly with its heat as she felt again the echo
of his hand taking hers, kissing her palm…the touch of his
flickering tongue…

Beneath the protectively thick towelling robe she could
feel her breasts tighten.

Angry mortification filled her. She could tell herself all she liked that it had been hateful to be treated like that, but she knew she was a liar.

Theo Atrides had had an effect on her that she had never encountered in her life before. It had overwhelmed her, blasted her out of the sky like a fireball...

She'd been helpless, totally helpless. If he'd wanted, he could have taken her hand and led her away from Demos— led her away to a private room and folded her against his body, lowered that hard, mobile mouth to hers and done anything he wanted to her...anything at all...

She stared down into her coffee, appalled by this shaming realisation.

A shudder went through her as she fought to throw his image, his memory, out of her mind.

'Lea—are you all right?'

She jerked her head up. 'I'm fine—fine. Just tired, that's all.'

Chris was looking at her closely.

'Did the bastard get to you, Lea?' he asked quietly. At his side Demos stiffened at this cavalier description of the cousin he had always looked up to, but he said nothing.

Leandra bit her lip. She could deny the way she'd reacted to Theo Atrides, but it wouldn't fool either of them for long. She might as well admit it now.

'Yes,' she acknowledged. 'But it doesn't matter—all that matters is that he leaves Demos alone now.'

She made her voice bright and cheerful and decided she had to just pull herself together. It didn't matter a jot that she had all but melted over Theo Atrides. It didn't matter that he was the most devastating male she had ever seen. It didn't even matter that he thought her nothing but a wind-up sex toy.

She would never set eyes on him again.

Theo Atrides had come and gone in her life. He wouldn't be back.

CHAPTER TWO

THEO stared moodily out over Hyde Park from the penthouse suite where he and his grandfather were staying. The trees had turned autumnal already; summer was over.

His mood was grim. Demos had just left, and the exchange with Milo had not been pleasant. When his grandfather had finished lecturing him on duty, responsibility, family and Sofia Allessandros waiting in Athens for him to deign to turn up, Demos had stubbornly repeated what he'd said to Theo the night before. He wasn't ready to get married. That was all. He was enjoying his bachelor life.

Then he'd walked out.

Theo turned back towards Milo.

'You are so sure of this marriage?' he heard himself ask.

Milo flashed him a dark look from eyes which, though wrinkled, were still keen and sharp.

'Demos needs a good marriage. Sofia Allessandros is just the girl for him.'

Theo paused. 'I know,' he said carefully, 'that you are in a hurry. But can't you give him more time? It's *his* life, Milo.'

The dark, shrewd eyes stared at him.

'I'm worried about him,' he said. 'I want to see him safe with Sofia Allessandros.'

There seemed to be meaning in his words. Theo frowned.

'This woman of his? A pillow-friend, nothing more. He won't marry her, if that's what's worrying you!'

The dark eyes snapped and Milo's mouth thinned.

'Young men are foolish!' He fixed Theo with a piercing, uncomfortable look. 'You would have made such a foolish marriage…'

The accusation hung in the air. For a moment Theo stilled. Then, with a deliberate shrug of his powerful shoulders, he said, 'Well, you and my father soon sorted that out, didn't you? And that other "minor complication" it involved!'

The accusation had been returned, and Milo felt it. His eyes snapped again. 'Don't take that tone! We did what was necessary. A woman like that—you should be grateful!'

Theo stilled again. 'Grateful.' The word fell heavily from his lips.

A harsh, impatient rasp sounded in the old man's throat. 'Money showed her true colours! It always does with women of her stamp!'

He shifted restlessly in the chair he was sitting in. Pain flickered briefly in his face. Theo saw it. Pity filled him. The past was gone—his grandfather and his father had done what they had thought best, by their lights. And they had been right, he knew. Money did show true colours. And he was grateful, just as Milo said he should be. Grateful to have had his illusions shattered.

Illusions were always dangerous. In business, and in bed.

Theo had no illusions any more. Never again. He knew what he wanted from women now. It was simple, pleasurable—and painless. As for taking a wife—no. No matter how much Milo pressurised him to continue the family name, he knew he would never trust a woman with his happiness again.

'Sofia will make Demos a good wife. You know that.'

Milo's voice brought him back to the problem in hand.

Yes, Sofia Allessandros would make Demos a good wife. She had been groomed from childhood to be the perfect wife for a rich man. And, like every well brought up Greek girl, she was as untouched as the morning dew.

Theo's brow darkened briefly. The image of Demos's lovely young pillow-friend slid into his mind, lush and enticing. Tempting men from their duties, their responsibilities—their families.

As if reading his thoughts, Milo spoke again.

'Demos won't look twice at Sofia while he's got a mistress to warm his bed.'

The grim look returned to Theo's face. Leandra's lush body swayed in his vision.

'That one would warm any man's bed!'

His grandfather's eyes narrowed. 'Yours, Theo?'

Theo gave a rasp of denial. But Milo hadn't built a business empire from scratch without being able to read men's thoughts. He gave a sudden rough laugh.

'Well, that would be one way of removing the obstacle!'

Theo's mouth set in a thin line.

'I was thinking of something a little more basic.'

His grandfather gave that rough laugh again. In his time, Milo Atrides had kept mistresses by the score.

'Nothing is more basic than sex,' he said bluntly.

'Except money,' corrected his grandson. He looked straight at Milo. 'That method never fails. You, of all people, should know that.'

If his grandfather heard the bitterness in his grandson's voice, he ignored it. He had done what he had had to do. The woman had been a danger to his family. As this one now was.

'Yes,' he agreed, relaxing back in his chair. 'Money's a good method.'

Theo nodded.

'I'll take care of it. She'll be out of his bed in a week!'

Leandra frowned in concentration. 'Can you just give me my cue again please, Demos?'

'Of course.'

He smiled obligingly, but Leandra could see that his eyes were troubled. The morning's interview with his grandfather had been painful, she knew. She felt so sorry for him. In the weeks she'd spent at his apartment she'd grown to like this young man who came from such a totally different world. Their only link was Chris. Why did his family keep trying to arrange his life for him? It was bad enough his grandfather pressurising him to marry—now even his cousin was joining in!

His cousin was totally unlike Demos, she mused. With Demos she felt safe and comfortable. With Theo Atrides she'd never feel safe or comfortable. She gave an inward shiver.

Then, resolutely, she turned back to the page. Demos was kindness itself in agreeing to help her learn this fiendishly difficult part. It would bring neither fame nor fortune, but it was a privilege to have been chosen for it. The Marchester Festival, highly specialised though it was, had an excellent reputation. Besides, the effort of learning it helped to take her mind off Theo Atrides.

And she needed all the help she could get. He was haunting her. She couldn't get him out of her mind. His hooded eyes were vivid in her brain, looking her over—setting her body on fire...

He intruded everywhere, even in her dreams. Which was ridiculous—she would never see him again. He'd go back to Athens with his grandfather, admit defeat over Demos, and that would be that.

He would admit defeat, wouldn't he? After all, in the end there was nothing either Theo or his grandfather could do to force Demos to marry Sofia Allessandros. All Demos had to do was stand firm.

Would Sofia mind being rejected by the man she was expecting to marry? No one seemed too concerned about *her* wishes in all of this!

'Demos,' she heard herself asking, 'are you sure Sofia won't be upset that you won't marry her? It sounds like she's spent her whole life assuming you will.'

He looked away uncomfortably. 'I can't help it, Leandra. You know I can't marry her. For me to do so would be to wrong her grievously.'

She bit her lip. Carefully, she said, 'Can't you tell her why? And your family?'

Demos's face shuttered. 'Do not ask that of me,' he answered. There was anguish in his voice, and guilt—Leandra could not press him. He had burdens of his own to carry. One day he would be able to set them down, but not now, she knew. He was not ready.

Instead, she asked another question.

'Demos, when is your grandfather likely to go back to Athens?'

The shadowed look in his eyes intensified.

'I am not sure,' he admitted. 'Theo wants him to see a Harley Street specialist while he is in London.'

'Oh. Then what would you like me to do? What would be best?'

'If you would be kind enough to stay here I would be most grateful, Leandra.' There was entreaty in Demos's voice.

She smiled reassuringly. 'Of course, if that is what you want. I can hardly complain about the standard of my accommodation! I'm in the lap of luxury here! And I'm happy to help out if there's anything I can do. There's a saying in English—in for a penny, in for a pound!' She tapped at the page of her script with a grin. 'But I'll drive a hard bargain, my young Greek millionaire! Back to work!'

He pored over the words with her, heads together. Suddenly she gave a laugh. Her amber eyes gleamed wickedly.

'Oh, if your cousin could see us now! He'd never believe it! Never!'

Remembering the look of unveiled contempt in Theo Atrides's eyes as he looked her over like a piece of sex-trash, she felt a sharp sense of satisfaction.

It was a beautiful day, even for central London. The mild, sunny autumn weather was still holding. Leandra swung down the Edgware Road, her body pleasantly tired and stretched from her dance class in Paddington. Acting was hard work. London heaved with struggling actresses, and competition for parts was fierce. Still, acting was what she had always wanted to do, and her very staid parents had been happy enough for her to work it out of her system— as they'd been sure she would within a few years.

Her eyes shadowed, grief showing in them briefly. Their death in a coach crash on holiday had been so sudden, so brutal. Even now, nearly two years later, the memory was like a knife in her breast.

Chris had been so kind to her, proving a true friend, taking her under his wing and looking after her while she was raw with grief and shock. No wonder she hadn't hesitated when he had asked her for a favour for Demos.

The blare of a car horn made her jump. The Edgware Road was clogged with traffic, and she was still quite some way from Demos's Mayfair apartment. She made an inward grimace. She would miss that fabulous apartment all right! Going back to her tiny studio flat on a noisy road south of the Thames—all she could afford at London property prices, even with the legacy from her parents—was not something she was looking forward to. For the first time she could understand why women would agree to exchange their self-respect for such a luxurious lifestyle.

Her amber eyes darkened. That was exactly the kind of woman Theo Atrides thought her—that much was obvious. The kind who latched on to men just because they were rich! Not for the first time she felt a stab of anger at him. Oh, she would love to see him eat his words! 'Delicious morsel of female flesh' indeed!

She should not have recalled them to mind. For with them came an image of the man saying them—tall, powerful, those dark, heavy-lidded eyes making her stomach flip over slowly, oh, so slowly as her legs turned to jelly...

Someone brushed past her on the crowded pavement. Automatically she moved to one side, and then, just at the same time, someone brushed her from that side as well. She glanced either way, frowning suddenly. London was safe enough on the whole, if you were sensible, but muggings happened all the time. She clutched at her shoulder bag more tightly, but even as she did so she felt her body crowded from both sides.

It happened so quickly. One moment she was being hustled on the wide pavement and the next, in broad daylight, on a busy London road, two men had caught her by either elbow, pulled her forward and then, before she could scream, she was being thrust into the gaping interior of a huge black-windowed limousine that was suddenly there, pulled up at the kerb. The door slammed behind her. Her head was tilted forcibly back, a pad pressed over her nose and mouth. Her eyes flared in terror and then, as the drug sucked into her gasping lungs, fluttered helplessly shut as consciousness drained away.

'Well, did he tell you how long I've got?'

Milo's voice was harsh, but Theo could hear the exhaustion in it. Milo was tough, but age was finally taking its toll.

'Six, maybe nine months. A year if you are spectacularly fortunate.'

Theo did not mince his words. He would not be thanked if he did.

Milo's eyes gleamed fiercely. 'Hah! Long enough to see a great-grandson on the way!'

Theo looked out of the window of the chauffeur-driven limo. They were nosing down Harley Street. Traffic was bad. Rush hour was all around them.

He did not answer his grandfather. Instead, he said, 'He wants to put you on a different drug regime. Says it could buy you time. He wants to start you straight away, but he'll need to monitor you for a week or two to see how you respond. You don't need to be in hospital. So I've taken the suite for another fortnight. I'll stay with you, naturally.'

His grandfather gave a rasp. 'Not in that damned hotel, you won't! And neither will I. We'll stay at the apartment. I want to see more of Demos anyway!'

Theo frowned. 'The girl is still there. I haven't had a chance to buy her off yet!'

Milo gave a harsh laugh.

'Save your money. She's been dealt with.'

Theo's head swivelled.

'I said I'd handle it—'

'Well, I've saved you the trouble. And my way was a whole lot cheaper! And more certain.'

'What do you mean?' Theo's words were slow, filled with foreboding. 'What have you done?'

Milo looked at his grandson with grim satisfaction.

'She's gone,' he said. 'She was in the way, so I had her removed.'

Cold snaked down Theo's spine.

'What…exactly…have you done with her?'

Milo gave another harsh bark of laughter.

'Don't look at me as if I'd had her murdered! She's perfectly safe. Sunning herself on a beach.'

Theo's brows drew together.

'She agreed to go on holiday?' He sounded sceptical.

'I didn't waste time asking her. I just sent her!'

The cold snaked down Theo's spine again.

'You *sent* her? How? Where?'

'How? I had her picked up and packed off. I had a tail put on her when she left Demos's apartment this morning. She was put in a car, kept quiet, driven to an airfield and that was that. Don't look at me like that, boy! I'm not incapable yet! I know agencies who will do such things and be discreet about it!'

But his grandson was staring at him with an appalled look on his face.

'Are you telling me,' he said, his voice hollow, 'that you had her abducted?'

Milo made a testy noise in his throat. 'I had her removed! That's all! She's perfectly safe—I told you!'

A word escaped Theo that was not in polite usage.

'*Where?*' he demanded urgently. 'Where is she, Milo?'

His grandfather gave his harsh laugh again.

'So eager to find her?' he jeered. 'Maybe you do want to replace Demos between her legs!'

Theo ignored the crude jibe. The cold had spread from his spine through every part of his body. Had Milo gone insane? Had he really had a British citizen abducted from the streets of London and flown out of the country?

'Where is she?'

Milo's eyes flashed. 'Don't take that tone with me! She's on that hideaway island of yours. The one you take your own pillow-friends to!'

Theo's eyes stabbed black fire.

'What?'

Milo gave another snort. 'Hah, did you think I did not know of the place? Of course I knew! But if you want to keep a place like that to yourself, who am I to interfere? A man wants to be private when he communes with Eros. I respect that. So you see—' he sounded well pleased with himself '—Demos's little tart will be perfectly at home there. She can improve her tan and pretty herself up for her next protector. And by the time I let her off the island Demos and Sofia will be engaged!'

He cast a triumphant look at his grandson, still staring at him appalled.

'Cheaper than a pay-off, and far more certain.'

'With only one slight downside.' Theo's voice was hollow. 'Abduction is a criminal offence.'

How Theo got through the next twenty-four hours he didn't afterwards remember. Milo, utterly oblivious of what he had done, had had to be taken back to the hotel. Then Theo had to confront a frantic Demos who had realised, when he returned to his apartment from his office, that Leandra seemed to have disappeared off the face of the earth.

'Milo did *what*?'

Demos had gone white.

'She's safe, Demos. That much is clear.' Theo spoke tersely.

'I'm going out there right away!'

Theo caught his shoulder. 'No! I will deal with it.'

Demos glared at him accusingly. Theo could read his thoughts. He shook his head. His smile was grim. 'Even I have my limits, little cousin.' For a moment they looked into each other's eyes. Theo had been like a big brother to Demos all his life.

'Trust me,' said Theo, holding his cousin's stricken gaze. 'You stay here and take care of Milo. Right now—' he inhaled sharply '—I don't want to be too close to him!' He shook his head. 'I knew he was desperate, but to commit such an act! He seems to have absolutely no idea of what he's done!'

Grimly, Theo knew that if he couldn't find a way to silence the girl she might drag the Atrides name through the criminal courts. Milo could even be facing a jail sentence.

As for what the press would make of it…

He snapped his mind away. His hand squeezed on Demos's shoulder.

'Trust me,' he said again, and took his leave.

But even then his problems hadn't been over. The Atrides jet had been stranded on the tarmac. UK airspace had been in chaos—the air traffic control system had gone down again. It wasn't until well into the next day that Theo had finally been able to get airborne.

Then, when he'd landed in Athens, he'd found Sofia's father, Yannakis Allessandros, had heard the Atrides jet was due and assumed it was Demos at last. Calming a justifiably exasperated Yannakis, and trying to assure him that Demos's continued absence was not an insufferable slight to his patiently waiting daughter, had taken yet more precious time.

The next blow had been to discover that the Atrides corporate helicopter stationed at Athens had developed a fault, and the others were scattered at other locations on various company business. Hiring a replacement he proposed to pilot himself—the fewer people who knew about Leandra

Ross's illicit presence on his island the better!—had meant having his own pilot documentation exhaustively vetted by a helicopter company extremely nervous of letting the head of one of the country's largest companies fly and possibly crash himself.

By the time he finally headed east out to sea the bright Mediterranean sun was low in the sky and Theo Atrides was in the worst mood he'd been in for a very, very long time.

Leandra sat on a rock, the sunlight pounding down on her. She stared doggedly out into the blinding sky, constantly scanning the heavens, then dipping back to the horizon again.

Her face was set, skin stretched tight. Her head ached.

In her stomach, fear coiled like a snake.

She had surfaced earlier that day to discover, through her drugged and groggy senses, that she was lying on a bed in a cool, shady room. Although there were few furnishings, it was very luxurious. The large double bed she'd been lying on was covered by an exquisite hand-stitched quilt, and the furniture was dark wood with an antique patina.

Her terror had been absolute. She'd fought for memory.

There was a car. I was pushed inside. Everything went black...

Fear had crammed in her throat. She'd staggered to her feet, lurching towards French windows dimmed with wooden slatted blinds. She had pulled them open. Beyond was a terrace, flooded with sunlight much brighter than it could ever be in England at this time of year. And the scent of flowers was wrong for England—heady and pungent, coming from fragrant blooms tumbling out of ceramic pots. She had lifted her eyes further forward. Beyond the terrace was vegetation—Mediterranean vegetation—and beyond she'd glimpsed bright azure sea.

The house she had emerged from seemed to be built as a long, low series of rooms, one after another, their French windows all closed. Then, suddenly, those of the room at the end of the terrace, where it ended in a vine-shaded patio, had opened, and an elderly woman had come out. She was dressed in black and carrying a bucket and mop.

She'd seen Leandra and nodded her head, smiling. She had set her things down and made some gestures with her hands, clearly ushering Leandra into the room.

Suddenly it had dawned on Leandra where she must be. *Greece! I'm in Greece!*

And if she were in Greece, there could be only one reason why...

Demos. This had something to do with Demos Atrides. It had to—it just had to.

Emotions had coursed through her. One, she knew, was relief. At the back of her mind a dark, hideous fear had been lurking, that she had been abducted and taken away to be white slaved to the Middle East, or worse...

But why had Demos brought her here? And by such extreme means? She wanted answers—fast!

'Demos?' she croaked.

But the woman only smiled and nodded, and made those movements with her hands again. With chilling realisation Leandra understood. The woman was deaf; she was signing.

A bubble of hysteria beaded in Leandra's throat. There was no way she could communicate in sign language with a deaf Greek woman! Then, as a wave of faintness washed over her, the woman was taking her arm and gently guiding her inside the room, sitting her down on a large, soft sofa in front of an empty stone fireplace.

Leandra shut her eyes in confusion and faintness, only to open them again a few minutes later when the woman brought in a tray of food. Hunger clawed in her stomach, and she fell to, swiftly devouring the delicious freshly made bread and soup, washing it down with hot coffee.

A magazine on the lower shelf of the coffee table caught her eye. It was a fashion magazine in Cyrillic. More relief washed through her. She was definitely in Greece and this must definitely have something to do with Demos! But where *was* he?

She combed the villa. It wasn't large, and it didn't take long to realise the only person in it other than herself was the elderly housekeeper. Fighting back fear, Leandra headed off outside. Demos had to be somewhere!

The grounds consisted of an attractively landscaped Mediterranean-style garden, with no lawn but a lot of little stone-paved paths and beautifully tended plants and shrubs. Olive trees were dotted here and there, perhaps remnants of an original olive grove. Instinctively she headed towards the sea, making her way down a little stone path until she emerged some few minutes later on to the edge of a perfect crescent beach.

Leandra stopped dead. It was absolutely exquisite! Gentle waves broke on golden sand. On either side of the beach the land curved protectively, white gleaming limestone brilliant in the sun.

Looking back, she glanced towards the little villa, half hidden by the olive trees.

It was a gem of a place! Very private, very rustic, but with a simplicity that caught at the heart as much as the eye.

But of Demos there was no sign.

Apart from the housekeeper the only other human being was an elderly man watering plants, who must be her husband—and from the way he would only sign to her Leandra realised that he too was deaf.

Her face tightened and she felt fear claw at her again. Instinctively she skirted around the villa, determined to make her way to a public highway and thence to a village or taverna with a phone she could call London from and find out what on earth was going on! At least she had her purse with her, and somewhere she must be able to change money.

She halted dead. She could see no entrance to the villa, no drive leading to a public roadway. Nothing.

The grounds just seemed to stretch on, rising slightly as the contours of the land led gently upwards. She found a pathway and set off. Maybe she could cut across land and find a road further inland. There must be some sort of traffic passing, however remote this villa was. Judging by the absolute silence—not the hint of a sound of traffic, even from far away—it must be pretty remote, Leandra found herself thinking worriedly.

Resolutely she went on, gaining the top of the rise. She paused and looked down. There, below, nestled close to the beach, was the little villa. Beyond it she could see a flat, bare area of ground, the modern metal-framed hangar and windsock declaring it to be a helipad. Just below the helipad was a small cove, with a stone jetty and boathouse, but no sign of a boat. To the front of the villa was the beach, a secret jewel. She swept her eye past the beach, bringing it round to the opposite direction. The sea went with her.

She went on sweeping her head round—and still the sea was visible.

As she completed her three-hundred-and-sixty-degree turn Leandra felt her insides dissolve.

There was sea visible in every direction.

As she stilled, like a statue frozen in disbelief, the truth hit her.

She was on an island.

Theo closed the throttle and cut the rotors. He'd landed. Finally.

As he shut down the controls with routine expertise he glanced out of the helicopter, sliding off his headphones as he did so.

The girl was there waiting for him.

He'd seen her running towards the helipad as he'd made his descent, alerted by the racket the rotors made which was audible all over the island, he knew.

He glowered balefully in her direction. What an infernal mess this was! Cheaper than paying the girl to leave

Demos? Theo snorted. It was going to cost an arm and a leg to sweeten her after her ordeal! And if she chose to press charges…

Sweat pricked beneath the collar of Theo's business suit. He wanted a shower, and a long, cold beer.

He slid the door back and stepped out on to the ground. There was no way he was flying back to Athens tonight. The chopper would need refuelling, for a start, and night was coming on. Besides, he was tired.

Tired physically and mentally.

And his temper was on a knife-edge.

He just hoped the girl wasn't the hysterical type. She must have been frightened by what had happened to her, he found himself thinking as he slid the door to and headed across to her. She was standing very still.

Theo hoped she wasn't going to start weeping and wailing all over him.

He hated that in a woman.

As he drew closer, walking with his customary rapid stride, it dawned on him that if he hadn't known it was Leandra Ross standing there he'd never have recognised her.

The clinging sex kitten was gone. Her lush, slender body, which had been so lavishly on show the other evening, was now almost completely concealed by a sweatshirt and jeans. Her glorious blond hair was pinned haphazardly on her head and her face was completely free of make-up. Yet she was still a stunner.

As he approached he felt his body responding. She had an unconscious grace, standing there, so very motionless— poised almost, he thought, like a nymph of mythical Greece, sighted by Apollo, or Dionysus, or any one of the Olympians in a mood for dalliance, deciding whether to flee from the approaching god or yield to his desire…

Again, just as it had at the gala, the vision that leapt in his mind was vivid. He saw her caught by his restraining arms, drawn close against him, so soft against his hardness, pressing her pliant body against him…

Brusquely he quelled the thought. It was an irrelevance. She was simply a complication—a deadly, dangerous complication now, thanks to Milo!—and she had to be neutralised as soon as possible. That was all.

He stopped in front of her.

CHAPTER THREE

LEANDRA was staring at him as if transfixed.

After hours of staring out to sea, up into the heavens, desperate to spot something, anything, heading towards the island, the approach of a helicopter had sent her hurtling down towards the helipad. Until its noisy rotors had cut through the silence the only sounds she'd heard had been the old man hammering intermittently as he mended an outhouse roof and his wife emerging from what must be their living quarters behind the villa to hang up washing.

Then, as Leandra had watched the machine land, a new terror had filled her. The helicopter bore no markings, no Atrides logo.

Oh, God, suppose this isn't anything to do with Demos! Suppose I really have been white-slaved!

She'd felt weak with horror.

Then, as the door of the helicopter had slid back and the occupant had emerged, her eyes had lit on a figure she knew all too well.

Theo Atrides, immaculate in a business suit that must have been handmade for him, his night-dark eyes veiled by a pair of aviator sunglasses, had shut the helicopter door with effortless ease and started to walk towards her.

Something had started to simmer inside her.

He looked so cool, so composed, so immaculate—so imposing. So damn *calm* that Leandra had felt her emotions boil up inside her as if the lid had just been taken off a pressure cooker heated in a furnace.

He'd kept on coming closer. His face set, his eyes hidden by the impenetrable sunglasses that half her mind registered, made him look so ludicrously sexy that she wanted to scream!

And if it hadn't been the sight of Theo Atrides heading towards her as if he could melt butter as he walked that made her want to scream, then something had. Something powerful, and black, and overwhelming, and absolutely, totally raging!

She had been through so much—terrified out of her mind—and now here he was, just sauntering towards her looking like a million dollars.

He stopped in front of her. And the lid flew right off the pressure cooker.

With a frenzied strength she hadn't even known she was capable of Leandra found her hands lifting and starting to pummel, insanely, at the broad chest, thumping and pounding as if she were possessed by all the devils in hell.

Her voice was yelling. She could hear it. Yelling right at Theo Atrides, letting out all the terror and anger and bewilderment and outrage she was feeling—had been feeling all day, since she had surfaced to realise that someone, *someone,* had kidnapped her right off the streets of London, drugged her out cold, and dumped her down a thousand miles away.

And that someone hadn't been kindly, troubled Demos at all! It had been his overbearing, arrogant, *contemptible* cousin, who'd looked at her as if she was dirt. *He* was the one who'd done this to her! And she knew why! To get rid of her! That was why! To make sure Demos couldn't hide behind her, so he could drag him back to marry Sofia!

How dared he? How *dared* he?

Then, abruptly, her hands were seized and held away from him. 'Be silent!'

Her face contorted even more. 'I will not be silent! You kidnapped me and I'll see you in *gaol!*'

'I said, be silent, you virago! Be silent and I will explain!'

Theo looked down at her, his hands like vices around her wrists to immobilise her.

She was a she-devil, a maniac!

Her eyes were flashing like swords trying to pierce him and her chest was heaving raggedly, the breath choking and panting in her throat. Her face was contorted with fury.

And he had thought she might wail and weep!

But at least she had stopped yelling at him. With a hard, heavy command he impelled her to step backwards, increasing the distance between them but still prudently holding on to her wrists all the while.

'Let me go!' she spat at him, writhing against his implacable hold.

'Only if you listen to me!'

Breath shuddering, she gasped, still venomous, 'What's to tell, Mr Atrides? You kidnapped me and I'll see you in *gaol!*'

He swore again. 'I did *not* kidnap you. I am *not* responsible for your presence here, which—' he gave a heavy intake of breath again '—I regret as much as you. Believe me!' he finished crushingly.

He eyed her balefully as she stood there, panting and dishevelled, face twisted like a demon. This was all he needed—a virago flying at him! The perfect end to an intolerable day!

'Now,' he went on, his voice commanding her as if she were the most junior minion in his employ, 'if your hysteria is finally spent, listen to me!'

Heart still pounding in her chest, every limb trembling, jerkily she nodded.

He let her go. Her eyes flashed. 'Well, go on,' she ground out, breath still painful. 'You said you'd explain to me! Go on. I'd love to hear you explain away what you've done to me, Mr Oh-So-Almighty Theo Atrides! And then you can tell it to the police!'

His face darkened at her hostile, vicious tone. No one spoke to him like that! His body stiffened, growing taller and even more imposing, Leandra felt, suddenly shrinking her to about a centimetre high.

'You will not speak to me in that tone,' he informed her coldly, every inch the head of the Atrides Corporation and a man held in respect by all who crossed his path.

It was the wrong attitude to take. The pressure cooker inside her head might have blown its lid, but there was still a whole lot of anger boiling away in the depths!

'Try saying that to the judge sentencing you for criminal abduction and false imprisonment!' she bit back, her chest still heaving with emotion.

He flashed a hand upward imperiously.

'Be silent! I had no part in this debacle, I assure you! And if you will finally condescend to listen to me I will explain what has happened.'

He glanced past her. 'But not here.' He glared balefully down at her. 'It has been a tiring day. I will speak to you in twenty minutes on the terrace. Be there.'

Then he was striding away towards the villa, leaving behind a fuming, shattered Leandra.

Slowly her hands fell to her sides. She could not credit what she had just heard him say.

He dismissed me, she thought incredulously. He kidnapped me, imprisoned me, and now he's just walked away.

Unbelievable, she thought. *Unbelievable!*

Twenty minutes later he walked out on to the patio where Leandra sat at an ironwork table, nerves still shot to pieces. Suddenly she had something else to make her breathing ragged. Her eyes fastened on Theo Atrides and could not move.

Dear God, but he was devastating!

He had obviously had a shower. His dark hair was still damp, gleaming like ebony, and he had changed out of his business suit into casual trousers, immaculately cut, and a polo shirt with a top designer logo discreetly on the pocket. His sunglasses had been discarded and now Leandra could get the full glory of those powerful, hooded eyes surveying her as he approached.

Just as he reached the table and sat down opposite her

the elderly housekeeper emerged from the living room immediately behind the patio, carrying a tray with a glass of beer on it and a pot of filter coffee.

Theo nodded at her, signing a brief response which made her smile and nod before backing away.

'Agathias is deaf,' said Theo, draining a generous portion of his beer as if he needed it, indicating to Leandra that she should help herself to coffee. 'So is her husband Yiorgos.'

'So I discovered,' Leandra said repressively. 'How very convenient to hire gaolers who can't hear their prisoners demanding to be released!'

The night-dark eyes flashed at her.

'As a non-hearing couple, especially of their generation, they find it easier not to be always amongst hearing people. This island they look after for me is a haven for them. But they will return to stay with their family on the mainland when the weather worsens in winter. And they are not, Ms Ross, my hired gaolers!'

'You just admitted this was your island!' Leandra shot back.

'Yes,' said Theo heavily, 'this is my island. But Agathias and Yiorgos are not here to be gaolers, only caretakers. All they know about you is that you were carried in from the helicopter insensible.' His jaw tightened. 'I'm afraid Agathias assumed you were drunk.'

An outraged expression formed on Leandra's face.

'Drunk?' she said furiously. 'I was *drugged,* Mr Atrides! Abducted from Edgware Road and forcibly knocked out! Don't even *think* of making out that I was drunk!'

'Of course I don't think you were drunk! I know perfectly well what happened to you.'

Her eyes widened, her expression instantly accusing.

'My God, so it *was* you who did it! It was you all along!'

A rasp sounded in his throat. 'No! *I* had nothing to do with this, Ms Ross. Absolutely nothing!'

She looked across the table at him, lips thinning.

'Oh? Then who, pray, is responsible? Do tell me!' she enquired venomously.

For a long moment he just looked at her.

'It was my grandfather,' he said quietly.

She started. 'Your *grandfather?* Is he completely mad?'

Theo sighed sharply and reached for his beer again. 'Not mad, no. But old, Ms Ross, nearing the end of his life.'

He looked at her directly. She looked nothing like the way she had at the gala, hanging on to Demos's sleeve!

The memory, which also sent an unwanted kick through his system, reminded him of why he was here. The only reason he was here. To separate her from Demos—and *not* he reprimanded himself grimly, to wonder how it was that her eyes could shift from amber to gold, then back to amber...

'My grandfather is determined not to die before he sees my cousin marry. Demos must surely have told you that he will shortly be marrying a Greek girl?'

He watched her face closely as he spoke. Had Demos told her, or was she wallowing in ignorance of the fact that their affair was going to hit a brick wall any time now?

For her part, Leandra was wondering how best to react. It had just dawned on her that she was going to have to stay in character as Demos's mistress—or completely destroy the whole charade. She thought fast. If she *had* been Demos's mistress, would he have told her about Sofia?

She gave a little shrug. 'I know his *family* want him to marry,' she returned. 'But that's up to Demos, isn't it?'

Her answer was a clear provocation, and Theo took it as such. He ignored her jibe and ploughed on.

'My grandfather is an old, sick man, Ms Ross, who has had much grief in his life. In his...urgency...to hasten the wedding he...' Theo chose his words carefully, as if he were conducting a press interview with news-hungry journalists '...may have overstepped the mark in this instance.'

Leandra felt a spurt of anger. Overstepped the mark?

Abducting and imprisoning her was 'overstepping the mark'?

'He had me kidnapped!' she threw at him fiercely.

Theo's face was unreadable. In his time he'd struck deals worth billions—and he knew how to conceal his feelings when he had to.

'That's a very harsh word, Ms Ross,' he said temporisingly.

'It's a very true one!' she whipped back.

He drank some more of his beer, giving himself time before making his next move. Leandra watched him, eyes narrowed.

'Ms Ross—' Theo moved in again '—I freely admit there has been a gross error committed. You have, most inadvertently, been subjected to an experience which has, I don't doubt, been very distressing...'

Right now, he thought privately, she looked about as distressed as a hangman—eyeing him up as her next customer!

Compunction filled him. She had every right to be angry, he knew. Milo had behaved unforgivably. But he *had* to persuade her not to press charges.

To that end he was prepared to offer her very substantial compensation—providing she also agreed to end her liaison with Demos. Then, at last, he could get Leandra Ross out of his hair and out of his life!

He opened his mouth to start working towards the offer he was prepared to make.

She pre-empted him totally.

'I don't care, Mr Atrides, who gave the orders to bring me here! I just want out. OK? As in out right now. Tonight.' Her demand was crisp, clear, and very insistent.

His expression hardened instantly.

'That's impossible, I'm afraid,' he said immediately.

The amber eyes flashed. He wished she wouldn't do that. It distracted him, and he needed his wits about him now. He didn't need to know how anger made her eyes glitter like gold.

Her riposte came swiftly.

'You flew yourself in, now you can fly me out. Simple.'

'Not simple at all,' he retorted dismissively. 'The helicopter needs refuelling, it's getting too late to fly, I haven't checked out the weather forecast, or logged a return flight with Athens air traffic control, and finally—' he held up a hand decisively '—I am in no mood whatsoever to go anywhere else today!'

Leandra's face whitened and her fingers gripped convulsively at the table surface. 'But I've got to get away from here! I've got to! I absolutely demand that you fly me back to Athens immediately and put me on a plane to London!'

There was a note of panic in her voice, beneath the peremptory order, but Theo ignored it. He was in no mood to do anything other than keep to his firm intention of staying right where he was. He pushed away his empty glass and got to his feet.

'I do not respond to orders—or pleading. No one is going anywhere tonight, and that is final! Now, if you will excuse me, I must contact my office. Please feel free to enjoy the facilities of my island.' An ironic gleam showed in his eyes. 'You may roam at will—be my guest.'

He strolled off, oblivious to the choking sound of Leandra Ross spitting with fury behind him at his parting jibe.

'Agathias will serve dinner in an hour,' he threw over his shoulder. 'Do not be late.'

He disappeared inside the villa and Leandra was left fuming disbelievingly. She was going to be stuck here all night with the insufferable Theo Atrides!

The prospect appalled her.

Changing for dinner did not take Leandra long. After showering in the *en suite* bathroom in her bedroom she could not face putting on the clothes she had worn for nearly two days. But the only other garment she could find was a thin, silky wrap hanging on the back of the bathroom door. Her lips compressed. Presumably it had been left by a former female visitor to the island.

It was pretty obvious to her now just what this island was all about! This must be where Theo Atrides took his high-profile celebrity lovers when they wanted to get away from the flashbulbs of the paparazzi. With only an elderly deaf couple to look after them, they could be as private as they liked.

She tugged the belt of the wrap tight. Well, Theo Atrides's glittering sex-life was nothing to do with her. His only use was to airlift her back to Athens.

Unfortunately, if she didn't want to starve, it looked as if she was going to have to put up with his company for dinner. Defiantly she padded down the corridor on bare feet and into the dining room which opened, she discovered, off the living room.

As she walked in Theo glanced round from opening a bottle of wine.

He stilled totally.

Leandra Ross stood on the far side of the room, wearing nothing but a thigh-length silk wrap belted so tightly at the waist that each breast was moulded in all its glory beneath the taut material. Her long hair streamed over her shoulders, loosed like liquid gold against the scarlet of the skimpy robe. From beneath its short hem her slender legs were like creamy silk. Her feet, arched and narrow, were bare.

Instinctively, just as it had when he had first set eyes on her at the charity gala, Theo felt his body responding to the vision she presented. Desire, hard and insistent, kicked in his guts.

Then another, dampening reaction set in.

Christos, but she was a fast worker!

His mouth twisted cynically. Did she think she could flash her body to get him to fly her back tonight? Was that what this tempting display was all about?

A contemptuous glint showed in his eyes. Or was she after something more than a ride back to Athens? Well, if she thought she could manipulate him the way she ran circles round Demos she was in for a rude surprise. *He* chose the women he bedded—they didn't choose him! And, however tempting a morsel Leandra Ross was, he had no intention—none whatsoever—of making this hellish mess even more complicated than it was already! The only relationship he wanted with her was via his chequebook. Clean and simple.

Even *thinking* of anything else was sheer lunacy!

From her side of the table Leandra saw the expression in his eyes. She bristled instantly.

He's doing it again! Looking at me like I'm trash!

Did he think she was wearing this wrap thing on purpose? Only hunger kept her from bolting back to her room. Defiantly she flashed a scintillating smile at him, as false as it was dazzling, and took her place at the table. What did she care what Theo Atrides thought? He was nothing to her!

There was a caustic look on his hard, handsome face as he sat down opposite her.

If he had been going to comment on her appearance he was prevented by the arrival of Agathias, entering through the door leading to the corridor and the kitchen beyond, carrying a tray bearing bowls of soup which she placed on the burnished table. The smell of food drove away everything else from Leandra's mind and, hardly waiting before Agathias had put a bowl of the creamy liquid before her, she set to.

She ate fast, driven by hunger. Besides, the soup was delicious. So, too, was the delicately flavoured fish which followed. Not bothering to speak to her dining companion, Leandra cleared her plate completely, reaching for a hunk of bread from the basket between her and her host and mopping up the last of the delicious juices. Eating had made her almost forget that she was dining in Theo Atrides's utterly unwelcome company.

Agathias arrived to clear the table, bringing coffee with her. Then she bustled out, leaving them alone once more.

Theo poured out more wine, refilling Leandra's glass. She realised, to her dismay, that she'd drunk rather more than she'd realised. Determinedly she ignored the wine glass and poured herself some coffee.

She felt better now, on a full stomach. The last of the drug seemed to have cleared from her system and her headache was gone. Maybe her mood was better because this time tomorrow she'd be back in London—to sanity.

A shudder went through her. The whole thing had been the most hideous ordeal! Now, calm and well fed, with a large glass of wine inside her, she was filled with incredulity that Demos's grandfather should have committed a criminal act and had her kidnapped.

Even so, her sense of fairness interposed, and she had to concede that no actual harm had come to her. Maybe, she thought unwillingly, she *had* overreacted when Theo had stepped out of that helicopter. She squirmed mentally as she recalled how she had gone berserk at him. After all, she thought grudgingly, he *had* flown straight out to take her back to London, and he did seem pretty appalled by what his grandfather had done.

'Mr Atrides,' she began, her voice slightly husky with nerves, 'I want to apologise for the way I behaved when you arrived. I…I was…very frightened…very confused…I…I didn't know what had happened to me…'

She trailed off. There was a closed look on his face—as though, she thought, he was evaluating what she had said. No, she amended, as if he were evaluating *why* she had just said what she had.

It confused her, making her stare at him wide-eyed, wondering what was going on in his mind.

Then, in a very foreign gesture, he gave a shrug, his broad shoulders moving with perfect musculature beneath the material of his polo shirt, stretched tautly across his chest. The movement distracted her, making her realise just how very perfect that pectoral musculature was. No running to seed for this captain of industry! However he kept fit, he kept very fit indeed...

She snapped her mind back to what he was saying.

'Please, do not apologise. It was perfectly understandable.'

The handsome acceptance of her expression of regret was so astonishing that Leandra simply stared at him. There was something different about him suddenly, she realised, and then worked out what it was. The cynical look in his eye had disappeared. The expression in it now was bland.

'Besides,' he went on, and she heard a new note enter his voice, 'you were, after all, entitled to a display of passion. No woman as beautiful as you should ever have to endure such an ordeal.'

Leandra blinked slightly. What had beauty to do with it? Being kidnapped would be terrifying for anyone!

Theo was talking again. That bland look was still in his eye, and his voice was smooth.

'It is time, I think, Ms Ross, to reach an agreement which will, I trust, conclude this...escapade...on a basis satisfactory to all.'

Escapade? He made it sound like some madcap adventure she'd deliberately got herself involved in!

He paused, curling his fingers around the stem of his wine glass and lifting it to his mouth. She watched, unable to draw her eyes away, as she saw the fingers press with only a fraction of their power around the slender stem, and how, when he drank, the strong column of his throat worked.

He set the glass down. He seemed to have noticed that she had been watching him.

He smiled.

Inside her breast, Leandra felt her heart give a little skip.

She had never seen Theo Atrides smile before. She knew that if she had she would have remembered it in absolute detail. The way his lips indented, showing white, even teeth, and carving deep lines between his nose and mouth.

It was an irresistible smile, one so potent, so devastating, that she could only sit and stare at him.

Suddenly she seemed very short of breath.

And very, very aware that she was sitting here in nothing more than a skimpy robe, an arm's length away from a man who had turned her bones to jelly the first time she'd laid eyes on him—and they were here, on Theo Atrides's very private island, a little piece of paradise where he brought the women he had selected for their beauty and allure to be his personal, intimate companions...

She felt weakness seeping through her, and a creeping, insidious heat.

What would it be like to be one of those women?

What would it be like to be brought here by Theo Atrides and wined and dined, taken out on to that moonlit terrace to feel his arms sliding around your waist, drawn back against the powerful strength of his body, to have those skilled, experienced hands stroke the softness of your flanks, cup the sweetness of your breasts, turn you into his arms and let his mouth plunder the softness of yours, until you were breathless, senseless, boneless...

The vision was so powerful she had to force it away from her. No! Theo Atrides could bring a hundred women here! She would never be one of them!

It didn't matter that he could sit there, looking at her through those dark, heavy-lidded eyes as if he could unveil the contours of her body and make free with them as he would...

She sucked her mind back to reality. And the reality was bleak, and blunt. She had nothing to do with Theo Atrides, nothing at all! He was just the pilot who would fly her back to Athens and put her on a plane to London.

He was talking again, and she forced herself to listen. He was speaking in that same bland, smooth voice, and somewhere deep inside a jiggle of unease began to tingle. She squashed it, and listened to what he was saying. He had leant back in his chair, one hand flat on the table, the other on the arm of his chair. He looked very relaxed.

His deep voice was mellow, and very composed. 'And so, as a gesture of…conciliation…Ms Ross, I am prepared to offer you substantial recompense in consideration of the…distress…you have undergone. I am sure I can count on you to accept it in the spirit with which it is offered, as a confirmation of…good faith…between us. Let us say…' his eyes rested on Leandra, his expression quite unreadable '…fifty thousand pounds.'

Leandra stared. What was he talking about?

'Of course,' he went on, and his voice as smooth as butter, but she could hear an adamantine thread beneath, 'you will appreciate, I am sure, that I must in return ask you to sign certain…assurances…which my legal department will draw up. In addition,' he continued, his voice like cream, 'I am prepared to add as much again as…consolation…for the dissolution of your liaison with my cousin.'

Leandra stared across the table at him. Theo wished she wouldn't. He liked to keep a cool head when he was negotiating, and having those amber eyes upon him was no help. What jewels would he drape her in if she were his? he found himself wondering. Emeralds for her blondness, perhaps? Or sapphires…?

'Say that again.'

There was something strange about her voice, but it was a welcome interruption to his inappropriate reverie. Leandra Ross would get no jewels from him—just hard cash. Fast, simple—and very basic.

'One hundred thousand pounds in all,' he confirmed. There was a note of finality in his voice. He was not about to be bled dry by a woman who had no business making him think of fastening a glittering necklace around the slender column of her throat as his eyes feasted on her lush, luscious curves…

'You're buying me off,' she said slowly.

He veiled his expression at her blunt description, concealing his own revulsion for what he was doing. But he just wanted the whole sordid, ugly mess sorted out.

'Fifty thousand not to complain about being kidnapped, and the same again for dumping Demos. Is that right?'

Her voice was flat.

He inclined his head in silent acquiescence. She looked at him. There was something in her eyes; he couldn't tell what.

'You expect me to accept, don't you?'

He met her gaze. 'It's a very generous offer, and I believe a fair one.' Beneath the smoothness of his voice he was watching her like a hawk. 'After all—' he pushed harder, wanting to put an end to this distasteful process '—my cousin means very little to you.'

Something moved in her eyes then, all right. He felt its sting, and before he could stop himself he heard his voice drawl, openly sarcastic, 'Or are you going to sit there and tell me you're desperately in love with Demos?'

'Of course not!' Leandra retorted.

Scornful triumph flashed in his eyes. Aghast, Leandra realised what she had done—blurted out a truth that would only make him think one thing. And he was obviously thinking it!

'So.' His voice was deadly, and very chill. 'It is, after all, just his money that interests you.'

She tried to recover, floundering to find words that would retrieve the situation, that would wipe that look of condemnation from his eyes.

'You're wrong!' she cried. 'I may not love Demos, but I'm...I'm very fond of him!' The words rushed out of her mouth.

The expression in his eyes changed to one of derision.

'Fond!'

She pushed her chair back and stood up jerkily. She wanted out of here, right now! But first she'd wipe that mocking, derisive look off his face! She folded her arms tight across her chest, quite unaware that it served to raise the hem of her robe dangerously high.

Theo did not miss it, though. His eyes dropped automatically. *Christos,* any higher and he'd be able to put to proof his guess that underneath that skimpy robe she wore nothing at all! He felt his body respond to the thought, and shifted uncomfortably in his seat. Damn the girl! Damn her for standing there and making him want to reach for her, slide her onto his lap and feel her clench his thighs with her long, naked ones...

And damn her for talking about Demos when he wished him to perdition. And the rest of the world too! When all he wanted, with painful aching, was that golden-haired temptress flashing fire at him!

'Yes. Fond. Anything wrong with that, Mr Atrides?'

It was a challenge she should not have issued. Should not have issued at all. Certainly not to him. Not now. Not when she was standing there displaying just about the whole treasure chest of her lush, soft body...

Her arms fell to her sides, loosening the tie at her waist so that the valley between her breasts opened towards the secret jewel of her navel, her hair flowing like gold over her shoulders, her beautiful eyes flashing amber, her soft, lush mouth parted, and her body—oh, that alluring, beguiling body—breasts like ripe peaches, thighs like slender columns leading to pastures of delight...

He felt his own body move. Forwards. Impelled by an urge he could no longer resist. Would no longer resist.

She stood, waiting for him, lips parted. *Christos,* she'd been asking for this all evening, and now she was going to get it!

A lesson he was going to teach her about what was needed between a man and a woman to hold them together...

Fond! She was *fond* of Demos! She stood there, looking like temptation itself, and thought *fondness* was what it was all about—the way to hold a man!

Leandra stared, her limbs as heavy as lead suddenly. She ought to move. Run. Flee like the wind. But she could not. She was as frozen to the spot as Daphne, rooted into laurel, trying to flee from the god Apollo as he came to ravish her.

The breath came hard in her throat. Her stomach was turning to jelly, her limbs to water. But in her veins a flame was running...

CHAPTER FOUR

HE CAME towards her. Stopped in front of her. She could not move. Theo Atrides, potent, overpowering, and she was weak, weak as a kitten, as she stood in front of him. Waiting for him to reach her.

'So…' His voice was a low, deep husk. 'You are fond of my cousin, is that it?' He was looking down at her. His eyes were different. There was not that look of contempt in them any more. Not that blank smoothness. Now there was nothing in them but something even she could not deny, blazing from them like a dark, black beacon.

He was so close to her. Far, far too close… She should step back, away, but she could not. Could not.

He reached towards her.

'But fondness,' he said, and the low, deep voice was a drawl now, slow and compelling, compelling her acquiescence as she stood, staring up at him, so dark and tall in front of her, 'fondness cannot hold a man to a woman. Fondness is far too weak, far too feeble. How can fondness…?' She saw his hand outstretch, felt those long, powerful fingers touch at her throat, sending flickers of debilitating fire through every millimetre where he touched her, stroked her. 'How can fondness match this?'

His fingers glided down the column of her throat, skimming the pulse which had started to beat with low, throbbing insistency. His fingers trailed fire, flickering, licking fire that burnt along her veins, her skin, penetrating deep, deep within her body…

He touched the silk revere of her robe, gliding at its edge along the path of her silky skin, taking the fire with it. Her breath caught, her eyes held by his, dark and lustrous, as

53

his cool, devastating fingers stroked at the faint swell of her breast, easing towards its instantly, insistently aching peak...

He smiled. A devil's smile. Knowing and expectant. Stripping away the lies between them and revealing only the truth—that her body yearned for his like a flower craving the sunlight flooding down upon it...

Her lips parted as she gazed at him, helpless, trapped in that knowing regard, and he smiled down at her, and stroked her tender, sensitive skin, closer, ever closer to its goal, until she thought she must faint with the pleasure of it...

She wanted him to touch her, cup his hand around the straining fullness of her breast, tease the delicate, aching tip to ecstasy...

'You see.' He smiled down at her, eyelids drooping over those knowing eyes that had seen so many women melt before him at his touch. 'You see now, don't you, my tender white dove? *This* is what holds a woman to a man.' His voice was low, speaking to her, only to her...

A primeval moan sounded softly in her throat. She felt her body sway towards him. Faintness drummed at her, and she could not move, not to save her life. Could only feel—feel the endless, endless pleasure of his touch...his soft, arousing touch...

And then it was gone.

Switched off, like a light. His hand was withdrawn and she was left standing there, swaying numbly.

And the smile was gone too. And the dark lustre of his gaze. And the husk in his voice.

He took a step towards the table, reaching out for his wine glass and raising it to his mouth, drinking deeply. As he set it down on the table again he spoke.

It was in a very different voice. Harsh and mocking and sardonic. She was too dazed, too devastated to hear the tight leash of control slammed down upon it by a man who had nearly, so very nearly, lost control altogether. Now he had to claw himself back to sanity by any means he could—whoever paid the price.

'So…' his voice crawled over her '…now we have established that your feelings for my cousin are quite insufficient to prevent you lighting up for any man who strokes that lovely body which you have been displaying to me so generously all evening, let us conclude this matter once and for all.' His voice was harsh now, grating at her like rough wire. 'Take your money—and go. I want you *out*—out of my hair once and for all!'

There was a resolution in his voice that brooked no argument. Had she finally got the message? Theo hoped so—he profoundly hoped so. The effort of walking away from her had been harder than he had anticipated. Much harder.

The harshness in his voice was as much for him as for her.

Folly to have succumbed to the temptation to prove her affections for Demos effortlessly alienable! He had come dangerously, dangerously close to throwing this whole damnable business into oblivion and seizing the one thing he wanted out of the whole godforsaken mess—Leandra Ross, melting that soft luscious body into his…

It had taken all his strength to put her aside. To draw his hand back from where it had ached to go, to curve around the soft heaviness of her breast and graze its thumb over that ripe, succulent nipple he could see thrusting against the raw silk that covered it so sheerly…

But he had done it. There had been no other option—unless it was to sink into a morass so deep only a fool would wade into it willingly.

Leandra Ross was trouble. He had thought so from the moment he had set eyes on her—and her near victory over him now only proved it over again. No woman manipulated him! No woman took him where he did not wish to go.

No more illusions. Never again.

His lip curled. About Leandra Ross he had no illusions. She clung to Demos for his wealth; that was all.

Money would show her true colours.

'Well?' he prompted, wanting this over and done with now, for there was a bad taste in his mouth, getting worse. 'Money is all I am prepared to deal in, Ms Ross. It alone must compensate you for your loss—both of liberty during these last thirty-six hours and of the luxuries you have enjoyed as my cousin's mistress. My offer is one hundred thousand pounds.' His voice was heavy. 'I suggest you accept it gracefully.'

He fell silent, and she went on looking at him.

Her amber eyes were completely empty, drained of all expression.

Then, with a flat voice, she said, 'And I suggest you show me the money first, Mr Atrides.'

'Very well.' His voice was as flat as hers. Something— he didn't know what—seemed to have tightened in his chest as she spoke. Something that closed like an iron grip around him. If he hadn't known better, if he hadn't known all along just what a woman like her wanted most out of life, he might have said it was disappointment.

'If you would wait one moment.' He strode from the room, heading for his office at the end of the corridor.

It did not take him long. When he returned she was still there, standing like a statue. He didn't think she'd moved at all, not a muscle.

Leandra watched him. He had a piece of paper in his hand. The size of a cheque. She held out her arm towards him, turning the palm of her hand upwards.

He placed the cheque in her hand.

She glanced at it, holding it up to check the amount. Yes—one hundred thousand pounds, payable to Leandra Ross. Drawn on the personal account of Th. Atrides, at a very prestigious private London bank.

She looked at it one last time. Then tore it into tiny pieces and let them fall through her fingers on to the floor.

'You—' her eyes had narrowed to fierce, livid slits '—are the most *contemptible* human being I have ever encoun-

ered!' Her chest heaved with seething emotion. 'How *dare*
you offer me money to buy me off? How *dare* you?'

Her voice rose. 'I can't believe you and Demos have any
genes in common whatsoever! How *can* he be related to
someone as vile as you?'

She was choking with fury now. Not only had he tried to
buy her off, he'd gone and accused her of trying to vamp
him!

Her voice was a hiss, venomous with rage.

'And for your information I am wearing this wrap purely
and simply because I've got nothing else to wear! Your
precious grandfather didn't bother to pack a suitcase for me!
So don't flatter yourself I'm wearing it for you! I wouldn't
have you if you came stuffed on a plate with an apple in
your mouth! You are the most *despicable, loathsome* human
being I have ever met!'

She backed away, her face contorted, eyes flashing like
laser fire that would shrivel him on the spot. At the door
she paused, and spat one last piece of venom.

'Burn in hell, Theo Atrides! Burn in hell!'

Then she was gone, and the door slammed behind her so
hard it made the room shake.

Behind her, Theo looked down at the fragments of his
cheque, all around him on the floor.

His mouth tightened in black anger.

And total disbelief.

In her room, Leandra sat on her bed, hunched and fearful,
hurting and furious. She felt sick. Sick right down to her
feet. Sick right to her soul. What a foul, foul man he was!
Offering her money. Trying to pay her off. And when he
couldn't…when he couldn't…he had resorted to exploiting
that dark, brooding sexuality of his, making her melt like
putty in his hands…

She blanked her mind, moaning in distress. No, she
mustn't, *mustn't* think of that—the way she had just stood

there, like a dummy, and let him stroke her—*fondle* her—as if she were a rag doll…

Colour stained her cheeks. She loathed herself. How, *how* was it that her body was so indiscriminate that it could let itself be aroused by a man like Theo Atrides? A man who used his wealth to buy his way out of trouble, thinking nothing of it!

Thinking women were for sale. Thinking *she* was for sale!

Rage replaced shame. That was better! That was much better! Making herself feel her rage and loathing for Theo Atrides was much safer. Feeling anything else about him was far, far too dangerous.

Angrily she made herself see not his dark, tall figure reaching out to touch her, but him standing there with that curl on his lip as he offered her a hundred thousand pounds to buy her off. Yes, *that* was the Theo Atrides she must remember! That and no other.

Keeping that image firmly in mind, she tore off the wretched silk robe, tossing it into a corner, oblivious of the exclusive designer label that made it warrant gentler attention. Hateful rag! To think he'd thought she'd worn it on purpose!

Her teeth ground together, eyes flashing furiously as she yanked back the bedclothes and dived underneath them, squirrelling herself deep underneath the covers as if she would totally shut out everything around her—everything on this benighted island, and especially the serpent that had struck at her tonight.

Sunlight slid delicate fingers of light across the cool, shady terrace running along the front of the villa on Theo Atrides's private hideaway island. It was early morning, and a hint of autumn was finally in the air, even in these warm climes. Dew glistened on the aromatic plants that bordered the paving stones, and brought a diamond beauty to the vine that arched over the patio at the far end.

Theo Atrides stood looking out over his domain. It was

only a fraction of what he owned, but it was very dear to him. He had found it years ago, when his heart was still bleeding—raw from the wound inflicted on it even before the terrible blow of his parents' death, along with his aunt and uncle, that terrible day eight years ago when their plane had plunged like Icarus into the bright Aegean sea.

Now it was the place he came to when he sought solace—but not solitude. In the years since he had been forced to take over the running of the Atrides Corporation he had used it as the one place he could ensure privacy when he conducted the brief, pleasurable affairs which were all he allowed himself these days.

I should come here more often on my own, he thought.

There was a beauty here, a remoteness, a timelessness that brought a peace to him. His mind cast back to all the women he had brought here—so carefully chosen, so eager to please him. So many.

Women from his own world. Rich women, heiresses, wealthy divorcees, film stars and supermodels and opera singers—women he could rely on to be as discreet about their lovemaking as he needed them to be. Women who understood that what he offered was dalliance—sophisticated, pleasurable dalliance. As transient as the waves that broke upon the sand, never reaching into the unplumbed depths of emotion, remaining in the pleasant, pleasurable shallows of his life. Anything more and they would be disappointed.

They had come here, he had enjoyed them, and then they had left. And he had moved on to the next one, and the next.

Their faces merged in his memory; their bodies melded into one another.

A frown creased his brow as he stood looking out towards the sea, so quiet, so still in the early hours of the day. Conjuring up a woman whose face would never blur into another woman's, whose body would never merge into another's.

A woman not from his world at all.

She formed in his vision like a second Aphrodite, rising from the sea, out of its secret depths. Like pale gold she shimmered in his mind, her hair flowing like water, her beauteous limbs gleaming creamily, kissed by the early sun, her breasts like flowers, her sweetness waiting to be plucked.

So much beauty!

Something tightened around his breath.

He tore it free. No, she was not for him! It was impossible!

Pay her and get rid of her!

His face tautened. But she wouldn't take the money he'd offered! Had thrown it back at him as if it were poison! Why? Why had she done that?

Was she trying to get more out of him? Was that it?

Or did she really feel insulted by it?

The thought, once there, could not be thrust aside—no matter how uncomfortable it made him. He didn't *want* Leandra Ross to be capable of feeling insulted at being offered a hundred thousand pounds to relinquish her lover and not see Milo punished for what he had done to her. He didn't *want* her capable of any kind of decency! He wanted her to be venal, and grasping.

Why? Why was it so important to him that she should be someone he could despise?

The answer came crowding instantly.

Contempt for her would keep him safe from his desire for her...

Leandra pulled on her clothes. They were rumpled and grubby but she didn't care. All that mattered was that they were good enough for flying back to Athens in.

With steely determination she kept her mind fixed on the one thing that was keeping her going—the fact that in a few hours she would be back in Athens and on her way home.

She tidied her bed, checked the bathroom was neat and

clean, picked up her shoulder bag and headed out on to the terrace. She would wait there until Theo Atrides appeared, and then she would stick to him like glue until she was safely sitting in his helicopter and lifting off from this benighted, accursed island.

It looked like paradise—but she was mistaken.

The sun was already quite high in the sky. With autumn approaching the days were getting shorter, but the warmth was still a blessing on her face. As she felt the heat of the south on her limbs a sudden brief regret that she would be leaving assailed her. She hardened her heart. It didn't matter how beautiful this island was—she had to leave it. The moment she could.

At the far end of the terrace, where it opened into a patio, she could see that Theo Atrides was already there. Breakfast things had been laid out on the table and he was sitting with his back to her, a phone against his ear. His free hand was gesticulating in short, sharp gestures.

Another minion getting an earful, Lea thought sourly, padding towards him on soft-soled shoes. Well, she didn't care. She wasn't going to speak a word to Mr Theo Atrides, and the only reason she was going near him now was because she was not about to miss out on breakfast.

She reached the table, went to the free side, pulled out a chair and sat herself down, reaching for the coffee pot and a cup in the same movement. She did not deign to look at her host from hell.

Anyway, he was still busy demolishing his hapless minion in terse, brusque tones. She helped herself to bread, butter and honey, doggedly casting her eyes down towards the beach and the sea beyond.

With a final curt command Theo disconnected, and set down the phone.

Hell and damnation! This was all he needed! Yet another crisis to sort out! Out of the blue the head of his US subsidiary was jumping ship. Now he would have to spend the day vetting a replacement and dealing with the inevitable buzz of financial journalists, Wall Street analysts, institutional investors, major customers and suppliers, all wanting to know what he was going to do about it!

He had already just given his media director a grilling over why, pray, it had taken a call at midnight from a prominent business editor in New York asking for his comment to alert him of the impending resignation in the first place!

Face dark, he realised he was staring straight at the figure of his other current first-degree mess. From the way she was ostentatiously ignoring him, she was obviously still fully astride that ridiculous high horse she'd charged off on last night.

Well, this was one mess he was going to clear up right here and now.

'Ms Ross—'

His call for her attention was so expectant of her instant compliance that she found, to her annoyance, that she had turned obediently back to look at him before she'd realised it.

His face was shuttered. Well, that suited her. Leandra schooled hers into similar immobility. She would not lose her temper with him again. She would remain calm and dignified, whatever the provocation. And totally focused on her sole end—getting off this island the minute she could.

And that might be very soon, she registered with relief, as she took in the fact that Theo Atrides was once more arrayed in his hand-tailored power suit, as if he were going to march straight off the tarmac and into a board meeting.

Good! That meant he'd be ready to fly out right away. She couldn't have been better pleased.

He surveyed her a moment, and she held his gaze—blank for blank. Then, abruptly, he spoke.

'You have had the night to reconsider your behaviour. Please understand that I have neither the time nor the inclination to draw this matter out further. I will now write out another cheque for the sum in question. You will oblige me by accepting it without any further hysterics. When we reach Athens my lawyer will present you with papers that he is currently drawing up. You will sign them, and then you will be returned to London where you may cash your cheque.'

He might as well have been speaking to his secretary as to a woman he was trying to extricate from his cousin's bed and prevent from breaking a hideous criminal scandal over his head. Leandra answered him in matching crisp fashion.

'I am not going to accept payment of any kind from you for any reason whatsoever, Mr Atrides,' she informed him in a clipped voice. 'Nothing you can say—or do—will change my mind. However, I am perfectly willing to sign any papers you want that refer to your grandfather instigating my abduction—and I will charge you nothing for signing them!' she put in pointedly.

She looked at him steadily across the table. 'You see, I have, Mr Atrides, absolutely no desire to have my name dragged across the newspapers—as must surely happen if my kidnapping comes to the attention of the police.'

The very thought of what the tabloids would make of a criminal court case involving the kidnapping of a woman painted as the mistress of Demos Atrides, ordered by his own grandfather, aided and abetted by the head of the Atrides Corporation, made her blood run cold.

'However,' she went on, and her voice was chill now, and quite deadly, 'I will brook no attempt by you whatsoever to sever my...relationship...with your cousin. That is no one's business but his own. I appreciate that it is difficult for you,' she finished sarcastically, 'to understand that your vast wealth cannot always buy you what you want, but on this occasion you must remain disappointed.'

Theo looked at her, hearing her out. She was different, quite different from any way he had seen her yet. He had seen her as the clinging sex kitten, the berserk virago, the temptress in *dishabille* last night—and the seething Fury again.

But this Leandra Ross was different again. She was cool, composed, calm and...dignified.

The word sounded strange applied to her. Dignity was not something he associated with women like her. And yet, sitting there, in nothing more than a crumpled sweatshirt, hair loosely tied back at her neck, she had the dignity of an aristocrat, a queen.

Turning his money down.

Money shows their true colours!

In his memory he heard Milo's cynical jibe.

By everything he knew about Leandra Ross, by everything he knew about women like her, she should have been clutching that cheque of his to her as if it were the most precious thing in her life, the very reason for her existence!

But she wasn't. She was turning his money down.

All of it.

Something went through him. Something that scorched through a shell so hard that he no longer noticed it was there.

It made him speak.

'Very well.' He nodded tersely. He didn't want to say more. And he didn't want to think why he didn't want to say more.

She went on looking at him. He reached for the coffee pot and poured out another cup, then glanced at her as he realised she was still looking at him.

'That's *it?*' she said.

He took a mouthful of coffee and set the cup down again.

'There was something else you wanted to say?'

Her mouth tightened. This cool, offhand manner of his was so alien she was confused by it. Then she recovered. If that was the way he wanted it to be, so much the better.

'Only to ask when we are leaving. I am ready to depart as soon as you want. I have no luggage to pack,' she pointed out, resisting the urge to make it sound too sarcastic a reminder of his unutterably false assumption last night about her choice of attire over dinner.

'I will be setting off very shortly,' said Theo Atrides. 'But you will not be accompanying me.'

Cold pooled in Leandra's stomach.

'What do you mean I won't be going with you? Of course I am going with you!'

He shook his head. 'I'm afraid that is no longer possible. Now that you have made it clear you will not accept any money for leaving Demos, I must point out to you that you cannot, at the moment, return to his apartment. My grandfather is staying there while he undergoes medical treatment and examination. You will appreciate, I am sure, that it would be quite impossible for Demos to entertain you as you would wish while he is attending to his grandfather. Accordingly,' he went on, in that same remote, cool voice, 'I must ask you to consent to remaining here a little longer.'

Her eyes stared.

'No *way!*' she bit back.

He raised an interrogative eyebrow. 'Where will you go, Ms Ross, if you arrive back in London with no possibility of resuming your co-habitation with my cousin for the next week or so? Had you accepted my financial aid, I am sure you would have had no problem finding alternative accommodation, however temporary, very swiftly. As it is, where will you go? Do you have resources of your own?'

She opened her mouth to say she had a perfectly good studio flat to go back to. Then abruptly closed it again. Did she want Theo Atrides intruding into her private life? He was bound to want to see her escorted there, whether in person or by one of his minions, and the last thing she wanted, she realised, was for Mr Insufferable Atrides to know anything at all about her real life!

If Milo Atrides was staying with Demos it was obvious she couldn't go back there! As for dossing down with Chris—no, that was too risky as well. Again, she had no wish to draw Theo's attention in that direction!

So what could she do? Where could she go?

As if taking her hesitation for confirmation that she would

be homeless if she arrived back in London, he got to his feet.

'As I thought. So, you see, it really would be much easier all round, would it not, for you to remain here a little longer? As my guest, Ms Ross, nothing more. The island, as you already know, is very beautiful—' he gestured expansively with his hand '—and you may regard your stay here as something of a holiday for you. Everything is at your disposal—why not enjoy a peaceful few days, relaxing in the sun? Please avail yourself of all the facilities—I am sure Agathias can find some swimwear for you. And now—' he glanced at his watch, a gleam of gold at his lean wrist '—you must excuse me. I can delay no longer. I have pressing matters of business to attend to.'

He strode off, heading down towards the helipad where the helicopter, already refuelled by him and Yiorgos earlier that morning, as soon as he had picked up the bad news from the US, waited for him.

As he went through the pre-flight routines the concentration they required was a balm to him. It stopped him thinking.

Not about who the devil was going to replace his man in New York, but what he was going to do now about that far more irritating thorn in his flesh—Leandra Ross.

The combination did not make for a good day. As well as orchestrating the urgent replacement of his US chief executive, he also had to endure Demos phoning him, urgent for news. Was his cousin never going to calm down about his missing mistress? Theo growled silently. Using the US crisis as an excuse to keep the conversation brief, he simply told Demos that Leandra Ross had decided to stay on the island for a few days' rest. He did not elaborate, and certainly did not say that he had tried to buy her off.

And failed.

That was another, very severe source of irritation to him. If she wouldn't take money, what would it take to sever her from Demos? He would have to come up with something fast—an imperative made even more urgent by an invitation he could not refuse: lunch with Sofia's father. It was the last thing Theo wanted to do, but he could not snub Yannakis Allessandros any more than Demos had already done, and to crown it all the man had brought his daughter along as well!

A sweet-natured, pretty girl, Sofia Allessandros sat quietly while her father discussed the business world with Theo.

'She'll make a good wife, *ne?*' The girl's fond father beamed. 'Knows to let men talk business without distracting them. Demos is a lucky lad!'

Theo agreed, as Yannakis clearly wanted, reassured Sofia kindly that Demos would soon be in Athens to claim her, and extricated himself as swiftly as possible.

To his even further irritation, Theo realised that Sofia's docility had not improved his mood. He found himself contrasting it with the flashing-eyed virago he had left behind on his island this morning.

Thinking of Leandra was a mistake. In his mind's eye he kept seeing her, wrapped in that skimpy robe she'd flaunted herself in.

He frowned. Except that she hadn't done it deliberately, apparently. What had she said? Milo hadn't bothered to pack a suitcase for her? His frown deepened. Holding up his hand to silence whatever it was that his group finance director was telling him, he called his PA across to him and voiced his requirement in crisp, low-voiced tones. She departed dutifully on her errand, face expressionless. Then, without missing a beat, he turned his attention back to his FD.

But the damage had been done. Now Leandra Ross had intruded into his consciousness again he could not get rid of her. He needed to see her—or at least let her roam at will through his imagination.

What was she doing? he found himself wondering. Sunbathing on the beach? A vision of her spread-eagled on the sand sprang instantly before him, every limb in perfect display for him. Naked beneath the sun—waiting for him...

He crushed it aside and doused the reaction of his body, shifting uncomfortably in his seat. By the time he had nailed down his new US chief executive he heaved a sigh of relief.

He got to his feet, gathering his papers.

'Gentlemen, forgive me. A pressing engagement. Thank you for your endeavours today on this matter. I believe we can make good progress from now on. I will conference call you tomorrow at ten. Good day.'

He was gone, striding out of the office on long legs.

Heading for a very pressing engagement indeed.

She was there, just as he had imagined. Well, almost. She was not quite naked. A scrap of material still covered that lush, round little *derrière,* but that was a trifling consideration.

She was deeply asleep, he could tell, and the rhythmic rise and fall of her torso showed no signs of disturbance at his soft-footed approach.

For a while he simply stood and looked at her. Pleasure and satisfaction surged through him. Yes, he had made the right decision! This was exactly the thing to do! It solved everything!

His keen brain had applied its usual incisive logic to the situation and come up with the perfect answer to the dilemma facing him. How to detach Leandra Ross from his cousin.

She would not take money—extraordinary as that was for a woman of her kind!—so, Theo reasoned, only one other way was left to him. She had already admitted she was nothing more than 'fond' of Demos. Well—a shaft of satisfaction speared him—let us see just how far 'fond' went!

It wouldn't go the distance, no question!

The way Leandra Ross melted every time he touched her proved that! Theo smiled with feline satisfaction, like a tiger eyeing up a foolish gazelle drinking at a dangerous pool.

He knew exactly what he could do. Would do—very definitely—starting right now. Here on his private beach, below his private villa, on his private island.

He would show Leandra Ross, totally, comprehensively and *consumingly* that she was made for *him,* not Demos! After he had done with her, worked her out of his system, as he had ached to do since he first saw and desired her, she would never go back to Demos! Never!

Leandra was dreaming. Sleep had come to her almost the instant she'd lain down on the soft sand, towel beneath her, the peace and quiet of the island so absolute that her battered spirits had found balm and restoration. Unlike Theo's, her day had been spent quietly—her initial indignation at being stranded here gradually giving way to relaxation, tension gradually draining from her during the long slow hours. As Leandra had lain beneath the warm Aegean sun she had been glad, after all, still to be here on the island. Did it really matter so much to be stranded here a few days longer, in this little piece of paradise? Theo Atrides was gone—and his insulting chequebook with him. There was no reason why she should not take her ease and recuperate from the stress and strain she had endured.

Which was exactly what she had done. After insisting, despite agitated signing to the contrary, on helping Agathias with her housework, she had eaten a light salad lunch on the terrace, which she had prepared with Agathias, and then, choosing the least revealing of the chic, designer labelled bikinis the housekeeper had produced, had headed down to the beach.

A leisurely, steady-paced swim back and forth across the little bay had cooled her nicely, and, pausing only to slather herself with sun-cream she had found in her bathroom cabinet, she had spread out the towel on the sand and herself on top.

And now she was dreaming.

The dream had formed out of the jumbled images tumbling around her exhausted brain. Her dance class, the terror of her abduction, even the noisy thudding of the helicopter seemed so loud it was almost real. And then she was not on board the helicopter but fleeing from it as it chased her across the island, dark and monstrous. Suddenly it had gone, but she still had to run, fleeing from something—something she could not face up to, something she must never succumb to. But she tripped, and fell, sprawling on the sand, winded, and then, as she lay there, the fear of being chased evaporated. It was gone, that threat to her, as if it had never been.

In its place was a voice murmuring softly, like warm honey, filling her with a sweet, soothing languor. It was wonderful! Almost tangible. It was like fingers, soothing down the length of her spine, gently, oh, so gently. She relaxed totally, all fear and tension draining away into the bliss she was feeling.

The lovely, sensuous touch smoothed along the graceful sculpture of her back, drifting like foam from the sea, so lightly she could hardly feel it. And then it was returning, sweeping up to her neck, to that sensitive, oh, so sensitive nape where a million delicate nerve-endings were set flickering.

It was so lovely, so beautiful a sensation, that she gave a soft little sigh, feeling her limbs dissolve into the warm sand.

She sighed again. Those gentling, skilful fingers were smoothing aside her hair, touching at the lobes of her ears, curving down her neck, stroking the hair from her cheek.

In her dream she felt a shadow lowering over her, blocking the warm sun, and as she gave an instinctive, involuntary little shiver it seemed to set all her nerves flickering once more.

Then, soft and soothing, she felt a kiss ease across her shoulder, slow and sensuous…

Her eyes opened.

This was no dream.

JULIA JAMES71

The shadow over her was real, all too real. And all too solid.

Theo Atrides lounged beside her, lifting his mouth from her back, his hand from the nape of her neck.

In blind, absolute shock she sat bolt upright, and as she did so she noticed the unfastened bikini top laying crumpled on the towel. She was baring her breasts to Theo Atrides!

CHAPTER FIVE

FOR one long, timeless, unbearable moment Leandra sat there, naked to her waist, while a mere handspan from her Theo Atrides lounged nonchalantly, feasting his eyes upon her uncovered breasts, her golden hair tumbled over her bare shoulders, a second Aphrodite cast up upon the seashore for his pleasure.

A high, strangled sound came from her throat. Then, with a cry of complete horror, she stumbled to her feet, clutching her towel to her. She ran on wings, pelting towards the shelter of the villa, desperate to gain the shelter of her room.

Panting, she fell inside through the French windows. Then, from behind her, her arms were caught, staying her hectic flight. Her sanctuary was destroyed.

'Leandra! It's all right! I didn't mean to scare you!'

He sounded amused as much as concerned.

His hands slid briefly up and down her bare arms.

'Foolish girl,' Theo said, his voice warm with amusement.

It was that that did it. His amusement. He thought it funny, did he? Funny that she'd lost her bikini top and given him a close-up eyeful? With a wild, broken cry Leandra tore away from him, collapsing on the side of the bed in a torrent of tears, hugging the towel to her for dear life.

She could take no more. This was it—this was absolutely it! She'd thought he'd gone, finally cleared off, leaving her alone—and all along—all along he'd just been biding his time. Waiting to come back and...and...*plague* her all over again!

And he'd struck paydirt! He'd finally got his eyeful, all

right—seeing her sit there stripped to the waist, totally on show for him!

Her tears ran hotter, burning and scalding, and she clutched the towel, hunched over, sobbing chokingly.

Theo looked down at her. His good mood had gone— evaporated instantly. What was wrong with the wretched girl? What was she throwing hysterics about now? He looked down at her, an expression of sheer exasperation on his face.

He loathed women crying. They only ever did it when they wanted to make him do something he didn't want to. They always wept so—so beautifully! Tears like pearls brimming over, never spoiling their make-up of course, a delicate little sniff of the nose, a few heart-rending sobs, and then some gentle dabbing at the eyes with a lace hanky. A stricken *Oh, Theo, how can you be so cruel to me?* to wring his heart.

And, oh, miraculously, how the tears stopped instantly the moment he gave in to them. Then it would be smiles and cooing again, and *Darling Theo!* until he was sick of that too!

He glared at Leandra. Oh, she was crying, all right! Tears pouring out of her. He frowned. She didn't look the way women usually did when they cried for him. Her eyes were not shimmering like pearls, they were turning red and puffy, and tears were dripping off her chin, which was wobbling ungracefully. And she wasn't giving off any delicate little sobs and sniffs either. Instead, her throat was making great gulps, and she was sniffing heavily in a quite disgusting fashion, trying to wipe her nose on her towel, which she was clinging to as if it were a life raft. And still she was crying and crying like a river in spate.

Theo looked at her. She looked a mess, that was for sure! The frustrated desire he'd been living with all night and all day had withered completely.

He went on watching her a moment. She really did seem to be genuinely upset. He frowned, trying to spot her covertly glancing at him to check his reaction, but she made no such calculating gesture, just descended into sobs that were quieter now, and more desperate-sounding for that very reason.

Not quite realising he was doing it, Theo found himself reaching into his breast pocket and pulling out his handkerchief. It was silk and pristine, monogrammed and gleaming white, quite unused, but he found himself shaking it out with a snap and closing the few paces between himself and the weeping girl.

'Here,' he said irritably, and thrust the handkerchief at her.

She took it with fumbling fingers, not looking at him, and wiped her eyes with a vigorous sweep, then blew her nose, loudly and inelegantly, still gripping on to that ridiculous towel for dear life, as if she were a blushing virgin, not a hot little number who could get him hard in seconds! Then she gave a sniff, rubbed at her tear-stained cheeks with her hands, scrunching up the now-sodden handkerchief.

'I'll wash it out for you,' she said, chin lifting. Her voice sounded thick and choky.

Theo negated her gesture with a dismissive flick of his hand. He looked her over. She looked awful—face all blotchy, skin red and damp, and her eyes were bleary and sore-looking. She looked a million miles away from the pampered little sex kitten who had hung on Demos's arm that night in the hotel's banqueting suite. As for remembering how he had slipped his hand inside that wisp of silk she'd worn last night, or how her sun-kissed body had been splayed out for him on the beach just now—that seemed even further away!

Theo frowned yet again. He was feeling something odd about the girl, but he wasn't sure what it was. It was an emotion he wasn't used to feeling, certainly not about women. Then he realised. He was feeling sorry for her.

He felt himself begin to step towards her, then stopped. He realised what he had been about to do. Smooth the tears from her cheek and draw her into his arms. Not to kiss her. Not to caress her. But to hug her. Tell her it was all right. That he was sorry. That he hadn't meant to make her cry.

Astonishment at his own intention halted him. A sobering thought came to him. He wondered when he had last hugged a woman. For comfort—his or hers. For affection. For kindness.

But why should he feel kindly towards Leandra Ross, who had done nothing but cause trouble and aggravation? It was just that she looked so damn *miserable* standing there, head bowed, face puckered up—no beauty at all...

'Why did you cry?' he asked. His question came out rather more curtly than he had intended. For a moment he thought he saw her flinch back from it. Then she recovered.

'Because I hate you!' she said fiercely. 'You just won't leave me alone!'

There was real vehemence in her voice. For a moment he was taken aback, and then an amused smile slid across his face.

'If you want a man to leave you alone, *pethi mou,* you should not light up when he touches you! Nor,' he added, his amusement deepening, 'should you display yourself to me as naked as a sea nymph, white-breasted like the foam, tipped with deepest coral—'

To his astonishment, at his words a blush started to stain her face. A vivid, violent blush. He stared, completely astounded. For a moment he thought he was mistaken—must be mistaken—for blushing, surely, was something a female like Leandra Ross was far, far beyond. Yet she was blushing all right. And it did as much for her as crying had done. It turned her red as a beetroot and twice as unappealing.

'Why are you blushing?' he asked. There was genuine incomprehension in his voice. 'Because you showed me your breasts?'

He sounded incredulous at the notion.

The blush deepened, running along her arms and suffusing her neck.

'But *why?*'

Leandra screwed her eyes tight shut, then opened them again.

'Because I feel embarrassed!' she let out in a rush, as though he were unutterably stupid to ask.

He stared at her disbelievingly.

'You have no need for any such embarrassment,' he told her. 'You have beautiful breasts, *pethi mou.* Exquisite. High and firm. Full but not heavy. Like mother-of-pearl. They are perfect—quite perfect. You need feel no embarrassment for them! I have seldom seen their like.'

Leandra felt her mouth fall open. He really thought her embarrassment was about having breasts that might not be up to his demanding standard! For the first time in all her sorry encounters with him she was totally speechless. She couldn't even *begin* to find the words to put him right!

As she stood there, gape-mouthed, he went on speaking. His brows had drawn together.

'There is something I wish to say to you,' he announced.

Leandra braced herself. Now what? A flattering reassurance that he found the rest of her body up to his demanding standard as well? A bubble of hysteria formed in her throat. She felt as if she'd just been through a force ten gale—totally battered.

What was he doing here anyway? Why had he come back? Why wasn't he in Athens, or wherever he lived when he wasn't trying to pay people to make them do what he wanted? He'd never warned her he was coming back to the island! If she'd known that she'd have stormed his helicopter this morning and hijacked it back to the mainland! Anything, *anything* rather than have him here again!

Theo steeled himself and spoke. It went against the grain, he admitted to himself, because apologising was something he did only infrequently, seldom having anything to apologise for. But right now he did. So he would do it. He would do it handsomely, and that would be that. It would clear the way ahead and let him get on with what he intended—which was to get Leandra Ross pulsing with pleasure under him as soon as the delicacies of seduction permitted.

'I wish to apologise,' he said, looking across at her. This was not entirely true. He did not wish to apologise, but he realised that he must. Any woman who had turned down a hundred thousand pounds would want to have her gesture appreciated. He was a generous man—he could apologise if it was necessary. And if it meant that at last, *at last,* Leandra Ross would lose the virago act and start to act like a normal woman, eager for his attention instead of fighting it the whole time, then it was an investment that was well worth making.

He frowned as he looked at her. She was still staring at him, lips parted, still clutching that ridiculous towel, his handkerchief screwed up in her hands. Her red colour was fading, and her beauty was beginning to be restored, but she had an expression on her face he could not recognise. He eyed her warily. Was she about to explode again into another bout of inexplicable histrionics? He had never known such an inflammable woman! Not even that opera singer he'd bedded had had such a temper on her! Well, that would soon be long gone. Soon, very soon, Leandra Ross would be purring like a cat beneath his touch…

Right now, though, she was looking at him as if he'd grown an extra head. Now what? he thought irritably.

'Apologise?' she got out. 'You want to apologise?'

His mouth thinned. She made it sound as though he'd just said he wanted to join a monastery or play the trombone.

'Yes,' he said tightly. He could do this. He *would* do this. He took a sharp breath and ploughed on. 'Last night—this morning—you felt yourself insulted when I offered you money. Please understand, I intended no insult. I merely thought that it was an outcome that you would consider…favourable. Clearly I was mistaken. I believe we may now both consider the matter closed.'

There, that should do! He went on, speedily, to the next item on his agenda.

'Now...' his voice changed '...you mentioned this morning that you are suffering from a dire lack of clothes. I have remedied the situation, and once you have...refreshed yourself...with a shower you may select what you wish! I trust you will find something in what I have brought that pleases you.'

He glanced at his watch. 'Perhaps you would like to join me for drinks in, say, an hour? On the terrace? Oh—' he had a sudden recollection as he headed towards the door. 'There should be all the toiletries you require as well. I told my PA your colouring so I hope they will suit.'

He paused again, looking back one last time. She was still standing there, taut as a whip.

'Leandra,' he said softly, 'relax—please. From now on between us there will be only good things. I promise you.' He held her eyes, his own softening. She really was very appealing, standing there with that lost look on her face, wary and confused.

'Trust me,' said Theo Atrides.

Then he was gone.

Trust him. That was what he had said. Leandra veered between bursting into tears all over again or saying an extremely rude word. Trust him? She'd trust a snake more! A serpent!

She shook her head. She was exhausted, she was shocked, she was confused. She didn't know what to do. For a few moments longer she just went on standing there, then with a long sigh realised that the one thing she could do was have a shower.

She padded through into the bathroom.

The shower certainly revived her spirits, and the routine of washing herself and her hair was soothing and calming. As she stepped out and started to dry herself she put her battered mind in gear and started to think.

What was she going to do? Theo Atrides had come back, and it didn't take a genius to work out why. That little scene on the beach had been a dead give-away.

Her expression hardened. Or was there more going on? Was this just the next round in the 'Get Demos Married' campaign? Well, if it was, she had better make one thing absolutely crystal-clear to him. Trying to pay her off with cash hadn't worked—and if he thought she'd meekly tumble into his arms—his bed—and conveniently 'forget' all about Demos then he'd better think again!

She marched out into the bedroom—and stopped short.

Agathias was there, hanging up the last few items of what seemed to be a wardrobe full of clothes. A pile of now empty flat boxes and carrier bags from fashion houses were strewn on the bed. Seeing Leandra, Agathias turned and smiled and beamed, gesturing to the beautiful clothes she was putting away. Then, with a last smile, she pointed towards the enormous vanity case on the chest of drawers, nimbly scooped up Leandra's own clothes, making reassuring washing gestures, and went out. Leandra was too stunned to stop her.

Freshly showered and shaved, wearing comfortable casual clothes, Theo walked out on to the patio with a spring in his step. His mood was excellent. True, Leandra had managed to confuse him again with all that extraordinary crying business, but it was probably just her hormones. Women got overwrought about things—who knew why? And, he conceded generously, she had had a lot to be overwrought about. But all that was over now. As he had told her—from now on there would be only good things between them.

Anyway, her mood would have improved by now, he knew. Agathias would have unpacked her new clothes for her and she would be in seventh heaven! The budget he'd given his PA had been generous indeed—and as for that other item he had brought with him, well, it would take her breath away. He had checked it personally, just now, before placing it in the drawer of the sideboard in the dining room. It was exquisite!

As, of course, was she!

Absently he reached out to check the temperature of the champagne bottle nestling in its ice bucket on the table. Which of the evening outfits would she choose? he wondered. He had asked for several, and, since the exclusive and extremely expensive fashion store he favoured stocked nothing like that tarty little number Demos had been foolish enough to let her wear for the gala, whatever she chose would look breathtaking.

He took a deep breath of the fragrant evening air, anticipating the pleasures of the evening ahead. How quiet it was, how peaceful! Only the cicadas chirruping in the bushes. He looked down towards the sea, dimming now at the end of the day. What more could a man want than a place like this? And a beautiful woman to please him—

Well-being filled him.

A step on the terrace alerted him. He looked round expectantly.

And as his gaze registered the woman approaching him his expression changed.

What on earth was she wearing?

It was definitely not an evening outfit. In fact, he saw as she got closer, it was a beach sarong. The long swathe of jungle-print cotton swept from waist to ankle, but instead of wearing what should undoubtedly have been a matching bikini top she was wearing a long-tailed, long-sleeved, high-necked white and blue striped cotton shirt that should have been paired with cropped pants. It looked totally wrong with a sarong!

He frowned. Did the girl have no fashion sense whatsoever? As his gaze travelled over her he realised she'd done worse than wear a totally wrong top with a totally wrong skirt—she'd hidden her hair underneath a patterned scarf that completely clashed with the sarong's swirling jungle pattern. And she wasn't wearing a scrap of make-up.

Leandra almost laughed out loud at the expression on his face as she approached! Oh, yes, he'd thought she was going to conveniently slip into one of those slinky, sleeveless, low-cut evening numbers he'd so thoughtfully provided! Just right for a spot of fondling later on in the evening! Well, there wasn't going to be any more fondling—let alone anything else!

She reached the table and sat herself down, eyeing the champagne bucket distastefully. Oh, get her liquored up first—was that the plan? Think again, friend!

'I'm afraid, Mr Atrides,' she began, in a prim, tight voice, 'that I don't care for champagne. And I'm also afraid I have bad news for you. I have absolutely no intention of providing your holiday entertainment. I am wearing clothes you bought me solely because I have none of my own to wear this evening, and I am here now solely because I don't intend to starve. I don't enjoy your company, and I wish to endure as little of it as I can! Is that clear to you?'

Her chin had gone up as she'd spoken.

It was a very firm chin, Theo found himself thinking. Firm and resolute. With the slightest hint of a cleft in it that he found extremely kissable. He heard her out.

As she delivered her speech he found he had to control his mouth quirking. *Theos,* but she *was* good entertainment, this Leandra Ross! He found himself highly appreciative. All those endless legions of women who simpered and cooed at him, or threw him sultry come-hither looks, now seemed a total bore!

'Well, I have to say I am relieved to discover that your highly bizarre choice of attire for this evening has a particular purpose,' he murmured, keeping his face straight. 'However, since you tell me champagne is not to your taste, what would you prefer?'

'Mineral water,' she snapped. She could see him trying not to laugh, and it made her cross. He wasn't supposed to be laughing at her.

'Of course,' he said blandly. 'If you will excuse me?'

He disappeared inside the sitting room, and returned a moment later with a chilled bottle of water and a glass.

'I chose sparkling,' he said baitingly, 'to match your eyes.'

Again she could see the humour quirking at his mouth.

She wished it wouldn't. She wished he simply just looked furious, the way he usually did at her. Not just because she was pretty sure he was laughing at her, at her defiance of his evident intention of seducing her, but because when Theo Atrides let humour light his face it made it even more gut-wrenching than it normally was when he was doing his Mr Powerful impersonation.

She shot daggers at him and sat herself down, sipping away at the water he'd poured out for her. For himself, he didn't seem to want anything to drink.

'No champagne for you?' she said sweetly. 'No point in wasting a bottle since I'm not going to oblige you tonight? Still, I'm sure if you phoned the mainland one of your minions would parachute you over a film star, considering I'm off the menu!'

The mobile mouth quirked again as Theo Atrides sat back to enjoy his guest in a way he admitted he had not expected to.

A light gleamed in his eye. 'Are you? But you must remember, sweet Leandra, the night is young,' he said expansively, 'and it is always a woman's prerogative to change her mind! Who knows what the evening will bring? Now, if you wish, let us go through.'

He stood up and gestured indoors. Stiffly she got to her feet and went in. At least he wasn't getting an eyeful tonight, she thought with grim satisfaction. Apart from her face and hands there wasn't an inch of flesh on show! She was covered totally from neck to ankle. She knew she looked daft, that none of the pieces worked together, but their sole purpose was to cover as much flesh as she could—plus her hair.

She took her seat at table. Tonight it was lamb, slow-cooked and meltingly tender, and Leandra ate heartily. Lunch had been a long time ago, and the island air seemed to give her a good appetite. Of the wine that Theo poured for her she drank sparingly, however.

Her host did not, she noticed. Though hardly drinking copiously, he made good inroads on the bottle, clearly savouring what she assumed was an extremely expensive vintage. Yet one more of the many good things in life he indulged himself with!

Well, bully for him!

She found herself watching him as the meal progressed. The fine olive-green crewneck cashmere sweater he wore clung lovingly to his frame, complementing the tanned hue of his complexion. She watched his face, with its strong nose and that wide, mobile mouth. His night-dark eyes, so heavy lidded, met hers from time to time, glinting as they did.

It was as if he could read her rebellious thoughts and found them amusing. It made her stomach tighten even more than watching his face did.

Conversation tonight was more expansive. Certainly it could hardly have been worse than last night. Tonight, Theo seemed to want to draw her out.

'Tell me about yourself, Leandra,' he asked, when Agathias had left the room after serving the main course. 'Are you from London?'

Leandra thought of the bungalow on the south coast she'd been brought up in. She'd inherited it when her parents had been killed, but it was let as holiday accommodation to help supplement her meagre income as a struggling actress.

'Yes,' she lied. She didn't want Theo Atrides knowing anything about her. Anything at all.

'What part?'

'Um—nowhere you'd have heard of.'

'Try me.'

She shrugged. 'Why? What interest can you possibly have?'

'It's called conversation, *pethi mou*. It's what people do when they are having dinner together.'

'I'm not having dinner with you. I just happen to be sitting at the same table as you!'

Theo's mouth quirked again. Taming her would be so very enjoyable. Soon, very soon, the spitting little cat would be purring in his arms.

Smoothly he went on. 'So, you are from London. But, tell me, do you enjoy travelling?'

'Only when I'm not shanghaied,' she returned sweetly.

He ignored her jibe. 'I shall be going to New York next week. Perhaps you would like to come with me?'

She stopped eating, a forkful of food halfway to her mouth.

'New York?' she echoed blankly.

'Yes,' he went on, his voice smooth. 'Come with me.'

His eyes rested on her.

Her mouth tightened. 'No, thank you.'

He smiled, not put out by her reaction. 'Then perhaps Paris would be more to your liking. Or Milan. There,' he said, and his eyes danced, 'you may choose your own clothes, Leandra, since those I have provided so clearly fail to meet with your approval.'

'I doubt it,' she said repressively, refusing to rise to his bait. 'Besides,' she went on, taking the war into his quarter, 'next week I shall be back in London with Demos.'

Right now, even a totally fictitious lover seemed like good protection.

Because, for all her defiance, for all her determination not to succumb to the passing lust of Theo Atrides, Leandra felt weak. He was dangerous to her—very dangerous. And now, tonight, when he seemed to have abandoned hostilities, he was even more dangerous.

Like now, when he smiled.

'Of course,' he agreed, but the glint in his eyes told her he found her reply amusing.

She wished he wouldn't look at her like that. Wished he

would revert back to being insufferable again, so that she could just sit there and loathe him. Of course, she didn't exactly approve of him the way he was now, so calmly assured she was going to fall into his arms like a ripe peach, but all the same the kind of attraction he was generating now was very potent. He was so damn confident of seducing her!

Would it really matter if he did?

The treacherous thought came from nowhere, like a knife to her spirit. Aghast, she crammed it down. Of course she mustn't let Theo Atrides seduce her! What on earth was she thinking of?

She was thinking of how it would be to stop fighting him, to meet his eyes and acknowledge, at last, what had been there from the beginning. To walk towards him and go into his arms, to feel them around her, strong, caressing, to give herself to him and let him do what he wanted with her...

No. No, no and no! She mustn't even *think* like that! It was far, far too dangerous. Theo Atrides was not for her. He never would be. Never.

Shaken by her own inner treachery, she reached blindly for her wine glass, drinking deeply. As she lowered it she met his eyes.

The amusement had gone. In them suddenly, searingly, was only one emotion.

Desire.

For one long, endless moment she just looked at him, her gaze held by his, and between them flowed something so powerful it made her feel faint.

He gave a slow, acknowledging nod.

'Yes,' he said, his voice deep and grave. 'Deny it all you want, Leandra. But it is there. And it will not go away. Whatever you do to fight it—to fight me—if you wore sackcloth and ashes I would still desire you. And I will have you.'

Slowly, very slowly, she shook her head.

'No, Mr Atrides. You will not.'

Humour flashed in his eyes, dissolving their dark, dangerous intensity.

'Well, certainly not if you insist on calling me Mr Atrides! Come, my name is Theo. You must get used to using it! And by the time the dawn breaks...' his voice dropped, husking in his throat, his eyes resting on her with that slow, dark burn in them '...you will be calling it in ecstasy, again and again, until we are both spent...'

The vision leapt in her mind. She saw them, bodies entwined, exhausted in the aftermath of passion, fused together as one being...

He saw it in her face.

'You see?' he said simply, and his voice was low and grave once more.

She stared at him, helpless.

'Why do you fight me, Leandra?' His voice was impelling. 'I am not your enemy. I never was. You have nothing to fear from me, I give you my word. I want only to give you pleasure. What is so wrong with that?'

Wrong...? she thought wildly. There was everything wrong with it! Everything! He was far too dangerous to her! Why couldn't she be immune to him? Why did she have to feel her insides dissolve when he looked at her like that? Why did her heart start to race and make her feel weak in all her limbs?

'Stop fighting me, Leandra, and let me give you the pleasure I know you ache for.' His voice was low and sensual. She felt fire flickering along her veins, stealing her sanity. She tried to fight it, but she couldn't. The noose of his dark eyes had caught her, and she was helpless.

What was the point of trying to fight him—fight herself? Ever since she had laid eyes on him Theo Atrides had set a flame alight within her—one she had never known existed—one she could not douse.

She had tried to douse it—dear God, how she had tried! She had tried to hate him and despise him. She had tried yelling at him and ignoring him. She had wept and she had blushed.

But it had all been for nothing. She knew that now.

The dark allure that was Theo Atrides held her in thrall. Somewhere, somehow, she must find the strength to fight it! To free herself.

But where could such strength come from?

What could save her from him now?

He smiled. A slow, knowing smile. Knowing her weakness to him, her helpless, debilitating weakness that made resistance futile.

'Now,' he said indulgently, 'you have played your little game with me, and it has amused me, but the time for games is over. Go and change, Leandra. Make yourself beautiful for me. Then join me in the sitting room. Agathias will serve coffee and then leave us to be private. Very private.' His voice dropped to a sensual note.

He was so sure, she realised, so absolutely sure that she would simply trot along and do what he wanted, then return and be seduced by him. How very, very convenient for him!

Her mouth tightened. 'No,' she answered, in the prim, controlled voice that at this stage of the game was beginning to irritate him, 'I don't think so. In fact, Mr Atrides—' she deliberately avoided his first name '—I am now going to retire. Goodnight.'

She got to her feet, neatly pushing her chair into the table. She would have liked a cup of coffee, but not if it came with Theo Atrides and being 'very private' with him on a sofa!

She walked towards the door, her canvas soles slapping on the tiles, head held high.

He caught her wrist as she passed.

CHAPTER SIX

LEANDRA tried to jerk it away, but his grip was strong. He turned her to face him as he got to his feet.

'Stop running,' he said softly. 'Stop fighting, stop running, stop...playing...with me.'

There was an intensity in his voice she had not yet heard. She looked up at him. He was so close to her she could inhale the tang of his aftershave, the scent of his raw, potent masculinity. She felt overpowered by him, overwhelmed.

'Let me go!' She pulled at her wrist again and he loosened his grip. His fingers soothed gently at her skin, sending a rich, deep shiver through her. She should pull away—he wasn't restraining her at all—but she could not. She could not.

'Foolish girl,' he said, in that soft, sensual voice, his dark eyes holding her more immobile by far than his fingers around her wrist. There was humour in them, humour and indulgence and desire.

With his free hand he tilted up her chin, cupping it along the line of her jaw, his thumb moving over the lobe of her ear. She felt herself tremble, grow weak.

Her defences fell, without a sound.

'No more games,' he murmured, and drew his thumb along the lush line of her lips, pressing gently until she parted them, with a little breath, a final weakness. He skimmed sensuously along the moist inner surface while her heart started to beat in slow, heavy strokes.

He drew her closer, so that her legs were pinioned between the strong columns of his thighs. She felt herself long to press forward, to feel the whole length of his powerful, hard body against hers.

She gazed up at him, helpless, quite helpless, and felt her captured hand slacken in his grip. He felt it too, and when she let it fall, like the sigh of a feather upon his shoulder, and let her hands curve around the strength beneath, his freed hand found other occupation. It found her hip, smoothing over its gentle curve, sliding behind.

He pulled her in to him.

She gasped, feeling his arousal.

Her reaction pleased him. He moved his thumb along her lip again, sensuously, speaking softly to her.

'You see how much I want you? Go then—go my sweet white dove, before I yield to what I want to do more than anything else and kiss you, and be totally lost... So go swiftly. Make yourself beautiful for me—and when you come back adorn your beauty with this.'

He drew back from her and she felt empty, bereft. What was happening to her? Why was she standing here, swaying as if in a dream, with every nerve on fire with longing— longing to give herself to this man who had such power over her she could not resist, could not...

He reached across to the drawer in the sideboard, sliding it open and taking out the slim, narrow case within. He handed it to her.

'For you, Leandra. For your beauty. For my desire of you.'

She stood a moment, as if dazed.

'Take it,' he said.

She was his, he knew. Relief surged through him. The fighting was over; the games were over. Now there was nothing left but passion and desire. Deep satisfaction filled him. Soon she would be in his arms and he would finally, finally have what he had been craving now for days...

She lifted the lid of the case. A diamond pendant, exquisitely wrought, lay on a velvet bed. It caught the light, flashing with rainbow iridescence. Leandra found herself lifting it out, letting the gold chain slide through her fingers. She looked up at Theo Atrides.

*I could have him tonight! He could be mine! I could lie
in his arms, his bed...*

A wild recklessness filled her. Everything about Theo that
she had spent the last days denying surged through her. She
wanted him badly, hopelessly—helplessly.

She stared across the table at him, lips parted, eyes wide
with longing. He was looking at her. Waiting. His eyes
slumberous with anticipation.

Coldness crept over her. Realisation came hard, riding on
self-disgust. She felt the heavy sharp-edged diamonds pressing into her skin. Theo Atrides was only offering her his
wealth. That was all he was tempting her with. Worthless
money. And that, Leandra realised, with a cold, silent shriv-
elling of all the heat that had inflamed her just now, was all
she was to him. She was nothing to Theo Atrides except a
body to be bought, an object to be enjoyed.

Worth nothing more than diamonds.

Slowly she closed her fist over the pendant, squeezing on
the sharp facets of the jewels as if this pain would obliterate
the pain stinging in her heart.

'Put it on, Leandra, and adorn your beauty for me,'
drawled Theo Atrides, his voice heavy with satisfaction, anticipation.

With a single, fluid movement Leandra hurled the necklace down the length of the table, her face contorted, her
rejection of it—and the man who had given it to her—total.
Then with a broken cry she ran to the sanctuary of her room.

Moonlight pooled on the floor in Leandra's bedroom where
she lay asleep. It was long past midnight. Theo stood, looking down at her.

Her beauty, in repose, was absolute. Her pale hair was
spread like a flag over the pillow, long lashes fringing the
alabaster curve of her sculpted cheek.

As he stood looking down at her an ache filled him.

Why? he thought. Why did he want her so much? Why

was she haunting him like this? Giving him no peace. Other women had never haunted him like this. Why this one?

And why had she run from him that evening, giving that broken cry?

He heard it again, and it caught at him. Piercing him like a needle sliding deep.

Why? Why did she always run from him?

Too many questions. Questions he did not want to ask. Did not want to answer.

He turned away and walked from the room, his face sombre.

It was Leandra who was up first the next morning, dressed defiantly in her crumpled jeans and sweatshirt. She sat at the table on the patio, hands clasped, keeping a vigil. Agathias brought her coffee and breakfast, but Leandra could hardly smile her thanks.

Nor could she eat. A heaviness filled her, crushing her.

She waited.

Time passed slowly.

Eventually, when the sun was already flooding out over the gardens, warming the stones where it reached beneath the dappled shade of the vine, she heard him come. Agathias came with him, setting out fresh coffee and breakfast, and whisking away Leandra's untouched tray with a shaking head.

Theo sat down. After all this time, all this waiting, she could not speak to him.

'Leandra—' His voice broke the silence. It sounded strange.

She looked up, her twisting hands stilling. Her face was bleak.

'Tell me,' said Theo Atrides. The bleakness in her face was like a blow. 'Tell me what I have done. What crime I have committed this time!'

He really didn't seem to know. That was the worst of it— the very worst. Just as he had handed her a cheque for a hundred thousand pounds to buy her silence, to buy her out of his cousin's bed—and thought nothing of it!—now, this time, he really didn't seem to know what his crime was either!

She knew what hers had been all right!

Folly! Unforgivable folly! To let him get so close, to be so *close* to succumbing to him. Well, that was what you got when you indulged in appetites you knew were bad for you, she thought punishingly. And desire for Theo Atrides, weak, helpless, aching desire, was a very bad appetite indeed...

He spoke again. 'Silence won't help, Leandra. If you don't tell me, I can't know!'

Her eyes flashed. No, in his book it wasn't a crime, was it? It was just 'normal practice'! Just like writing out cheques was normal practice! Paying people off.

Buying them for sex.

A cheque, a diamond pendant—what was the difference? Nothing.

'Let's just say,' she replied grittily, 'I appreciate being bought with jewellery as little as I appreciate being paid off with a cheque on your personal account!'

His face darkened.

'I am not trying to buy you! You insult me!'

She stared. 'I insult *you?* Good God, you hand me a diamond pendant and don't think that's an insult?'

'Of course not! Leandra, I gave you that pendant because I know it will look beautiful on you. I gave you those clothes for the same reason. Your beauty cries out for adornment!'

'Yeah?' she jeered. 'Well, pal, *timeo Danaos—et dona ferentis.*'

He stared.

'It means,' she went on in that same gritted voice, '*I fear the Greeks even when they bring gifts.* The Trojan Horse, you know?'

His eyes snapped. 'Of course I know! But how on earth—?' He stopped, looking at her. Then he made a noise in his throat. 'Little cousin Demos, I assume, amusing himself with you.' A hard glint appeared in his eyes. 'And did you object just as much when he gave you those diamond earrings you were flashing that evening?'

She opened her mouth to deny it—then closed it again. She couldn't say that the earrings had simply been hired for the evening—it would expose the charade she'd paraded.

'Ah,' said Theo heavily, leaning back in his chair. 'So my cousin gives you diamonds and you accept prettily. I give you diamonds and you consider yourself insulted!'

She recovered. 'Yes, I do!' Her voice was fierce. 'You insult me all the time! You've insulted me ever since you first laid eyes on me! I can't *believe* you're Demos's cousin!'

'You don't love him. You admitted it.' His voice was scathing.

She glared at him.

'No, I don't. But I'm fond of him. You think that counts for nothing, but it doesn't, Theo Atrides! "Fond" goes a long way.'

'"Fond" is for lap dogs!'

'Don't sneer at him! How dare you? Demos has something you couldn't have in a million years! He's *kind,* and he's considerate. He's a million times nicer than you are!' Her voice had risen. 'So take your jewellery, and your designer clothes, Mr Atrides, and go and give them to someone who wants them, who thinks they're important—more important than kindness or consideration. And don't try and throw sex in my face! I don't care if you're the hottest thing between the sheets since Casanova! I can do without you!'

His eyes narrowed. He did not want to hear her praise Demos to him. He did not want to hear her scorn his gifts and, most of all, he did not want to hear her deny her desire for him!

'I could make you care, *pethi mou.* I could caress your body till you melted from the heat!'

'And then you'd give me another shiny little bauble to

reward me! So much more *tasteful* than handing over money! Men who try and buy sex make me *sick!*'

A rasp of exasperation escaped him.

'Leandra, since gifts from me obviously upset you so much, I give you my word you shall never have the price of a coffee from me! Will that calm you down? You've taken insult where I truly did not mean it. It's my experience that women like being given jewellery. They don't think I'm paying them for sex!'

'That's because they're rich in the first place!'

'Yes, very probably. But the point is I was *not* trying to equate a costly piece of jewellery with spending the night with you! You're a beautiful woman; you know you are! Clothes and jewels adorn beautiful women—that is all. Now—' he raised his hand '—please, let us consider this subject closed.'

His voice changed. 'What would you like to do today?'

'Go home!'

He sighed heavily. 'That isn't possible. You know that.'

'Then you can go home!'

He drew back from reaching for the coffee pot.

'This happens,' he said tersely, 'to be *my* island. Look…' He made a real effort, because everything had collapsed in shards around him and he didn't know what else to do, didn't begin to know how to make Leandra Ross stop fighting him, how to make her yield to him—and the mutual desire that scorched between them.

'Can we not reach some form of…of truce, Leandra? I would like, if it is possible, to spend a quiet, relaxing day. Can you not agree to that without going off the deep end all the time?'

'It's because you keep pushing me into the deep end!'

He sighed again. She was such hard work, this one, but she would be worth it, he knew, finally—finally—when he took her to his bed. 'Right, well, if I try very hard not to do so, will you consent to calm down and accept my peace offering—which involves no gifts, Leandra, no Trojan Horses!—simply a quiet, relaxing day together?'

She eyed him suspiciously. 'I don't want you pouncing either!'

He held up his hands in submission. 'Very well. In exchange for a quiet, relaxing day, I will agree. So, do we have our truce?'

He held out a hand towards her. She looked at it warily.

'Leandra?' he prompted. There was a strange light in his eye.

Slowly, cautiously, as if she was taking a step that might change her whole life for ever, she placed her hand in his.

'A truce,' she said. Then, with a last marshalling of her defiance, she rushed on, 'But don't confuse a truce with surrender!'

He gave a slow, wide smile that reached his eyes, which drooped suddenly, tellingly, at the corners. 'A surrender? Oh, no, *pethi mou*—when you surrender to me you will not, I assure you, confuse it with anything less!'

His eyes dwelt on her face, lambent, expressive, and made her breath catch—before it turned into a choking sound of protest.

'But right now—' he held up a hand to silence her '—I will be content with a truce.'

Leandra twirled in front of the long looking glass set into the armoire in her room. The sun-dress was almost unbearably pretty and beautifully feminine. Despite its designer label it was very simple, in a buttercup-yellow print with tiny white flowers. With its modest halter-neck bodice and gathered waist, floating down to a generous mid-calf length, there was nothing she could possibly object to about it.

Except that Theo Atrides had asked her to wear it.

A truce, she had discovered, meant compromise. And he had asked her nicely—very nicely, in fact, with a wary humour in his face—whether, considering they were going to have a quiet, relaxing day together, she might consent to choose something from the collection he'd brought for her to replace her own tired clothes.

Truth to tell, she was glad to get out of her own clothes. Pausing only to stipulate that she was simply going to borrow something to wear, and had no intention of taking a single garment he'd provided home with her, she had gone in to leaf through the contents of the wardrobe.

The sun-dress had caught her eye immediately—she hadn't been able to resist it. Now, as she twirled, her hair loosened, floating round her shoulders like a golden veil, she felt her spirits lift. She slipped her feet into a pretty pair of sandals—when had Theo Atrides paused to check her shoe size? she wondered—and headed out to the terrace.

The smell of freshly baked bread caught at her. Suddenly she felt hungry. As she approached the table Theo stood up, courteously going round to draw her chair back for her, as if she were a duchess.

'May I tell you that you look enchanting?' he said, and there was that wary humour in his eye again, as if he really did think such a compliment might cause her to bristle.

'Maybe,' said Leandra, almost as wary, taking her seat.

He smiled, and their eyes met, fellow conspirators in this delicate, tentative truce.

She chose a good breakfast—fresh bread and butter, and sweet Cretan honey—and as they ate she asked him about the island, and who had lived here before he had bought it.

'No one,' he told her. 'It is too small for a small holding, but olive trees were planted, and goats grazed here from time to time. The villa is new, but made from old stone I had imported from a ruined building I bought elsewhere. Agathias and Yiorgos' sons work for me, and they were willing—glad, even, as I mentioned—for the remoteness of the place.'

She looked around. 'It is very beautiful,' she said.

'Very beautiful,' he agreed, but his eyes were not looking at his island. Only at her.

She was a chameleon, this girl. She was someone new

again, someone he hadn't seen before. In that dress she looked—she looked enchanting, just as he had told her. Desirable, of course—always that—but the way she sat there, looking as pretty as a picture, he knew he still wanted her, but he also wanted...

He wanted more.

He didn't know what the more was. But whatever it was, he wanted that too.

And Theo Atrides always got what he wanted. He made sure of it.

Leandra's wariness of her host was reaching new heights—and new lows. The reason for the heights was easy to identify. Theo Atrides was exerting himself to be charming to her.

And he was succeeding in spades.

That was the reason for the lows.

She was torn between the two. On the one hand she could obviously appreciate that a man like Theo Atrides, effortlessly running both a vast business empire plus an ever-changing stable of fabulous females, should be well-skilled in the art of making himself agreeable when he chose. On the other hand it was equally obvious he used his charm as a weapon to get his own way—whether in business or in bed.

The trouble was, she realised, that just because she could see what Theo Atrides was doing it did not mean she was immune to the effect. He was pulling out all the stops to charm her. She could see him doing it, know why he was doing it—and still be charmed all the same.

Dimly, she realised that it made him even more dangerous than ever.

This Theo Atrides—the charming, exquisitely mannered, good-humoured, well-behaved version, who sat looking at her, rather than looking her over, as if she were nothing more than an exceptionally pretty girl whom he wanted to admire rather than pounce on—was far, far more dangerous to her than the practised seducer.

Why, she didn't want to think. Wouldn't think.

Would only let herself enjoy, very warily, the day spent in his company.

When they had both finished breakfast Theo left her briefly to call his office, receiving the happy news that all was going well within his empire, including the matter of his new US chief executive. Telling his PA he did not wish to be disturbed except in an emergency, he emerged to find Leandra. He ran her to earth in the kitchen, helping Agathias wash up.

His brows drew together. The chameleon had changed colour yet again! In a hundred years he would not have thought a female like Leandra Ross willing to soil her hands with housework. And she certainly seemed to have won Agathias over—the housekeeper was beaming at her in approval, though she seemed most concerned that Leandra might splash her pretty dress.

He whisked Leandra out to the patio, where Yiorgos had set up a sun-lounger at his bidding in the dappled sunshine beneath the vine. As he settled her upon it he handed her a sheaf of glossy English-language magazines and some popular bestsellers he'd extracted from a cupboard in the sitting room. It wasn't Leandra's usual reading matter, but it was better than nothing and she fell on them hungrily. For himself, he opened his laptop and started to work.

A pleasant hour or so passed, interrupted only by the arrival of mid-morning coffee served by Agathias. Leandra lay, legs extended, warm in the autumnal Aegean sunshine, half shaded by the vine winding overhead, browsing through the magazines while Theo Atrides assiduously worked his way through whatever he was doing, a look of focused concentration on his face. She might not have been present. It suited her, though, for it allowed her ample opportunity to do something she had never yet done to satiation. Feast her eyes on him. Drink him in, soak up the masculine glory that was Theo Atrides.

It came to her, with a shaft of piercing sadness which was really quite illogical, that this time together on his private island was going to be the only time in her life she shared Theo Atrides's company. The sense of sadness—impending loss—intensified. It started to grow into something else, but she did not realise it, caught up in the pleasure of watching him.

Only once did he glance up absently, clearly preoccupied with some business matter, and with a flicker of his dark eyes catch her surveying him. The slightest glint showed in his eyes, the slightest indentation of his mobile mouth smiled at her, and then he focused back on his work again.

All around, the soothing chirrup of cicadas, the rustle of the breeze in the olive trees and oleanders, and the occasional bird song, made the mild warmth very peaceful and relaxed.

Eventually Theo Atrides logged out of his laptop, closed down the lid with a click, tidied up his papers, and looked across at Leandra.

'You're very soothing company,' he informed her. There was a note of surprise in his voice. 'It's a rare trait in a woman.' He looked at her approvingly, and for all her determination not to care tuppence about his opinion of her, she felt herself flushing pleasurably at the mild compliment. He saw her reaction and smiled.

It was a real smile. Not mocking, or amused at her ploys to stop him bedding her, but a real smile. He got to his feet, holding out his hand towards Leandra. The sun had climbed noticeably, and a light little breeze had sprung up.

'Come,' invited Theo, 'we've sat around long enough. Time to take a little walk.' He glanced down at her. 'Hmm, enchanting as your dress is, perhaps it is not quite suitable for an island stroll.'

She went indoors to change, and when she emerged he had too. Gone were the immaculately cut chinos and knitted polo shirt. He had exchanged them for well-worn sawn-off denim shorts, and a white T-shirt which lovingly moulded every muscle in his broad chest and back.

Her breath caught, and she stared openly. Then realised he was doing likewise. She hadn't thought the turquoise shorts particularly tight, or particularly brief, but by the way his eyes were resting on her exposed slender thighs she thought so now. Fortunately, her appliquéd matching top was capaciously cut, with a boat neck and loose elbow-length sleeves.

She dragged her eyes from drinking in his long, muscled legs, fuzzed with dark hair, and his equally exposed biceps and forearms. She would not goggle at him as if he were a pin-up! Nevertheless, she was grateful when, with a decided glint in his eyes, he tossed her a pair of sunglasses—and even more grateful when he veiled his own eyes with another pair.

'Are you wearing sun-block?' he asked. 'You must not burn that lustrous skin of yours, *pethi mou.*'

She nodded in the affirmative. A light tan was one thing—sunburn quite another.

'Let's go, then,' said Theo smoothly, and headed off.

She paused only to knot her hair up into a high swinging ponytail, slide on the sunglasses and hurry after him.

It was a surprisingly pleasant excursion. They talked little, enjoying the silence and the endless views out over the dazzling azure sea. From time to time he took her hand over the rougher terrain, and in his large, warm grip she felt a strange sense of safety. Once he stopped dead, and soundlessly pointed to a lizard, splayed motionless on a rock. It darted away and they went on. Leandra stooped to pluck a twig of thyme, which grew everywhere, rubbing the tiny green leaves between her fingers to release its heady, pungent smell. Theo waited for her companionably.

At the furthest point of the island they paused, looking out to sea.

'Is there anything more beautiful?' he asked.

It was a rhetorical question, and Leandra knew he did not require an answer. This time his eyes really were for the landscape and seascape all around him.

He belongs here, she found herself thinking. He belongs to the sea, and the white brilliance of the land, and the blaze of the sun. This timeless, ancient place whose roots descend for thousands of years. And he is part of it. The thought of it gave her a little tug, somewhere in her insides.

He turned back to her, and his gaze swept past her to encompass all his domain.

'It is a little piece of paradise, *ne?*' he said softly, and then his gaze dropped to her. Again she felt that little tug inside, almost in the region of her heartstrings.

'All you require now is that parachute drop of a couple of film stars!' Her voice was tart, quelling that strange little tug.

A smile quirked at his lip. 'I prefer them one at a time, *pethi mou.*' His brows drew together suddenly, as if something had just struck him. Could that be the reason why she was so reluctant to succumb to him?

'One beautiful woman is enough for me, Leandra,' he said soberly, studying her expression. 'Did you think my appetite ran to more? No, be assured I have no tastes in that direction—or for any other perverse sexual indulgence. One man, one woman—and mutual passion and pleasure between them. That is all that there should ever be. You may rest easy, if that has been worrying you!'

The expression on her face was strange as she heard him speak, and he wondered at it for a moment. Then, as if with effort, she replied lightly, 'Providing they're rich and famous enough, of course!'

His mouth quirked again. 'Ah, so that is your complaint! It is true, I have confined my interests to women who move in my world. But that is for our mutual benefit and protection. This island is as much a haven to them as it is to me, for they live their lives in the glare of gossip and paparazzi.

But that does not mean...' his voice softened teasingly '...I cannot make an exception in your case...'

Something flared in her eyes. 'Oh, slumming, are you, in my company?'

He heard the hurt in her voice and cursed himself.

'No! I did not mean that, Leandra. It was a joke—a clumsy one.'

'Hilarious,' she said, and turned away.

He caught up with her. 'I have offended you—I am sorry.' He took her hand and raised it to his lips. 'Forgive me,' he said.

There was a sincerity in his eyes she'd never seen. It made those strings that were tugging at something very deep inside jerk again. She felt her throat tighten.

She withdrew her hand and he made no attempt to retain it. Well, he wouldn't, would he? She'd got him to promise he wouldn't pounce. It had been rash of her to bait him with those women—even though the answer he'd given had disturbed her. Not about the slumming so much as about his distaste for any kind of sexual perversion...

She had no more time to dwell on this worrying aspect of Theo Atrides, for he was leading the way forward again.

On the way back from their almost completely circular tour, they descended down the low cliff to the jetty on the north side of the island beyond the helipad. There, neatly moored, was a powerful-looking motor boat. It seemed to have appeared by magic, but had presumably been extracted from the boathouse by Yiorgos earlier. A picnic hamper and fishing equipment was on board as well.

'Time to feel the wind in our hair,' Theo remarked, heading for the boat. 'And time to catch our dinner as well.'

He handed Leandra in to the expensive vessel—clearly a millionaire's toy if ever there was one—undid the moorings, jumped lithely aboard and took the helm. Gunning the engine, he carefully nosed the boat away from the jetty, heading for the open sea.

It was fabulous. The Aegean bobbed beneath the gleaming hull as they creamed across the waves. Leandra sat, hanging on to the gunwale, trying not to pay excessive attention to where Theo Atrides stood, legs apart, steering the launch with effortless grace, the wind ruffling his dark hair, buffeting his features. At one point he turned, pointing out the villa as they rounded the south of the island, and grinned.

She felt her heart lift, and grinned back. She knew she shouldn't be having fun with Theo Atrides, but it was too exhilarating to matter any more. He shouted something, but the wind whipped it away. She lifted her face into the onrushing breeze, feeling the spray tingle all over her bare arms and legs. It was wonderful! Glorious!

Theo zipped the launch through the water, evidently relishing its power and manoeuvrability, his masterful control over the sea and the craft. He looked exhilarated as well. He reached the spot he was aiming for, cut engine and dropped anchor. Instantly silence surrounded them. At Theo's direction, while he busied himself setting up his fishing lines, Leandra unpacked the hamper.

It was a simple feast—fresh-baked bread, cheese and cold meats, tomatoes and olives, a bottle of cold white wine, with peaches and pomegranates for dessert.

They ate companionably—Leandra with her bare legs stretched out along the wooden seat in the stern, Theo with his powerful legs splayed where he sat on the starboard bench. Leandra tried hard not to look at the muscled sinews in his thighs, or the way his denim cut-offs strained across his groin. There was a lot of well-developed kit stored away under the tautly moulding material, she reckoned, and then looked away hurriedly, out over the sun-silvered sea. She did not see Theo observe the faint colour staining her cheekbones, or realise that he had witnessed her covert observation of his lounging body.

He felt his body start to stir, roused by her awareness of him, and mused upon whether to dare to sweep away her restrictions—which he would sweep away anyway tonight;

he was determined on it—and take her here, now, on the sea's gently swelling bosom, in the bright clear air, with all her limbs kissed by the mellow sun. The idea was attractive...

One of the fishing lines jerked, and he was diverted.

When they set off back to the island, at a gentler speed this time, Leandra leant back, letting her hair stream in the breeze, her fingers trail in the water. She felt wonderful. Calm and relaxed. As though all the tumult and the tension had been blown out of her, leaving her tranquil and still in the singing silence of the sea.

This is heaven, she thought, closing her eyes and lifting her face into the sun, and quite forgot that she was not here in Greece of her own volition, that she had never asked for the company of Theo Atrides.

As he rounded the headland she watched him steer. He looked so good. She just liked to sit back and watch him. He twisted one hand over the wheel and slewed the boat into a new heading.

'It looks easy!' she exclaimed, before she realised she was voluntarily opening a conversation with him. 'Can I try? I've never driven a boat before!'

Theo glanced over his shoulder and slowed the boat right down.

'Come here,' he said, and she came forward. He positioned her hands on the wheel, letting her feel the pull of the boat on the swing of the sea. Slowly he let the throttle out.

'Steer straight into the sun,' he told her.

He stood behind her, his large frame encircling hers, their legs apart to keep their balance. She could feel his hair-roughened thighs against her, feel her spine pressing back into the breadth of his strong chest, warm and powerful.

Belatedly, she realised this had been a very bad idea.

But it was so exhilarating to drive a boat! As if understanding, he let the throttle out more, his hands over hers on the wheel, and they were warm and powerful too, capturing her fingers with a sweet imprisonment...

The sea and the sun and the salt spray flashed past them. The water thumped against the hull as it parted the sea beneath it. Her hair whipped in her eyes and all she could feel was speed, raw speed! Then, deciding they had left the island far enough behind, he closed the throttle down and came to a halt again.

Hastily she freed herself, and sat down in the gunwale.

'Well?' Theo asked, holding the wheel steady with effortless ease.

'Fantastic!' Leandra grinned. 'Just fantastic! Thank you!'

He cast her a sardonic look. 'So, finally I have found a way to give you pleasure, *pethi mou!*'

Their eyes caught, and held. For a moment complete silence held them as the little boat rocked gently on the swell, caught in a great noose of light from the golden sun.

Something passed between them. She didn't know what. Could not tell. Dared not ask. But it was something so powerful, so strong, so impelling that her breath caught in her throat.

No! Please, no! I can't bear it! Don't let this be happening!

But it was happening. Here, now, under the bright Aegean sky, she was falling in love with Theo Atrides.

And she was utterly helpless to stop it.

CHAPTER SEVEN

IT WAS a sober journey back to the island. The *joie de vivre* had gone out of the day. In its place was a stillness, an expectation. The air was heavy between them, with a strange intimacy, yet not once did Theo touch her, or look at her seductively, or even make her aware of any part of her body.

Yet she was totally, tinglingly aware—and of his as well.

Studiedly she helped him moor the boat and lift off the fishing gear and hamper before they set off back to the villa.

She made sure she walked a little apart from him, not wanting even casual contact with him. That hyper-awareness of him was even more vivid, even more disquieting.

As the villa came in view Theo spoke, breaking the tangible silence between them.

'I must give Agathias our catch. Then, would you like to swim? Shall I meet you on the beach?'

An instant memory of their last encounter there flashed in front of Leandra's eyes. She tried to ignore it.

'Yes—yes, a swim would be great. I'll see you there!'

She almost dashed off, hurrying to get away.

It was typical, she thought in exasperation some few minutes later, as she surveyed the collection of swimwear—it contained no one-piece swimsuits at all, and every bikini was more minuscule than the last. Maybe going swimming with Theo Atrides was a bad idea!

But she couldn't resist a swim for all that. Now that the breeze from the open sea was gone she was heated, and wanted to cool down and refresh herself. The sun was golden and sinking in the sky, and when she padded down to the beach the sand was hot under her feet. There was no sign of Theo yet and, thinking herself lucky for that, she dropped her towel and T-shirt and ran lightly down into the water.

A vigorous, energetic swim back and forwards across the bay did her good. It was only when she was ploughing across for the dozenth time that she felt the water stirring behind her, and in seconds Theo's much larger form was effortlessly overtaking her, with powerful, rhythmic strokes.

Competitive instincts aroused, she increased her own pace, and though he obviously outclassed her she gave him as good a race for his money as she could. At the furthest reach of the bay he hauled himself out on a large flat rock tumbling down from the land.

'Here,' he said, and held down a hand to help her out as well.

She clambered out, winded, and collapsed, gasping. Theo laughed.

'You swim well! But I don't want to tire you out too much, *pethi mou.*' His eyes danced. 'I want you to save some energy for later.'

She threw him a quelling look as she sat herself up, wringing out her hair. It was certainly supposed to be a quelling look, but halfway through, as she met his eyes, it changed. She faltered, the hands squeezing her hair stilling.

'Don't,' she said faintly.

'Don't what?' he echoed. His eyes weren't dancing any more. She wished they were. Dancing seemed safer.

Safer than the way he was looking at her now.

'Don't look at me like that.' Her voice was strained and husky.

Something caught in him. Something about that husked voice of hers, something about the way she was looking at him—something about those slender sun-kissed limbs, that sea-glistening perfect body of hers displayed almost completely, so tantalisingly…

And something more. Something more about her caught in him. It was that strange, elusive *more* again, that he had wanted this morning. He hadn't known what it was, only that he wanted it.

She held the secret to it. He didn't know what it was, but she would show him. He knew that now. Certainty filled him.

Just as he knew that now, tonight—finally—she would come to him.

He laid one long, gentle finger across her mouth.

'Hush,' he said.

And then briefly, swiftly, like the fleetest touch, his lips brushed hers.

A second later he was gone. Plunging into the azure sea, a perfect arrowed dive. Leandra watched him head back to shore, cleaving the water.

He did not look at her as he made his way back across the beach. She could see his body, that powerful, lithe body, gilded by the westering sun. He swept a towel off the sand beside hers, slung it round his neck, and kept on walking.

Alone on her rock, Leandra stared after him until he had disappeared from view inside the villa. Then, slowly, with a strange, helpless feeling, she touched her mouth where he had touched it with his.

That night she wore one of the dresses Theo had had brought for her. It was very simple, very lovely, a column of azure chiffon, like the sea, shot with gold. It fastened at the shoulders with tiny tie straps, then, with a softly folded neckline, drifted down to her ankles. The chiffon hushed around her legs as she walked out to the patio.

There was no sign of Theo. She looked around and then, looking further, saw him on the beach. She walked down to him. He was looking out to sea, into the heart of the setting sun, hands plunged in the pockets of his chinos.

He had spread out a cotton throw across the sand, and nestled an ice-bucket with champagne in it.

Almost she smiled, and then, as Theo turned, the smile died. There was a look in his eye she had never seen before.

It was hunger. Raw, terrible hunger.

For one long, timeless moment their eyes held, exchanging the message that Leandra could no longer deny. Then, with a faint, acknowledging smile, he released her from his gaze and walked up to the throw, to hunker down and open the champagne with a twist of his strong wrist.

The golden liquid frothed into the waiting glasses and he handed her a glass.

Champagne on the beach at sunset—with a handsome millionaire beside me! I ought to think it corny, thought Leandra, sipping the icy golden bubbles.

But it wasn't corny. It was simply—

The word came to her, and she could not unthink it.

Romantic.

But it *isn't* romantic! she thought desperately. Romance is for lovers!

We aren't lovers! We mustn't be lovers!

Why?

The treacherous thought slid into her brain. She groped around, trying to marshal her reasons—her quiverful of reasons—but they evaporated like foam, insubstantial, unimportant.

Instead, she simply gazed at him, eyes huge.

They hardly talked, simply sitting there, letting the mood of the moment ease over them, watching the sun slip into the sea like molten gold pouring over the lip of the world. She sat, legs curled delicately under her like a cat, keeping her distance from him. And he sat, legs bent, slanting outwards, his wrists cupped loosely around his knees, tilting his champagne glass. Behind them in the vegetation the cicadas sounded. A zephyr breeze lifted the ends of her hair, toying with them as if with fingers. She saw his eyes, watching.

And could not meet them.

When the final band of gold had spread out in one last, liquid line along the horizon's edge, and the sun was gone, they watched a moment longer, then, lightly, Theo got to his feet. He held his hand down to help her up. Only for the briefest moment did she let hers slip into his, and let it go again as soon as she had her balance. He scooped up the champagne bottle by the neck, swinging it idly as they walked back to the villa.

The interior was cool, and Leandra gave an involuntary little shiver, pausing to fetch the matching chiffon scarf that still lay on her bed and swathe it around her bare shoulders. When she returned Theo was in the dining room, waiting to take his place. Her champagne glass had been refilled.

Agathias came in, carrying *mezzes,* tasty and appetising, to soak up the champagne, and then Theo fetched the opened red wine, left to *chambrer* on the sideboard, while Agathias served the freshly caught fish, grilled simply with lemon and olive oil and herbs, eaten with delicately flavoured rice.

They talked, but desultorily. It was almost dream-like, Leandra felt. The champagne had lifted her spirits, placing them on a level just out of the stream of things. She felt disassociated, as if reality were somewhere else tonight. She drifted on, as if she were a boat with moorings cut, carried by a slow, inexorable current, heading she knew not where.

Or knew, but would not say.

'Come,' said Theo at the end of the meal, and stood up, holding out his hand to her.

She took it, then let it slip from her. He guided her through to the sitting room, and there a fire had been lit in the huge stone fireplace against the chill of the night. Coffee had been set out on the long, low table before the fire.

I'll drink my coffee, thought Leandra, and then I'll go to bed. Yes, definitely after I've drunk my coffee.

She settled herself down at one end of the sofa while Theo hunkered down to pour out coffee. He was wearing dark trousers tonight, with a black shirt. Leandra had done her best not to look at him over dinner, but now her gaze slid to him, seeing how the material strained across his braced thighs, how the turned-up cuff of the shirt cut the strong sinews of his forearms, how the open collar revealed the column of his throat, hinting at the curl of hair still covered by the shirt...

She took another sip of her wine, which she had brought through to finish. After the champagne perhaps it was not wise, but drinking it kept her dreamy state of mind in place, made her feel as if she were moving through a mist, that reality was still very away.

Theo placed the coffee in front of her, taking his own, then sitting on the sofa. Though at the other end from her, he seemed to dominate the space. Unconsciously she drew her legs away a little, unwilling to be quite so close.

Leandra looked into the dry, crackling flames in the hearth. Outside, she heard the sound of Agathias heading back to her own cottage, her work done. It was only her and Theo now.

The silence surged around them. Drawing them together.

'So,' said Theo in a low voice, 'you must tell me, Leandra, what it is to be. This is your moment of choice. Come to me of your own free will—or tell me otherwise.'

She lifted her eyes across to him.

His voice had sounded solemn. His eyes rested on her. There was a message in them she could not deny. *Did not want to deny*.

Not any more.

She wanted to speak, but she could not. There were no words to say. What was between them was not for words. Not for reason, or logic, or sense.

For something much more powerful...

He spoke again, his voice low and resonant.

'Silence is consent, my sweet Leandra—'

Her eyes were huge, unbearable, drinking him in, absorbing him into her brain, her heart.

His night-dark eyes consumed her.

'It must be of your own free will. Nothing else. I have made too many mistakes with you, Leandra. If you come to me now it must be because it answers the desire between us—the flame between us.'

He leant towards her. She could not move.

He lifted the wine glass from her, placing it on the table without looking at it, without taking his dark, compelling gaze from her.

'If that is not so,' he said, his voice as low, his gaze never leaving her, 'if there is no desire between us, no flame burning, then tell me—tell me now, Leandra.'

He touched her mouth with his fingers, touched along the line of her lips, as gently as gossamer. She could hardly feel his touch—but where she felt it was not in her mouth, but deep, deep inside.

'Tell me to go,' he said. 'Tell me to stop. Tell me not to do this—'

He brushed his finger along her lip, moistening it.

'Or this—' He slipped his hand around her neck.

'Or this—' He drew her towards him, boneless, unresisting.

'Or this—' His mouth covered hers.

His kiss was ecstasy. His mouth moved over hers, easing her lips to yield to him, gently, so gently, she thought she must die of it.

He drew her to her feet, never breaking the kiss, only folding her body against his when they were both standing, the whole sweet, soft length of it, against the strength and power of him.

He held her against the cradle of his hips, feeling himself surge against her.

As if at a signal his kiss deepened, opening her mouth to his like a soft, sweet peach, to taste the succulent fruit within. His hand wound into her hair, holding her mouth to his while he savoured her to the full.

His other hand curved around to span the swell of her bottom, pressing her into him.

He heard her moan, high and helpless, unable to fight him any more, and triumph surged through him.

And relief. Profound, shuddering relief.

She was his!

A growl sounded in his throat and he settled into a slow, pulsing rhythm, laving her mouth, her lips, sucking and grazing, as she gave little moans and lifted her face to his. Her eyes were shut; her long, beautiful eyelashes lay on the pale, opalescent skin. Her hair was falling back off her face, cascading down her spine. Her breasts were swollen against him, and he could feel their hardened tips grazing through the insubstantial gossamer of her dress.

Her hand had wound around his neck, and he could feel her fingers brushing the sensitive skin over the vertebrae at his nape. Her other hand was clutching his waist, holding him against her.

Thunder drummed through Theo as he feasted on her. The moment of possession had come at last! The relief was exquisite. She'd held him off so long, but now, *now* was the hour of satiation. He felt the familiar urgent tension mounting in him, and realised through the dim drowning of his senses that if he did not pull back, and fast, the frustration he'd been suffering since he'd admitted his desire for her in the first moment of seeing her would explode, physically, within him.

And that was not the way he wanted it to be.

He wanted much, much more.

Slowly, with infinite control, he eased away from her, loosening his hold. It was agony. His loins ached as they lost contact with the flesh they sought. He wanted to catch her back, slide the filmy chiffon up her silken legs, lift her up and impale her, sinking himself into her swollen, waiting flesh. Bury himself again and again within her until the stars exploded and the oblivion of bliss embraced him.

But that was yet to come.

He eased her back, catching her shoulders with a swift movement to steady her, for she was swaying on her feet. Swaying with a look of such blank shock on her face that he almost gave a laugh of triumph.

Her eyes fluttered open and met his, pouring down into her.

'Oh, my Leandra,' he breathed, and their breath mingled hotly. 'That, *that* is why you are mine! Your body has known that from the moment I first beheld you, though you have wasted so much time denying it! But now...' He paused, drinking her in. 'Now you will deny me no longer.'

His hands slid down her arms and took hers, holding them gently.

'Come,' said Theo Atrides softly, and led her away.

She followed blindly. In the room behind the coffee grew cold, and the fire in the hearth died slowly down.

Elsewhere, new fires were raging.

He took her to his room, leading her to the side of the bed, his hand holding hers, and she went with him. She could not help herself. She knew with her brain that this was madness. Nothing but madness! Whatever it was that Theo Atrides wanted of her, it was not for all time. Perhaps only for tonight.

But when an eternity without him stretched in front of her, tonight was enough. Tonight was now, and now was all there was. All there ever would be. She would have this of him, then nothing more.

He stood beside the bed and looked at her. She stood in front of him and looked at him. His face was strange. She could see sexual desire imprinted there, blazing with a fierce, dark sensuality that made her bones turn to water. But there was more in his face that she could not read in the dim light.

No matter. For them, the only currency could be desire. Everything else had been burnt away. The rest of the world no longer existed. There was only this moment—now.

'Leandra—' His voice was low, and very husked. He stood tall above her, dark and overpowering. He had overpowered her helpless resistance to him, and now held her with the strongest bonds of all. The bonds of passion and desire.

'Leandra—' His hand reached out and with long fingers stroked down the side of her face, traced along the line of her throat, to pause a moment, his thumb on the beating pulse at its base.

'Your blood beats for me like a wild bird,' he told her, in that low, husked voice.

The fingers traced along the delicate folds of her scarf, dipping across her shoulders, and his wide, mobile mouth smiled.

'This veil inflames me—you inflame me. After all my waiting, now it is time to lift your veil and show me all your beauty.'

He brushed the chiffon from her shoulders and it floated free. His hand slid to her bared shoulder and down the length of her arm, over her warm flank, the soft swell of her hip. As it touched it left a trail of soft fire. His hand slid on, round to her back, gliding up her spine, which arched towards him, to find the concealed zip of her dress.

In one long, smooth movement he had undone it, drawing the delicate material with it. The azure chiffon fell from her.

His breath caught.

She stood in front of him in the dim light as naked as Aphrodite born from the foam. As beautiful. For a moment he did not touch her, only with his eyes. Drinking her in. Desiring her absolutely.

She gloried in it. After all her fears, all her resistance, it had come to this. She stood before him, naked and beautiful. Woman to his man. Desired to his desiring. Knowing that now…now…Theo Atrides, the man she most desired in all the world, was taking her to his bed to make her his. To possess her absolutely.

He touched her slowly.

His hands cupped her shoulders, his fingers resting lightly on the curve of her upper arms, then slowly brushed down the length of them. At her elbows he paused, just holding her there a while as he looked at her—her face, her breasts, which tightened beneath his look alone, even before his thumbs reached out to span the aching peaks which flowered beneath his skilful touch. The pads of his thumbs rested there so gently she could feel no pressure, yet her nipples swelled to him, the tiny indentations on their tips tumescent and as sensitive as swansdown. His fingers slid from her elbows and cupped underneath her full breasts.

He stroked across her nipples, tiny, brief little strokes that turned her spine to liquid and made her sway, weak with desire. She moaned beneath his insistent repeated strokes, as he brushed them rhythmically, arousing them to a hardness she had not known they could possess. Then reluctantly, lingeringly, his hands smoothed downwards, abandoning her breasts which felt cold, bereft, though heat was firing through every vein.

His hands spanned her waist, stroking at her belly button with the edge of his thumbnail before splaying out and down to fasten her by her hips. Again his thumbs moved inwards, touching lightly, so lightly, the tight curls at the juncture of her thighs.

Excitement seared through her. Anticipation. She trembled.

He made a soft noise in his throat, then swiftly, suddenly, he had dropped to one knee. His head bent towards her and she felt, fleetingly, the brush of his mouth on her skin, just above where his thumbs were resting.

It seemed to her to be a kiss of homage—homage to her womanhood.

Then he stood again, swiftly releasing her.

'Lie down for me—lie down for me, my sweet white dove. Let me feast my eyes and then my body—' His voice was low. Impelling.

She lay down on the bed for him, her body limned with light. She lifted an arm above her head whilst the other hand rested laxly, curved at her hip, fingers just edging the curls of her pubis—the unconscious pose of a woman watching her lover—waiting for him. She lay and let him watch her, his dark eyes narrowed, unable to tear themselves away. She felt the power and the glory of her sex, the beauty of her womanhood. Displayed for him—for him alone. No matter if a thousand other women had lain for him, this moment was hers and hers alone. He wanted her and she, oh, how she wanted him. Her nipples tautened again, and the fire laced through her veins.

He stripped his clothes off, steadily, with no visible sign of hurriedness, yet the total unconcern with which he simply let them lie where they fell betrayed his inner urgency. As his naked body revealed itself to her she felt a flush of pleasure wash through her. He was magnificent—a paean to polished muscle, sinew and taut skin. In the dim light that threw into relief the shadows and his strength he was the ultimate male.

As her eyes flickered over his absolute nudity she quailed momentarily. Fleetingly she realised that he assumed she was as richly experienced in the act of consummation as he was. Would he expect an expertise she could not provide? Feel cheated by her exchanging well-practised skill for the only thing she could offer him—absolute desire? The slightest tinge of alarm singed her. Could she even accommodate all that powerful, thrusting masculinity into her unpractised body?

Then all wonderings, all anxieties were over—he moved onto the bed and knelt over her.

A powerful thigh pressed each side of hers. His torso loomed over her. Each hand was lifted and moved, held down by his, either side of her head. She could feel the rearing baton of his sex resting on her belly. Resting before its labours in the long night ahead.

His eyes held hers even as his body held hers.

'Now I have you, my lovely Aphrodite—'

His smile was feral, and a shudder went through her. Of pure sexual excitement. As his dark hooded eyes gleamed down at her something moved within her—powerful, exciting. Dangerous.

'And what will you do with me?' she heard herself whisper, looking up at him, lips parted.

He laughed. Low, triumphant.

'What will I do with you?' he echoed softly, mockingly. Huskily. 'Why, anything I want, my lovely goddess—anything I want…' Slowly his head bent to hers. 'Anything…' he breathed, and his mouth claimed hers.

He kept his word. He was a voracious lover, exacting her absolute surrender to him with the skill of his mouth, his hands, preparing her body for him until she was pleading for his possession, feeding her hunger with his own, bringing her to the brink of ecstasy, unleashing all her restraint, laving her and stroking her until her senses were a single, aching flame of tormenting desire.

He paused just before the moment of absolute consummation. As she lay desperate for his possession, caged beneath his powerful, aroused body, poised to enter her, he looked down at her.

'Is this safe?' he husked.

Safe? This wasn't safe! she thought wildly. This was the most dangerous thing she had ever done in her life! Giving herself to Theo Atrides…

Then radiance illuminated her face. What had safety to do with desire? This rich, wild, sweetness that filled her throbbing flesh? This was beyond sense, beyond reason. This was for wonder, for enchantment—for the emotion that welled like a great tide within her, consuming her.

She would give herself to that. Yes! She would give herself to desire, to wonder and enchantment, to everything that Theo was, to everything he wanted…

'Yes,' she breathed, the word an exhalation. A promise. 'Yes!'

She closed her eyes, lifting her mouth to his. He caught it, possessing its sweetness, possessing her desire. Fulfilling his.

He plunged within her.

She was ready for him, her hips arching in supplication, pleading for the searing invasion of her flesh by his.

For a moment only her body resisted him, then her arousal opened her body to him completely, enclosed around him.

'*Christos*—you're so tight!'

His words were slurred with shock, incomprehension. For a moment, an instant, she felt him hesitate. Withdraw infinitesimally. It was immediate agony. Deprivation. Her clutching fingers pressed into his shoulders. Pulling him back to her.

'I want you!' she breathed, her voice hoarse, gritty. 'I want you, Theo. Oh, God, I want you, I want you!'

Her hips lifted higher, twisting around him. With a low, triumphant laugh he surged again, meeting her twisting hips with a yet more powerful thrust, driving into her. Her senses swam and he thrust again; she cried out, gasping with delight as he filled her completely, her swelling muscles stretching around him, caressing him even as his fullness caressed her. He withdrew a little and she cried out with loss, clutching his shoulders to draw him back. He laughed in triumphant male possession and came down on her again, plunging in to fill her, fuse himself within her, and she cried out again and again as he withdrew and plunged, withdrew and plunged in a pounding rhythm that became the pounding of her blood in her veins. And then, in one final crescendo of sensation, the pulsing spasms of her body convulsed around him. Her throat opened, arching back, and her cry of fulfillment rent the air, mingling with his gasp of triumph as he emptied himself into her. Her straining body collapsed, exhausted beneath him, filled with his seed, fulfilled by his desire for her. By hers for him.

She lay beneath him, panting, dazed. As though she had just taken a journey to an unknown world.

'I never knew... I never knew...'

Her voice was weak, her limbs slack, hands sliding off his shoulders slick with sweat.

'I never knew…' Her exhausted echo trailed away, suffused into a joy so intense it dazzled her.

He lifted himself up on his elbows, only the rapid inflation and deflation of his chest betraying his own exhaustion, his own fulfillment.

'And now you do,' he told her.

His eyes blazed down at her in absolute possession.

CHAPTER EIGHT

BUT not satiation. As she lay beneath him, still so dazed and dazzled that all she could do was stare up at him, bemused, adoring, he dropped soft kisses on her face—her brow, her temples, the corners of her mouth. Kisses that sealed his possession, that marked his territory. She lay passive, sweating, supine. Totally possessed. His hands, loose around her wrists, held either side of her head. Then, as he went on kissing her, murmuring to her in his own language, marking her for his ownership, the kisses started to deepen. At the corner of her mouth he slid across, biting her lower lip softly, but insistently, until she opened her mouth to him again and he drank from that well of nectar.

And as he drank his body quickened within her, and as his tongue moved within her mouth so he moved within her body, hardening himself as he moved, so that she stretched around him, still slick from his seed, and he started to slide, rhythmically, insistently, stroking her, arousing her, himself, building the desire again to red heat, and still more. She moaned beneath his mouth, their tongues twining. Her wrists were held fast now. He was holding her supine beneath him so that he could take and enjoy she who was already his.

This time was slower, with a controlled possession that was a victory lap for his ultimate triumph and pleasure, of which an essential part was bringing her with him. She had to feel exactly what he could do for her, to her, had to moan and writhe and beg for the moment of release that he alone controlled until he judged her ready—not as she thought she was ready, but as he knew she could yet be if she were denied, again and again, past all bearing.

121

When he let her come she was senseless with desire denied, sobbing at him to give himself to her and so give her her own release. And as he let her go where she ached to go, sobbed to go, he sank inside her, swollen against her flesh, and let her use him for her pleasure as he used her for his, so that she overflowed all around him, through every vein, until her whole body was one engorged, pulsing mass, inflamed and throbbing.

He took her again after that, allowing her no rest, his own body recovering even before hers had ebbed away, so that she was still aroused when he began to caress her again. His caresses turned to sensual teasing and he began to toy with her, stroking the swollen, throbbing entrance to her body with taunting forays of his rigid shaft. She tried to catch at him, clutching his hips, his hard-muscled buttocks, but he laughed again, dark eyes like devils, effortlessly resistant to her urgings to return to her, to sink his tumescent length into her aching flesh and let her feel him hot and thick within her.

'Do you want me, my enticing nymph of the sea?' His question mocked her. She moaned incoherently beneath him, clutching at him again to no avail.

He rolled her over, plunging deep inside her again as he did so, and the rotation and the relief of finding him inside her once again made her incapable for a moment of realising that he had placed himself beneath her. She lifted her head, blind with sensation.

'Lift yourself—come astride me,' he ordered, using the muscled strength of his hands still linked to hers to impel her upright. She sat over him, her thighs slipping down on either side his hips. He moved her slightly, very slightly back, until she was exactly in the position he wanted her to be. Immediately he slid within her, to the very deepest yet, and her lips parted in a gasp. He was pressing to the ultimate, the very neck of her womb.

'Now ride me.' His voice was hoarse. Insistent.

Excitement blazed through her and he could see it in her face. He laughed again.

'You like that, *ne?* Well, so do I, my lovely wanton nymph, with her long golden hair and her naked body, taking her pleasure of me.'

He lifted his head and shoulders with the effortless power of his iron-hard abdominal muscles. His torso was fuzzed with dark hair, the beads of sweat catching the light. Taking each hand in his, he turned them over and softly bit each mound beneath her thumbs.

'Ride me—' he commanded.

She rode him. He held fast her hands, so that she had to grip with her knees for balance, and as she stroked him with her body, rising and falling to impale and re-impale herself on him in wave after wave of mounting pleasure, his eyes glazed with an intensity of pleasure she had not yet beheld in him. It transfixed her, and once in her steady riding she paused in her stroke. Immediately his eyes widened and fixed on her. Again he lifted his head and laved the tender mounds below her thumbs.

'Ride me—'

Dumbly, she obeyed, incapable of resisting a command so absolutely at one with her own desire. Soon her eyes too had the same glazed look about them, and her entire being focused on the intensity of the sensations aroused in her exhausted, over-stimulated body.

She rode him, on and on and on, until her whole body fused into incandescence, igniting over him, around him, and she had to pause in her motion, leaning back as if to rein him in, but only shooting pleasure through herself as his angle of penetration changed and exploded her into a backdraft of searing heat.

She swayed in her saddle as the ecstasy rolled through her and through her, every muscle clenching. His hands gripped hers, keeping her going, keeping her astride, in the saddle of his loins, while her orgasm rolled and roiled, and she pitched and yawed, bucking over him in her extremity.

A long, long time later she stilled, hunched over him, her hands still caught tight, but pressed now between her breasts and the hard wall of his chest. She was still impaled on him, but lassitude overcame her and she began to slip away.

Immediately, insistently, he jerked her back.

'You have had your ride, Leandra,' he told her. 'Now it is my turn.'

He jerked again, bringing her upright again. A grunt of primal satisfaction escaped him as he filled her to her ultimate capacity.

'Ride me—'

Almost she could not obey him—had not the strength left in her body. But his powerful, controlled movements impelled her into her own response.

'Ride me—'

She rode him, rising and falling with a steady, remorseless, pitiless rhythm that took him higher and higher, deeper and deeper. Now freed from the enslavement of her own desires, it was her turn to watch as his eyes glazed to blindness as his whole being focused on this one sensation, this one compelling point of pleasure which mounted and mounted with each impaling stroke until, her hands still held by his, she suddenly saw his face contort and witnessed that almost unbearable moment—his release into ecstasy. He shuddered into her, his expression translated, and watching him come into her suddenly made her weak with awe and mute worship. At that moment he was all-powerful—and all-vulnerable. Utterly dominating her, yet entirely at her mercy.

Wonder flooded through her—wonder and a wild tenderness. As his body jerked beneath her, enslaved by its own desire for hers, she swooped down suddenly, scooping his head between her cradling hands, folding his clenching body to her breasts, holding him close to her, filled with an overpowering devotion to him, an overwhelming desire to hold and guard him from his own vulnerability to her.

She hardly heard her own voice, crooning...

'Theo, Theo, Theo, Theo…'

She hunched over him while he emptied himself into her, utterly spent. Utterly fulfilled.

She folded herself against him, knees gripping his sides, fingers grasping each side of his face, pressed close against him until finally, finally he had stilled, and was hers to hold.

For ever.

Or only for tonight.

It was extraordinary. Leandra's limbs felt as heavy as lead, every muscle exhausted. She could hardly move. Yet she was floating on air. Soaring high into the stratosphere.

It was the Theo effect. The magical, wonderful, incredible, glorious, *radiant* Theo effect!

She stretched languorously, luxuriously. Morning had come after a night of enchantment so strong, so wild that she could not believe it. Yet even though the bright Aegean sun streamed through the window she knew it had been no dream, no fantasy. Last night had been real—searingly, scorchingly real.

Happiness suffused her. She grinned helplessly to herself.

'Theo… Theo… Theo…'

She repeated his name like an incantation.

As if summoned by her calling, the door to the bedroom opened and Theo, a short towelling robe barely covering his powerful body, reversed into the room, carrying a groaning breakfast tray.

Eyes shining, Leandra lifted her arms to him, then let them fall back on the tumbled bed.

'Theo—I've no strength left in me!' she moaned.

He gave a low laugh and set the tray down on the bedside table.

'I will feed you to restore your energies,' he declared. Another promise filled his dark, lustrous eyes. 'You will need them again soon, believe me…'

He sat himself down on the bed, his weight depressing the sturdy mattress. He reached out a long finger and traced the soft outline of her areola as she lay, naked as the goddess of love, in his bed. At his touch her nipple hardened.

He laughed again. A low, husky sound, filled with anticipation.

'Very soon...' he promised.

He fed her morsels of bread dipped in honey, bending to lick away any traces on her lips, deliberately refusing to let her deepen his embrace as she soon, oh, so soon hungered to do.

Once she had broken her fast it was her turn to feed him. He lay back on the pillows like a pasha, powerful, indolent, glorious. She fed him like an adoring odalisque, until he caught her fingers and sucked them into his mouth, then curled his hand around the nape of her neck and drew her down to him.

It took them a long time to surface and pour their coffee.

As he finally levered himself up to perform that office Theo looked down at the woman in his bed.

Her legs were tangled, arms spread out laxly, her hair tumbled across the pillows, her mouth swollen and bee-stung, breasts still half aroused. Her skin had the silken sheen of sweat upon it, still marked in places by the suffused bruising of his lovebites, and the absolute exhaustion of her muscles almost melted her body into the bed.

Theo's heart swelled as he looked at the woman who was his at last. He felt like a king. The emperor of the world! There hadn't been a woman like this for him for a long, long time. In fact, his dazed mind registered, he couldn't think of a woman who had ever had such an effect on him— who left him breathless with desire the moment she had slaked it. A woman he could not get enough of.

A woman who blew his mind away, and a lot else besides. Oh, a lot, lot else besides.

Into his memory a name rang, but he pushed it away roughly. No, this woman—now, here, in his bed—who had fought against his desire for her, his need for her, was nothing like that other one. Nothing at all!

His cousin's dark, accusing eyes swam into his mind's eye. He pushed them away roughly too. Demos had a bride to collect—his bachelor days were over. Leandra had no place in his cousin's life any more. Only mine! thought Theo triumphantly. Mine for as long as I want her—without impediment or obstacle. The future shone brightly with a golden glow.

'I want to remember you like this,' he told Leandra, his eyes lambent, voice purring. 'Imprinted on my memory. Mine, absolutely mine.'

Leandra gloried in Theo's possession. She was his, absolutely, and for this time, while she amused him, he was hers.

She knew, somewhere in the realms of reality, far below the radiant stratosphere she inhabited now with Theo Atrides, that this was only an interlude in time. A brief, precious span of time while he wanted her—before he grew bored and sought new pleasures.

But it was enough.

Later—later would come the pain of losing him. But losing him had been inevitable from that firm moment she had yielded to him. She would endure it, the pain of losing him, but the memory of paradise would last her all her days.

All I have is now. All I have of him is here.

Joy filled her heart as she clung to him, holding him now for all the years to come when he would be lost to her.

After a timeless while, gently but remorselessly, he unpeeled her clinging hands, holding her away from him so that he could nuzzle at her breasts.

'Theo,' she said faintly, 'I can't—no more…'

'I want you again,' he growled. '*Thee mou*, but I want you!'

His skilful lips closed over her nipples, sucking and arousing. She felt her exhausted body respond. Soon he was nuzzling at her with more than his lips, between her thighs. But as he came over her fully, to penetrate her, she suddenly froze.

'Theo—no! I can't!'

His grip on her wrists tightened.

'Do not toy with me, Leandra!'

She heard the frustration in his voice, but her own fear overcame her. She stared up at him fearfully, flinching her body away from where he was trying to impale her yet again with his.

'Theo! I can't! It...it hurts!'

He drew back, frowning. Then, as if seeing for the first time the fear in her eyes, he soothed his hand over her brow.

'Be still—I will not hurt you,' he assured her, withdrawing from between her thighs. He looked down at her musingly. 'You were very tight last night, *pethi mou*. Perhaps that is why you are so...weak now. At first I thought I was imagining things—for there is no reason for you to feel almost as a virgin must! And then I remembered that you dance, and I realised the discipline must have strengthened all your muscles, made you capable of great ...dexterity. It was...' his mouth brushed her temple '...very arousing. Very arousing...'

His mouth worked at her skin, moving down in tiny skimming caresses to her mouth.

'*Very* arousing...' he murmured, and again she felt his body stir against hers, automatically seeking to probe at her.

She tensed once more, fearful of the pain she knew would accompany his penetration. He stilled, and sighed. A fond, regretful sigh.

'Ah, well,' he breathed into her mouth. 'It seems, my lovely nymph, that we must, perforce, move on to more...sophisticated pleasures.' He kissed her once more, then drew back. He rested on his elbow, looking down at her, his finger tracing the outline of her lips. 'Now,' he mused, 'where shall we begin?'

Before the Aegean sun had reached its zenith that day Leandra had become a skilled initiate into just what he had in mind, and whatever last remnants of shyness and reserve had held her back vanished completely.

Theo would permit neither. Nor, as he demonstrated after a long, lazy lunch on the terrace, would he permit any modesty. On the warm sand of the beach, exposed to the sky and the sun, he took her again—so very gently there was not a breath of pain—and then carried her sated body into the shallow water to bathe her in its foaming waves. Then he lay with her, still both naked, under the sun, while she slept in his arms.

When they awoke, as the sun stretched fingers of molten gold over the turquoise sea, he led her back to the villa. They walked through the gardens like the gods of old, in their own private paradise.

Of the serpent there was no sign.

'All right, then, twice in a row! Go on! You said you could!'

'I never promise what I cannot perform—do you not know that yet, *pethi mou?*'

Theo smiled at her, mocking her doubt, and then, with a quick, decisive movement, flicked the pancake high into the air. It landed with a flap, and then soared up again, higher still, so that Leandra gasped.

He caught it expertly in the pan, and grinned at her.

'Three times!' she challenged him, hugging her knees.

They were in the kitchen—she in a pair of casual pastel trousers and a cotton sweater he had bought her, and he, naked to the waist, in denims so tight they outlined every muscle in his buttocks and thighs. And lovingly cradled the bulging pouch of his manhood.

Her breasts prickled. She wore no bra, and the soft, expensive fabric of her sweater revealed the swell of her breasts and the erect buds of her taut nipples.

She ached for his possession again. Their aqueous lovemaking had only whetted her appetite, but he had been cruel. She had begged him to shower with her, but he had denied her.

'No,' he had told her, putting her away from him, where she had clung to his body, pressing her hips into his and circling them enticingly. 'I want you much more desperate for me than this.' He put a finger over her mouth, admonishing her. 'You must learn hunger, Leandra.' His dark eyes roved over her.

She caught his finger in her mouth and sucked on it. He pulled it back, administering the slightest, lightest tap to her cheek. She caught his reproving hand and bit it softly.

'I'm hungry now,' she whispered.

He pulled his hand free and laughed, soft and low.

'Then I will feed you,' he promised her.

But he had brought her to the kitchen, and the commands he'd issued there were focused on sating a quite different hunger.

'Milk, eggs, flour,' he announced, fetching each item and presenting it to her. Then he extracted a food processor, measured the quantities, and told her to switch it on. As the pancake batter frothed he told her to fetch cheese, ham, fruit, cream, syrup, chocolate.

'Food for the gods.' He laughed. 'Simple, quick, nutritious and very versatile. Stand back! This pan is hot!'

It *was* a feast fit for the gods, full of laughter and appetite, as they sat across from each other at the scrubbed table, demolishing their stack of pancakes, helping themselves to the array of savoury and sweet accompaniments.

She had never in all her life enjoyed a meal more.

They washed it down with vintage champagne.

Then they went back to bed, and Leandra discovered exactly, *exactly,* what hunger could do when it was unleashed on a naked, aroused body.

Their coupling was like a burning forest fire, consuming them. All night, again and again, satiation yielded to renewed desire until once more her body was a mindless pulp of inflamed arousal. Again and again he took her to the brink, and plunged over with her, so that their cries mingled in the dark night air, echoing to the starry heavens.

Once he led her outside, and in the chill air leant her back against the still sun-warmed whitewashed wall of the house and took her beneath the stars themselves, lifting her body up on his like a homage to the heavens. Then, released again, her ecstasy burnt out, she ran with bare feet, bare body, like an elven creature of the night, down to the beach.

'Catch me!' she cried, her hair streaming in the starlight.

He sprinted after her, allowing her the pleasure of evading him until he chose to close the distance and bring her down with a tackle that drove the breath from her body. They collapsed upon the sand, rolling over and over, breathless with laughter, until he clasped her to him and scooped her up, ran with her to the tumbling waves and tossed her laughing in.

Her shriek was drowned in water, and he dived after her. She shrieked again and lurched away from him, diving down and under, and up and through the waves and the inky water, until he caught her by her wet streaming hair and kissed her, and picked her up and carried her out of the sea, like Aphrodite herself, and back to his bed for his possession.

She was an inhabitant of paradise.

But in the morning the serpent returned, destroying all her bliss.

*   *   *

She had no warning of it.

They had just made love. Leandra was lying in the fold of his arm, wrapped around her shoulder, spent and languorous, her cheek against his hair-roughened chest as he held her loosely to his side.

'Tell me,' he said, his voice low and sonorous, 'have you been to New York?'

'No.' She smiled, letting her hand play idly over the taut muscles of his abdomen.

'Good.' He sounded satisfied. 'Then I shall have the pleasure of showing it off to you—and you to it! I told you I would need to go there next week.' A frown creased his brow momentarily. 'Do you have a passport?'

'Uh-huh,' she murmured drowsily.

New York! The words glowed before her eyes. He could have told her he was taking her to Death Valley and her bliss would have been the same.

He wants me to go with him!

Happiness and relief seared through her. However brief, however transient this time was with Theo, to know that it would not end here, on this island paradise, was a wonder and a joy to her!

As she rejoiced that he had not yet grown weary of her she felt his hand brush at her arm. He was speaking again.

'I will have your passport brought to Athens. The agency my grandfather used to bring you here managed to evade the immigration formalities, but you will need it if we are to travel.' A frown creased his brow. Her passport must be in Demos's apartment, and the reminder that she had once been part of his cousin's life was unwelcome. Then his brow cleared. That was gone now—all gone. Leandra was his— and would remain so for as long as he wanted her.

And *how* he still wanted her! His appetite for her was insatiable! She was as fresh and sweet for him now as she had been the first time he had taken her!

And more so! There was something about her—something about Leandra Ross—that captivated him! He still didn't know what that elusive 'more' was that had so drawn him to her, but he would find out. Oh, he would find out!

However long it took, he would find out what it was that he wanted from Leandra Ross—more than the absolute sensual consummation that he already possessed, supreme though that was.

He would keep her until he had it. However long it took. The thought bathed a radiant, glorious light over him.

Another thought struck him, banal in the extreme, but while he was in practical mode, he might as well deal with it—and then… He could feel his body hardening already, recovering from its total exhaustion of a few minutes ago. Then he would put aside all banalities and sink once more into the bottomless well of desire…

'Is there anything else you need from London, Leandra?' he asked. 'Personal effects—that sort of thing. I don't mean clothes—I will buy you everything you need! Oh, and you had better tell me if you have sufficient supply of the Pill. I can have your doctor contacted for a repeat prescription if you need more—or you can see a doctor in Athens if you prefer.'

He smiled down at her, his heavy-lidded eyes dark and lustrous. She looked up into his eyes, feeling her breath catch. Bliss filled her.

'Well?' he prompted absently, busying himself with brushing her arm idly.

'What?' she murmured, distracted by the delicious sensation he was arousing.

'The Pill—do you need any more or have you got enough?'

Her skin was tingling with soft pleasure where his fingers lightly touched.

'I'm not on the Pill,' she replied. She pressed her mouth

against his chest, shifting her weight a little on her hips so she could turn her body into his more closely.

A hand gripped her elbow. The stroking had stopped.

'Then what are you using for contraception?'

CHAPTER NINE

HIS voice was different. She lifted her mouth away and tilted her head towards him.

He was looking at her, head lifted off the pillow. There was no indulgence in his face, only a demand to be answered.

'You told me it was safe.'

She stared at him. What did he mean? He sat up, pulling away from her.

'Before I made love to you. You told me it was safe.'

His voice was still different. Fear licked at her. What was happening? Why was he being like this? What had she done?

Contraception. He was talking about contraception. She had not thought about it. Had blanked it out. She had realised belatedly, some time in the long hours of that first night together, that Theo had used no protection himself. She knew she should care, but she did not. Could not. She gloried in the freedom it gave their lovemaking—and she was safe enough. Her period was due any day now—surely she was safe?

Abruptly he got out of bed. Pulling on his towelling dressing robe, he knotted the belt tightly. When he looked at Leandra again his face, she realised, had simply closed.

'Theo—' Her voice sounded strained, fighting down panic. What was happening?

He did not answer.

'I have been away from my office too long,' he announced. 'Forgive me, but I will have to leave you alone today.'

She studied his face anxiously. Something had happened. She knew it had.

And she knew what it was. As she watched him stride off into the bathroom and shut the door behind him her stomach started to churn.

He was worried because she had used no contraception.

Well, of course he's worried! What do you imagine? And you should be worried too!

Dismay flooded her, and shame. How could she have been so stupid as not to think about the consequences of what she had done? She had done the one thing that no woman anywhere ever did—she had had unprotected sex with a man, carried away by her own selfish self-indulgence! She had behaved like the most irresponsible teenager in the world! Shutting out anything that might interfere with the reckless abandon that had consumed her. Thoughtless, selfish, feckless…

I could be pregnant!

She waited for the horror to strike her as she made the admission to herself—but instead of horror a huge, ballooning wave of delight filled her. Pregnant—pregnant with Theo's child!

For an instant, as brief as it was blissful, she felt filled with such happiness she could not believe it. She could be carrying Theo's child!

The balloon burst. Fool—you fool! How irresponsible can you be? Wanting to bear a child for a man to whom you are nothing more than a seductive interlude! Oh, don't give yourself grand ideas, my girl—he's all over you now, but you knew—you *knew* it meant nothing to him…you *knew*…

And his reaction just now is all the proof of that you need. Did you see bliss on his face when you blurted out you weren't on the Pill? Did you? You think a man like Theo Atrides wants his passing fancies to get pregnant? And that's all you are to him! Nothing more…

She stared out over the sunlit terrace. Paradise had just turned to ashes all around her.

*   *   *

Theo was not horrible to her—but he simply retreated into an impersonal, remote politeness that she could not break through. Not that she tried. She felt so guilty for having been so stupid, so irresponsible, that she could not blame him for the way he was behaving.

Only as he was about to leave did she catch at his sleeve and blurt out, 'Theo—my period—it's due in a couple of days. Please, please don't worry!'

He merely smiled briefly at her perfunctorily and excused himself, heading out to the helicopter.

It was a long, endless day. Leandra was filled with restlessness. As she paced the terrace, or tried to relax by swimming, she felt her tension mount like a clock spring. She missed him already. Missed his lovemaking, missed his laughter—missed *him*.

An ache opened up in her heart. *Come back to me! Oh, come back to me as quickly as you can!* After all, she thought with ruefully wanton desperation, he could easily buy condoms in Athens...

As the sun westered in the sky she took to the highest part of the island and scanned the horizon, straining her ears for the sound of rotors. As she sat and waited she thought of that first day she had sat in this same place, terrified out of her wits about what had happened to her.

Her life had changed totally since then. Turned upside down and inside out. Changed utterly.

She had fallen in love with Theo Atrides.

For she knew that that was what had happened. Knew that that was why she had gone to his arms, his bed, unable to deny the overwhelming feelings that had swept through her, blowing away all caution, all suspicion.

Oh, she knew he did not love her back! Knew that that was impossible. But for her the falling had been irreversible.

She would never stop loving him.

Her eyes went back to conning the skies.

But Theo Atrides did not come home that night.

Alone in his bed, Leandra tossed and turned, aching for his large warm body beside her, inside her...

She was sitting on the terrace the next morning, disconsolately reading one of the books Theo had found for her, when the sound of rotors came to her. Eagerly she rushed down to the landing pad, but when the helicopter landed the man who emerged was not Theo.

'Ms Ross—Mr Atrides requests that you return to Athens, if you please,' said the polite young man. He looked at her incuriously, Leandra realised, and with a flush she knew that he saw nothing unusual in his boss depositing or collecting bed mates from his private island.

In Athens, she was driven by chauffeured car through the teeming streets until they reached a quiet, but expensive part of the city. She looked about, hoping to see Theo, but the aide simply ushered her into a tall, anonymous building. It was, she swiftly realised, a private medical clinic.

A nurse came forward to greet her. She was polite, but unforthcoming. The doctor who saw her, however, was far more open. He made a complete internal examination of her, asked her detailed questions about her menstrual cycle and made notes. Then he smiled impersonally and handed her over to the nurse to perform a pregnancy test. Leandra tried to explain that it was far too soon for anything to register, but the nurse simply smiled and went ahead anyway. Leandra gave in.

Afterwards, she was conducted back to the waiting room, where Theo's aide was waiting. Politely he escorted her from the clinic, and took her to a large, luxurious and quite impersonal hotel in Athens.

'Mr Atrides will call on you later in the day. Please do not leave the hotel,' he instructed her politely, before departing.

It was as well she was warned, because otherwise Leandra would have plunged out into the streets of Athens, desperate to divert her mind from the brooding fears which had been growing ever since Theo had left her. As it was, cooped up in the luxurious room, she had nothing to do but pace up and down, idly flicking TV channels.

What was going on? *What was going on?*

Questions buzzed round her brain. Why had the nurse taken a sample for a pregnancy test when surely nothing could show this soon after making love? She had told them her period was due soon, and her own familiar body changes were affirming that. What worried her most, however, was Theo's absence. She tried to be reasonable about it, reminding herself that Theo Atrides was a captain of industry, that he had a vast business empire to run, that men like him worked long hours, with little time for romantic dalliance... She must simply wait patiently until he could leave his office and come back to her.

And when he did she would be ready for him!

Eyes lighting in happy anticipation, she spent the next couple of hours having a huge deep bubble bath and attending to a scrupulous beautifying programme. Shortly after she had been deposited in the hotel a bellboy had arrived with a suitcase full of her clothes from the island, as well as a vanity case containing everything she could possibly need to make herself as lovely for Theo as she could.

As she stared at herself, wearing one of the beautiful silk negligees Theo's PA had included in her purchases, her spirits recovered. Her golden hair, freshly washed and dried, streamed down over her back. Her make-up was subtle, but enhanced her natural beauty. Her body was soft and creamed—and aching for Theo.

When he came she would beg his forgiveness for having been so reckless, so thoughtless as to neglect contraception. He would forgive her! Surely he would forgive her, understand that she had been so overwhelmed by his lovemaking that it had driven out all thought of anything else!

And then, when that had all been sorted out, he would smile at her again, and that troubled, brooding look would leave his face and she would be his again—for as long as he wanted her...

Because she wasn't pregnant—was sure she wasn't! Her body simply felt lush, and wanton, that was all.

And aching for his possession.

Impulsively, she ordered a bottle of champagne from Room Service, storing it in the mini-fridge in the room. She shaded the windows, drew back the bedcovers. Surely Theo would not be long now!

He came in the early evening. Leandra heard the card slice in the door lock and whirled around as the door opened. She stood, poised, and feasted her eyes on him.

Theo stood in the doorway, quite still. His eyes were locked on her. A nerve was ticking in his cheek. He looked as tense as a whip.

And sexy as hell.

She went towards him. She couldn't help it. She had been deprived of him for thirty-six hours and her starvation for him was absolute. She needed him—needed him now!

She pressed her body against his, glorying in the hard, solid feel of him, crushing up against him, winding her arms around his neck.

'Oh, Theo, I've missed you so much!' Her voice was a soft little cry. She lifted her mouth, to catch at his and feed on the sweetest nectar of his kiss.

His body stiffened, every muscle taut as a bow. Then, his hands closing on her arms like steel bands, he put her away from him.

'No, Leandra—don't touch me.'

His voice was heavy. She stood, eyes puzzled, anxious, not understanding.

He closed the door with a snap and walked across the room, increasing his distance from her. She stared after him, heart thumping. What was happening?

He enlightened her.

'It's no good, Leandra.' His voice was heavy still. 'Your tricks won't work any more.'

'Tricks?' she echoed faintly.

His eyes looked bleak suddenly.

'What else would you call them?' he intoned.

His face was shuttered, the way it had been when he had asked her about contraception the morning he had flown back to Athens.

'Perhaps,' he went on in that same flat voice, 'you might call them an insurance policy. A meal ticket, perhaps. A golden one. For life.'

Consternation filled her.

'Theo—please—what are you saying? I don't understand! Look, if you are angry or upset about my being stupid enough not to think about contraception, then I'm sorry—I truly am! It was rash and foolish of me, I know. But...well—' she tried to smile, but it didn't work somehow '—I was just too carried away to think about it.' She made another attempt at a smile, but that didn't work either. 'You made me forget about everything—except you, Theo...'

Her voice trailed off. His face was still closed, impenetrable. He looked older, suddenly, she realised, as if the weight of the world were on him. Nervously she twisted her hands together.

He saw the gesture, and the bleakness in his eyes intensified.

'Leandra,' he said heavily, 'if it had been just the first time I might, *might* have believed you! I might just have thought that, yes, contraception was the last thing you were thinking about. God knows,' he said with mordant self-accusation, 'it was the last thing I was thinking about!'

He took a breath that sounded painful in his throat. 'But you cannot stand there and tell me that for two days you just "didn't think" about contraception. We made love so often that you *must* then have given it some thought! It was obvious to you by then that I was not taking any precautions—if you were similarly unprotected why did you not say something? As for me—' his voice flattened even more, and a bitter, yet more self-accusing note entered it '—knowing that you were Demos's mistress, and that he must therefore have checked you were clean, gave me a sense of lib-

eration I could not resist! I indulged myself in naked sex
with you because I trusted you, Leandra. I trusted you.'

His eyes slid over her. Seeing her body—but nothing else.
'And you betrayed me.'

A cry of rejection escaped her. He ignored it.

'You cannot seriously expect me to believe that for two
days you "forgot" about contraception—and that means—'
his eyes hardened '—there is only one explanation for your
silence on the matter. It was deliberate. You deliberately
indulged in unprotected sex with me.'

She shook her head. 'No! No, Theo—I didn't—truly, I
didn't!'

He slashed his hand in impatience. 'Leandra—you are not
some naïve teenager! You are a very sexually experienced
woman! You have been my cousin's mistress! Of course
you knew what you were doing! You wanted me to think—
as I did—that you were on the Pill. What else should I think
of a woman who had been living with Demos for weeks?
And what should I think of you now but that you deceived
me deliberately?'

'No,' she said faintly, so faintly.

She couldn't believe this was happening. Couldn't believe
that a simple, stupid mistake was having such a terrible
effect.

Theo was talking again. His voice was like stone. Condemning her.

'And to what end, Leandra, would you have deceived me
in such a fashion? Why would you deliberately indulge in
unprotected sex with me? I can think of two reasons—and
both are unforgivable.'

His dark eyes looked across at her. Repulsing her.

'You were either pregnant already—or hoping to become
so.'

A gasp escaped her. She shook her head in instant denial.
'No! No, Theo!'

A rasp sounded in his throat. 'Well, on the first count you
have been discharged. The doctor at the clinic you visited

today assures me you are not pregnant. So—' his mouth twisted '—it seems that you are not already carrying Demos's child, as I at first suspected.'

She stared at him disbelievingly. 'Demos's child?' she echoed faintly. Was *that* what he had feared? Was *that* why the clinic had done a pregnancy test on her today?

He shrugged. 'Yes, why not? That could have been your plan all along. Who knows? Getting pregnant by Demos would have stopped his engagement in its tracks and given you a wealthy man to look after you financially all your life. Of course—' his voice hardened again '—when your liaison with my cousin was so abruptly ended, and you realised that his engagement to Sofia Allessandros was only a matter of time, you might well have decided that I would be quite adequate as a substitute father! The blood relationship is close enough for you easily to pass off Demos's child as mine, and certainly I am even richer than he is!'

Leandra's mouth was dry as dust. What he was telling her was appalling! He could not believe it—surely he could not? Dismay filled her. She tried to speak, but he went on in the same dispassionate tones that chilled her more than anything else.

'But it seems you are not pregnant by Demos, so that, at least, I must be grateful for. Now all I have to do is wait and see if a fate almost as bad awaits me. Fathering a child on you myself.'

She flinched as if he had struck her. He saw her recoil and smiled thinly. There was not a trace of humour in it.

'Oh, don't look anxious! There is no need! For if you are indeed pregnant, Leandra, then you will have your golden meal ticket for life, never fear! No child of mine will be rejected, or born illegitimate—whatever I think of its mother! Any such child will be secure, and safe, and loved by me! So I will marry you, be assured. And as my wife, the mother of my child, you will in live in luxury all your days. There—is that not a pleasing prospect for you?'

She paled. It was a hideous prospect—hideous! To be

married to Theo because he had no other option, simply because he felt he must do his duty by a child he had never wanted, never intended to conceive, was anathema!

She shook her head. It would never happen. She had already, in the long, long hours of his absence, made her mind up on that. If she were indeed pregnant, if her own rash foolishness had resulted in a baby, then she would make no claims on Theo whatsoever. She would go back to England and bear the child on her own, be a single mother. Oh, it would be difficult, but she would manage. Her career would have to go, but that was no matter. She had her parents' house by the sea to live in—she would do bed-and-breakfast in the summer, take in lodgers in the winter. She would get by. And she would never see Theo Atrides again. Her heart squeezed. After all, it was not as if she was going to see him once he had tired of her, once the novelty of bedding her had worn off. She did not fool herself she meant anything to him…

She would not have Theo—whatever happened she would never have Theo—but she would have his child…

Longing, sweet and piercing, rushed through her as she thought of holding Theo's child in her arms…

His words cut through her reverie. They were crisp and businesslike. Chilling her with their deadly dispassion.

'If your period is late, then you will have another pregnancy test immediately afterwards. If the result is positive we shall be married without delay.' His mouth twisted again. 'I did not think that I would beat Demos to the altar—and with such a bride at my side.'

She flinched again, at the cold derision in his voice. She had to make him see that he was wrong! Completely wrong! That she had never deliberately courted pregnancy!

She took a step towards him, face working.

'Theo, please, please believe it was nothing more than an accident! Forgetting about contraception!'

His lip curled.

'An accident? No, I think not. I know the ways of ambitious women better than you think, Leandra. Why do you think I have confined myself to women who are rich in their own right?' He lifted an eyebrow. 'Do you think you are the first to use her womb in a moneymaking scheme to enrich herself at the expense of the Atrides wealth?'

His voice sounded hollow.

'But you were certainly the cleverest. I grant you that. Oh, I grant you that.'

He looked at her across the room, across a gulf so wide she knew now, with a blooming of bitter despair in her heart, that it could never be breached. That it was so wide it had swallowed up everything that had flowered between them, so gloriously—so briefly.

Nothing was left.

He was talking still, and the words came like knife-cuts at her.

'Like all cheats, you played on my weaknesses, Leandra. You realised I despised you as a woman who chooses her lovers for the size of their bank accounts, and realised that I would never bed such a woman. So you took on the mantle of a woman of virtue! You took a gamble, turning down a safe hundred thousand pounds to net a much bigger prize!'

His voice rose and fell in those dispassionate, deadly tones, and Leandra stood there, letting it wash over her like a tide of coruscating acid, eating away at something so precious she felt a physical pain as it was destroyed in front of her eyes.

'And then you played the same hand all over again, with the diamond necklace. That time it was tears, not rage, that you turned on for my benefit. And it worked, Leandra—oh, it worked! As did your indignation over the clothes I bought for you, and your oh-so-convincing reluctance to succumb to me! Yes, so clever, Leandra—playing me inch by inch, on your silken web, reeling me in...'

Her heart was like a stone, as heavy as lead.

He was speaking again, and she forced herself to listen. Her world was crashing down around her and she felt sick,

sick right into the very core of her, because everything had gone wrong, so hideously, hideously wrong.

'You had me running circles around you, confusing me, making me stupid, senseless with aching for you! Until I was besotted with you! Putty in your hands! Just the way you planned all along...'

His voice was coming from very far away now. The other side of the world.

'And once you had me in your trap you couldn't lose, could you Leandra? Whatever happened you profited! If you weren't pregnant—if I started taking precautions myself— then you would be my pampered mistress and I would shower my wealth upon you. And if it was your lucky day— or night—and you conceived, then your profit margin would be even greater! You would be financially secure for life even if I never married you. And if I did marry you—and there was a good chance I might, for did you not know that my grandfather was desperate for an heir? So what if it was his other grandson who provided it— Well, as Mrs Theo Atrides the world would be yours for the buying!'

His voice dropped. His eyes burned like cruel flames.

'Or did you have one final scheme in mind? One final pay-out?'

A rasp sounded in his throat like a knife-blade. His voice sank to a low, harsh thrust.

'Did you prefer to make your fortune without even losing that lush, luscious figure of yours, Leandra? Did you think you could hold out your hand for a cheque with enough zeroes on it to ensure that you took a trip to an abortion clinic...'

Faintness drummed at her. She pressed her hands to her ears to cut out the vileness of this last, most repulsive accusation.

'No!' Her voice tore from her throat. Denying everything he had said of her. 'No! Everything you've said! It's not true—none of it!'

Theo's face was like stone.

'None of it? So I'm imagining it, is that it? I'm imagining that you knowingly, deliberately, had unprotected sex with me, time after time... And never once, not *once* thought to mention the fact?'

The scorn in his voice was unconcealed.

She looked at him helplessly.

How could he have said such things to me? Accusing me of scheming to deceive him, get money from him! How could he even think them after all we have had together?

She searched his face, looking for the man who had opened heaven's gate to her. There was nothing there—no trace of the man she had given herself to so rapturously. No trace of the man who had possessed her in the fires of passion. No trace of the man who had held her in his arms, against his heart...

Just a stranger. Worse than a stranger.

Something died inside her. Withered and died.

She stood, head bowed, defeated.

'It wasn't like that, Theo—truly to God it wasn't.'

It was all she could say, the only truth she could cling to as her world crashed around her. But it was not enough.

He made a noise in his throat and shook his head.

'It doesn't matter, Leandra. None of this matters any more. Only one thing matters—are you or are you not carrying my child? That is all I need to know. Nothing else.'

He looked at his watch. She saw the sleeve of his jacket ride back, saw the strong, powerful twist of his wrist. Felt the weakness go through her as her body yearned for his.

His mouth tightened.

'I must leave you now. I have a business engagement for dinner.' He spoke in distant, dispassionate tones. 'Tomorrow I must fly to Milan. I will be there several days. If your period has not arrived by the time I return I will accompany you to the clinic for a pregnancy test, and then—' his breath inhaled sharply '—we shall take it from there.'

He glanced around. 'You are comfortable here? You have everything you want?'

His voice was courteous—as courteous as a complete stranger.

She nodded, unable to say anything. But what was there to say? Nothing—there was nothing to say to Theo Atrides. Ever again.

'Good,' he acknowledged. 'Very well, I shall take my leave. If you wish to sightsee a car will be at your disposal. Your passport has arrived, but if you don't mind I shall keep it until we know the results of your pregnancy test. Please do not attempt to leave Athens, Leandra—I do not want to waste my time tracking you down. As for Demos—' his voice hardened '—I ask you not to contact him. My grandfather is still with him, and his PA has instructions not to put you through if you phone his office. His life is complicated enough as it is without your plaguing him again.'

He took another sharp inhalation of breath. 'I think that is everything. I will bid you good evening.'

He walked past her. As he did so she caught a faint elusive scent of aftershave, of the scent of his own, masculine body. He did not touch her. He did not look at her. He simply left.

In the silence after the door had closed behind him, in the emptiness of her room, in the emptiness of her life, slow tears started to seep from her eyes.

The lift doors closed on Theo. Claustrophobia clawed at him. He felt crushed, annihilated. What a fool he had been! What a stupid, unforgivable fool! He had thought he had found paradise—it had been a mirage.

Just like before.

Deceived. He had been deceived! Putting his trust in a woman—like a fool. Just as he had been before! Like time rolling back he felt again the shock and the pain of that first time. He had thought Leandra, who had delighted him, captivated him beyond all reason, all expectation, was nothing like that other one...

She was exactly the same! False. Totally false.

She had denied all his accusations, looked stricken as he'd thrown them at her—even that last, most terrible one— but so what? She was a clever woman—knowing how to appeal to what he wanted to find in her! Knowing how to pretend to be the woman he had been so overjoyed to find! So exultant at possessing! But he would not be taken in again by her. Never again. From the moment when, lying with her in his arms, his guts had turned to ice as the realisation had dawned on him that he had just spent two days in rapture with a woman who had deliberately, knowingly, had unprotected sex with him, from that bleak, unforgiving moment the scales had been ripped agonisingly from his eyes. He could see through her now—see every twist and turn she had made to fool him! Her deceits were over…

And so was the happiness he had found with her—that searing, burning, liberating happiness that had cut the chains of the past, opening a future to him that he had never thought he could have…

Illusions! More illusions! He must rip them from him mercilessly, ruthlessly.

Or they would destroy him.

Darkness closed in on him. Blinding him to everything— everything but the nightmare that was consuming him, taking away all that he had once thought he had. Leeching out the happiness he had found with her, draining it from him, hour after hour, until there was nothing left. While he prayed, prayed desperately that there might be some reason, some totally innocent reason, for why Leandra had not told him she was unprotected.

But no innocent reason existed. Only a guilty one.

She had done it on purpose, as a means to extract money from him.

I should have known that a woman who had already been the mistress of one rich man would do anything to enrich herself at the expense of another!

Pain seared at him. More than pain. Despair.

The lift moved down. Towards hell.

*   *   *

Three days later Leandra knew she was not pregnant. She phoned the clinic, as she had been instructed to do, and dully relayed the information. An hour later one of Theo's aides arrived to conduct her to the clinic—the doctor, she presumed, was under strict instructions to check out her claim personally. Her word alone was not good enough.

When it was all over she sat in the waiting room. She stared at the walls. She was numb, totally numb.

After a while Theo arrived.

Seeing him was like a stab to the heart. She did not move.

He spoke with difficulty. 'I understand you are not pregnant.'

She nodded briefly, saying nothing.

He seemed ill at ease, restless. She watched him from very far away.

There was something in his eyes that hurt her.

'Well—very well,' he began. He paused, then looked at her. He took a breath. 'Leandra—'

'I want to go home!' Her words burst from her, sharp and staccato.

He stilled.

'Right now! Today! Give me back my passport! I'll take a taxi to the airport and fly out on the next flight! You can't keep me here any longer—you can't!'

Something flickered in his face. It might have been pain. She didn't know. She didn't care.

'I want out, Theo! Out right now!'

Her voice had risen. Pressure had forced it higher. There was pressure in her whole body, squeezing her, crushing her from the inside.

'Leandra—'

She stood up, silencing him. 'No! I don't want to hear anything else you have to say! Nothing! You've made your opinion of me crystal-clear! And now I've spared you the onerous task of marrying me I don't have to stick around any longer! So I want out, right now!'

He frowned. 'Where will you go? You cannot go back to Demos!'

A hiss sounded from between her teeth. 'Oh, don't worry! He's safe from me!'

For a moment, a brief, vicious moment, she wanted to throw the truth at his head! To tell him that his precious cousin had always been safe from her! Hope flared in her. Raw, desperate hope. If she could tell Theo that Demos had never been her lover then perhaps she could convince him he had no right to throw any of those vile accusations at her!

But even as hope flared it died. Extinguished by a truth she could not deny. So what if she had never been a rich man's mistress? She was still guilty of a crime that condemned her in Theo's eyes, that turned her instantly into the scheming, deceitful female he thought her. A crime that damned her totally—being so reckless, so irresponsible as not to worry about contraception when he had swept her into his arms, his bed. How could she ever prove to Theo she had not hoped to conceive his child, to get some kind of hold over him by which to extract his precious wealth from him? An impecunious actress, she thought with slicing bitterness, was just the kind to want to enrich herself at the expense of a passing Greek millionaire who fancied her in his bed...

And what if she told him that other truth? The one she had been denying even to herself but which had welled up in her hour by hour, day by day, in Theo's arms, in paradise? That lost, poisoned paradise.

The truth that now stabbed as cruelly as an assassin's knife in her side, piercing her very heart.

What if she told him that she had fallen in love with him? That she had committed the unspeakable folly of falling in love with a man who stood there, accusing and condemning, and to whom she could never plead her innocence.

She did not even have to think to answer. He would simply think it one more scheme to make money out of him.

As if he had read her thoughts, he spoke again.

'If you need funds—' he began.

Her face set stormily. 'No, thank you,' she clipped out viciously, cutting him off.

His wealth had destroyed everything that had been between them.

His voice was heavy. 'I will, of course, see to the expense of your return flight to London.'

'Don't bother!'

His eyes flashed. 'It was not, I believe, your fault that you ended up here in Greece. Therefore it is the responsibility of the Atrides to return you at no cost to yourself.'

She closed her eyes. 'I don't care. Just get me out of here. Just let me go home. Let me go home.'

She looked so defeated. So broken. For a moment, a long, terrible moment, Theo wondered if he had been wrong about her.

Then he hardened his heart. This was a woman who had clung to his cousin's arm like a limpet, who had worn his cousin's diamonds, warmed his bed. Oh, she might look like innocence personified, like a golden-haired nymph of the sea, but he knew better now! Oh, he knew better. It was all an act, nothing but an act!

Money shows their true colours!

His grandfather's words burned like acid. Some women, like this one now, were too cunning to be caught in so simple a snare. They played for higher stakes. Played on the hapless emotions of the men they caught in their toils…

Made fools of them.

'Very well.' His voice came brusquely. 'You can go home. You can do whatever you want. Be whatever you want. Catch another besotted, gullible fool with your beauty and your cunning. As for me—' his voice twisted and broke '—I wish to God I had never laid eyes on you!'

Leandra stared blindly out over the rooftops of south London. Theo had not come near her again, leaving it to his aide to collect her from the clinic and take her to the airport, where her passport and airline ticket had been waiting for her.

Demos and Chris had met her in London, taken one look at her ravaged face and exchanged appalled looks.

'What did Theo do to you, Lea?' Chris asked in low tones, taking her hand. Her fingers clutched his desperately.

Demos knew his cousin. Knew him all too well. *Trust me,* Theo had said to Demos.

Trust him to do what?

'If he has dishonoured you,' he said to Leandra, sitting at her side in the huge limo, 'he will marry you. I promise you that!'

A shudder jarred through her and she gave a stifled, frightened cry.

Chris and Demos exchanged worried glances again.

'Please,' Leandra begged in a strained voice, 'just take me home! Take me home!'

After the opulence of Demos's Mayfair apartment, and the rustic beauty of the island, her studio flat seemed bleak and drear. It suited her mood.

Unrequited love. The phrase seared in Leandra's head. What a joke! What a vicious, agonising joke! It had always seemed such a romantic condition. Poignant. Soulful. The traditional fate of every heroine in drama. In reality it was nothing like that. It was a tearing, ugly agony, more cruel than Medea's poisoned cloak, lacerating her body, her heart. Day after agonising day. Week after agonising week.

A wound that could never heal...

Work was her salvation. Her hold on sanity. The rehearsals for the Marchester Festival had started, and were extremely mentally demanding. Leandra could only be grateful, for her absorption into her difficult role helped to block out her own raw, bleeding emotions over Theo Atrides.

She was trying to pull the gaping edges of her shattered heart together and get on with life.

Even if she felt that her life was over—that the pain would never leave her.

The world was empty without Theo Atrides in it. And he was gone from her for ever.

Only in her dreams could she possess him still—but they were torture to endure. In her dreams, alone in her bed, Theo's presence filled her, body and soul, and in her dreams she relived, over and over again, the incandescent rapture of their union, so that morning after morning she woke with her cheeks wet with tears shed for what she had lost.

One other bitter pill she was forced to swallow: Theo Atrides had washed her out of his life like dirt on his hands.

He had moved on to pastures new.

Leandra had to watch, in a blaze of publicity, one of the world's great solo artists, Diana Delado, parading Theo Atrides on her arm, certainly as her lover, even perhaps— so the columnists speculated wildly—her next prospective husband. A scandalous liaison with a prominent and very married US senator had ensured that whatever Diana Delado did—and especially whoever she did it with—was hot news on both sides of the Atlantic.

As autumn slipped into winter, Leandra had to endure seeing pictures of the stunning, sultry singer accessorised by the man who had, a lifetime ago, taken her to her own private Eden. Before proving himself the serpent in its midst.

Leandra found one picture of them inside a glossy celebrity magazine that encapsulated all the heartache she was enduring. Side by side on the steps of the casino in Monte Carlo stood Diana Delado in glittering evening dress and Theo, dazzling in a tuxedo. He was smiling down at the petite singer, who was looking out of the photo. The sight of Theo's dark, glossy head, his strong features and the lazily amused smile on his sensuous lips, all turned knives in Leandra's heart. She stared at it a full moment, then carefully cut out the picture, pinning it to the inside of her wardrobe door. From time to time she would open the door, stare at the photo and remember what he had done to her.

Then, slowly, she would close it again and get on with her life.

The first night of the Marchester Festival arrived. Chris and Demos were there to see her. Though both of them were still concerned about her, blaming themselves for ever having involved her so disastrously in their scheme to prevent Demos's betrothal to Sofia Allessandros, she had seen little of them since coming back to London for they were an agonising reminder of Theo Atrides.

But it was good to see them again as they came to wish her luck before the performance. She hugged them both.

'I have some news,' said Demos, watching Leandra carefully. 'Sofia Allessandros has become engaged to someone else. She has washed her hands of me. I believe,' he said cautiously, 'she is very happy with her father's new choice. He lives in Athens, and I know she never wanted to move to London.'

Leandra smiled. 'I'm glad it has worked out for her. And for you, Demos.'

Demos was still looking at her. 'I wanted to thank you again, Leandra, from the bottom of my heart, for your kindness to me.'

She shook her head. 'It was nothing.'

'No,' he disagreed. 'It was not nothing. I know the price you paid for helping me.'

His dark, kind eyes rested on her, so like his cousin's. But Theo had never looked at her with such kindess...

Her heart constricted.

'It wasn't your fault, Demos. It was my own.'

'Demos wants to tell Theo that it was all just a charade between you,' said Chris.

Her eyes flared. 'There's no point,' she said bleakly. 'It doesn't matter what he thinks of me.'

Behind her head Chris and Demos exchanged glances.

'Theo has not been himself, Leandra,' said Demos slowly. 'These past weeks he has been...different. He stopped off in London on his way to New York—he wanted...' He paused, his eyes on Leandra. 'He wanted to know if you were back with me again. I told him no. He looked... relieved.'

She gave a shrug. 'He would. After all, separating me from you was what it was all about, wasn't it?' Bitterness crept into her voice. She wanted them to stop talking about Theo. Wanted never to hear his name again.

Abruptly she changed the subject.

'Is your grandfather very upset, Demos? About Sofia marrying someone else?'

Demos accepted the diversion. He had seen the pain flare in Leandra's eyes when he spoke of his cousin.

'I feel bad,' admitted Demos, 'but what can I do? I can never give him the heir he craves.'

Anguish flooded through Leandra at his words.

I might have done that...I could have given him the heir he wants so desperately!

Then icy water deluged her heart. She could hear Theo denounce her all over again...

Once more she changed the subject deliberately—to something Theo Atrides had nothing to do with at all.

'I want to thank you again, Demos, for all the coaching you gave me for my part. I could never have learnt it without you!'

He laughed self-deprecatingly. 'I am happy to have helped—and I wish you the very best fortune for tonight.'

'Knock 'em dead, Lea,' said Chris cheerfully, getting to his feet with Demos and preparing to leave her to get ready for the performance. 'It's not my thing—but slay 'em, all the same!'

Both congratulated her—and all the cast—hugely when the performance ended. Leandra felt drained—it was an exhausting role, mentally and emotionally. But she was filled with the glow that always came at the end of a good performance, and her mood had lifted dramatically. Her hard work had paid off and the production was deemed a success.

The cast and highly specialised audience unwound in a refined celebration afterwards. As first-night parties went it was very sedate, so much so that at the close Leandra happily went off with Chris and Demos, ending up in Demos's suite at the best hotel in town. Demos produced champagne, and by the time it was finished Leandra was happy to crash out on the sofa in the sitting room, with empty champagne glasses on the coffee table in front of it. Chris laughed, tossed a spare blanket from the bedroom over her, and let her be.

She surfaced, late and bleary, the next morning, still buoyed up. The sheer exhilarating pleasure of having given a good performance, and in such a difficult role, was like a rush of endorphins through her, for once smothering the clawing pain that she woke to every morning when her fervid, frantic dreams of Theo Atrides—dreams in which she relived over and over again the erotic bliss of their congress, where he gazed down into her eyes with tenderness, cherishing and, most unreal of all, a blaze of love—gave way to harsh cruel reality.

She stood up, pushing her hair back off her face, and grimaced because she was still wearing the jade-green evening trouser suit she'd slept in, sadly crumpled after a night on the sofa. No, she told herself decisively, stretching her limbs and blinking to clear her head, don't think about him. Think about last night—tonight, the night after. Your performance is all—your art is all. Dedicate yourself to your art, and that alone.

It's all you have left...

A shower revitalised her, and half an hour later she was curled up on the end of Demos's bed finishing a hearty breakfast. She was wearing a hotel bathrobe and her loose hair streamed down her back. Demos, looking very elegant in monogrammed black silk pyjamas, was drinking coffee, propped up against the pillows.

'A pity there are no reviews,' he said to her. 'They would be glowing, I know!'

She laughed. 'The festival's far too small for that. The production might make the local paper next week, I suppose, if they're a bit short of news!' She gave a languorous stretch. 'I must head off—if the rest of the cast discover I've spent the night in a luxury hotel instead of in the hostel with them I'll be lynched!'

She set the tray down on the floor and was just about to rebelt her robe, which had fallen loose across her breasts, when there came the sound of the outer door to the hotel corridor opening sharply into the suite's sitting room. She paused, glancing at Demos.

'More Room Service?'

'I didn't order anything—' he began, mystified.

The door to the bedroom was flung open. An instant later the tall, commanding figure of Theo Atrides stood framed in the doorway, tension in every long line of his body.

CHAPTER TEN

FOR a moment nobody moved, frozen into a tableau. Then, in a hard, curt voice, Theo Atrides spoke. Not to his cousin, who was staring at him transfixed, but to Leandra.

'Get dressed.'

His voice was terse, and seemed to be strung like wire about to snap. His dark eyes bored into her like a drill.

She stared, wordless. Her heart was hammering inside her chest—she felt bereft of breath. A mix of fear and—far, far worse—searing, incandescent joy at seeing him again soared through her.

'Get dressed,' he ordered brusquely again. 'We're going.'

His words made no sense. She went on staring—drinking him in—drinking in the long, lean, powerful body, the dark crisp hair, the hooded eyes and that wide, sensual mouth, set now like steel between the deep lines carved from the base of his nose.

It was Demos who recovered first. 'What the hell do you think you're doing here—?' he began.

His cousin cut him short. Swiftly, ruthlessly.

'I'm taking Leandra,' he said roughly. 'She's mine—not yours. She always will be. I want her and I'll take her. She's not going back to you! Never!'

His eyes went to Leandra, his expression devouring. She went on clutching her bathrobe, incapable of speech, incapable of thought, just staring, helplessly, hopelessly. Heart hammering.

He gave a harsh laugh and advanced towards her. He stood in front of her.

'I want you back,' he told her simply. 'I cannot be without you. Not one more day without you. You will have all the luxury you crave—all my wealth to spend! My Leandra—'

Numbly, as if she had no will of her own, she let his hands close around her upper arms and draw her to her feet. His closeness, his male scent, made her bones weak.

'Theo—I—' Her voice was a thread.

The bathroom door snapped open. A new figure appeared in the bedroom. Blond, impossibly handsome, wearing nothing but a towel wrapped around narrow hips, his bare, smooth chest still damp from his shower.

'What the hell—?' said Chris, joining the frozen tableau staring at Theo Atrides.

As his head whipped round and his eyes focused on the semi-naked young man emerging from the bathroom Theo Atrides stilled. Like stone. Leandra's faint breath caught in her throat, and closed it tight. She had seen that expression only once before on Theo Atrides' face—the moment he realised she had used no contraception.

For a long, timeless moment the man who had taken her to heaven and left her in hell stared at Chris. Then his eyes slid back to Leandra, via Demos, sitting in bed wearing his black silk pyjamas. Theo's hands slipped from her arms and he stood back, as if in the presence of something loathsome.

Something moved in his eyes. Moved, and died.

A word crawled from him. She did not understand it, but the way he said it made her blench. Demos understood it, and gave a shocked inhalation of breath.

Theo ignored him. He ignored Leandra. His eyes glanced from the half-naked blond man by the bathroom door to the dark-haired man in the bed. His lips twisted. It might have been a smile. But it was not. He looked back at Leandra.

His expression could have obliterated her on the spot.

'And to think,' he said slowly, as if every word were coated in foul slime, 'I once thought to reassure you that I had no taste for perversion!' His mouth twisted in revulsion. 'No wonder you did not answer me! I thought you shocked...'

His eyes dragged from her, dragged to the two men still staring horrified at him.

'And all along…'

He trailed into silence, then, with an odd, choking sound in his throat, he slammed from the room.

For an eternity, it seemed, the tableau in the bedroom held. Then, like a wash of acid through her, Leandra felt hot, burning colour stain her skin from toes to forehead.

'Lea—did he just say…?' Chris's voice was a croak of disbelief.

Behind her she could hear Demos suddenly spring out of bed, Greek spouting furiously from him.

She was galvanised, shooting to her feet, launching herself towards the door.

'Lea!' croaked Chris again, alarm in his voice now. 'Don't! Leave him to us! Leave him to—'

It was too late. She had wrenched the door open and erupted into the sitting room like an avenging angel.

'Don't you *dare* walk out of this room!' Her voice was a scream of white-hot fury.

At the door to the corridor Theo Atrides froze, hand on the handle. His body tautened. He did not turn around.

'Don't speak a word, Leandra—not one word,' he said in a voice so soft, so quiet—so cruel—it slayed her where she stood. 'I would strangle you with my bare hands if touching your depraved flesh would not soil them!'

With a little cry she snatched up an empty champagne glass and hurled it at his back. It bounced off, breaking as it landed on the floor. His shoulders tensed, but he did not turn, merely exerting pressure on the handle to open the door and walk out on her—the woman he had just accused of taking two men to her bed at the same time.

'Turn round and face me, you disgusting, vile-minded bastard!' Leandra screamed at him, hurling another champagne glass at him. It caught his shoulder this time, shattering on impact.

He whirled round, face contorted.

'How dare you?' she lashed at him. '*How dare you?* How dare you even *think* what you just said—let alone say it to my face? You have the vilest mind of anyone I know! You know nothing—*nothing!*'

His lips twisted. 'The evidence speaks for itself, *pethi mou*. One woman—one bed—two men. With all three of you—how shall I put it?—in *dishabille*.' His voice dripped contempt. More than contempt. Utter disgust. 'And to think I had come to believe that it was Demos who had led *you* astray. He is an innocent compared with you! Tell me— were you playing your little threesome party tricks with Demos and that blond hunk before or after you opened your legs for me?' His words, his voice, flayed the skin from her flesh. His eyes burnt into hers like hot irons branding her. 'I'm sorry I was so boring for you—if I'd known your tastes I'd have had some handsome young men flown in for you, to keep you happy. But you'd have had to count me out, I'm afraid. Not my scene.'

He turned to go again. She hurled the last glass at him. It missed, and smashed on the wall beside him. He gave an exaggerated flinch and opened the door.

'Go back to my cousin's bed, Leandra—he may enjoy your perversions. I don't. You sicken me. You all sicken me.'

His voice was flat. Final.

Rage convulsed her. The words hurled from her throat. 'I have *never* been in your cousin's bed! I have never been his *lover!* I have never slept with him *or* Chris! Neither of them would damn well want me! They're sleeping with each other, you moron!' Her breath caught, choking in her throat. 'That's why Demos could never marry Sofia! He's gay— he's in love with Chris—and this is such a God-awful, hideous mess I...I...' Her voice shook and her hands moved helplessly, hopelessly.

Then, with a cry that broke from her heart, she turned

and belted back into the bedroom, rushing through into the bathroom and slamming the door shut. She locked it against all the world. For ever.

The bar in the hotel was empty, all except one small table, tucked right away at the back. Even the barman had made a discreet withdrawal. At the table, two men sat. One was hunched over a glass of neat single malt whisky. The bottle, more than half empty, stood on the table beside it. It was mid-afternoon.

'What am I going to do?' asked the man clutching the whisky glass within the cage of his strong, long fingers. 'What the *hell* am I going to do, little cousin?'

He spoke Greek, and his voice was slurred. The whisky might have done it, but it was not the only cause. Demos opened his mouth to answer, but Theo just went on talking.

'I've screwed up everything. *Everything!* Dear God, how could I have got it so wrong? Got *her* so wrong! So totally, completely wrong! I've fouled up everything—all down the line!'

'Yes,' said Demos.

Theo lifted bleared eyes, wanting to kill the man who'd just agreed with him. Then his expression shifted. He looked haunted. Haggard.

'How?' he asked his cousin. 'How could I get it so wrong?'

'Because you thought the worst of her. Judged and condemned her. Every time,' said Demos. He had no mercy in his voice. He knew how deep a wound Theo had inflicted on Leandra. He'd seen it in her anguished eyes.

Theo's head lifted sharply. He came back fighting. '*Christos,* you wanted me to think she was your mistress! Clinging on to you! Wearing your diamonds! Nothing but a bimbo airhead hanging on to you for your money!'

Demos shrugged—a little uncomfortably, to be sure. 'Leandra's an actress, Theo. She was just acting a part! That wasn't the real her.'

Theo Atrides fought back again, like a drowning man.

'Did you pay her?' he demanded aggressively. 'Did you pay her to act as your mistress? Did she take your money for that?'

For a moment he thought his placid younger cousin would strike him. Then Demos controlled himself.

'No,' he said levelly, 'I did not pay her to act my mistress. She did it out of kindness. She's known…Chris…' he hesitated only slightly over his lover's name '…for years. They've been friends since drama school. When he told her of our…predicament she agreed to help out. I wish to God,' he said, suddenly savage, 'I'd never sucked her into this.'

His soft eyes flashed angrily. 'When Milo lost his head and abducted her you told me I could trust you, Theo—and I did! I trusted you! And what did you do?' His voice was condemning. 'You seduced her! I should have known, Theo! Known what you were capable of!' His voice was grim. 'I told her I'd make you marry her for dishonouring her! She looked petrified at the thought, but I swear to God, Theo, if she even once says yes, then you'll marry her! You'll marry her if I have to hold a gun to your head myself!'

There was a long silence. Theo's dark, shadowed eyes shifted away, staring into the darkness that was in his soul.

'She'll never have me now. Not now. I've blown it. Totally blown it. For the rest of my life.' He picked up the whisky glass and downed its contents in one. Then he poured himself another, setting down the bottle with a crack on the surface of the table. He tried to look at his cousin, and failed. 'I've lost her,' he said, and his voice was as bleak as Arctic wastes. 'I love her and I've lost her.'

He picked up the glass and put it to his lips, to knock it back. It was taken suddenly from his hand. His head snapped up, a snarl on his face.

'No,' said Demos sharply, getting to his feet and removing the glass and the bottle. 'On your feet, Theo. On your feet. You're a self-pitying, undeserving piece of junk right now—but I'm family, and you're going to get another chance.' He yanked his cousin to his feet—no mean achievement, given his cousin's much heavier build and inert muscles. Ignoring Theo's slurred protests he said roughly, 'And don't think it's for your sake I'm doing this—it's not! It's for Leandra—I want her to have the pleasure of seeing you crawl!'

He got Theo to the lift and pushed him ungently inside. As they ascended Theo slumped back heavily against the wall, lost in whisky fumes and brooding thought, his face haggard and drawn. Suddenly he looked his cousin straight in the eyes, as if remembering something that had hitherto slipped his mind.

'Demos—why the hell didn't you just tell me you were gay?' His voice slurred again, incomprehension in it. 'Why all this garbage you handed out to me about a mistress?'

'You wanted me to marry Sofia, remember?' replied his cousin tightly.

'Well, not if you're gay, for God's sake!' Theo reacted explosively. He ran his hands through his thick black hair. He stilled a moment, and once more looked his cousin in the eyes. Right in the eyes. 'This guy you're in love with—Chris—tell me, little cousin, did it hurt when you fell for him?'

'Yes,' said Demos. 'But not any more. Now,' he said, looking at Theo with compassion for the first time, 'now we're the whole world to each other.'

Theo's face buckled.

The entrance to the Faulknerian Library in Marchester was via an imposing sweep of shallow steps leading through a Corinthian portico to an echoing lobby. George Augustus Faulkner had made a fortune in the sugar trade in the eighteenth century, and had bought himself respectability by making lavish endowments to Marchester's Institute of Arts and Mechanical Instruction. Now the Institute was the University of Marchester, and the grand neo-classical library one of its centrepieces.

'I don't believe this,' growled Theo Atrides in a low,

incredulous voice to his cousin as they ascended the flight of steps. 'You throw me under a cold shower to sober up, pour water down my throat and a ton of coffee, put me to bed like an infant to sleep off the whisky and then drag me out for *this?*'

'Atrides plc is the sponsor,' his cousin told him, unmoved by Theo's objections. 'I have a duty to show up—so do you.'

'I never chose to sponsor it!'

'No, I did. Marchester's reputation is second to none in the country. It was a good choice for us. You'll see.'

His cousin rolled his eyeballs. 'I can think of a hundred better ways of spending the evening!'

'Can you?' returned Demos, as they walked inside. 'Tough.'

His cousin made an indefinable noise in his throat. Demos continued to be unmoved.

Some ten minutes later, civilities over, they were seated in the small but perfect Oval Saloon, with its celebrated Adam ceiling. Theo Atrides leant back in his tiny gilt chair—excruciatingly uncomfortable for a man of his large frame—and looked forward to an evening of purgatory. Only courtesy for his hosts held the expression of intense boredom from his face.

'A bunch of English amateurs—wonderful!' He contented himself with muttering to his cousin out of the corner of his mouth as the proceedings started.

'Not all of them are amateurs,' said Demos cryptically.

The drama started.

For all his native Hellenic doubts about the ability of English actors to recreate the glories of the fifth-century Attic stage in the original tongue, Theo Atrides had to allow that the library's neo-classical setting was perfect for an indoor performance of the play. Besides, Sophocles's pitiless drama of the princess Antigone, so tragically caught between private and public responsibilities, torn between loyalty to her family or to her community, was as relevant today as when the play had first been performed under the bright Aegean sun so long ago. But as the traditionally masked character of the young Princess Antigone made her entrance, and began to speak the very words Sophocles had written over two millennia ago, Theo Atrides sat suddenly bolt upright in his chair.

'Tell me I'm dreaming,' he said to his cousin in a hollow voice.

'No,' said Demos quietly. 'It's Leandra playing Antigone.' He paused. 'She has a Classics degree from Marchester University and she was invited to take the part in this specialist production.'

'Oh, my God,' said Theo Atrides in a hollow voice, of the woman he'd once thought nothing more than a scheming, gold-digging, sexy, airhead bimbo.

'Shh!' said the man sitting behind them irritably—Leandra's old professor of Greek.

Demos hushed. He'd made his point.

Theo felt his guts kicked in. All over again.

It took every ounce of Leandra's professionalism to get through the performance. There was no formal stage, and if she'd wanted she could have taken three steps and touched Theo Atrides with her bare hand. Or thumped him from here to Christmas. Only the recollection of the expression on his face when he'd recognised her kept her from doing just that.

'*Timeo Danaos?*' she'd gritted inwardly, grateful for her stiff, concealing mask, remembering how Theo Atrides had assumed Demos must have taught her the phrase like a parrot, when she could have spouted whole stanzas of Virgil's *Aeneid* in the original Latin if she'd wanted to. '*I don't think so, chum!*'

As the performance proceeded towards its tragic climax she was intensely grateful that it required total concentration for her to act in a highly stylised fashion, speaking an antique, foreign language, and convey Antigone's agonising emotions as the tragedy unfolded and she obeyed her conscience at the price of her life.

By the end of the drama she felt drained. She was also filled with a sense of dread. She did not know why Demos had brought Theo here. Was it nothing more than a sense of corporate duty from the festival's sponsor? Demos had made no mention of it, but then, she acknowledged, he had been more concerned to assure her that neither he nor Chris were upset by her storming revelation that morning.

'We should have been brave and come out months ago,' Chris had said.

'We had no right to embroil you in our problems,' his lover had agreed.

Both of them had put their arms around Leandra, but neither had mentioned Theo's name to her.

Now he was here, not six feet from her.

She knew she had to face him. She could not throw the truth in his face, as she had done this morning in her furious rage, and not expect him to want answers.

As she changed out of costume, chatting quietly to the other cast members, she felt a shaft of guilt go through her. Merely to justify herself in Theo's eyes, and give free reign to her fury at his vile accusations, she had betrayed Demos and Chris. Despite their reassurances, what damage had she done to Demos's relationship with his cousin?

They might be sitting next to each other tonight, but was that just for public consumption? Could a man as rampantly macho as Theo Atrides ever tolerate a different orientation? He'd denounced her supposed sexual debauchery as perversion—would he be as ruthless towards his cousin?

Heart heavy, she bade goodnight to the rest of the cast, who were off to supper, telling them she might join them later. Then, clad in jeans and sweatshirt, hair in its customary plait, skin free of make-up, she went back out into the Oval Saloon.

It was deserted apart from Theo Atrides.

As she came in his head turned towards her. Instantly,

though she would have paid a million pounds for it not to be so, her bones felt weak as water just from seeing him again. Her breath caught in her throat.

He looked breathtaking. His face was shuttered, but the familiar strong planes and the dark hooded eyes and oh-so-sensual mouth made her breath catch. He was wearing a charcoal business suit, formal tie and pristine white shirt, a slim gold watch glinting on his strong wrist. His tall, lean body overwhelmed her. A terrible impulse to run to him, wrap her arms around his long length and never let him go for the rest of her life, made Leandra's limbs tremble with the ferocity of her urge.

The vivid, searing lines of the Greek poetess Sappho leapt in her mind—'''Fire runs like a thief in my veins...'''

She must have spoken them aloud, and in the original.

Theo's taut expression tensed even more as he heard the tongue of his ancestors on her lips once more.

'Even I know those lines—every Greek schoolchild does,' he said harshly. 'Why didn't you tell me, Leandra? You had chance enough to throw it in my face!'

'Throw what?' she returned, her voice faint, holding it steady by force of will alone. Half the distance of the room separated them. And much, much more.

His eyes darkened. 'That you were just acting a part!'

Her face tightened. 'I had no choice. I had to protect Demos.'

'You put me through purgatory, letting me think you were his mistress!' he threw at her. The stark outline of his face was gaunt, his voice bleak-edged, but she felt no pity for him. 'Letting me think you were the kind of woman who would—'

She didn't let him finish. 'I...I put you through purgatory? My God, Theo Atrides, you are beyond belief! After everything you said to me—every foul accusation you laid at my door—!' Taking a deep shuddering breath, she steadied herself. Her chin lifted. Her expression was glacial.

'For the record, Mr Atrides—' her words were chill, precise '—despite being an impecunious actress, I did not participate in unprotected sex with you in order to impregnate myself with your child so I could extract money from you in any of the vile ways you outlined for me in such detail. I was stupid, yes, careless, yes, in being reckless enough to have sex with you without proper precautions, but believe me, your precious money was the last thing I was thinking about at the time! And also for the record, Mr Atrides,' she went on remorselessly, watching his face whiten beneath its customary tan as he moved to say something back to her, 'I would not willingly bear a child to you if you went down on your knees and begged me to marry you! I couldn't think of a fate worse than marrying you! Even in exchange for the immense privilege—' her sarcasm slashed at him furiously '—of spending all your money!'

She took a deep shuddering breath. He started to try and say something, but she cut him short again, tossing her head up.

'And now that I've cleared up that little fact with you, I'll tell you right now that I am here for one reason and one reason only—to warn you to lay off Chris and Demos! They've had enough pressure on them and they are both good friends of mine—so don't even *think* of trying a replay of your charming tactic by offering Chris money to leave Demos!'

Theo's face darkened. 'I would not dream of doing so!'

'Why not?' Leandra threw back at him. 'You thought it a good enough way of getting rid of me when you thought I was sharing your cousin's bed! Why so squeamish just because Chris is a man? Or is it,' she bit, 'because you don't happen to want to go to bed with him?'

A hand slashed through the air. 'Enough!' said Theo Atrides. He strode towards her, emotion working in him powerfully. She backed away. He stopped dead. 'I don't,' he told Leandra, 'want to talk about Demos—or his lover, whoever he is providing it is not *you!* I only want to talk about us!'

Her mouth trembled. 'There is no us. There never was.'

'There was always an us,' said Theo quietly. His expression changed. 'There was an us from the moment I saw you pressing up against Demos in that sexy little black dress you were half hanging out of! If I hadn't believed you were my cousin's woman I'd have whisked you up to a hotel room and you'd have been in bed with me that same evening! I wouldn't have waited a day to take you, Leandra—not an hour...'

His voice had dropped, its timbre sending coils of debilitating weakness through her as those hooded eyes surveyed her. Memory flared in her—hot and humid—of that first electrifying encounter with him. He saw her remembering it, and something changed in his eyes. Something of their Arctic bleakness ebbed. He took a step towards her.

'I wanted you then, Leandra—and I didn't want Demos to have you. I told myself it was because he had to be free to marry Sofia, but even then I knew it was because I wanted you for myself. Only myself.'

His eyes were dark, desiring. Leandra's heart started to race—fire laced her veins. Oh, God, he was so dangerous, so deadly—if he moved now—if he simply closed the distance between them and took her in his arms—she'd melt over him, into him, under him. It didn't matter what he had said to her, what he had done to her... She was helpless to resist him.

Theo Atrides went on talking to her, and she drank it all in—his words, his voice, the vision of his irresistible body standing there a few steps away from her. So close.

'I thought it would be so simple. But instead you spat and raged and threw diamonds in my face! You fought me all down the line. You infuriated me, enraged me, exasperated me—until I realised...' his voice changed, took on a rueful, caressing note '...the real reason I didn't want you to fight me.'

He looked her in her eyes, and Leandra had the strangest feeling she was seeing right into him for the very first time.

'Not because I wanted you to submit to me—but because I wanted you to love me. As I...' He faltered, then went on. 'As I was starting to love you.'

His voice changed again. 'I have known many women, but none—not one—did for me what you did when I finally took you. It was passion, but it was more—something in you touched me in a way no woman has, no woman could. Something that could only ever be between you and me— that we had never shared with anyone else. And suddenly,' he went on, his voice strange, 'no other lover mattered— neither mine nor yours! I knew that what we had was for us alone. And I rejoiced! I knew then that I would keep you at my side, in my bed—in my life.' He looked at her, his eyes resting on her. 'You made me the emperor of the world, Leandra.'

His voice tightened, like a garrotte around her hopes. 'And then, just as I was yielding to my delight in you, everything was ripped from me! I discovered what a fool I had become! What a gullible, besotted fool! When I realised you had used no contraception I thought only one thing! I thought that despite everything we had been to each other it was all just a lie! That it had meant nothing to you— nothing at all! That all I was to you was a yet richer source of treasure. It wasn't me you wanted—just my wealth. And you were plotting to win yourself a rich prize from me by the deliberate, cold-blooded creation of an Atrides child.

'And so,' he finished, a deadly stillness about him, his voice an Arctic waste, 'I got rid of you.'

Leandra stood there, very still, every nerve and sinew motionless.

'Yes,' she whispered. It was a thread of sound. Inaudible. 'You got rid of me.'

He didn't hear her. He was locked in his own memories. His eyes were inward looking, and something in his face was so terrible it made her breath catch.

'When I sent you back to London I vowed, Leandra, never to think of you again. Never to remember you. To wipe you out of my life, my heart, my memory, as if you had never been. And it took me a long, long time to face up to why I so desperately needed to do so.' As he spoke his voice grated, drawing his own blood.

His eyes focused on hers, and for the first time she knew she could see the pain in them. Reflecting her own.

'I had fallen in love with you, and I thought you had betrayed me. Made a fool of me. I would not, could not forgive you that!'

A deep, shuddering breath went through him.

'I tried to forget you,' he said, his voice as quiet as a grave. 'But you would not let yourself be forgotten. You haunted me, Leandra. Haunted me by day and by night, giving me no peace. You invaded my dreams, tormented my waking hours with wanting you. Craving you. And gradually, day by day, night by night, I realised that whatever you were I wanted you back. I wanted to hate and despise you for what you were—what I thought you were—but I could not. I could only want you—all of you. Because I had no peace without you.

'A thousand memories assailed me—not just of your lovely, throbbing body spread for me, but more—much more. I saw you dance out on to the terrace in that yellow dress, your hair floating around you like a golden mist— you enchanted me! I saw you splashing in the waves, breasting the sea with your soft white breasts—you beguiled me! I heard your sweet laughter as I showed off to you, tossing pancakes in the air for your delight—you captivated me! I felt you cling to me in the aftermath of passion, trembling in my arms—you awed me with the intensity of your response. And I could not do without you any longer. Despite everything I still thought you, I could not do without you.'

He paused to take a long, heavy breath. 'When Demos told me you had left to go your own way I rejoiced! He had no hold over you—so I was free to claim you back. And then, yesterday, in Athens, Demos's PA, whom I had asked to keep me posted, phoned to tell me he was coming here to meet you. I flew to England at once and raced here, determined that you should not go back to him—that you should come to me! I came after you, to take you on any terms I could. And lost you all over again.'

He turned away. Something had broken in him. It hurt her unbearably to see it so.

'When I saw you in Demos's room I didn't care. I had taken you from him once and I would take you again. I knew that once I had you in my arms, my bed, burning for me alone, he would mean nothing to you! And I would forgive you everything! You were poor—it was natural you should want a rich man! I understood that—I excused it! I would make you my wife and you would be mine for ever! And I would shower you with my wealth and your craving for a golden meal ticket for life would be assuaged—you could get as pregnant as you liked and I would only rejoice!

'And then—' his voice tautened, like wire pulled beyond its breaking strain '—the bathroom door opened and another man walked in, and I realised my world had just ended.' He looked at her, straight in the eyes. 'I saw my illusions about you stripped to the bone all over again. I saw a woman who sees nothing vile in being the sexual toy of two men together! Such a woman could only sicken and revolt me. For such a woman there could be no excuses, no forgiveness. Her depravity was absolute.

'And so,' he echoed, 'I rejected you again. This time for ever.'

The silence stretched between them. Tangible. Unbearable.

When he spoke his voice was as bitter as gall.

'But the joke was on me, Leandra. And now you may laugh all you wish. For you have not been one—' he spelt it out heavily, each word weighing more than she could bear to hear '—not even one of all the things I thought you. Not one.'

He took a heavy breath that razored in his throat. 'I misjudged you totally, Leandra. Presumed the worst about you—always—about everything. From beginning to end. I was a fool, and worse. A thug—a brute.'

He turned and walked away from her. Not looking back. He reached the tall double doors to the saloon and took the gilt handles in his grip to open them.

'I'm paying the price for having done what I did to you, Leandra, for what I thought about you in my arrogant presumption which always looked for the worst in you—and found it! Well, the last of my illusions is stripped from me— the illusion that you could ever want me in your life after all I have done to you, said to you, accused you of! You can take pleasure, as Demos told me he wanted you to, in seeing me crawl to you. And you can have one last pleasure from me as well—I now look forward to the inestimable pain of loving a woman who can only think of me with loathing!'

He gave a long, shuddering sigh that racked his powerful body. Then, in a harsh, husked, low voice, proud head bowed, he said, 'Goodbye, Leandra. Take care of yourself. If you should ever have need of anything an Atrides can provide you must let me know. I have an eternal debt to pay you.'

He did not look back at her. He simply walked out of the room and was gone.

CHAPTER ELEVEN

THE low Aegean sun was dipping towards its winter horizon as the helicopter made its whirring way over the darkening waters. Theo's face was set. This was a journey he did not wish to make. There was no reason for such a trip—Demos hardly needed a personal guided tour over the island that his cousin was making over to him. Theo never wanted to set foot on it again. Going there would be an exquisite form of torture.

But Demos had been insistent, so Theo had steeled himself and climbed aboard, curtly telling his cousin to pilot the machine himself. Throughout the journey they did not speak. Theo flicked open his briefcase and buried himself in his work.

Work was the only salvation he could find, and then it was painfully inadequate. The raging pain within him would not be stilled, it ate at him like a cancer. It would get worse, too, Theo knew. It was nearly Christmas by the Latin calendar, and the thought of having to join the family for the orthodox celebrations early in the New Year was gruelling. Once, a lifetime ago, he had imagined the joy he would bring his ailing grandfather by presenting his own bride to him. Demos might never give Milo great-grandsons, but he, Theo, would instead!

But there would be no Atrides bride to lighten Milo's last months on earth. Or give meaning to his grandson's empty existence.

Theo went back to studying his business papers. Profit and loss.

But especially loss.

It was late afternoon by the time they landed. At least

they would not be able to stay long. Theo wanted this ordeal over and done with. With the light going, Demos wanted a tour of the island first. Morosely, Theo accompanied him. He tried hard not to look about him, to keep his mental eyes shut from his surroundings. But the memories came all the same.

Demos, damn his soul, seemed oblivious to his cousin's sombre, painful preoccupation, talking about banalities such as water supply and telecommunication links. His cousin made terse, minimal replies, staring out sightlessly over the choppy wave-tossed seas. Winter had come. For Theo, it would never be spring.

A thousand memories fought for entrance to his locked, unseeing mind. Memories of Leandra at his side, his arm around her shoulder as they strolled around his domain, their private Eden—then him turning her to him and kissing her.

Then their hurried, urgent return to the house—their bed. Their sensual, ecstatic coupling.

Pain stabbed him again. Worse than ever. His loss was unbearable. Exile from paradise.

As they approached the landscaped gardens the pain of loss got worse yet. He remembered Leandra sitting under the vine, sunning herself on the terrace. Leant back against the wall, face lifted to the starry heavens, legs hugging him, gasping as he emptied himself into her soft, shuddering body. Clinging to him, naked as he, as he held her against his heart. Beating so wildly—but only for her. Only for her.

But I didn't know it, he thought bleakly. I didn't know it until it was too late.

Too late. The worst words in the world.

He wondered where she was, the woman he had loved too late too win. That she was somewhere under the same sky that sheltered him upon the wide earth was his only comfort. How strange, he thought, that love does this to you. How powerful it is. The most powerful thing in the world.

Except grief. And loss.

Abruptly he realised that his footfall on the winding steps

leading down to the sheltered garden of the villa from the higher rough ground beyond was falling alone. He glanced back. There was no sign of Demos. Frowning, irritated by yet more delay, he turned to re-ascend the rise. Then, suddenly, he heard the distinctive ignition of the helicopter's engine and the noisy rotation of the rotors. A moment later he saw the machine lift off behind the villa, hover momentarily, then veer and head back across the sea.

Disbelief stunned him. What the hell was Demos playing at? Stranding him here! Didn't he know the motor boat wasn't moored here at this time of year and that Agathias and Yiorgos were at home with their family on the mainland? Face grim, stunned with anger, he headed down the steps towards the villa. Now he would have to get the generator working, power up his computer, get the telecom kit going and summon another chopper to lift him off.

If this was some kind of stupid joke that Demos was playing on him there'd be hell to pay!

As the sound of the helicopter's engine died away, echoing into the distance, the silence of the drear evening lapped around him again. Then, into the silence, there was a new sound—a slight click. He stopped dead. The glass doors to the sitting room opened.

A woman stepped through, on to the terrace, catching the last of the frail winter sunlight.

She was like a vision, a dream. A mirage of lost happiness. Her dress was black velvet, sweeping in a bell down to the ground. From the night-dark bodice her shoulders rose like snow. A white rose nestled at her breasts. Her pale blond hair was caught in a low chignon at the nape of her neck.

She was the most beautiful woman Theo had ever seen. The most precious to him.

She stood looking at him, and his heart turned over.

'You've been kidnapped,' said Leandra to Theo Atrides. He stood stock still.

'Have I?' His voice husked.

'You're my prisoner,' she told him. Her words were a whisper. A promise.

He took a step towards her. Only one.

'On one condition,' he replied.

She shook her head, the light catching the beauty of her face. Her perfume reached him. He used all his self-control and stayed where he was.

'No conditions,' she told him. Her eyes were like glowing stars, answering the starlight as Venus glowed, hanging low in the sky. The goddess of love.

She was the goddess incarnate.

'One condition,' he repeated. Cruel. Harsh.

Her eyes widened unbearably, lips parting. Fearing what he would say.

'I want a life sentence,' said Theo Atrides to the woman he loved.

Her eyes were brighter than jewels. Brighter than stars. Bright with tears.

She gave a little choke. Such a little one. But he was there, the distance between them gone. Gone for ever.

He cradled her face in his hands. Long, and strong, and so absolutely tender.

'I love you, *thespinis*. I love you and I don't deserve you. But if you give me a second chance I will prove myself worthy of you if it takes all my life!'

She gazed up at him. The tears were still unshed, but hovered on her eyelashes. They were long and dusky. Not caked with mascara, the way they'd been when he'd first seen her. When he'd wanted to wipe off the layers of jarring make-up from her beautiful face and reveal the true loveliness beneath. She'd been the woman he would love even then, but he'd been too blind, too stupid, too arrogant to see it!

He saw it now.

'Can you forgive me, Leandra? Will you forgive me? Will you let me be your prisoner all my life?'

She shook her head.

'No,' she whispered. 'I will only let you be my lover.'

He smiled. A smile that lifted his haggard face and reached his eyes, his heart. Her heart.

'Oh, I am that—I am that for ever, Leandra. My Leandra. My lover and my love. My bride and my wife. The mother of my children. The jewel of my heart. My life. My heart. My eyes. My everything.'

She saw the tears gleam in his eyes. And drew him to her.

Later—an eternity later, an eyeblink later—after they had gone indoors, to where the fire burned in the grate and the iced champagne awaited them, after they had toasted Demos for his cunningly executed plan to bring them together, after *Antigone*'s brief run had finished, here on the island where they had first found happiness, and after Theo had led her through into the chilly bedroom and into the bed, which they warmed with their love until they both burned in the flames they had ignited in each other, then he held her to him, against his heart.

'How can you forgive me?' asked Theo Atrides, once so arrogant, now humbled by love. 'After everything I did to you—everything I said to you—'

Leandra smiled into his searching, doubting eyes, and told him the truth

'Because I love you,' she said, and the simple words were all he needed to hear, all she needed to say. A sly, teasing smile slid across her face. 'You see, Virgil also said, "*Omnia vincit amor,*"' she said softly. 'Shall I translate?'

A rueful look filled his eyes. '*Love conquers all.*'

'Very good,' she said approvingly, the teasing smile in her eyes now. 'You're not such a bad classics scholar yourself, Theo Atrides.'

The rueful look intensified.

'It's Demos who's the scholar in the family.'

'I know. He was an excellent coach—I could never have learnt *Antigone* without him!'

The rueful look changed to wonder—tinged with self-mocking chagrin.

'To my dying day I'll remember how I felt when I realised *Antigone* was you,' he said.

An unholy smile twitched at her lips. 'So will I,' she assured him. 'I have to confess, I was thinking pretty mean and nasty thoughts about you when I saw you sitting there next to Demos!' A questioning look clouded her eyes. 'Theo—about Demos…and Chris. Do you mind? I was so afraid you would. So were they.'

Theo stared at her uncomprehendingly. 'How can I possibly mind?' A glint entered his dark eye. 'You may think me an unreconstructed male chauvinist, *thespinis mou*,' he said baitingly, 'but knowing you have never slept with him fills me with deepest satisfaction! I was eaten with jealousy of him! And every time you praised him it was like a blow to me!'

'How will your grandfather react to Demos being gay?' she asked tentatively, her heart glowing with his possession.

'We have decided not to tell him just why he paraded you as his mistress to avoid marrying Sofia—there is little point now that he is so near death. Particularly now that she has become happily engaged to someone else.'

She smiled. 'I'm glad for her. I always felt sorry for her, waiting for Demos who could never marry her. But I hope Milo won't be too disappointed in losing a granddaughter-in-law.'

Theo's eyes gleamed. 'But he will be gaining one, *matia mou*. And such a one! Milo will be beside himself with joy. Not only is his obdurate, philandering older grandson finally doing his family duty and marrying, after he long ago washed his hands of me, but I am bringing home the perfect bride! Not only is she as beautiful as foam-born Aphrodite—' his hand tenderly caressed the soft roundness of her belly, where even now his seed was seeking its fruition '—not only is she eager to bear our child as soon as possible—' he kissed her gently, joyously, delighted that she had agreed to hasten the arrival of Milo's great-grandchild without delay '—but to crown her perfection she can spout Sophocles to him! She can even, I believe—' he smiled conspiratorially at her '—manage a little modern Greek as well, no? How fortunate,' he finished dryly, 'for your charade that Agathias and Yiorgos are deaf and you could not speak to them.'

He sobered, self-accusation in his eyes.

'It took me so long to realise you were not in any way the woman I took you for. Can you truly forgive me for being blinded by my own prejudices?'

It was Leandra's turn to look guilty.

'I held the truth back from you, Theo—in that I deceived you. I was trying to protect Demos—I couldn't break his confidence—he was so screwed up about telling you, in case you disowned him.'

'He and Chris love one another—and how can we, loving each other, condemn that?'

His generosity of spirit warmed her.

Then a frown creased the perfect happiness of her brow.

'Won't Milo mind, Theo—that I am the woman he thought was Demos's mistress?'

'Mind? He'll be insufferably pleased with himself. He sussed straight away I had been smitten with you! And since you're nothing like—'

He stopped.

She felt his sudden tension.

'Theo—?' Alarm was in her voice.

He held her against him, more tightly still.

Then, as if slowly releasing the poison that had long, long ago seeped into his bloodstream, he began to talk. She held him in the safety of her arms, the harbour where he now finally found shelter, and safety, and love.

'I was twenty-one,' he said slowly, staring sightlessly at the ceiling, memory taking him back down a bitter path. 'I was in Paris. Her name was Mireille. She was—' his mouth twisted '—a dancer in a nightclub. She was twenty-eight—

nearing the end of her career—but I never noticed that. She did, though. I was…besotted with her. I wanted to marry her. She told me she was pregnant. I phoned my parents that night and told them I was bringing home my bride. It was the happiest moment of my life.'

He stilled. His eyes looked out into the past.

'My father arrived in Paris the next day. Milo had sent him. My father paid Mireille three million dollars and took her to an abortion clinic. She went willingly. Then she flew to South America with her money. I never saw her again.' The baldness of his words could not hide the bleakness within. He took a short, tight breath, and went on.

'My father told me Mireille had confessed the child was not mine but another lover's—she had quite a few, he told me, all far more experienced than a twenty-one-year-old boy. He called the abortion—' his voice tightened unbearably '—a "minor complication". Between us all,' he said, his voice empty of all but bitterness and guilt, 'we created and killed an innocent child—whoever fathered him. To save the good Atrides name from unpleasant scandal.'

He paused. 'I vowed that day that never again would I be caught…or used…to create a child conceived purely because of someone's greed for the Atrides wealth. And that is why…that is why…' His voice choked.

She put her hand over his mouth. 'It's all right, Theo. It's all right. I understand now.' Her voice was very gentle.

He looked at her, turning his head so that her eyes looked into his, understanding all, forgiving all. He kissed her softly in gratitude.

Then not in gratitude at all.

As his kiss deepened his body hardened against hers.

'Pethi mou,' said Theo thickly, lifting his mouth momentarily from hers. 'I am crazy about you—just crazy, my sweet, enchanting Leandra!'

'I think it's mutual, Theo,' she moaned faintly, yielding her mouth to his again with an eager wantonness he found extremely arousing. Almost as arousing as he found it to

slide his body down alongside hers, his strong hands stroking her flanks as he positioned her to his satisfaction prior
to some serious lovemaking. As his kiss deepened his eyelids fluttered shut, long silky lashes splaying. In his loins
the engine of passion started to rev with pleasing precision.

'*Yineka mou*, but I want you again,' he murmured thickly,
not for the first time that evening—and certainly, he intended, not for the last. His lips moved to explore the tender
morsels of her earlobes.

This was a mistake, for it gave Leandra a chance to speak.
She knew they would never again need to speak of the
wound that had poisoned him so long ago, but there were
still two things preying on her peace of mind. She wanted
them banished for ever.

'Theo?'

He lifted his head, opening his eyes. There was a questioning look in hers, a note of anxiety in her voice. He
wanted to kiss it away from her. She must never look questioning or anxious again. He had hurt her so badly, but from
now on her life must be perfect in every detail. He, Theo
Atrides, would see to it. It would be his life's mission. The
prospect made him want to shout with joy and exultation.
He was the emperor of the world once more!

He moved to kiss her mouth again, but she drew back a
little from him, albeit with reluctance.

Theo stilled the swift burgeoning need in his body. His
own most beloved of women wanted to ask him a question.
He wanted to make love to her until she was breathless, but
in this, as in everything now, Leandra's needs must come
first.

'What is it, *thespinis mou?*' he said with great forbear-
ance.

That forbidden anxious look was still there. She bit her
lip. Theo wished she wouldn't. If anyone's teeth were going
to nip that tender flesh of hers they were going to be his!

'Theo,' she began diffidently, 'I...I may not have been
Demos's mistress, but I have...I have had other lovers,' she

finished in a rush. 'Two,' she admitted. 'One was at university—my first. We were, well, sort of experimenting. He was nice, but we broke up in the second year. The other was when I was on tour in rep. He was Darcy in a stage version of *Pride and Prejudice*. He looked a knock-out in knee breeches. But when the run was over I went off him terribly. That's all,' she said.

Theo received her confession with sublime unconcern.

'From now on there will be only me,' he informed her with happy possessiveness.

She grinned stupidly. The anxious look was gone. Theo never wanted it to come back.

'I think that will do for me,' she teased.

'Good,' he said, and decided it was definitely time to put this admirable policy into immediate practice. But as his hands slid up to shape her breasts, which they had been wanting to do for longer than was physically comfortable, she held him off again.

'And what about you? Does the same rule apply to you?'

He stared at her, outraged. 'Of course it does! Why should I want any woman but you? My beautiful white-breasted Aphrodite.'

He lowered his mouth purposefully to those very orbs. Leandra intercepted him and laid her fingers over his mouth.

'Theo?' she said for the third time.

Torture, thought Theo. That's what this is. He caught her fingers with his and kissed them lightly, before setting them aside to answer her.

'Yes, delight of my heart?' he answered, with gritted teeth and every muscle aching with self-control.

'What about Diana Delado?'

He stared at her blankly.

'Who?'

'Diana Delado?' repeated Leandra. 'You were all over the press with her!'

Theo grimaced at the note of accusation in her voice. Perhaps some ravishing lovemaking would improve her mood. His fingers made for the nearest nipple. She lifted his hand away.

'Won't one of the most beautiful and glamorous women in the world miss you accessorising her?' Leandra jibed. She was trying to sound brave about it, but Theo knew her soul now, and he heard the fear in her voice. Fear that his past would poison their future.

That must never happen. Theo lifted his weight back on to his elbow and gave an exaggerated sigh.

'Diana Delado,' he intoned patiently, 'is going to marry her senator, whose wife has filed for divorce in order to marry a twenty-six-year-old tennis pro. I merely diverted press attention until Diana could reveal her true intentions. We did not,' he said emphatically, gazing down at her, 'sleep together—I have touched no other woman since you, Leandra, and I never will again. There is only one woman I love, only one that I want, and by the grace of God, and her own forgiving heart, she is with me here, in my arms. And now, my own beloved, is there anything else you'd like to know?'

'Yes,' said Leandra. She was smiling now. Knowing that the man you loved could be so casually indifferent to one of the world's most beautiful and glamorous women was really very reassuring.

Theo Atrides held on fast to his self-control. This was the woman he loved. He had lost her through his own arrogant folly but she'd let him win her back. He would never do anything ever again to lose her—he would indulge her every whim. Even the ones that were driving him insane—like asking asinine questions at a time like this.

'What would you like to know, *thespinis mou?*' he enquired in a restrained, exquisitely courteous fashion.

'I'd like to know,' said Leandra, opening her eyes very wide and letting the tip of her tongue lick lightly at her lower lip, hooking her thigh over his and rubbing softly, while her hand wandered south again over his suddenly clenched abdominals until it reached its target, stroking it languorously with her finger, 'when you're finally going to get on with making love to me. You're keeping me waiting, Theo.' Her long eyelashes swept down, and then up again. 'And I don't like to wait,' she husked, with the most tempting smile playing on her lips, and a wicked, wicked light in her eyes, as her hand closed caressingly around him, feeling him jerk uncontrollably in her arousing grip and guiding him towards her own aching loins with growing urgency. 'I don't like to wait one little tiny bit, Theo darling...'

She didn't have to any longer. He fell on her like a starving man. She gave him the world, and heaven too.

Mediterranean Men

Let them sweep you off your feet!

Gorgeous Greeks

The Greek Bridegroom by Helen Bianchin
The Greek Tycoon's Mistress by Julia James
Available 20th July 2007

Seductive Spaniards

At the Spaniard's Pleasure by Jacqueline Baird
The Spaniard's Woman by Diana Hamilton
Available 17th August 2007

Irresistible Italians

The Italian's Wife by Lynne Graham
The Italian's Passionate Proposal by Sarah Morgan
Available 21st September 2007

www.millsandboon.co.uk

M&B

THE ROYAL HOUSE OF NIROLI

*...International affairs, seduction
and passion guaranteed*

Volume 1 – July 2007
The Future King's Pregnant Mistress by Penny Jordan

Volume 2 – August 2007
Surgeon Prince, Ordinary Wife by Melanie Milburne

Volume 3 – September 2007
Bought by the Billionaire Prince by Carol Marinelli

Volume 4 – October 2007
The Tycoon's Princess Bride by Natasha Oakley

8 volumes in all to collect!

NIROLI/LIST/5–8 V2

THE ROYAL HOUSE OF NIROLI

...International affairs, seduction and passion guaranteed

Volume 5 – November 2007
Expecting His Royal Baby by Susan Stephens

Volume 6 – December 2007
The Prince's Forbidden Virgin by Robyn Donald

Volume 7 – January 2008
Bride by Royal Appointment by Raye Morgan

Volume 8 – February 2008
A Royal Bride at the Sheikh's Command by Penny Jordan

8 volumes in all to collect!

From international bestselling author Nora Roberts

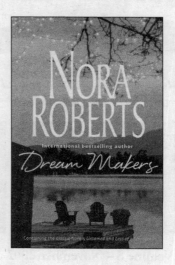

Featuring two classic novels

Untamed

Jo Wilder couldn't deny the attraction between her and her charming new boss, Keane Prescott. Though his kisses left her breathless, it was his tenderness that threatened to tame her heart…

Less of a Stranger

Despite the passion David Katcherton aroused within Megan Miller, she wasn't about to fall for this irresistible stranger who was after her grandfather's business…

Available 3rd August 2007

In the heat of the desert, two women find love in the arms of their Arabian princes

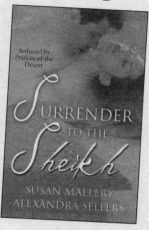

THE SHEIKH'S SECRET BRIDE *by Susan Mallery*

Malik Khan, Crown Prince of El Bahar, had been determined to possess Liana Archer from the moment that he saw her. But should Liana trust the man who could give her anything – everything – but love?

SHEIKH'S TEMPTATION *by Alexandra Sellers*

Sheikh Arash Khosrari was the only man who had ever touched Lana Holding in one night of unbridled and electrifying passion. But would the obstacles in their path be enough to take the heat out of their white-hot desire?

Available 7th September 2007

Romancipation

ro·man·ci·pa·tion *noun*
The freedom for women to love whom they choose
whilst retaining their own space and identity

Maggie is living the life she's always wanted.
Her career is taking off and, thanks to Japanese
straightening technology, her hair is lying down.
Maggie even has a funny, caring boyfriend – but
there's one problem: he wants Maggie to move in.

Maggie's not sure she's ready to move from "me" to
"we"… As she examines the relationships around
her, Maggie has to decide: is she ready to face her
fears and embrace her own romancipation?

Available 17th August 2007